Further Praise for Catherynne M. Valente

"A marvelously original story . . . Immensely rewarding."
—*RT Book Reviews* on *Deathless*, 4½ stars, Top Pick

"A terrific, complicated retelling of a Russian folktale . . . Fast-paced with a strong protagonist who keeps the engaging storyline focused; readers will appreciate this intriguing look at Bolshevik Russia through a fantasy lens." —*Midwest Book Review* on *Deathless*

"*Deathless* made me happier than my first shot of vodka. Valente writes novels that are bold and brash and beautiful, complex and subtle: all qualities that suit the Russian mind-set admirably. She maintains the complexity and the subtlety and tone of the Russian fairy tale, over-laying it onto the iron of Russia's history with the deft hand of a master in Fabergé's workshop . . . or a quantum physicist resolving the paradoxes at the heart of the world."
—Helen Pilinovsky, Slavic folklorist, Columbia University

"A glorious balancing act between modernism and the Victorian fairy tale, done with heart and wisdom." —Neil Gaiman on *The Girl Who Circumnavigated Fairyland in a Ship of Her Own Making*

"Stories can live again—but only under very special circumstances. They must be revived by the miraculous touch of a very rare class of being, a kind of multiclassed genius/scholar/saint who can restore them to life. Catherynne M. Valente is such a being."
—Lev Grossman on *Ventriloquism*

"Valente just knocks me flat with her use of language: rich, cool, opi-ated language, language for stories of strange love and hallucinated cities of the mind." —Warren Ellis on *Palimpsest*

DEATHLESS

Catherynne M. Valente

TOR®

A Tom Doherty Associates Book
New York

DEATHLESS

Copyright © 2011 by Catherynne M. Valente

Anna Akhmatova translations copyright © 2011 by Catherynne M. Valente and Dmitri Zagidulin

Edited by Liz Gorinsky

A Tor Book
Published by Tom Doherty Associates, LLC
175 Fifth Avenue
New York, NY 10010

www.tor-forge.com

Tor® is a registered trademark of Tom Doherty Associates, LLC.

The Library of Congress has cataloged the hardcover edition as follows:

Valente, Catherynne M., 1979–
    Deathless / Catherynne M. Valente.—1st ed.
        p. cm.
    "A Tom Doherty Associates book."
    ISBN 978-0-7653-2630-0
    1. Young women—Fiction. 2. Russia—History—20th century—Fiction. I. Title.
    PS3622.A4258D43 2011
    813'.6—DC22

                                                                2010036670

ISBN 978-0-7653-2631-7 (trade paperback)

First Edition: April 2011
First Trade Paperback Edition: February 2012

Printed in the United States of America

0 9 8 7 6 5 4 3 2 1

For Dmitri,
who spirited me away from a dark place

From the year nineteen forty
I look out on everything as if from a high tower
As if bidding farewell
To that from which I long ago parted.
As if crossing myself
And descending beneath dark arches.
                                        —ANNA AKHMATOVA

PROLOGUE

Don't Look Behind You

Woodsmoke hung heavy and golden on the shorn wheat, the earth bristling like an old, bald woman. The apple trees had long ago been stripped for kindling; the cherry roots long since dug up and boiled into meal. The sky sagged cold and wan, coughing spatters of phlegmatic sunlight onto the grey and empty farms. The birds had gone, arrows flung forth in invisible skirmishes, always south, always away. Yet three skinny, molting creatures clapped a withered pear branch in their claws, peering down with eyes like rosary beads: a gold-speckled plover, a sharp-billed shrike, and a bony, black-faced rook clutched the greenbark trunk. A wind picked up; it smelled of clover growing through the roof, rust, and old, dry marrow.

The boy stood sniffling, snot and tears dripping down his chin.

He tried to knuckle it away, rubbing his nose red and scratching his belly with the other scuffed-up hand. His hair was colorless, his age vague, though no fuzz showed on his face, no squareness set his jaw, and his ribs would have been narrow even if they had meat on them. His eyes drooped, too tired to squint in the autumnal light. The sun slashed through his pupils, stirring shadows there.

"Comrade Tkachuk!" A young woman's voice cut through the brisk, ashy wind like scissors. "You have been accused of desertion, gross cowardice in the face of the enemy. Do you deny this?"

The boy stared at the pair of officers and their polished tribunal bench, dragged from a truck into this wasted field for the purpose of punishing him, as though the army were a terrible stern mother, and he a child who had not come to dinner when called. His nose dribbled.

"On the eighteenth of June," continued the staff sergeant, her pen scratching against her notepad like a bird in the dust, "did you report for service when Lieutenant-General Tereshenko opened his books to the village of Mikhaylovka so that all might know glory on earth through the gift of their bodies to the People?"

"N-no . . ." mumbled the boy, his voice thick and slurred, an illiterate voice, a field hand's lazy vowels. The officer's nose wrinkled in distaste.

"Why not?" she barked, the buttons on her olive uniform blinking like eyes in the sun.

"I . . . I'm . . . eleven, ma'am." The sergeant frowned, but did not open her arms to him, did not gather him up or smooth his hair or feed him bread. He hurried on. "And I got this bad leg. Broke when I were six. I . . . I falled out a cherry tree. The man come with his big book, and I run and hidded with the pigs. Don't want t'be in the army. Wouldn't be no good soldier anyhow."

The staff sergeant's gaze sharpened itself on the boy's fumbling speech. "The service of your body is not yours to give as you please. It belongs to the People, and you have stolen from us by means of your weakness. However, the People are not unkind. Just as you chose to hide among pigs rather than serve among lions, you may now choose your reprimand: execution by firing squad, which is no more than you deserve, or service in a penalty battalion."

The boy stared, his eyes glassy and mute.

"That will be the front lines, son," said the senior officer, her rough voice honey-full of infinite mercy. The rook ruffled her feathers; the shrike clacked her beak. The plover called, mournful and high. A wind kicked at the grasses, then, sudden and brief, neither warm nor sweet. The senior officer's thick, dark hair was plaited around her head like a corona, her stare hard and tired. "You probably won't survive. But you might. You're small; we all were, once. You could be missed in the ranks. It has been known to happen."

The staff sergeant looked bored. She made a note on her pad. "Comrade Tkachuk, what is it you want?"

The boy said nothing for a moment, his gaze moving between the two officers, seeking mercy like a boar snuffling for mushrooms in the loam. Finding nothing, he simply started to cry: thin, dry, starved tears cutting through the dirt on his face. His little chest heaved jerkily; his shoulders shook as though snow was already falling. He rubbed his nose furiously on a bare arm. Blood showed pinkish in the mucus.

"I want t'go *home*," he sobbed.

The plover shrieked as though pierced with long thorns. The shrike hid her face. The rook could not bear witness—she opened her black wings to the air.

Major-General Marya Morevna sat impassively and watched the child weep. The staff sergeant tapped her pen impatiently.

"Go," Morevna whispered. "Run. Don't look behind you."

The boy looked at her dumbly.

"*Run,* boy," the major-general whispered.

The boy ran. Flecks of dead earth flew up behind him. The wind caught them, and carried them away towards the sea.

PART 1

A Long, Thin House

And you will arrive under a soldier's black mantle
With your fearful greenish candle
And will not show your face to me.
But the riddle cannot torment me for long:
Whose hand is here, under that white glove
Who sent this wanderer, who comes in darkness?

—ANNA AKHMATOVA

1

Three Husbands
Come to Gorokhovaya Street

In a city by the sea which was once called St. Petersburg, then Petrograd, then Leningrad, then, much later, St. Petersburg again, there stood a long, thin house on a long, thin street. By a long, thin window, a child in a pale blue dress and pale green slippers waited for a bird to marry her.

This would be cause for most girls to be very gently closed up in their rooms until they ceased to think such alarming things, but Marya Morevna had seen all three of her sisters' husbands from her window before they knocked at the great cherrywood door, and thus she was as certain of her own fate as she was certain of the color of the moon.

The first came when Marya was only six, and her sister Olga was tall as she was fair, her golden hair clapped back like a hay-roll in autumn. It was a silvery damp day, and long, thin clouds rolled up onto their roof like neat cigarettes. Marya watched from the upper floor as birds gathered in the oak trees, sniping and snapping at the first and smallest drops of rain, which all winged creatures know are the sweetest, like tiny grapes bursting on the tongue. She laughed to see the rooks skirmish over the rain, and as she did, the flock turned as one to look at her, their eyes like needle points. One of them, a fat black fellow, leaned perilously forward on his green branch and, without taking his gaze from Marya's window, fell hard—thump, bash!—onto the streetside. But the little bird bounced up, and when he righted himself, he was a handsome young man in a handsome black uniform, his buttons flashing like raindrops, his nose large and cruelly curved.

The young man knocked at the great cherrywood door, and Marya Morevna's mother blushed under his gaze.

"I have come for the girl in the window," he said with a clipped, sweet voice. "I am Lieutenant Gratch of the Tsar's Personal Guard. I have many wonderful houses full of seed, many wonderful fields full of grain, and I have more dresses than she could wear, even if she changed her gown at morning, evening, and midnight each day of her life."

"You must mean Olga," said Marya's mother, her hand fluttering to her throat. "She is the oldest and most beautiful of all my daughters."

And so Olga, who had indeed sat at the first-floor window, which faced the garden full of fallen apples and not the street, was brought to the door. She was filled like a wineskin with the rich sight of her handsome young man in his handsome black uniform, and kissed him very chastely on the cheeks. They walked together down Gorokhovaya Street, and he bought for her a golden hat with long black feathers tucked into its brim.

When they returned in the evening, Lieutenant Gratch looked up into the violet sky and sighed. "This is not the girl in the window. But I will love her as though she was, for I see now that that one is not meant for me."

And so Olga went gracefully to the estates of Lieutenant Gratch, and wrote prettily worded letters home to her sisters, in which her verbs built castles and her datives sprung up like well-tended roses.

The second husband came when Marya was nine, and her sister Tatiana was sly and ruddy as a fox, her sharp grey eyes clapping upon every fascinating thing. Marya Morevna sat at her window embroidering the hem of a christening dress for Olga's second son. It was spring, and the morning rain had left their long, thin street slick and sparkling, jeweled with wet pink petals. Marya watched from the upper floor as once more the birds gathered in the great oak tree, sniping and snapping for the soaked and wrinkled cherry blossoms, which every winged creature knows are the most savory of all blossoms, like spice cakes melting on the tongue. She laughed to see the plovers scuffle over the flowers, and as she did, the flock turned as one to look at her, their eyes like knifepoints. One of them, a little brown fellow, leaned perilously forward on his green branch and, without taking his gaze from Marya's window, fell hard—thump, bash!—onto the streetside. But the little bird bounced up, and when he righted himself, he was a handsome young man in a handsome brown uniform with a long white sash, his buttons flashing like sunshine, his mouth round and kind.

The young man knocked at the great cherrywood door, and Marya Morevna's mother smiled under his gaze.

"I am Lieutenant Zuyok of the White Guard," he said, for the face of the world had changed. "I have come for the girl in the window. I have many wonderful houses full of fruits, many wonderful fields full of worms, and I have more jewels than she could wear, even if she changed her rings at morning, evening, and midnight each day of her life."

"You must mean Tatiana," said Marya's mother, pressing her hand to her breast. "She is the second oldest and second most beautiful of my daughters."

And so Tatiana, who had indeed sat at the first-floor window, which faced the garden full of apple blossoms and not the street, came to the door. She was filled like a silk balloon with the flaming sight of her handsome young man in his handsome brown uniform, and kissed him, not very chastely at all, on the mouth. They walked together through Gorokhovaya Street, and he bought for her a white hat with long chestnut-colored feathers tucked into its brim.

When they returned in the evening, Lieutenant Zuyok looked up into the turquoise sky and sighed. "This is not the girl in the window. But I will love her as though she was, for I see now that one is not meant for me."

And so Tatiana went happily to the estates of Lieutenant Zuyok, and wrote sophisticated letters home to her sisters, in which her verbs danced in square patterns and her datives were laid out like tables set for feasting.

The third husband came when Marya was twelve, and her sister Anna was slim and gentle as a fawn, her blush quicker than shadows passing. Marya Morevna sat at her window embroidering the collar of a party dress for Tatiana's first daughter. It was winter, and the snow on Gorokhovaya Street piled high and mounded, like long frozen barrows. Marya watched from the upper floor as once again the birds gathered in the great oak tree, sniping and snapping for the last autumn nuts, stolen from squirrels and hidden in bark-cracks, which every winged creature knows are the most bitter of all nuts, like old sorrows sitting heavy on the tongue. She laughed to see the shrikes scuffle over the acorns, and as she did, the flock turned as one to look at her, their eyes like bayonet points. One of them, a stately grey fellow with a red stripe at his cheek, leaned perilously forward on his green branch and, without taking his gaze from Marya's window, fell hard—thump, bash!— onto the streetside. But the little bird bounced up, and when he righted himself, he was a handsome young man in a handsome grey uniform with a long red sash, his buttons flashing like streetlamps, his eyes narrow with a wicked cleverness.

The young man knocked at the great cherrywood door, and Marya Morevna's mother frowned under his gaze.

"I am Lieutenant Zhulan of the Red Army," he said, for the face of the world had begun to struggle with itself, unable to decide on its features. "I have come for the girl in the window. I have many wonderful houses which I share equally among my fellows, many wonderful rivers full of fish which are shared equally among all those with nets, and I have more virtuous books than she could read, even if she read a different one at morning, evening, and midnight each day of her life."

"You must mean Anna," said Marya's mother, her hand firmly at her hip. "She is the third oldest and third most beautiful of my daughters."

And so Anna, who had indeed sat at the first-floor window, which faced the garden full of bare branches and not the street, was brought to the door. She was filled like a pail of water with the sweet sight of her handsome young man in his handsome grey uniform, and with a terrible shyness allowed him to kiss only her hand. They walked together through the newly named Kommis- sarskaya Street, and he bought for her a plain grey cap with a red star on the brim.

When they returned in the evening, Lieutenant Zhulan looked up into the black sky and sighed. "This is not the girl in the window.

But I will love her as though she was, for I see now that that one is not meant for me."

And so Anna went dutifully to the estates of Lieutenant Zhu-lan, and wrote properly worded letters home to her sisters, in which her verbs were distributed fairly among the nouns, and her datives asked for no more than they required.

2

The Red Scarf

In that city by the sea which was now firmly called Petrograd and did not even remember, under pain of punishment, having been called St. Petersburg, in that long, thin house on that long, thin street, Marya Morevna sat by her window, knitting a little coat for Anna's first son. She was fifteen years, fifteen days, and fifteen hours of age, the fourth oldest and fourth prettiest. She waited calmly for the birds to gather in the summer trees, waited for them to do battle over thick crimson cherries, and for one of them to lean perilously forward on his branch, so very far forward— but no bird came, and she began to worry for herself.

She let her long black hair hang unbraided. She walked barefoot over the floorboards of the house on Gorokhovaya Street to preserve her only shoes for the long walk to school—and Marya, like a child whose widowed mother has married again, could never remember to call the long, thin street by its new name, having known it as Gorokhovaya for all her youth. There were other families in the house now, of course, for no fine roof such as this should be kept to one selfish patronym.

It was obscene to do so, Marya's father agreed.

It is surely better this way, Marya's mother said, nodding.

Twelve mothers and twelve fathers were stacked into the long, thin house, each with four children, drawing the old cobalt-and-silver curtains down the center of rooms to make labyrinths of twelve dining rooms, twelve sitting rooms, twelve bedrooms. It could be said, and was, that Marya Morevna had twelve mothers and twelve fathers, and so did all the children of that long, thin house. But all of Marya's mothers laughed at her aimless manner. All her fathers looked troubled at her wild, loose hair. All their children stole her biscuits from the communal table. They did not like her, and she did not like them. They were in her house, in her things, and though it was surely virtuous to share, her stomach had not marched in any demonstration, and did not understand its patriotic duty. And if they thought her aimless, if they thought her a bit mad, let them. It meant they left her alone. Marya was not aimless, anyway. She was thinking.

It takes a very long time to think through something as peculiar as the birds. One cannot simply leave it to the usual bash and bustle of memory and its underhanded tactics. And so, as it became clear that no shrike would come and take her away from her over-crowded house, the incessant noise of all those Blodnieks cooking or Dyachenkos fixing up the staircase; away from her hair growing thinner and more brittle as the communal table had to stretch further and further, from Comrade Piakovsky's sweaty staring in her direction; Marya's mind marshaled itself to the task of sorting out the whole business. No matter what she appeared to do—

sweeping out the leaves or studying her history or helping one of her mothers sew a shirt—her heart raced with problem of the birds, trying to outrun it into someplace where everything could make sense again.

Marya pinned out her childhood like a butterfly. She considered it the way a mathematician considers an equation. Given: The world is ordered in such a way that birds may be expected to turn into husbands at a moment's notice and no one may comment upon it all. What conclusions can be drawn? *That everyone already knows this, and it is only unusual to me. Or else only I saw it happen, and no one else knows that the world is like that.* Since neither her mother nor her father nor Svetlana Tikhonovna nor Yelena Grigorievna had ever made reference to their husbands having been birds, Marya rejected the first conclusion. However, the second conclusion led only to more delicate and upsetting hypotheses.

First resolution: Perhaps one was not meant to see what a husband looked like before he made himself more or less presentable. Perhaps the republic of husbands was a strange and frightening place full of not only birds, but bats too, and lizards, and bears, and worms, and other beasts waiting to fall out of a tree and into a wedding ring. Perhaps Marya had broken a rule of some sort, and visited that country without papers. Were all husbands like that? Marya shuddered. Was her father like that? Was Comrade Piakovsky like that, following her with his wolfish eyes? What of wives, then? Would she turn into something else when she married, the way a bird could turn into a handsome young man?

Second resolution: Rules or no rules, it was certainly better to see these things than not to see them. Marya felt that she had a secret, a very good secret, and that if she took care of it, the secret would take care of her. She had seen the world naked, caught out. Her sisters had been rescued from the city as beautiful girls are often rescued from unpleasant things, but they did not know what their husbands really were. They were missing vital information. Marya saw right away that this made a tilted kind of marriage, and she wanted no part of that. *I will* never *be without information*, she determined. *I will do better than my sisters. If a bird or any other beast comes out of that uncanny republic where husbands are grown, I will see him with his skin off before I agree to fall in love.* For this was how Marya Morevna surmised that love was shaped: an agreement, a treaty between two nations that one could either sign or not as they pleased.

When Marya saw something extraordinary again, she would be ready. She would be clever. She would not let it rule her or trick her. *She* would do the tricking, if tricking was called for.

But for a long while she did not see anything but the winter coming on and folk squabbling over bread, and her own arms growing so skinny. Marya tried not to come to the third resolution, but it hung there in her heart until she could not ignore it. Birds did not come for her because she was not as good as her sisters. Fourth prettiest, too lost in her own thoughts to steal back bread from the horrible little twins with their matching, cruel laughters. They did not come for her *because* she had seen them without their costumes on. Perhaps marriage was meant to be tilted, and she was spoiled for everything now, all because she had spied where she ought not to have. Still, she was not sorry. *If the world is divided into seeing and not seeing*, Marya thought, *I shall always choose to see.*

But thoughts are not food. Alone and birdless, Marya Morevna wept for her sisters who had gone, for her empty stomach, for the overfull house, which she could hear groaning at night like a woman laboring to bring twelve children into the world all at once.

Only once did Marya Morevna try to share her secret. If it was wrong to hoard a house, surely it was wrong to hoard knowledge. She was younger then, only thirteen, past the plovers and the shrikes. It was at thirteen years old that Marya Morevna learned how to keep a secret, and that secrets are jealous things, permitting no fraternization.

In those days, Marya Morevna walked to school with her red scarf tied around her neck, like all the other children. She loved her scarf—in the midst of the dreary house, turning grey with so many people scrubbing their laundry in it and sweating in it and boiling potatoes in it, her scarf was bright and gorgeous—and it meant that she belonged. It marked her as part of the young workers' committee, one of the loyal, one of the true. It meant she was one of the good children at school, the children of the revolution, handing out pamphlets or flowers with her classmates on street corners, adults smiling at her scarf, at her goodness.

Besides her scarf, the great love of Marya's young life was books. By extension, she loved her lessons, since they meant discussing books and the wonderful things inside them. The one miracle of the twelve families in her house was that they had each brought at least one suitcase of books with them, and all those new books with all their new treasures were meant to be shared among all. Having once seen the world naked, the engine which drove Marya Morevna through the long, thin streets of Petrograd was a terrible hunger for knowing things, for knowing everything.

Particularly, Marya Morevna loved the dashing Alexander Sergeyevich Pushkin, who wrote about that naked world she knew, where anything at all might happen and a girl had to be ready, had to be ready for that anything to bash onto the streetside once more. When she read the great poet, she would say softly to herself, *Yes, that is true because I saw it with my own eyes.* Or, *No, it's not like that, when magic comes.* She measured Pushkin against the birds, against herself, and believed the poor dead man to be on her side, the two of them steadfast, shoulder to shoulder.

That morning when Marya was thirteen, she had been reading Pushkin while walking to school down the endless cobbled streets, deftly avoiding men in long black jackets, women in heavy boots, newspaper boys with gaunt cheeks. She had become quite good at keeping her face hidden in a book while never faltering in her steps, never swerving from her path. Besides, a book kept the wind out. Pushkin's coppery words rang in her heart, warm and bright, almost as sweet as bread:

> *There, weeping, a tsarevna lies locked in a cell.*
> *And Master Grey Wolf serves her very well.*
> *There, in her mortar, sweeping beneath the skies,*
> *the demon Baba Yaga flies.*
> *There Tsar Koschei,*
> *he wastes away,*
> *poring over his pale gold.*

Yes, Marya thought, the smell of woodsmoke and old snow pushing back her long black hair. *Magic does that. It wastes you away. Once it grips you by the ear, the real world gets quieter and quieter, until you can hardly hear it at all.*

Bolstered by her comrade Pushkin, who surely understood her, Marya broke her usual rapt classroom silence. Her teacher—a young and pretty woman with large, nervous blue eyes—led the class in a discussion of the virtues of Comrade Lenin's wife, Comrade Krupskaya, who was neither young nor pretty. Marya found herself speaking without meaning to.

"I wonder what sort of bird Comrade Lenin was before he bounced up to become Lenin? I wonder if Comrade Krupskaya saw him fall out of his tree. If she said, *That is a beautiful hawk, and I will let him put his claws into my heart.* I think he must have been something like a hawk. Something that hunts and gobbles things up."

All the other children were staring at Marya. She flushed, realizing she had spoken all that aloud. She touched her red scarf nervously, as if it would keep off the staring.

"Well, you know," she stammered. But she could not say what they should know. Could not bring herself to say, *I saw a bird once that turned into a man and married my sister, and the sight of it bruised my heart so that I cannot think about anything else. If you had seen it, what would you think about? Not laundry, or whether it will rain, or how your mother or father is getting on, or Lenin or Krupskaya.*

After school the others were waiting for her. A throng of her classmates with narrowed eyes and angry expressions. One of them, a tall blond girl Marya thought especially beautiful, walked up to her and slapped her hard across the face.

"You're a crazy girl," she hissed. "How can you talk about Comrade Lenin like that? Like he's some kind of animal?"

The rest of them took their turns slapping her, pulling at her dress, yanking on her hair. They didn't speak; they did it all as solemnly and severely as if it were a court-martial. When Marya fell to her knees, crying, bleeding from her cheek, the beautiful blond girl shoved her chin up and tore Marya's red scarf from her neck.

"No!" Marya gasped. She snatched at it, but they held it out of her reach.

"You're not one of us," the girl sneered. "What does the revolution need with crazy girls? Go home to your mansion and your bourgeois parents."

"Please, no," wept Marya Morevna. "It's my scarf, mine; it's the only thing I don't have to share. Please, please, I'll be quiet, I'll be so quiet. I'll never talk again. Give it back. It's mine."

The blond girl sniffed. "It belongs to the People. And that's us, and not you."

And they left her there, scarfless, her nose running, sobbing and shuddering, shame flooding her skin like scalding water. One by one they spat on her as they went to their suppers. Some called her bourgeois, a traitor; some called her worse, a kulak, a whore—though she could not be all those things at once. It didn't matter. She was a person, but she was not one of the People. Not to her old friends, not anymore. The last of them, a boy with glasses, his own scarf voluminous and thick against his neck, pulled her book of Pushkin's poems from her hands and tossed it far into the snowdrifts.

After that, Marya Morevna understood that she belonged to her secret and it belonged to her. They had struck a bloody bargain between them. *Keep me and obey me,* the secret said to her, *for I am your husband and I can destroy you.*

3

The House Committee

Marya noticed it first because she paced while she was thinking, and paced while she was reading, and paced while she was speaking. Her body never wanted to sit still, never wanted to be calm or measured. Thus, she had an immaculate knowledge of the dimensions of the upper floors of her house, even as the space that could be called hers had shrunk. Only a month previously it had taken her five steps to walk from the cobalt-and-silver curtain to the green-and-gold curtain that marked the beginning of the Dyachenko family and their four boys, each as blond as birchwood. Then, suddenly, without anyone posting a notice of intent or collecting twelve signatures, it took seven steps to get there.

She counted her steps very carefully, both with slippers and without. She kept up her counting for twelve days and nights, though the Abramov twins pounded on their ceiling with brooms and pots, bellowing for peace, and old Yelena Grigorievna threatened to report her twice. On the twelfth night, when Marya Morevna was four steps across the floor, poised halfway between cobalt and green with her leg extended like a parade soldier, she heard a little breath beneath her own, so quiet she had to stretch her ears around it, a tiny sound, a faucet hissing in a thunderstorm. She looked down, her black hair spilling over her shoulder like a curious shadow. Thus Marya Morevna first saw the domovoi, and the face of the world changed again.

At her feet stood a little man, frozen in midstep, his leg, like hers, stuck stiffly into the air, his arm caught in a comic martial upswing. He had long, thin hair and a long, thin mustache that was split down the middle and flung over his shoulders, where it was tied to his hair with neat red bows. His white beard was full of dust, yet it did not seem unkempt; rather, he wore the grey dust like an ornament. He had a thick red vest, which looked as though it was made of tiny roof shingles, over a work shirt the color of concrete, and his trousers were crisscrossed with black stripes like window sashes. They were also split in the middle to allow a long, thin tail to escape, bald as a possum's.

Marya and the domovoi stared at each other for a long moment like two wild animals drinking from the same stream, both deciding whether or not to run and hide from the other. *This is it*, Marya thought, her heart leaping inside her. *The world is naked again, the underside of the world, and I wasn't crazy, I wasn't. I shall be clever, and I shall not let him go.*

Finally, she spoke.

"Where are you going to, Comrade?"

"Where are *you* going to, Comrade?" he repeated snappishly. His enormous eyes crackled hearth-red, ember-gold.

"I am measuring the house with my feet." Marya put her foot down, and the domovoi followed suit, pertly brushing his vest clean.

"I *was* on my way to a meeting of the Domovoi Komityet, the House Committee, which is why I have worn my most marvelous clothes, but I thought there was a military tattoo, and so I hurried to take my place in the ranks before I was reprimanded."

Marya longed to tug at the little domovoi's mustache and pinch his cheeks. She wanted to clap him up in her arms and tell him to take her away to whatever country he came from, where no one would slap her for knowing things, where there was enough bread and vodka to give him that round belly. Even if this was her husband come for her, unbounced and untransformed . . . but she did not think that was what the little man was about. She kept her face very grave. Her heart tripped over her breath. "You were right," she said finally, with what she hoped was stern authority. "And you should immediately take me to your superior officers, for I have discovered discrepancies in the state of the house."

The domovoi saluted. His eyes shone with delight. "Excellent! All house matters must immediately be brought to the attention of the komityet! Come! We will make a report! We will file *paperwork*! We will make *formal complaints*!" The domovoi's voice rose, higher and higher, like a teakettle boiling, until it was little more than an ecstatic squeak. "Follow me! Comrade Chainik shows the way!"

Marya thought she knew the house on Gorokhovaya Street. After all, she had lived there all her life. She had sipped 3,070 bowls of soup in the kitchen with black tile. She had eaten 2,325 entire fish at the cherrywood table with three knots in its center. She had dreamt 5,475 dreams in her little bed with its red blankets. She lived inside the house—she belonged to it. But little Chainik led her past the cobalt-and-silver curtain, past the green-and-gold curtain, down stairs grown rickety with the leaping ministrations of children. He led her creeping, tiptoeing around the rose-printed walls of the parlor (now the Malashenkos' room, piled high with mirrors, lipsticks, and combs, trophies of Svetlana Tikhonovna's days as the great beauty of the Kiev stage) and through the ragged linen sheet the Blodnieks had nailed over the kitchen to give their four daughters a kind of rough privacy. Though truly, having the luck to be allocated to the kitchen, where the warm iron stove puffed out ruddy heat, no one pitied the girls in the least.

Chainik scrambled over the sleeping bodies of the Blodniek daughters. The four of them curled together on two mattresses flopped onto the tile, amid a ruin of stumpy candles, saucers, shoes, discarded dresses, and the girls' prize possession clutched in the youngest sister's dreaming hands: a London fashion magazine, ten years out of date. Their long hair mingled, brown and rich, flowing back over the bed linens, the color of bread. The domovoi stopped on the shoulders of each to give their ears a little kiss. Marya Morevna held her breath and stepped over each of them, then their mother, her braid tight and severe even in sleep, and finally their father, resting in the position of honor next to the great benevolent stove, its rosy glow dim and delicious. Chainik wedged himself behind the stove and shoved—the stove creaked away from the wall. Papa Blodniek spluttered in his sleep, but did not wake. Chainik shoved again—the little domovoi had a donkey's strength! The stove scraped forward once more. Mama Blodniek sighed for dreams of days long dead, for rowan berries in her hair and sweet cream on her table. Chainik gritted his yellow teeth and pushed with all his vigor to let Marya squeeze in between the stove and the wall, for she was so much bigger, and the poor imp was not accustomed to making room for anyone but himself. Four daughters turned over in their sleep, each after the other, like a wave rolling across the sand.

Behind the stove was a little door. It was a fine, rich door, arched and tapering to a peak, carved over with the flowers of a happy garden, whose polleny centers were stamped in polished brass. It was as tall as a cathedral entrance for a creature of Chainik's size, but it barely rose to Marya's shin. Chainik knocked softly—three times, then two, then three again. The door creaked open.

"Comrade Chainik," Marya whispered. "I am too big! I shall never fit through!"

"We must all tighten our belts!" hissed the domovoi, and yanked on the sash of her nightgown. Marya spun like a spool; she had the peculiar feeling of a huge hand pressing down on the crown of her skull, of her ribs being squeezed as though Chainik were lacing her into one of her mother's old corsets. When he tucked her sash back into place, Marya faced the carved door once more. She had dwindled down until she was just barely small enough to fit inside the door, if she ducked. Marya fought to keep herself from laughing out loud—magic, Pushkin's magic, real magic, and done to her!

"Your bones are so stubborn!" snorted Chainik. "It's almost as though you don't want to shrink at all! Brazen thing, why do you want to be so tall?"

"I should never reach the top bookshelf otherwise," she protested, and the domovoi shrugged as if to say: *The ways of girls and other big folk are arcane and incomprehensible.*

He led Marya through a dank hall, past three layers of padded wall, a stony escapement, and a loamy passage with bits of worm and grass-root poking through the clayey dirt. Finally, these gave way to floorboards and a curious wallpaper: dozens upon dozens of Party pamphlets plastered against the earthen wall, holding back stone and mud.

The Workers Have Nothing to Lose but Their Chains! cried a painted earnest man with his fist in the air.

Beware Mensheviks, SR Loyalists, and Tsarist Generals! Bishops and Landlords Follow Closely Behind! warned a child beset by demon-faced soldiers.

Down with Kitchen Slavery! Give Us a New Life Under Socialism! announced a woman in a red kerchief, brandishing her broom.

Elect WORKERS to the Soviet! Do Not Elect Shamans or Rich Men! admonished a group of white-clad young voters.

Marya touched the papery faces of young girls with rosy cheeks. *ALL Society Must Transform into a Workers' Collective!* they told her.

The hall opened onto a broad room with its own high birch rafters and a cheerful hearth, small rugs on the floor, and a curious, fabulous flotsam jammed into every corner: heavy, gold-rimmed mirrors; polished silver doorknobs; china plates with tiny violets on their rims; copper teakettles; garden shears; thick goose-down pillows; an emerald-colored smoking jacket and a wide assortment of pipes; delicate snuffboxes with enameled lids; a heavy silver hairbrush with boar bristles and combs with tiny glass gems set into their teeth; a phonograph with a great golden bell; a croquet set with bright balls; a black lace fan with a long blue tassel. All this odd treasure surrounded a large table at which sat twelve little men, all like Chainik in their red vests and split mustaches, except that some of them had black hair and some blond, and some of them were women—though they had fine, thin mustaches as well, but no beards.

"Comrade Chainik, why have you brought this giant with you? She ought to be safe in her bed, dreaming of strawberries and laundry!" cried one of the other domovoi, who had an enormous golden medal on his chest—though when Marya peered closer, she saw it was nothing more than a disassembled pocket watch, made to hang down beautifully like a medal of courage.

"Chairman Venik!" Marya's guide replied in wounded tones. "She has a report to make! I would not rob the komityet of the

opportunity to hear delicious testimony, to make piquant judg-
ments, to carry out policies sweeter than oatcakes!"

The table sighed in relief and nodded vigorously to one another.

A domovaya raised her hand and was recognized by Venik. "I
am Comrade Zvonok," she said in a brash, ringing voice, tugging
at her silky blond mustache. "And I formally invite the giantess
emissary from the House Above to deliver her report."

"Hear, hear!" shouted the komityet, rapping the table with their
knuckles.

Marya still towered over most of them—seated, they came to
her waist, and she felt it was only polite to sit down on the floor, so
that she did not shame them.

"First, you must understand," she said, suddenly shy, "I did not
believe in domoviye before tonight."

Silence, bricked-up and mortared over, greeted her.

Marya hurried to fill it up, to appear wise and learned so that
they would not banish her when she had only just arrived. Her
cheek warmed where a child had slapped her once, years before.
"I mean to say: I believed that there might be domoviye in the
world—there might be anything in the world. But my education
was . . . rather specialized, and I did not assume that the presence
of birds who turn into husbands indicated domoviye and a door
behind the stove."

"Who," coughed Zvonok, "do you think broke your favorite teacup last fall? The one with the cherries on the handle?"

"I was careless, Comrade Zvonok. I left the window open and a
storm blew through."

"Incorrect! I broke it because you left me no cream and no dry
biscuits, and when your old boots wore through, you burned them
up for heat instead of giving them to me!"

"Hear, hear!" the table erupted in approval once more. "Well done,
well done!"

"I'm surely very sorry—"

"So is your teacup."

"Comrade, I don't understand. I have read my books and listened to my grandmother as well as any girl. I know very well that each house is only meant to have one domovoi. How did there come to be a committee of house imps?"

Chairman Venik straightened his beard like a vest, and brushed his vest like a beard. "Before the Party, each house only had one family. We have all had to adjust our thinking towards more correct principles, child. I came with the Abramovs when the White Guard drove them out of Odessa. What was I supposed to do, abandon the twins because our house burned down? They have such sweet little cheeks—they've grown so much! I saved the hallway mirror and Marina Nikolayevna's snuffboxes." He gestured to the piles of belongings around them.

Another domovoi, with a beard like a chimney brush, stood. "I came with the Ofonasevs from Moscow. Old Papa Kolya was a Menshevik, and his property was confiscated—nothing to be done, he had a big mouth. But they gave me nice old boots every Christmas, and his wife was a Party woman, no blame to her. So I snatched up her fan before they came and hitched a ride to Petrograd on the roof of the train."

Chainik patted Marya's hand. "I watched the Blodniek girls grow up in Sevastopol. They were even pretty as babies, and always with salty biscuits for me after supper. Is it their fault there was no work? Those girls had nothing to eat—no turnips, no bread, no fish. In Petrograd, maybe, they thought, there would be fish. I brought their plates, I was so full of hope. But here we are, and *ha!* No fish."

"I would have been happy to stay in Kiev," huffed a shrunken old domovoi, his skin almost blue with age, "but blasted Svetlana Tikhonovna knew the old ritual. She went out into her pumpkin rows in her best black lace-up boots with the sweet little heels, laid out a big round of cheese, and hollered, 'Grandfather Domovoi! Don't stay in this place, but come with our family!' The old bitch."

A groan rose around the table, with much nodding and sympathetic tears wiped away.

Each by each, all twelve of the domovoi told their tales, of the lost Dyachenko fortune; of the tragic Piakovsky children, who had lost their older brothers to the war; of the Semeoffs' disgrace.

"You must see," chirped Chairman Venik finally, "that a communal house requires communal domoviye, and communal domoviye require a committee. We are happy to do our part! It is a new world, and we do not wish to be left behind."

"Of course, I've been here since before you were a baby," said Comrade Zvonok. "This house is my husband, and we eat warmth together by the stove." Her broad face grew sly. "I saw the birds come, too."

Marya started. In all her life, she had never expected to meet another who had witnessed her sisters' seductions.

"Deliver your report, girl!" shouted Chairman Venik. "We haven't got all night to reminisce!"

Marya drew herself up. She tried to calm her little heart. Though they had merry mustaches and very fine vests, when they spoke she could see the domoviye's long yellow teeth, sharp and jagged.

"I . . . I wish to report that I have examined the . . . the matter carefully, and I think, I am fairly sure . . . I am *certain* there can be no doubt that the house is at least two steps larger than it was a few months ago, and possibly more. I cannot investigate the Dyachenkos' room, which adjoins ours."

"Too right you can't!" bellowed a domovaya with a glossy brown mustache that had been curled with a tiny iron. "It's not your business!"

Chairman Venik hushed the Dyachenko domovoi. "Is that all, giantess? Do you really think there is anything about this house we do not know? You have selfishly allocated excessive size to yourself, and forgotten to steal a bigger brain to go with it!" He polished his watch-medal proudly. "We are widening the house! We conferred over a period of six months, and determined that the Revolution requires more from us than mere mischief and teacup-breaking. If such a great number of people must hold the house, the house must hold a great number of people!"

Chainik clapped his hands. "From each according to his ability, to each according to his need!" he crowed.

"Well said, Comrade! We have abilities we have hoarded, self-ishly, because we did not understand that we owed them to the People, that we had become decadent, lazy bourgeoisie, in love with wealth and houses and ignoring Great Duties, High Philosophy!" Chairman Venik thumped the table with his little red fist. "No longer! The domoviye belong to the Party!"

"But surely," protested Marya, "if you widen the house the houses on either side of us shall be crushed."

"Child," said Comrade Zvonok in a patient tone, "we are not architects. We are imps. We are goblins. If we could not make a little room on the inside without budging the outside, we would not be worth our tails. After all, we have been making our little homes in the walls for centuries."

"We will open up the floors like untying a stack of newspapers—pop!—out they will spring! The house on Gorokhovaya Street will be a secret country in the midst of St. Petersburg! They will plant turnips in the kitchen, and grow wheat on the ceiling, and we shall all have biscuits till we are so fat we will roll and never walk!" burst out the Piakovsky domovoi deliriously.

Silence forked across the table like ice cracking.

"It's Dzerzhinskaya Street now, Comrade Banya," the chairman said quietly. "It's Petrograd."

"Of . . . of course." Banya sat down, abashed. His face grew bright red, and he began to tremble.

"Oh, don't worry!" Marya cried, wanting desperately to save the poor creature from embarrassment. "I can never remember!"

"It is our duty to remember," said Chainik coldly at her side.

"You must not tell anyone what we have done," interrupted the chairman. "You understand? We will report you to the House Committee, the other one, the Big Committee, and you'll be carted away, faster than you can yawn!"

"I won't, I promise," Marya said hurriedly. "Though you ought not to report people. It's not neighborly, and really rather horrid of you."

Chairman Venik grinned, and all his yellow, jagged teeth showed, like the teeth of a wolf-trap. "Don't misunderstand us. We are very sweet when you have cream for us, and biscuits, and boots, but you have brought us *nothing*, and so we owe you *nothing*. The Party is a wonderful, marvelous invention, and it has taught us wonderful, marvelous things—chiefly, that we can cause more trouble with less effort by filing complaints than by breaking teacups."

Marya began to tremble herself. Her stomach felt cold. "But a domovoi can't file a complaint. . . ."

"Who's a domovoi?" laughed Comrade Banya, her teeth out, too. "I'm Ekaterina Piakovsky."

"I'm Pyotr Abramov," chuckled Chairman Venik.

"I'm Gordei Blodniek," smirked Chainik.

"It takes two of us to hold the pen, but we manage," giggled the Malashenko domovoi.

All the domoviye were laughing at her; all of their teeth were shining in the candlelight. Marya Morevna buried her face in her hands.

"Stop it, Venik!" snapped Zvonok. "You old stove-snort! You're frightening her, and she's mine, so I say stuff your chimneys!" Her mustache quivered with rage. She left her seat to stroke Marya's nightgown. "There, there, Masha dear," she cooed, calling her by her old pet name. "If you like I shall mend your teacup. Would that make you feel better?"

But Chairman Venik was leaning over the table, his grin wider and wider, until the sides of his mouth met somewhere behind his ears. "Just you wait," he hissed. "Just you *wait*. Papa Koschei is coming, coming, coming, over the hills on his red horse, and he's got bells on his boots and a ring in his pocket, and he knows your name, *Marya Morevna*."

Marya could not help it; she screamed. The domoviye's mustaches were all blown back.

Zvonok whirled on him. "Venichek, you are a *hedgehog's ass*. You weren't supposed to tell! Is it worth it to scare a poor girl?"

"Zvonya, I *live* to scare poor girls! Their tears smell like the freshest, warmest cakes with cherry jam smeared all round them. Of course it's worth it!"

"We'll see, when Papa gets here," warned Comrade Zvonok.

The domoviye drew away from Venik slightly, as if waiting for him to turn to ash before their eyes.

"You all saw," quavered Banya, twisting her mustache, eager to make up her fault. "I didn't tell! It was Venik!"

"It's been recorded in the minutes," Zvonok said darkly.

"I don't understand," said Marya, her tears drying on her cheeks. "How do you know my name?"

"Don't worry about it, dear," said Zvonok brightly. "It's far past your bedtime. Let's get you to sleep, shall we?"

All Marya's fingers and toes were numb. She let herself be led away from the cackling komityet, shaking as though she had been drenched in water dragged in frozen buckets from the Neva. The domovaya pulled her past a grim Lenin demanding: *Have YOU*

Volunteered for the Front Lines? Marya had a moment of panic: What if she could not get big again, and was to be stuck down here forever with the goblins and frowning paper Lenin staring her down? Suddenly she wanted very much to see the front of the stove again, and her own bed.

"What did he mean? Who is Koschei?" she asked softly.

"You know, you've been very careless, Masha. I try to watch out for you, even though you've never given me boots or cream, and I think that's a testament to my generous soul, but you insist on drawing attention to yourself."

"But I don't! I'm *so* quiet the Abramov twins tripped over me last week." Since the affair of the scarf she had tried very hard never to be noticed by anyone.

"Marya Morevna! Don't you know anything? Girls must be very, very careful to care only for ribbons and magazines and wedding rings. They must sweep their hearts clean of anything but kisses and theater and dancing. They must never read Pushkin; they must never say clever things; they must never have sly eyes or wear their hair loose and wander around barefoot, or they will draw his attention! Safe in a house and a husband, that's where you belong! But it's too late now, too late! Fool child, the house and I tried so hard to raise you right!"

"But who is *he*?" Marya pleaded—yet she did know that name, didn't she? The name pulled at the back of her mind, bending her toward it.

But Zvonok had gone knuckle-white with fear and anger, and would say nothing. When they passed through the flower-carved door and back into the space between the stove and the wall, she yanked on Marya's sash once more. Marya spun like a spool, and she felt the peculiar sensation of a great huge hand pulling her up by the crown of her skull, of her bones yawning and stretching. When she stopped spinning, she faced the stove, and was quite her own height again. And she found herself disappointed, only a little. It was over. The extraordinary thing was over and it had taken minutes. She had gotten big again with no trouble, and how long would she have to wait now for some other scrap of the naked world?

"Here," whispered Zvonok. "This is the best I can do for you." The little domovaya reached into her red vest and drew out the silver hairbrush Marya had seen in the flotsam at the komityet. It grew larger and larger as she pulled it out, until it was taller than Zvonok but perfectly sized for Marya's hand. "It belonged to Svetlana Tikhonovna. Did you know she was a dancer when she was young, with the ballet? Comrade Stoylik calls her names, but when she sleeps, he comes out to curl up in her hair and sleep next to her ear. He says she smells like Kiev."

"Won't he know you took it?"

"I'll slap the bottoms of his feet until he says it was yours all along. But you keep it safe from old Svetlana—she'd love to have it back."

"I already have a hairbrush, though," protested Marya.

Zvonok winked, first with one eye, then the other. She put one hand over her left eye and spat.

"You need this one."

And with that, the domovaya hopped up onto one foot, spun around three times, and vanished.

4

Likho Never Sleeps

In a city by the sea that was certainly never called anything so bourgeois as St. Petersburg, there stood a long, thin house on a long, thin street. By a long, thin window, a young woman in a pale blue dress and pale green slippers watched her new neighbor arrive in the house next door. An old woman clutching her suitcase, shrouded in a black wool dress, very tall and thin, whose waist was so stretched and skinny that Marya could have put both her hands around it. The woman's fingers were amazingly long, her nose sharp and spiked, and her white hair pulled tightly back into a bun. She walked with a limp and a hunch, but Marya suspected that this was to hide how tall she truly was.

"That's Comrade Likho," said one of Marya's twelve mothers, darning an ancient stocking. "A widow with no children. She says she'll take in all our laundry, the dear old thing. I thought it might be nice if you visited her after school. She could tutor you, watch out for you while I'm at the factory."

Marya did not like this idea at all. In a classroom she could think her own thoughts and no one would bother her—no teachers called upon her anymore. With a tutor, she could not avoid being asked her opinions. She frowned down at the hunchbacked Likho. The crone stopped and looked up at the window, the turn of her head fast and sharp, like a bird's. Widow Likho's eyes were black and huge, as though they had drooped and melted and slid down into her cheekbones. Her gaze was barbed and biting. The cherry trees dropped their blossoms across Likho's black dress, and she scowled.

"You shouldn't be frightened of old ladies," admonished another of Marya's mothers—the one, by coincidence, who had borne her. Marya knew she should not show favoritism, but her mother's hands looked so thin, the skin so dry, she wanted to clap them between her own, to warm them and make them red again. "You'll be one someday, you know."

The widow Likho stared up at Marya's window. Slowly, like ice sliding across a plate, she smiled.

Marya had heard no more from the domoviye. But she had very carefully put out her favorite boots, her black ones with fine black ribbon, and tucked a precious biscuit into each. *All my fine things belong to the House, which is the same as saying the People.* She placed them neatly at the foot of her bed. *Besides, I have no place now to wear anything that makes me look like a rich man's daughter.* When she woke in the morning, the shoes were gone.

In their place was a little teacup with cherries on the handle, glued inexpertly back together. When she picked it up, the handle fell off.

Each evening, she brushed her hair with Svetlana Tikhonovna's brush. Her hair rustled dryly, strand against strand, no longer so soft or shining as it had once been, but not yet falling out. Nothing of note happened. Perhaps Zvonok had been making a commentary on the state of Marya's own ragged, wooden comb. *It's not my fault my hair is so tangled it broke off two of the teeth.* She sniffed.

Marya wanted very much to send a message to the House Below. At night, she whispered into the pipes: *I hate it here. Please take me away, let me be something other than Marya, something magical, with a round belly. Frighten me, make me cry, only come back.*

Despite Marya's pleas to the contrary, all twelve of her mothers insisted she visit old Widow Likho after her lessons every day. *And take her some nice rolls; she's old and can't walk to the bread line.*

Marya stood very still in front of her neighbor's door. Her toes had gone clammy and blue in her threadbare shoes, and her stomach chewed on itself. She wanted to go home. She ought to have gone behind the stove and called out Zvonok or Chainik to go with her. They would not have come—they never answered her tapping. But she would have felt better. She didn't need a tutor, or looking after. She knew her algebra and her history and could recite two hundred lines of Pushkin from memory.

Widow Likho opened the door and stared down at Marya like a vulture on a hawthorn branch. Marya half expected her to open her mouth and caw or screech like one. She stood so tall that she could not get through the door without bending down beneath the jamb. Her long hands clutched the sides of the door—she had sharp, pearly fingernails, without a hint of yellow or age. In fact, though her face was wrinkled and withered, her hands were young, firm, certainly able to snatch a girl from the street without trouble.

Widow Likho said nothing. She turned around and walked slowly down her hall, her black dress trailing behind her like a stain. She pushed aside the curtain that divided her room from the next family's, and Marya crept in behind her, hoping only to be invisible, for the old witch to take a nap while Marya read until she could politely leave. She laid out yesterday's bread ration, wrapped in slick brown paper, on a little brass table with cherubs winging its legs. Widow Likho did not touch the food. She merely stared at Marya, inclining her head faintly. She folded her long hands together in her lap—so long the tips of her middle fingers grazed her forearm.

"My mother said you might like to tutor me, but if you're tired, I can read to you until evening. Or make you tea, or whatever you like," Marya stammered nervously.

Likho curled up her thin pale lips into a smile. It seemed to take some effort.

"I never sleep," she said. Marya shuddered. Her voice was deep and rough, like black heels dragged over stone.

"Well . . . I suppose that saves time."

"Lessons." Her voice dragged across the room again.

"You don't have to."

"On the contrary. Lessons are a specialty of mine." Widow Likho inclined her head in the other direction. "Shall we begin with history?"

The crone turned, her bones creaking and popping as she did, and pulled a large black book off of the shelf. It was so wide that the edges hung off Widow Likho's lap, polished and gleaming. She extended it towards Marya.

"Read," she rumbled. "My voice is what it used to be."

"Do you mean 'isn't what it used to be'?"

Likho smiled again—the same blank, distant smile—as though she had thought of something amusing that happened a hundred years ago.

Marya was grateful not to have to look at her. She opened the massive black book and began to read:

> *The Causations of the Great War were several. First, the avid student must be aware that when the world was young it knew only seven things: water, life and death, salt, night, birds, and the length of an hour. Each of these things had Tsars or Tsaritsas, and chief among these were the Tsar of Death and the Tsar of Life.*

Marya Morevna looked up from the book.

"Comrade Likho, this is not the history of the Great War," she said uncertainly. "This is not a book approved by my school."

The widow chuckled, and the sound was a heavy stone falling into a shallow well.

"Read, child."

Marya's hands shook on the black book. She had never seen a book so beautiful, so heavy and rich, but it did not seem friendly, like the books in her mother's room, or in Svetlana Tikhonovna's or Yelena Grigorievna's suitcases.

"The world is a slow learner," Marya Morevna read.

> *And only after eons did it master the techniques of the sun, earth, sugar, the length of a year, and men. The Tsars or Tsaritsas retreated into mountains and snow. They stayed far from each other out of family respect, but had no interest in these new things, which were surely passing fashions.*
>
> *But the Tsar of Death and the Tsar of Life greatly feared one another, for Death is surrounded by souls, and is never*

lonely, and the Tsar of Life had hidden his death away in a place deeper than secrets, and more secret than depth. The Tsaritsa of Salt could not reconcile them, though they were brothers, and the Tsaritsa of Water could not find an ocean wide enough to place between them.

After a space of time longer than it takes the stars to draw breath together, the Tsar of Death was so well loved by his court of souls that he became puffed up and proud. He bedecked himself in onyx, agate, and hematite, and gave bayonets of ice, and cannons of bone, and horses of drifting ash with eyes and nostrils of red sparks to each of the souls that had perished in the long, tawdry history of the world. Together this great army, with shrouds flying like banners and trumpets of twelve swords lashed together marched out across the deep snow and into the lonely kingdom of the Tsar of Life.

Marya swallowed. She felt as though she could not breathe.

"Comrade Likho, the Great War began because Archduke Ferdinand was shot, and the West would have crushed a noble Slavic people to dust underfoot if we had not intervened."

Likho chewed her cheek. "You are a very clever child," she said.

"Not really, everyone knows that."

"If you are so clever that you know everything, why did you call me?"

Marya sat back in her chair. The black book slid perilously forward on her lap, but she did not reach out to catch it.

"Me? I didn't call you! You're a widow! You were allocated housing!"

"Your hair is so long and tidy," sighed Widow Likho, as if Marya had not even spoken. Her breath rattled like bones in a cup. "However did you get it to behave?"

"I . . . I have a silver brush. It belonged to a ballerina before me. . . ."

"Yeeeeessss," the crone said, drawing the word out longer and longer, until its end flapped like a broken rope. "Svetlana Tikhonovna. I remember her. She was so beautiful, you cannot imagine. Her hair was the color of water in winter, and her bones were so delicate! She hardly had any breasts at all. When she danced, men killed themselves, knowing they would never again see such beauty. She had four lovers in Kiev, each richer than the other, but her heart was so cold that she could hold ice in her mouth and it would never melt. We could all have taken lessons from her. And then, one New Year, her second lover, who owned a cosmetics company and a fleet of whaling ships that harvested ambergris for perfumes and lipsticks so red they would leave spots in your vision, made her a present of a silver brush with boar bristles. Who knows where he found it? A peddler woman, maybe, hunched and thin, in a black dress, hauling her cart along a larch-lined road. Svetlana loved the brush; oh, how she loved it! The longer she spent brushing her hair, the more terrible and beautiful she grew. So she let her lover comb her pale hair over and over, and I heard the sound of strand against strand on the other side of the snow. I came to her immediately; I wasted no time for one such as her. And when she performed for the Tsar's daughters, the ribbons of her shoes were just a little loose—such an infinitely small difference—but she fell, and shattered her heel. Her four lovers left her, since she could no longer dance so that they wished to die. But, ah, bad luck! She was pregnant, and though ice would not melt in her mouth, she hurried to marry the first bricklayer who didn't care about dancing, and had four children who ruined her beauty. Then her house burned during the purges. Terrible to happen to such a sublime creature, but tscha! Life is like that, isn't it?"

Marya wanted to run out of the house, but she could not move. Her throat dried up. "Who are you?" she whispered.

"Say my name, daughter. You know who I am."

"Widow Likho."

"*What is my name, Marya Morevna?*" the crone roared, her black voice bending the windows and rattling the books on the shelf.

Marya quailed, shrinking away into the upholstery. "Widow Likho! Comrade Likho! Comrade . . . oh . . . oh. *Likho.* Bad luck."

The old woman leaned forward. "Yeeeeessss," she said again, stretching her voice like dark glue. "And you have my brush. You called me to you."

"No . . . I didn't mean to!"

"Intent is trivial," barked Likho. Suddenly she stood up with a swiftness no young woman could match. She towered; the ceiling forced her to bend at the waist, but beneath it her back was straight, without a hunch. She hovered over Marya, her huge black eyes crackling violet. "But never you fear me, Marya Morevna!" Her voice turned crooning, sibilant, her breath sawing back and forth. She took Marya's face in her impossibly long hands. "I cannot touch you. You are not for me. Papers have been drawn up in your name, silks and candies allocated. Everyone knows to make way. But you called; I had to come. I am here to educate you, to make you ready. There is no better teacher of rough necessity than bad luck, and you will have great use of me, I promise. Keep your bread. Keep your tears. Neither will help you, and you will work hard to outgrow need of them. Go home. Pat your mother's hand and kiss your father's cheek. Drink out of your broken teacup." Likho grinned. "Don't forget to brush your lovely black hair. And come to me when the sun is low. Come to me and be my pupil, my pet, my daughter."

Marya bolted from the room. She ran down the long hallway,

bumping her arm against the wall, and out into the long, thin street, panting and crying, her heart hiding behind her ribs.

She still clutched the book to her chest.

Every evening, while the sun dripped red wax into the Neva, Widow Likho stood outside the house on Dzerzhinskaya Street and looked up at Marya's window. Her hunch returned—she seemed just a simple old woman again, but she watched the window like a raven with white hair, and smiled unwaveringly, silent, utterly still.

Marya did not read the book. She hid it under her bed. She shut her eyes so tightly her brow ached and recited Pushkin until she fell asleep. And at the rim of her sleep, at the edge of her reciting, there the black name sat, hunched, waiting: *There Tsar Koschei, he wastes away, poring over his pale gold.*

Spring became summer in this manner, and Marya's own mother, not the one who tucked her in on Tuesdays and Thursdays, nor the one who cooked supper on Fridays and Wednesdays, but the one who had carried her for nine months, began to visit Widow Likho, embarrassed that her daughter was so rude and neglectful. Marya begged her not to, but the two women shared tea and sour cherries from their tree every night when Marya's mother returned from her shift. And, though she had never been clumsy or careless, Marya's mother began to stumble on the stairs, to get splinters in her fingers, to lose her left shoes. Her work at the munitions factory became sloppy, faulty bullets slipping past her on the line, and she was reprimanded twice.

Marya thought she knew why—but whenever she thought she was brave enough to face the Widow once more, the awful vision of the crone bending over her filled her heart, and her skin went cold. Did everything that had magic have teeth? She had liked the world better when it served up sweet-looking birds and sweet-looking men. Likho was too much; Marya's mind could not even touch the edges of that blackness. Her body clenched itself and refused to let her act, no matter how tired her mother looked each day. When, just once, all her courage piled itself hand over hand, and she made it so far as the door, the moment her fingers grazed the knob she vomited horribly, her stomach emptying itself of anything good she might have had to eat and wanted to keep.

Was that magic, or am I just a weak and stupid and cowardly girl? Marya did not know, could not know, and she felt frozen all over with shame as she cleaned her sickness from the carpet.

And then, in June, Marya's mother tripped over a crack in the sidewalk and broke her ankle. While she convalesced in the great, tall house (slowly growing greater and taller), the close air gathered in her lungs, and she began to cough up dust, awful, racking sounds in the night. And like a fever, Marya's fear broke.

"I'm *here!*" screamed Marya Morevna into Widow Likho's curiously empty house. No other families greeted her or told her to shut up, for heaven's sake. "Do you hear me? I'm here! I brought your book! Leave my mother alone!"

Likho stepped quietly into the hall and turned her head to the side to face Marya without moving the rest of her long black body.

"I haven't done a thing to your mother, child. She's such a nice lady, bringing an old woman tea and sweets in the evening! What a shame her daughter has no manners."

"Bad Luck, I know you! It's your fault she broke her foot, and your fault she's coughing, and it will be your fault when she loses her job at the factory!" Marya shook—she felt like she might throw up again, but she savagely bit the inside of her lip, willing her body to obey her.

Likho spread her long white hands. "I am what I am, Marya Morevna. You cannot be angry with a stove for heating the house. That is what it was built for."

"Well, I'm here now. Leave her alone."

"It's dear of you to visit your old *baba,* little one, but there's no need. It's too late; the time has passed."

"Too late for what? What's going on? Why do the domoviye know my name? Please tell me!"

Likho laughed harshly. Her laugh bounced off of the parlor lamp; the bulb shattered.

"When the world was young, it knew only seven things. And one of these was the length of an hour. Such a pity little Marya doesn't know it. You had an hour to learn at my knee, and an hour, if I wish it, can be as long as all of spring. But the hour has chimed. He is coming; I am leaving. We try to stay out of each other's way. Family occasions can be so awkward."

Marya's mind surged ahead of itself. Her cheeks burned. The black book was warm in her arms.

"You're the Tsaritsa of the Length of an Hour."

"Bad luck relies absolutely on perfect timing." Likho grinned.

"Who is coming?" pleaded Marya Morevna. The Tsar from the poem? But that was only a story—but so were domoviye, and yet. She could not put it all together. She was missing vital information, and she hated it. When she knew and others didn't, that was better. "Tell me!" Marya tried to command the Widow; she tried to bellow and grow taller in her shoes.

But Likho only shuddered, and folded up her body like a suit-case, and the black of her dress became the black pelt of a tall racing hound, its ribs tucked up into its dark belly. It barked once, so loud Marya clapped her hands over her ears, and then disappeared with a crackling, crushing sound.

5

Who Is to Rule

In a city by the sea, there stood a long, thin house on a long, thin street, and by a long, thin window, Marya Morevna sat and wept in her work clothes, and did not look out into the leafy trees. The winter moon looked in at her, stroking her hair with a silver hand. She was sixteen years of age, with seventeen's shadow hanging heavy on her every tear. Old enough to work after school, old enough to be tired in her joints and her heels, old enough to know that something irretrievable had passed her by.

If she had looked out the window, she might have seen a great, hoary old black owl alight on the branch of the oak tree. She might have seen the owl lean perilously forward on his green-black branch and, without taking his gaze from her window, fall hard—thump, bash!—onto the streetside. She would have seen the bird bounce up, and when he righted himself, become a handsome young man in a handsome black coat, his dark hair curly and thick, flecked with silver, his mouth half-smiling, as if anticipating a terribly sweet thing.

But Marya Morevna saw none of this. She only heard the knock at the great cherrywood door, and rushed to answer it before her mother could wake. She stood there in her factory overalls, her face turned bloodless by moonlight, and the man looked down at her, for he was quite tall. Slowly, without taking his eyes from hers, the man in the black coat knelt before her.

"I am Comrade Koschei, surnamed Bessmertny," he said with a low, churning voice, "and I have come for the girl in the window."

The house on Dzerzhinskaya Street leaned in and held its breath. In the corners of the chimneys, the domoviye waited to hear what she might say. Marya held hers, too. Her breast filled to bursting, but she could not let her breath go. If she did, what might happen? She wanted several things at once: to run; to cry out; to shrink and crawl away; to throw her arms around him and whisper, *At last, at last, I thought you would never come;* to beg him to leave her alone; to faint in a ladylike fashion and escape the whole incident. Her heart shook, beating abrupt and hot, all out of time and measure. He took her hand, and she stared down at this man getting snow on his trousers and how big his eyes seemed, how black, how unforgiving, how sly, how old. And yet he was not old. Older than she, but if he were more than twenty she would eat the curtains. He had long, smoky lashes like a girl, and his hair flew about in the wind like the fur of a wild dog. Marya did not often think men beautiful, not in the way she thought the Blodniek sisters were, or hoped that she herself might one day be.

"Invite me in, Masha," Comrade Bessmertny said softly. The street drank up his voice, sunk it into the snow, disappeared it.

Marya shook her head. She did not know why. She wanted him

to come in. But it was all wrong: He should not call her by her pet name; he should not kneel like that. She should have seen him fall from the tree; she should have been more clever, more watchful. She should have seen what he was before—this was not how it was supposed to go. It was too familiar, and a little lascivious, how close he crouched to her. She knew already he would not take her walking down Dzerzhinskaya Street or buy her a hat. She was not filled up with the sight of him, the way she had seen her sisters fill up, like silk balloons, like wineskins. Instead, he seemed to land heavily within her, like a black stone falling. She did not feel it would be at all safe to kiss him on the cheeks. Marya Morevna shook her head: *No, not like this, when I have not seen you without your skin on, when I know nothing, when I am not safe. Not you, whose name all my nightmares know.*

"Then get your things, and come with me," said Koschei, unperturbed. His eyes sparkled in the cold, the way distant stars will when the night freezes. And Marya's heart stopped—that was what *they* said. When they came for you, because you were not good, because you were not worthy of a red scarf. *Get your things and come with me.* Perhaps he was not like her sisters' husbands at all.

But the shape of Comrade Bessmertny's lips fascinated her and made her feel sick all at once—and that was what magic did to her. His lips shone bright and dark, soft and heart-shaped. She felt, looking at him, that she could not see him at all, but could see only the things that made him unlike a man, the lushness of his face and the slowness of his manner. Though he frightened her, though the house moved in its sleep around her, no doubt dreaming of this very creature the domoviye called Papa and feared as though he might come wielding a belt, he also seemed familiar, a thing already part of herself, like herself even in the shape of his lips and the curve of his lashes. If she had spent her hours knitting a lover instead of coats for Anna's son, the man who knelt before her would have sprung from her needles, even down to the ghostly flecks of silver in his hair. She had not known before that she wanted all these things, that she preferred dark hair and a slightly cruel expression, that she wished for tallness, or that a man kneeling might thrill her. A whole young life's worth of slowly collected predilections coalesced in a few moments within her, and Koschei Bessmertny, his lashes full of snow, became perfect.

Marya shivered and, without really thinking about it, she took her hand from the man in the handsome black coat and withdrew into the house. He had come for her—for good or ill, she had little choice in it. *When they come for you,* her mother had once warned, *you have to go. It's not about wanting or not wanting.*

She pulled a suitcase—not her own, and perhaps this was the first humble sin in her ledger—from the hall closet. She had little enough to take, but in went a few dresses, work clothes, her grey cap. Marya paused, hovering precariously over the suitcase as though she might pitch herself in at any moment. Finally, she squeezed her eyes shut and placed Likho's great black book very gently beneath the clothes. The latches made small, hushed smacking noises as they closed.

Very suddenly, Zvonok the domovaya was sitting on the lid of the suitcase. Her boots shone new and polished, and her mustache had been beautifully oiled.

"I am not coming with you," the house imp said grimly. "You understand that. I am married to the house, not to you. Even if you went out into the fields and offered me dancing shoes and called to me, I would not come."

Marya nodded. Speaking seemed like such tremendous work just now. But at least Zvonok knew the man; at least he was only some demon-king of the domoviye and probably more besides, and not an officer come to carry her off to oblivion.

"Will you even say good-bye to your mothers?"

Marya shook her head. What would she say? How could she explain? She couldn't even explain to herself. *Mother, I have been waiting for something to happen to me my whole life, and now that it has I am going, even though it is a tilted kind of thing, and I meant to be so much better at it than my sisters.*

"What a dreadful girl I have raised! Still, if you don't ask their permission, they can't say no. That's our sort of logic." The domovaya gestured for Marya to crouch down so that they could talk face-to-face, on equal footing. "But if not your mother, who will tell you how to behave on your wedding night? Who will twine flowers in your bridal braid?"

From somewhere deep in her muscles, Marya Morevna pulled up her words. "I'm not getting married," she whispered.

"Oh ho! Easy to say, devotchka; not so easy to keep the house standing when the wolf comes thumping his tail in the grass. Listen, Masha. Listen to old Zvonok, who knows you. The domoviye have been marrying up and out and over each other just about as long as girls and boys. Prick your finger with a needle and let the blood fall over your threshold—it will hurt less, and you will dream of daughters. Men, they feel nothing like what we must endure. You have to make room in yourself for him, and that is the same in a house as in a body. See that you keep some rooms for yourself, locked up tight. And if you don't want to get big in the belly . . . Well," Zvonok wrinkled up her wide nose, "I don't suppose that'll be the same trouble for you as it is for the rest of us. The deathless can't play our little genealogical games. Just remember that the only question in a house is who is to rule. The rest is only dancing around that, trying not to look it in the eye."

Zvonok patted Marya Morevna's face with her little hand. "Ah! My heart! I warned you about reading Pushkin! I would choose another husband for you, I would, if the choosing of it were mine. I could have hoped for a different life for my Masha than his mouth on her breast like a babe, sucking her pretty voice down, her little ways, 'til she's dry and rattling. But you like him already, I can tell. Even though we showed our teeth and were very clear about his being wicked. That's not your fault. He makes himself pretty, so that girls will like him. But if you must insist on being clever, then *be clever*. Be brave. Sleep with fists closed and shoot straight." Comrade Zvonok shrugged and sighed with a little whistling sound. "But I am selfish! I must learn to give the best of my house away."

The domovaya hopped up to her feet and kissed Marya roughly on the tip of her nose. She did a shuffling, cock-legged little dance and laid her finger aside her own nose. "Who is to rule," Zvonok hissed, and disappeared.

Marya blinked. Tears dropped from her eyes like tiny, hard beads. Her legs, all against her head, longed to straighten and take her to the door, to Comrade Bessmertny, still kneeling there in the cold like a knight. She ruled nothing, Marya knew. Nothing and no one.

Marya Morevna ran out onto Dzerzhinskaya Street, which had been Kommissarskaya Street, which had been Gorokhovaya Street, her black hair long and loose, her cheeks lashed red, her breath a hanging mist in the air. Snow crunched beneath her boots. Comrade Bessmertny smiled at her without showing his teeth. *The birds never hurt my sisters*, Marya said to her galloping heart. *He is not a bird*, said her heart. *You weren't careful, you didn't see.* He held open the door of a long, black car—a sleek, curving thing, the kind Marya had only glimpsed rumbling by, always followed by the grumbling of her neighbors regarding the evils of the merchant class. The car growled and snorted, a baleful red peeping through the vents. Marya dropped gratefully into the car, relieved to have done it, to finally be inside the magic instead of looking at it through a window. To never have to hear again that something black was coming for her—it was here, and it was handsome, and it wanted her. She couldn't change her mind once the door shut—*ah, and there it went, nothing to be done now.* She shivered in the backseat. The car was as cold as a forest, and she had forgotten her good fur hat.

Marya jumped a little as Comrade Koschei slid in beside her. The car, driverless, roared ahead down the street with a whine and a screeching whinny. Koschei turned, gripped Marya's chin, and kissed her—not on the cheek, not chastely or unchastely, but greedily, with his whole, hard mouth, cold, biting, knowing. He ate up her breath in the kiss. Marya felt he would swallow her whole.

6

The Seduction of Marya Morevna

The black car knew the forests like a boar knows them. It sniffed at the bone-bright birch trees and blared its low, moaning horn, as if calling out to fellow beasts within the pine-slashed shadows. Marya Morevna shuddered to hear it, but when she shuddered, Koschei held her nearer to him, twined his hand in hers.

"I will keep you," he said softly, as sweet as black tea, "and I will keep you warm." But his own skin had frosted over; his fingernails shone pearly blue.

"Comrade," Marya said, "you are colder than I. I fear your flesh will freeze me."

Koschei studied her as if she were a terribly curious creature, to crave warmth so. His dark eyes moved over her face possessively, but he did not release her. If anything, the cold of his body deepened, until Marya felt as though a pillar of ice clung to her, sending out silver tendrils to cover her, too, in the stuff of itself.

That first night, the black car wheezed, spat, and coughed triumphantly as they entered a clearing around a little house whose ruddy windows beamed through the sharp, clear night, whose eaves bowed under fresh straw, whose door stood ever so invitingly ajar. A peasant house, to be sure, nothing like her own tall, thin home, but squat and pleasant as a grandmother, a brown chimney puffing away. Koschei helped her, shivering, out of the car and slapped its fender fondly, whereupon the automobile leapt up cheerfully and scampered off into the dark.

The house had made itself ready for dinner. A thick wooden table sparkled with candles and a neat spread: bread and pickled peppers and smoked fish, dumplings and beets in vinegar and brown kasha, mushrooms and thick beef tongue, and blini topped with little black spoonfuls of caviar and cream. Cold vodka sweated in a crystal decanter. Goose stew boiled over the hearth.

Marya would have liked to have been polite, but the sight of so much food dazzled her. She fell to the bread and fish like a wild thing.

"Wait, volchitsa," said Koschei, holding up his hand. "Little savage wolf! Please, sit at my table, brush the snow from your hair. No one will take your meal from you."

Marya started to apologize, to explain how scarce food had been in Petrograd, how her belly had felt like a clenched fist with nothing inside.

"Comrade, I am so hungry—"

"There is no need for you to speak tonight, Marya Morevna. That time will come, and I will hang on your words like a condemned man. But for now, please, listen to me, and do as I say. I know that is difficult for you—I would not have chosen you if you found it easy to be silent and pliable! But we are going to do an extraordinary thing together. Do you know what it is we are doing? I will tell you, so that later, you cannot say I deceived you. We are taking your will out of your jaw—for that is where the will sits—and pressing it very small between our two hands, like a bit of dough. We are rolling it, and squeezing it, until it gets very small. Small enough to fit into the eye of a needle which is hidden inside an egg, which is hidden inside a hen, which is hidden inside a goose, which is hidden inside a deer. When we are finished you will give your will to me, and I will keep it safe for you. I am very good at this thing. A savant, you might say. You, however—" Koschei poured vodka for her. It trickled into her glass like music. The sides of Marya's throat stuck together, so dry, so thirsty. "—are a novice. Less than a novice. And like a good novice, you must swallow your pride." Koschei raised his glass. Marya raised hers more slowly, unsure. Her hand shook a little. She did not like to be ordered. She wanted to say a hundred, a thousand things. She wanted to leap upon him and demand he explain it all: Likho, the domoviye, the birds, her whole life. *I have to know, I have to, or else you will just rule me until the end of everything because you know and I do not*. But he only smiled at her, encouraging, benevolent, serene as an icon. "To life," he said, and drank his vodka down in a long swallow.

"Now. Taste the caviar first, I must insist. I know that you would like to save it for last, to savor the delay because it has been so long since you tasted such a thing. But if I may teach you anything, it will be to relish everything, to devour it all—the richest things first, for they are your due. You have read your Pushkin— what is it old Aleksey says about me? *There Tsar Koschei wastes away, poring over his pale gold*. Tfu! That boy needed a haircut. But oh, Marya, Marousha, I *do* pore over my treasures! And some of them are glistening sturgeon eggs like piles of onyxes, and some of them are vials of vodka glittering like diamonds, and some of them are beets heavy and red as garnets, and some of them are beautiful girls from Petrograd, sitting in my house, silent as gold, because I asked them to be silent, which is the sweetest silence of all. And in the dark, I *do* pore over my riches, my impossible bounty."

Beautiful girls? Marya heard his plurals. Had there been others? Questions hammered at her lips, but she wrestled with them, and kept her peace. *If I do this,* she reasoned, *perhaps I will earn my answers.*

Koschei cut a thick slice of bread from the loaf. The crust crackled under his knife, and the slice fell, moist and heavy, black as earth. He spread cold, salted butter over it with a sweep of the blade, and scooped caviar onto the butter, a smear of dark eggs against the pale gold cream. He held it out to her, and she shyly reached for it, but he admonished her. And so Marya Morevna sat, silently, as Koschei fed her the bread, and butter, and roe. The taste of it burst in her mouth, the salt and the sea. Tears sprang to her eyes. Her empty belly sang for the thickness of it, the plenty. Suddenly, it was a relief not to have to speak, to make conversation, while her body exhausted itself in poring over the delights of salt and heavy bread.

"Now the beets, *volchitsa*. And look at them first, how bloody they are, how crimson, how they leave trails behind them, like wounded things. Sip your vodka, and then bite one of the peppers—see how the vinegar and the vodka mix on your tongue? This is a very marvelous thing. A winter thing, when everything is pickled and preserved under glass. You can taste summer in this mixture, summer boiled down and soaked in brine, mummified, packed with spices to be born again on this table, in this place, in this snow. Now, a spoonful of kasha to smooth your excited palate." He slipped the silver spoon into her mouth, his thumb grazing her chin. Marya felt as though she had never eaten before, never considered her food at all. She liked this better than Likho's angular, hard magic. This magic filled her up, made her belly ache with fullness. "As you swallow the cow's tongue, think for a moment about how strange and holy that is, to devour the tongue of another. To steal from it all its power to speak, to low at the moon, to call to its calf. To be worthy of such food you must guard your own words carefully, speaking only the wise and clever ones, lest your tongue end up likewise, on the plate of a rich man. Of course, rich men have been made obsolete by the Party, but if you learn a second thing from me tonight, let it be this: The goblins of the city may hold committees to divide a single potato, but the strong and the cruel still sit on the hill, and drink vodka, and wear black furs, and slurp borscht by the pail, like blood. Children may wear through their socks marching in righteous parades, but Papa never misses his wine with supper. Therefore, it is better to be strong and cruel than to be fair. At least, one eats better that way. And morality is more dependent on the state of one's stomach than of one's nation."

In this way, over hours, Marya Morevna ate her supper. The firelight dazzled her, the marrowy broth of the stew made her drunk, and Koschei's low, inexorable voice, a voice like black tea, rose and fell like a ballad, lulling her, pulling at her, stroking her. Her mind chattered away, since her mouth could not: *What kind of bird are you really, under your skin? Are you truly the domoviye's Papa? Likho's brother? I am not fooled by you pretending Bessmertny is your surname! Likho taught me better than to think names are only names and mean nothing! Koschei the Deathless, that's what it means, and that's you, it must be you. But what does that mean for me now? What will you do with me?*

But she said none of these things. The drowsy, easy pleasure of allowing herself to be fed, to be spoken to without speaking, overwhelmed her. She felt like a fierce woodland creature, a volchitsa in truth, a little wolfling, brought inside and brushed and petted and fed until it seemed the most natural thing in the world to fall asleep by the fire. She looked out the little round window of the hut and, in her dreamy, satisfied glow, thought she saw not a long automobile parked outside, but a huge black horse bent over a trough of glowing red coals, chewing them thoughtfully. Sparks fell from its velvet mouth.

Finally, Koschei placed a teaspoon full of sour cherry jam on Marya's tongue and instructed her to sip her tea through the lump of fruit. When she had swallowed, he kissed her, their mouths warm and sweet with tea and cherries, and Marya Morevna fell asleep in his arms, with his lips still pressed to hers.

Somewhere deep in the well of the night, she woke, her belly aflame, scalding, and while Koschei slept cold and insensate, Marya Morevna rushed out of the hut to retch all her marvelous supper onto the frozen ground. She tried to do it quietly, so that he would not know that she had lost all the lovely things he had set out for her. *It's not my fault,* she thought furiously, unable to speak even now, when he was sleeping. *Bellies trained on dry bread rations and salt fish cannot bear all this richness!*

Marya Morevna looked up. The great black horse watched her calmly, his eyes burning phosphorescent in the dark.

Shame flowed into her mouth, sour and thick. She crept back into the little house so softly, like a thief.

In this way they traveled, across thrice nine kingdoms, thrice nine republics, the whole of the world, between Petrograd and Koschei's country. The sleek, driverless car, which never seemed to need gasoline or maps, sped them on through wild, brambly woods and snowy mountains like old bones. It remained cold as midnight within the automobile no matter how bright the sun outside. Marya's teeth ached from chattering. Yet each evening they would unfailingly discover a little house cheerily aglow in a larch forest or amid razor-spiky firs. Each evening a table would be set for them, the food growing finer and finer as they proceeded east and the snow grew deeper. Roast swan, vareniki stuffed with sweet pork and apples, pickled melons, cakes piled with cream and pastry. Each evening Koschei would ask her not to speak and then feed her with his long, graceful hands. Each evening she would sneak into the woods to throw it all up again, the muscles of her stomach sore with eating and retching, eating and retching.

"The vineyards that gave us this wine also provide the wine for Comrade Stalin's table," he said one night with a sly grin. "You will remember what I said about children and Papas, and who eats first, and who eats last." Koschei the Deathless made a face as he tasted the wine. "It is far too sweet. Comrade Stalin fears bitterness and has the tastes of a spoiled princess. I savor bitterness—it is born of experience. It is the privilege of one who has truly lived. You, too, must learn to prefer it. After all, when all else is gone, you may still have bitterness in abundance."

Marya Morevna thought this did not sound quite right. But the glistening swan meat and the vodka so pure it tasted only of cold water spun her faster and faster, and the faster she spun in his arms, the more sense he seemed to speak. And because her body could not keep the sumptuous food down, she found herself all the more ravenous whenever he lifted a spoon of roast potato to her mouth.

He placed honey on her tongue, and pear jelly, and brown, moist sugar. She swallowed his steaming tea. And he kissed her, again and again, sharing sweetness and heat between them. Outside the hut, the strange tall horse nosed at his trough of embers every night, watching her secret sickness without blinking. Only now his coat was red, with a mane like fire. And whenever she woke from her deep, downy bed, the automobile would be waiting in the mist, puffing exhaust, it, too, no longer black but scarlet, like beets, like blood.

But Marya was only a girl, thin and young, and the constant lurching from frozen car to warm, crackling fireside began to eat at her. She began to cough, only a little at first, but then harsh and sharp. She became feverish and sickly until, finally, she could not even eat the little candied quails or holiday bread piled with apricot syrup. She had to push the spoons away or else spill out her guts on the fine fur rugs.

Marya lay on the floor by the fire in the latest cheerful, obedient hut, her knees drawn up to her chest, sweating and shivering all at once. If she had wanted to speak, she could not have. Her eyes glassed over; the room swam. Koschei looked down at her, his dark hair wet with melted snow. "Poor volchitsa," he sighed. "I have been in such a hurry to get you home. I have been too impatient, and you are only human. But you must learn to keep up with me."

Koschei the Deathless knelt at her side and unbuttoned her work shirt. Even through her fever, Marya would always remember how his fingers shook as he pushed and peeled her clothes away until she lay naked by the hearth, trying to hide her breasts in her hands. But Koschei turned her over onto her stomach, and Marya heard the clinking of glasses. She smiled against the plush pelts laid over the floor. Her mother had done this when she was very little. *Banki.* She could feel the movements, so terribly familiar: Koschei set rubles on her skin and lit matches on the coins so they would not burn her, then caught up the matches in little vodka glasses so that her flesh was sucked up into the vacuum. It was meant to pull out her fever, to suck the illness away from her chest. When she was very small, before the birds or the war or

Dzerzhinskaya Street, her mother had done this for her when she fell ill. Soon Koschei had several glasses on her, and when Marya moved she jingled like sleigh bells, glass against glass. She imagined herself a great beast, lumbering through the steppes with sparkling glass towers on her back, roaring at villagers, stamping down whole forests with her paws. Her fever carried these images far, making them lurid, loud, playing before her eyes as though they were real. She moaned. Koschei did not speak this time, did not lecture or instruct. He simply murmured to her, stroked her hair, called her volchitsa, medvezhka, koshechka. Wolfling, she-bear, wild little kitten.

The next night, the car brought them smokily to rest, not at a rustic hut full of food, but at a banya, a bathhouse. It had no food for them. On a little green marble table waited a black jar and a neat pile of long, linen bandages. The bottle of vodka remained. Koschei undressed Marya again and sat her on a wooden slab. He rubbed her skin with those long, thin fingers, suddenly hot and not frozen at all. He brushed her long hair, hundreds of strokes. And with every stroke, the dry, brittle, broken strands became soft and shining again, as though she had never had so little eggs or milk to eat that her hair had dimmed and frayed. Marya nearly fell asleep sitting up, calmed by the brushing and his snatches of sad little songs about biting wolves and uncareful girls. When her hair shone, he gathered it up into a deft braid, and laid her down on the slab.

Then Koschei arranged the bandages over her so that no skin showed. When he cracked the seal on the black jar, Marya's poor, raw nose was assailed with the prickling, slashing scent of hot mustard. Oh, how she had feared this when she was small! She would conceal any cold or sniffle from her mother, for if she was discovered, out the mustard plasters would come, smelling of burning and sickness. Marya Morevna had imagined that if hell had a smell, it smelled like mustard plasters. Koschei smeared the mustard over the wrappings. Marya's eyes smarted and wept, her skin sweated, and in her fever she cried for her mother, for Zvonok, for Tatiana and Olga and Anna, for her red scarf and poor Svetlana Tikhonovna and lastly, more softly than the rest, for Koschei. At the sound of his name he took away the mustard plasters and held her in his arms.

"Drink, Marousha," he clucked gently, like a mother, and put a glass to her lips. "Your lungs want vodka." Obediently, she drank, and coughed, and drank once more.

He picked her up in his arms and carried her to the bath. Calling her his wolverine, his lioness, he scrubbed her skin with harsh salt until it was red, then sunk her in a hot bath. He held a handful of water to her nose and ordered her to breathe it in. She spluttered, and gagged, but did it anyway, so accustomed had she become to his voice. Finally, Koschei made her stand, and took up a long birch branch. Marya marveled at the catch in his breath as he brought it down against her skin, first gently, then harder, then stopping to rub her down with oil and whipping her again. At first she shrank away, but by his last blow, Marya Morevna found herself arching her back to meet the branch, as though the forest itself were commanding her body to heal.

Finally, hot and aching and wrung out, Marya let Koschei lead her to the wood stove, where he had made a bed for her, tucked up against the warm bricks. She slept, and dreamed of the London fashion magazine the Blodniek sisters had so cherished. The magazine had grown as huge as a museum hallway. She wandered through the pages, cowed and small next to the beautiful tall women with their crisp coats and feathered hats.

One of them turned to her. She wore a bright blue turban and waved a golden fan.

"All the girls are wearing their deaths this year," the model said haughtily. "It's just the thing for a plain country girl hoping to make her fortune."

The woman gestured at her turban. In the folds rested a hen's egg, white and gleaming.

When Marya woke, the red car had gone, and in its place a sparkling white one rolled towards them, its fenders arcing with a swan's grace. She felt much better, though she had a headache and her back still throbbed where the birch branches had struck her. Still, her skin hummed with heat, and she leaned gratefully against Koschei as the icy, mountain-hunched world slipped by, as though everything had been caked in salt to wait for spring.

That night, the last night, the car ground through the rocky snow to another low little house, its eaves carved like icing, its door thick and red. Koschei lifted her up and carried her. Marya lifted her head sleepily to look over his shoulder and saw the white car roll up the path, only to bounce on a hard, icy lump of snow and spring up a great pale horse, his mane twisting in the wind. The horse whinnied happily and trotted off in search of supper. *At least I caught the car changing,* she thought dreamily. *At least I can still see the naked world, even if it will only show me an ankle or a flash of wrist now.* She had grown used to silence, and it had grown used to her. And because she had relaxed into muteness and ceased to think about it very much, because she was dizzy and warm and not at all vigilant, Marya Morevna slipped.

"Marya, we are nearly there, nearly at the borders of my country. I will have you healed before all the hustle and busyness there."

"Really, I'm feeling much better," she assured him before she knew she had spoken.

Like lamps extinguished, Koschei's eyes darkened. He put her down, less gently than usual.

"I have asked you not to speak, Masha," he said. His voice was as twisted as a rope. Marya fell silent, abashed.

A simple supper steamed on the table: turnip greens, bread, mashed eggplant, and salted chicken jelly with bits of meat suspended in it. Soft, bland food for her wrung-out body. Marya still could not eat much.

"This is our last night alone, Marya," said Koschei. "Tomorrow you will be beset with my relations and my serfs and all manner of tasks at hand. I shall miss this, our selfish private hours, secreted away from the collective share. But so it always goes in marriage. Half of matrimony is given over to those with no stake in our bed. I suppose you wonder if your sisters fared so, with their handsome bird husbands; if they grew sick or thrived, if they traveled so far, so fast. All those lieutenants were my brothers, my comrades, and though they did not have so far to go so fast, nor did they travel so well, they too had their moments with borscht and vodka and birch branches. It is a mating dance all birds know. I wish you would have looked out the window, Masha! I was such a lovely owl for you. I fell so hard onto the streetside. So that you would be comforted; so that what you expected would happen just as you wished it to. That is how much I want to please you. But *tscha*! You missed it! Perhaps if you had seen me that way everything would have happened differently. Perhaps *you* would have commanded *me* to be silent. It was a risk I took. I confess it excited me, the possibility of being caught out. But no, I got to keep my secrets after all. A chance passed is a chance passed. Oh, I will be cruel to you, Marya Morevna. It will stop your breath, how cruel I can be. But you understand, don't you? You are clever enough. I am a demanding creature. I am selfish and cruel and extremely unreasonable. But I am your servant. When you starve I will feed you; when you are sick I will tend you. I crawl at your feet; for before your love, your kisses, I am debased. For you alone I will be weak."

On her bed by the stove, Marya lay down, her naked back red as a ruby in the firelight. Like a magic trick, Koschei pulled an egg from behind his ear—but not a hen's egg. A black egg, embossed in silver, studded with cold diamonds. Marya smiled, for her father had done this once when she could not sleep, had rolled an egg along her body to soak up all the nightmares into the yolk and away from her heart.

"You do not understand this yet. Not yet, not yet. You are not ready. You would be rough with my gift. But it is our last night, and I shall soak up all your fears and nightmares and proletariat city-girl terrors. You must have room to fear new things. I shall make you all new, my own revolution, neither red nor white, but black."

Koschei the Deathless rolled his egg over Marya's skin. She felt the crackling of the delicate shell against her bones, the jewels scraping her skin.

When he had finished, he pulled her up roughly and crushed her to him, kissing her again. His mouth was cold, and there was no passing of pear jelly or cherries between them. But all the same, Marya Morevna tasted sweetness in his empty kiss.

Suddenly, the sweetness fled and pain forked through her lip— Koschei had bitten her. She stared at him, hurt, raising her hand to her mouth. Her fingers came away bloody. Koschei's lips were smeared with it. His eyes sparked and glowed.

"When I tell you to do a thing, you must do it. It is not about wanting or not wanting. It is about the will in your jaw, and the egg on your back."

Marya balked; her vision swam; her lips pulsed hotly where his long, thin teeth had cut her. She felt herself tottering on a needle-tip: *If I let him do this to me, what else will I allow?*

Anything, anything, anything.

Koschei the Deathless wiped the bright redness from his lips.

He looked down at his finger with Marya's blood upon it. Without taking his eyes from her, he lifted his hand to his mouth and tasted it hesitantly, as if waiting for her to stop him.

Marya Morevna held her breath, and made no sound.

PART 2

Sleep with Fists Closed and Shoot Straight

There is no such thing as death.
Everyone knows that.
It has become tasteless to repeat it.

—ANNA AKHMATOVA

7

The Country of Life

Where is the country of the Tsar of Life? When the world was young the seven Tsars and Tsaritsas divided it amongst themselves. The Tsar of the Birds chose the air and the clouds and the winds. The Tsaritsa of Salt chose the cities with all their bustle and heedless hurtling. The Tsar of Water chose the seas and lakes, bays and oceans. The Tsaritsa of Night chose all the dark places and the places between, the thresholds, the shadows. The Tsaritsa of the Length of an Hour chose sorrow and misfortune as her territory, so that where anyone suffers, there is her country. This left only the Tsar of Life and the Tsar of Death to argue over what remained. For a time, they were content to quarrel over individual trees, stones, and streams, giving each other great whacks with that scythe which Death wields to cut down all that lives, and that hammer which Life wields, which builds up useful and lovely things such as fences and churches and potato distilleries. However, Life and Death are brothers, and their ambition is precisely equal.

Their rivalry soon encompassed whole towns, rivers (which rightly belonged to neither, but neutrality is no defense), provinces, and beachheads, until the struggle of it consumed the whole of the world. If a town managed a granary of fine brick and half a head of good cabbage to share between them, then Death arrived with white banners like bones, and withered the place with a single stomp. If a village were hollowed out by plague or war, its streets lit by skulls hoisted up on pikes and blood poisoning the well water, then still green shoots would grow wild in the offal-rich gutters, still the last woman standing would grow great in the belly. There could be no agreement between them.

At last, with every inch of earth divided and subdivided, the loam and clay themselves could bear no more. The mountains yielded up their iron and their copper, and the Tsaritsa of Salt slyly taught men her most secret mechanisms, for of all her brothers and sisters, the Tsaritsa of Salt best knew civilized things, things made and not born. Up rose looms and threshers and plows and engines, stoves and syringes and sanitation departments, trains and good shoes. And so the Tsar of Life triumphed, and children upon children were born.

But the Tsar of Death is wily. Soon the looms bit off the fingers of their minders, and smoke clotted breath, and the great engines spat out explosives and helmets and automated rifles as well as shoes. Soon folk of the city requisitioned the grain of the villages, and stored it up in great *vaults, and argued over its distribution while it moldered, and wrote long books on the righteousness of this, and Death, iron-shod, copper-crowned, danced.*

The rapt pupil will be forgiven for assuming the Tsar of Death to be wicked and the Tsar of Life to be virtuous. Let the truth be told: There is no virtue anywhere. Life is sly and unscrupulous, a blackguard, wolfish, severe. In service to itself, it will commit any offense. So, too, is Death possessed of infinite strategies and a gaunt nature—but also mercy, also grace and tenderness. In his own country, Death can be kind. But of an end to their argument, we shall have none, not ever, until the end of all.

So where is the country of the Tsar of Death? Where is the nation of the Tsar of Life? They are not so easy to find, yet each day you step upon both one hundred times or more. Every portion of earth is infinitely divided between them, to the smallest unit of measure, and smaller yet. Even the specks of soil war with one another. Even the atoms strangle each other in their sleep. To reach the country of the Tsar of Life, which is both impossibly near and hopelessly far, you must not wish to arrive there, but approach it stealthily, sideways. It is best to be ill, in a fever, a delirium. In the riot of sickness, when the threatened flesh rouses itself, all redness and fluid and heat, it is easiest to topple over into the country you seek.

Of course, it is just as easy, in this manner, to reach the country of the Tsar of Death. Travel is never without risk.

Zemlehyed the leshy squinted at the great black book. With one gnarled, mossy hand, he shook it by its corner. A few leaves fell on it from the canopy of birches. Sunlight spilled down through the white branches, cool and golden and crisp. The coal-colored spine of the heavy volume glittered where the waxy autumnal light struck it. Dubiously, the leshy gave the cover a good gnaw. He wrinkled his burl-nose. Zemlehyed looked more or less like what you would get if a particularly stunted and ugly oak tree had fallen passionately in love with a boulder and produced, at great cost to both, a single child. His mistletoe eyebrows waggled.

"Why she read this none-sense? It's got no pictures. Also, boring."

Naganya the vintovnik rolled her eye. She had only one to roll, since her left eye was less an eye than a rifle scope, jutting out from her skull, made of bone and glassy thumbnail. Nevertheless, she wore half a pair of spectacles over the other eye, for she felt naked and embarrassed without some sort of lens to look through. The imp's walnut skin gleamed from attentive polishing, though her blackened, ironwork sinews showed through in places: her elbows, her cheek, the backs of her knees.

"Don't you pay attention? Likho gave it to her." Naganya sniffed ostentatiously. She produced a grey handkerchief and wiped a trickle of black oil from her nose. "Still, *I* don't approve. Histories are instruments of oppression. Writers of histories ought to be shot on sight."

Zemlehyed snorted. "Who's this Tsar of Life? Never met the man."

"Who do you think, rock-brain? He's not called Deathless for nothing." Naganya peered at the book for a moment, clicking her tongue against her teeth. It made a horrid mechanical noise, like a gun cocking and uncocking. "You're right, though. It *is* boring. Overwritten. I'm surprised you can read it at all."

"Nor good to eat! Shit! Why not tear it up and bury it? Some nice tree have a good munch, eh?" Zemlehyed spat a glob of golden sap on their picnic blanket. Naganya grimaced.

"Why the tsarevna lets you blunder after her is a mystery to me. You're disgusting. But if you want to wreck her things, be my guest.

At least the evisceration will be amusing. What *do* leshiyi look like on the inside? All mud and sticks?"

"Paws off, gun-goblin! *My* insides; *my* property!"

"Property is theft!" snapped Naganya, her cheek-pistons clicking. "Therefore, just by sitting there you're stealing from the People, Zemya! Bandit! Ring the alarms!"

Zemlehyed spat again.

"But Zemya," she whined, "I'm *bored*! Why don't I interrogate you again? It'll be fun! I'll leave my safety on this time, I promise."

The leshy gnashed his stone teeth with their rime of muck. "Nasha, why you only bored when I'm around? Get bored with someone else!"

Through the bramble-thicket two horses exploded, their riders flattened against their backs. The black one raced ahead, a young woman shrieking laughter in her green enamel saddle, her dark hair streaming, braided wildly with garnets and rough sea amber, her hunting cloak a red sail. She darted expertly between the pale, bony birches, ducking boughs heavy with yellow leaves and thin, brown vines sagging with ruby-colored berries. Behind her leapt a white mare and a pale lady riding sidesaddle, every bit as keen and fierce as the black rider, the swan feathers in her snowy hair flying off in pale clouds. Their stamping hooves set up whirlwinds of old orange leaves as they galloped past.

"Did it come this way?" cried Marya Morevna, her eyes blazing, reining her dark horse in and circling impatiently.

"Who?" barked the leshy.

"My firebird! Got moss in your ears again, Zemya?"

"You're too slow," sighed Naganya. "It blew through here over an hour ago. Singed my hair, which naturally incinerated most of our lunch." Naganya's hair glistened, wet and dark with gun-oil, reeking of gasoline.

"Well, then," said Madame Lebedeva, leaping lightly from her horse and adjusting her elegant white hat, which still had several of its swan plumes attached. At her throat, a pearly cameo gleamed, showing a perfect profile of herself. "I, for one, shall have a cup of tea and a rest. Firebirds are such frustrating quarry. One minute it's all fiery tail feathers and red talons and the next, nothing but ash and a sore seat." She knotted her mare to a larch tree and settled down on the slightly sappy picnic blanket, brushing invisible dust from her white jodhpurs and blazer.

Marya leaned her hunting rifle up against a fire-colored maple and fell in a heap onto the blanket. She hugged Zemya vigorously—which is the only way to do anything involving a leshy—and planted a kiss on his oak-bark cheek. The hunt had gotten her blood and her hungers up—she vibrated with excitement.

"What have we to eat?" Marya asked cheerfully, her jewel-strewn hair falling over one shoulder. She wore a smart black suit, half uniform, half hunting dress.

"Burnt toast, burnt pirozhki, onions both pickled *and* burnt. I believe even the tea has a distinct smoky flavor," sighed the vintovnik.

"We can't leave you alone for a second." Madame Lebedeva scowled.

"Three hours, vila!" groused Zemlehyed, scratching his knees. "And she were interrogating me again. Look!" He displayed his hands, each of which had a neat bullet hole through the leafy palm. "The price of cronyism, she says!"

"Well, now, you have to admit, you do hew fairly close to the heels of the Tsar's favorite." Madame Lebedeva smiled.

"And you don't? Where's *your* price, eh?"

"I am very careful not to be alone with the zealous Nasha." The vila sniffed. "This is the best way to avoid interrogations, I find."

"Peace!" Marya Morevna laughed, holding up her hands. On each finger gleamed silver rings studded with rough, uncut malachites and rubies. "If you don't behave, all of you, I shall not tell you any more stories about Petrograd!"

Naganya's limpid eye filled with greasy black tears. "Oh, Masha, that's not fair! How shall I further the Party's interests in the hinterlands if you will not teach me about Marx and Papa Lenin?"

Zemya scowled, his mouth little more than a gap in the rock of his chin. "Who is Papa Lenin? *Tfu!* Zemlehyed has *one* Papa: Papa *Koschei*. He needs no nasty bald Papa Lenin!"

Marya Morevna's face brightened and darkened all at once. She twisted the rings on her fingers. When she thought of Koschei, her blood boiled and froze all together. "Well, I'm sure that puts an end to the debate, Zem. Nasha?"

Naganya sighed dramatically. "I ought to go to Petrograd myself!" she wailed. "What use has a rifle imp out here where the best diversion for my sort is common hunting? How I long for real utility, to hunt out enemies of the People and put holes in them!"

Madame Lebedeva yawned and stretched her long arms. Her beauty was impossibly delicate and pointed, birdlike and nearly colorless, save for her dark, depthless eyes. "When is he going to marry you, Mashenka? How tiresome for you, to wait like this!"

"I don't know, Lebed, my love. He is so occupied with the war, you know. All day and night in the Chernosvyat, poring over papers and troop allotments. Hardly a good time for a wedding." In truth, Marya was tired of waiting. She squinted in the frosty sunlight, wishing to be Tsaritsa, to be safe here, to know she would not have to go home, back where she did not have a horse or firebirds to hunt, where she did not have such friends.

"Maybe he doesn't love you anymore." Naganya shrugged, her mouth half-full of pirozhki.

"Squirrel crap! Smashed snail's got more sense than you," growled Zemlehyed. "Papa can't marry nobody. Not 'til *she* approves. Not 'til Babushka comes."

"I wish she'd get a move on!" sighed Madame Lebedeva. She nibbled a bit of blackened onion. "I want to apply for the magicians' dacha this summer. It's quite competitive, and I can't concentrate on my application while I'm worried half to death over Masha's trousseau. The entrance essays are *brutal*, darlings."

Naganya sniggered. "What's a Petrograd girl's trousseau? Horse shit and half a pint of Neva washing water?"

"I'm sure it's no business of an imp," Lebedeva snarled. "Leave it to those of us with a teaspoon of refinement to spare."

"As if a vila witch knows anything but hair curlers and squinting for fortunes in a cup of piss!"

Naganya narrowed her monocled eye and spat. A neat little bullet erupted out of her mouth and punched through Madame Lebedeva's swan feathers, blowing her hat quite off her head. She shrieked in indignation, her ice-white hair singed black at the tips. Madame scrambled after her hat.

"You *beast*! Marya! You *must* punish her! You made her swear not to shoot anyone this morning, and just look at her thwarting you!"

Marya Morevna pulled on a very solemn expression. She beckoned the vintovnik to her side with a crooked, jeweled finger.

"Nasha, you know you ought not to disobey me."

Naganya fell silent. Her hands trembled; her ironworks clicked nervously in her cheek.

Suddenly, Marya's hand flashed out and caught Naganya's mouth and nose. With the other hand she grabbed the back of the vintovnik's head. Naganya's chest heaved, searching for breath, but Marya did not let go. She forced the imp to the ground, clamping her face in her fierce hand, leaping astride her, the better to pin her to the forest floor. Marya's heart leapt and exulted in her. All unbidden she thought of a book of poems tossed into the snow, and a red scarf torn in half. She bore down harder. Slowly, black, oily tears pooled in Nasha's eyes and trickled down over Marya Morevna's knuckles as Nasha struggled, squirmed, and finally went still beneath her. Marya grinned, her braids brushing her friend's walnut arms. Finally, she let Naganya up. The imp gasped and spluttered, chagrined and hoarse, wiping at her tears.

"Let that be a lesson," Marya Morevna said cheerfully. "Mind your trigger in mixed company! When I tell you to do something you must do it." *Perhaps all a Tsaritsa is is a beautiful cold girl in the snow, looking down at someone wretched, and not yielding.* Marya thought these thoughts, her breath and pulse calming. Of late, she had felt that coldness in herself, and though she feared it, she loved it too, for it made her strong.

Naganya sat shaking. Her breath came in gulps. She sniffed pitifully and pawed at her nose.

"Oh, Nasha!" Marya cried, feeling suddenly not cold at all and a little embarrassed. Perhaps she had gotten carried away— but imps listened to no one who could not thrash them soundly. A good Tsaritsa speaks her subjects' language, after all. "Don't be sad! I'll find you a nice rusalka to snatch out of her lake in the middle of the night and throttle for information! Won't that be lovely?"

Naganya smiled a little, mollified. A high walnut-colored blush rose in her cheeks, and Marya knew that she had enjoyed being punished, if only a little. She turned to the leshy.

"Now, Zemya—oh, give me back that book! You've bitten it half to pieces! Zemya, who is this Babushka you mean? I thought I had met everyone here!"

At that moment, a high, gorgeous cry echoed through the forest. An orange flame circled the clouds, so far up in the air that it seemed little more than a speck of fiery dust. Before Naganya could shout, Marya had snatched up her rifle, knelt, and fired.

With a searing, crackling crash, a firebird fell from the sky.

"Why *do* they call this place the Isle of Buyan?" Marya mused as the four of them strode back down Skorohodnaya Road. The sun set over the city ahead, spilling light over warm white cupolas carved from smooth, gleaming bone. The first dusting of snow glinted on the road, promising the sweetness of winter to come. "It's not an island at all, as far as I can tell."

"Used to be one," said Zemlehyed, who was by far the oldest of them. "The unstopping salt sea. Your Lake Baikal? *Tscha!* Puddle! *Our* sea had fists, back in the yore."

"It continues to be a marvel to me," said Madame Lebedeva, her musical voice causing even her white horse to step lighter, "that leshiyi ever learned to speak. What sort of process was it, I wonder? Did a lonely hedgehog bash on a rock until it made noises?"

"Leshiyi learned from trees singing songs what birds taught, what birds learned from worms, what worms learned from dirt, what dirt learned from diamonds. *Pedigreed,* that's us."

"Well, I'm sure *you* were a very poor student, Zemya. You haven't got the vocabulary of a salamander. In any event, Masha, darling, the Isle of Buyan was once, indeed, an island, in a great sea where fish the size of galleons swam in golden waves. They sang, those fish, such songs at sunrise. If you had a hundred balalaikas and a thousand gusli, you could not play a song equal to the least of theirs."

"What happened?" Marya Morevna coaxed her black horse on ahead. He pulled a silver net behind him. Flaming feathers tufted out of it at every angle, scorching the earth beneath it as it dragged along.

Madame Lebedeva sighed. "What happens to anything beautiful? Viy ate it up. First the great fish went belly up, one by one, their stomachs practically islands themselves. Then the water turned black and green, with mud currents all through it. Then the waves caught fire, and burned down to the seabed. The flames seared the stars—and then it was gone. Vapor and steam. All the whole of it, gone down into the coffers of the Tsar of Death. You can bet that in *his* country, there's a ghost-sea full of ghost-fish still singing their songs, in a different key, with different words. And in our country, if you walk far enough out onto the plain, you'll see great bones sticking out of the earth where the seabed used to be. Mountains lined with rib bones, valleys full of jaws."

Marya rode in silence. Each time she learned something of the long history of Koschei's country and the war with the Tsar of Death, she loved Buyan a little more fiercely, and feared the war a little more sharply.

"Shall we go mushroom picking tonight?" said Naganya softly, still abashed and thrilled by her punishment. "There'll be a moon out, big as a bull's-eye. And I've a belly for chanterelles."

The motley party passed through the city gate, a palisade of tangled, towering antlers, each prong crowned with a grinning skull. Marya no longer thought it grisly or shuddered as she passed beneath the empty eye sockets. Now, the skulls seemed to smile at her, to say, *We who were once living can guard you still, and love you, and keep you living safe and whole. Nothing ever truly dies.*

Once the gates had shut behind them, shops and houses beamed within, their windows lit with red, happy fires. The Chernosvyat sprawled ahead, its black towers and red doors glinting. It looked so like the Kremlin that Marya had often thought the two must be brothers, separated at birth and set apart, one on either side of the world. Koschei lived in the biggest tower, its cupola drenched in garnets. But most folk lived somewhere in the Chernosvyat, in the smaller citadels and chapels and anterooms. The place grew by years, like a tree, like the house on Gorokhovaya Street—on Dzerzhinskaya Street. The old names swirled in Marya's mind, flowing together and apart again until she could not remember which had come first.

The broad plain hosted many other houses and halls and hearths and hostelries rippling out from the black Kremlin like water. Marya hardly noticed anymore that the houses and halls had been patched together from the skins of many exotic and familiar beasts, their roofs thatched with long, waving hair, their eaves lined with golden braids. Fountains spurted hot, scarlet blood into glass pools, trickling pleasantly in the late afternoon light. A rich steam floated from their basins, and the occasional raven alighted to sip. Once Marya had screamed when a bloody fountain geysered up in its noontime display. Once she had felt sick when she saw the wall of a chapel prickle up in a sudden wind, just like skin. But the fountain had been much embarrassed, and she had been introduced to the chapel, whose name was Avdotia, and these things now seemed only right and lovely to Marya, just living things in the Country of Life, where even a fountain breathed and flowed with vital stuff. That was so long ago now, anyway, like the dream of another life.

"I think I am too tired for mushrooms, Nasha," she said finally. "I will go to Koschei instead, and see if he has need of me. But," she added magnanimously, "you may sleep with me tonight if you like, and have a tart with icing." Did she enjoy punishing or rewarding more? Marya could not say. Everything in Buyan had a different pleasure to it, if only one learned how to find it.

The vintovnik brightened and danced a little down the long cobbled road. Zemlehyed grunted and punched the ground with his mossy fist.

"Cronyism!" he spat.

8

Sleep by Me

In the deepest, most hidden room of the Chernosvyat, whose ossified cupolas shone here and there with silver bubbles and steel cruciforms, Koschei the Deathless sat on his throne of onyx and bone. His eyes drooped, redly exhausted, from weeping or working or both. Before him, on a great table formed from the pelvic dish of some impossibly huge fish, lay scattered maps and plans and letters, papers and couriers' boxes, photographs and sketches, books wedged open, upside down, splitting their spines.

Marya Morevna entered, her hunting costume half-open in the heat of the place. The dark walls of the Chernosvyat often seemed to breathe, and their breath came either brutally hot or mercilessly cold. Marya never knew which to expect. Silently, she walked around the long table and let a single golden feather drop. It drifted lazily down to rest on a requisition form. It no longer flamed, but glowed with a soft amber light.

"I would have preferred it living, volchitsa," said Koschei, without looking up.

Marya shrugged. "It only died just now, as much of exhaustion from the hunt as the bullet."

Koschei rose from his papers and drew her to him, bending to kiss her collarbone.

"I am proud of you, of course, beloved, baleful. But you must realize that you have only added a firebird to Viy's cavalry. A black, flameless thing, its bony wings bearing ghost-pilots with their arms full of ordnance."

Marya Morevna shut her eyes, savoring his lips on her skin as she savored the slab of black bread, buttered and spread with roe, once, long ago.

"It was hiding a clutch of eggs," she breathed as he gripped her hair and tilted her head to show her throat, pale and bare. "In a short while we shall have enough firebirds to pull a siege tower, and still have one or two left over to light the hearth when we return." His weight against her chilled and wakened her skin. She smiled against his dark glove. "Besides, it was tradition, once, for a suitor to fetch a firebird's feather to show their good and marriageable qualities."

"I know your qualities."

Marya said nothing. She did not feel an urgency to marry, exactly—nothing like her sisters, who had longed for it like the prize at the end of a long and difficult game. But she did feel that as long as Koschei kissed her and kissed her and did not marry her, she remained a child in Buyan—a cosseted tsarevna, but not a Tsaritsa, not a native. A human toy. She did not care whether he gave her a ring—he had given her dozens, of every dark and glinting gem—but she did not wish to be a princess forever.

Koschei picked up the knife he had been using to open couriers'
seals and looked up at her speculatively. Reaching up, he slowly
sliced off the buttons of her hunting dress.

"If you keep cutting at me I shall have no clothes left," said
Marya Morevna. The gems in her hair clattered against one another as he cupped her skull in one large hand. With the other, he
cut away the skirt of her dress in a stroke, like peeling the skin off
a red, red apple. His hands burned coldly on her. She felt, as she
could always feel, the bones of him beneath the skin of his fingers,
his hips. Then he hardened, his skin becoming warm and real and
full. A skeleton, always, embraced her first, and then remembered
to be a man. She understood—had he not told her? *To be Deathless
is to treat with death in every moment. To stave death is not involun-
tary, like breathing, but a constant tension, like balancing a glass on the
head.* And each day the Tsar of Life fought in his own body to
keep death down like a chastened dog.

Koschei dug his nails into the small of Marya's naked back;
blood welled in tiny drops. Marya cried out a little, her breath
thin and quick, and he lifted his thumb to his lips, suckling at the
little smear of her blood. His cheeks, always gaunt, hung with
shadows, and he watched her with a starveling's eyes. But that did
not frighten her anymore. Her lover often looked starved, hounded.
She could kiss those things from him, and often did, until his face
waxed seraphic, soft, smooth—as anyone can do for her mate when
the day is long and hard, and solace far off. She thought nothing
of it now, of kissing him alive. Everything in this place was livid
and lurid and living, and when he loved her and hurt her all at
once she lived, too, higher and harder than she had thought she
could. *Yes,* she thought, *magic is like that, when it comes.* Like the
fountains of blood, the houses of skin and hair, Koschei had long
since become home. So Marya smiled as he bit her shoulders, feeling infant bruises bloom invisibly under her skin. *Tomorrow I shall*

wear them like medals, she thought as he lifted her up onto the wreckage of field maps and mechanical diagrams.

"Koschei," she whispered against his neck, where his dark hair curled. "Where do you keep your death?"

Koschei the Deathless lifted the calves of Marya Morevna around his waist and sank into her with the weight of years. He moaned against her breast. It stopped her breath, how like a child the Tsar of Life became when he needed her. The power she had over him, that he gave her. *Who is to rule, that is all.*

"Tell me," she whispered. She wanted that, too. She wanted so much these days, everything she touched.

"Hush, you Delilah!" He thrust against her, the bones of his hips stabbing at her soft belly.

"I keep nothing from you. I befriend your friends; I eat as you eat; I teach you the dialectic! If you will not take me to wife, at least take me into confidence."

Koschei squeezed his eyes shut. He winced with the force of his secret, his climax, his need. As he gripped her tighter and tighter, Marya thought his face grew rounder, younger, as though breathing in her own youth.

"I keep it in a glass chest," he gasped finally, pushing her roughly back over the stacks of predicted troop movements, his fists caught up in the infinite mass of her hair. "Guarded by four dogs: a wolf like you, a starved racing hound, a haughty lap pup, and a fat sheepdog. All their names begin with the same letter, and only I know the letter." He shut his eyes against her cheek as she arched toward him like a drawn bow. "And only someone who knows their names can reach the chest where I keep my death."

Koschei cried out as though he were dying. He leaned against his love, his chest shaking. She held him, like a baby, like her own. And it did not escape her that speaking of his death excited

Koschei somewhere deep inside, as if the proximity of it, even the word itself, sizzled electric in his brain.

"Will we win, Koschei?" she whispered. The room went suddenly frigid, frost gathering at the tall windows. "Will we win this war?"

"War is not for winning, Masha," sighed Koschei, reading the tracks of supply lines, of pincer strategies, over her shoulder. "It is for surviving."

Naganya the vintovnik curled against Marya that night in Marya's own bedchamber, which was curtained in wine red velvets and silks. Living in Marya's little room was like living inside a heart. She liked it that way, though it gave Madame Lebedeva a headache. And she liked her privacy, to be among her own things. Her enormous bed, its four black pillars disappearing into the ceiling, sank both girls in pillows and down. Naganya, always warm to the touch, sighed in the shadows, and Marya Morevna held her tight so that Nasha would know she wasn't angry anymore. Had never really been.

"Tomorrow," Naganya said, "it would be marvelous to go out into the central square and both of us shoot as far as we can, and then go running to see what we have shot! Once I played that game with a boy, and he shot a frog right through the throat. And the strangest, ugliest thing happened. The frog turned into a girl, and she started crying, all covered with mud and naked." Naganya paused to allow Marya to be impressed. "She wore a green dress when they married, and made wedding bread like nothing you'd believe. The crust was all full·of honey and sugar and hard little candied bilberries. She cried when the banns were read, too. The same tears as that day when he shot her. Perhaps she didn't want to be married to him, but who would not want to be married to an expert marksman? I cannot believe it. She must have cried for some secret amphibian reason. Then her dress caught on fire while they danced, and there was a mess, but that's neither here nor there."

"If we shoot in the city, we may hit someone who is not playing our game," said Marya sleepily. The small of her back still burned pleasantly from Koschei's nails.

The vintovnik struck the pillow with her walnut fist. "That's the fun of it! Ah, well, if you want to be a baby about it, we can go out into the wood. Probably won't get anything but squirrels, and none of *them* ever turn into girls."

"All right, Nasha. And if I get a frog, she's all yours."

The imp snuggled closer. "Do you still love me, then, Mashenka?"

"Of course, Nashenka. Punishment doesn't mean you aren't loved. On the contrary. You can really only punish someone you love."

Naganya clicked her ironworks happily.

Marya opened her eyes in the dark, staring up at the carved ceiling, which showed a scene of a great fringed wyrm beset by boyars. "Have I ever told you about the first time Koschei punished me?"

"Koschei punished *you*?"

"Oh yes, many times. But the first time was because he asked me not to speak, and I spoke anyway. I didn't say anything much; I just told him I was feeling better. But it wasn't what I said, it was that I'd broken my word. Even if you think it was cruel of him to tell me not to speak, I had promised."

Naganya wriggled, fretting. Even though the punishment was long done, she could not help worrying for her friend.

"And so when I first came to Buyan, he did not let me come into the Chernosvyat with him, or have supper, or meet any lovely rifle imps with names like mine. He left me at the stables to look after his horse because I had broken my promise."

"Well. You could still breathe, I'm sure." Naganya could not help needling—it was her nature.

"Some things are worse than not breathing," Marya said softly. "When you are so far from home, and frightened, and have been sick a long time, and no one knows you at all, and you miss your mother and your old house, and you don't know if you are to be married or killed, to be left in a stable alone without a word is very bad. But I got out the shovel all the same, even though the blade was half as tall as me. I mucked out the horse's stall—and that beast makes a mess, I can tell you, all manure and exhaust and broken mufflers! After a while I was hardly crying at all, but my arms ached like death. I brushed his coat and rubbed him down with oil, with him snorting and his eyes glowing all the while. He was still white and cream-colored, as he was while I was sick.

"'Why do you change colors like that?' I said, not expecting an answer. 'It makes it hard to choose the right oil!'

"And he rumbled at me, 'I'm not the horse who fetched you in Petrograd. That is my sister, the Midnight Nag. Then you rode my brother, the Noontide Horse, who is red as sunrise. You and I have only just met. I am the Dawn Gelding, and you must ride all of us to get here. My name is Volchya-Yagoda.'

"'He named you *wolf-food*?' I asked, since I didn't know Koschei's humor then.

"Volchya snorted again, and sparks flew out of his nose. 'Aren't we all?' he said.

"I began to brush his horribly tangled mane. Every time I pulled his scalp he nipped me, and Volchya's nips are like the bites of a sword. I wept a great deal, I recall. And in the cold, even weeping hurts. It comes in jerks and hitches, and your tears half freeze to your face. I didn't know how to keep from crying then. When I finished, his hair shone red with my blood, and he looked like his brother. Night had gotten fat and black outside, and the city frightened me. Where did Koschei live? Where could I get food? Where could I drink or sleep? So I reshod Volchya, to put off having to decide those things. I pulled off his old tire-tread horseshoes and hammered on fresh iron ones. I knew how to do this, for when I was young and I wore a red scarf, we all had to learn to maintain the policeman's horses after school. In case of another war, you understand. So I ran my hand along his fetlock—so soft and hot!—and he put his leg right into my hand. When I had finished, Volchya-Yagoda looked at me with those huge, fiery eyes and lay down right there in his clean stall.

"'Come,' he said. 'Sleep by me, and he will fetch you in the morning. Share my water trough and my oat bag.'

"Well, Nasha, I drank and I ate, even though the oats were dry and tasteless. I found a sugar lump in the bag, and Volchya let me have it. I lay down next to his big white belly and shut my eyes. It was like sleeping next to the stove in my old house. Because, Nasha, even when you have been wicked, sometimes there is a warm bed and a warm friend somewhere, if only you know where to look. I learned that from Volchya, though I don't think it's precisely what I was meant to learn. And just as I was drifting off to sleep, broken and exhausted and still bleeding a little from a nip or two, Volchya-Yagoda said softly in my ear, 'Sleep well, Marya Morevna. I think I like you best. None of the other girls gave me new shoes.'"

"And did he come for you in the morning?"

"Oh yes, and all was forgiven. You cannot punish someone unless you wish to forgive them, after all. What would be the point? And I told him what Volchya said."

"And? What did Papa say?"

"He said, 'You must have been mistaken. There have never been any other girls.'"

In the dark, Naganya the vintovnik frowned and clicked her tongue against her teeth.

Marya Morevna slept with her fists curled tight, held at the ready, next to her chin.

9

A Girl Not Named Yelena

Madame Lebedeva exhaled a thin, fine curl of smoke from her cigarette, nestled in its ivory holster. She reclined in a plush blue chair, her angular body sheathed in a sleeveless gown of swan feathers, speckled with tiny glass beads. Madame busied herself with flamboyantly not eating her cucumber soup. Bits of chervil and tarragon floated in the green broth, lonely and unattended. Lebedeva leaned in confidentially, but she needn't have—the crowded cafe produced enough din to hide any secret she cared to share.

"I'm thrilled to my bones to be able to bring you here, Masha, dear."

Marya thanked her again. Madame Lebedeva had made up her eyes specially for their luncheon, or more precisely, for the komityet that controlled entry to the exclusive magicians' restaurant. Her lids glittered, frosted with the lightest onion-green powder. She had chosen it to match the soup, which she had decided to order weeks ago. Marya could have eaten in the little chalet whenever she liked, of course, being forbidden nowhere in Buyan. But Lebedeva had earned her privilege, and hand in hand, the pleasure of lording her privilege over her friend. "I'm *insensate* with rapture, I tell you. It's all on account of my having produced a ci-kavac, of course. A trifle, really. For one possessed of such grace as I, to conceal an egg under the arm for forty days and shun the confessional is barely worth mentioning! Such a dear little creature, too. But the reviews! Oh, they have savaged me, Masha!"

"Savaged?"

Lebedeva tapped her cigarette; ash drifted. "*Savaged.* They said it should have looked like a parakeet, not a 'ridiculous miniature pelican.' Apparently, I shouldn't have cut my nails during the forty days, which is why it understands animal tongues but doesn't grant wishes. And my selling it to that vodyanoy was an act of blatant mercantilism and I ought to be questioned. Critics, my darling, are never happy unless they are crushing something underfoot. A pelican! I ought to eat his eyes."

A waiter in a crisp white shirt appeared noiselessly at their side. He bowed with genteel solicitude. "More soup, Madame?" His bald head shone in the lamplight, save for the strip of wild white hair that flowed down the center of his skull like a horse's mane. Lebedeva's face blossomed.

"How delightful to meet another vila! One's countrymen are always a comfort. No, dear." Madame Lebedeva smiled, her charm perfect, ripe, chill. She had practiced in the mirror for days. "I have a delicate constitution. Marya will certainly have another bowl of your captivating ukha, however! Humans are so robust. Is that sturgeon I smell in the broth?"

"Very perceptive, Madame. And the chef sends his compliments on your production of Tuesday last. Pelicans will surely be all the rage next season."

Lebedeva scowled. The waiter turned his attention to Marya, his pale eyes moist with anticipation. For her own part, Marya wanted no more fish stew, though it warmed her with a delicate, salty, dill-rich flavor. She was quite full—but she loved to make Madame Lebedeva happy, and what made her happy, chiefly, was ordering others about.

The waiter bent to speak more intimately with them. His skin smelled like frozen pine sap.

"If Comrade Morevna would be interested, I myself have been working on a small glamour she might enjoy. It's nothing, really," he demurred before Marya could say anything at all. "But if you like it, perhaps you could whisper a word to the Tsar?"

"I . . . I'm hardly a judge. I know nothing about the business of magicians."

"Marya," whispered Lebedeva, "surely you know how this works. We took extensive notes on our visits to Moscow."

"Yes, but in Moscow this sort of cafe is for *writers*." Lebedeva and the waiter both looked pleasantly perplexed, disliking to be shown up, but gladdened all the same, certain now to receive a lesson from the source. "Writers?" Marya said encouragingly. Speaking to the folk of Buyan was like walking on ice—they could be conversing just as smoothly as you please, and then suddenly Marya would fall through into their alien ideas, shocked at what they did not know. "Novelists? Poets? Playwrights?" Lebedeva sucked on her cigarette, which never seemed to get smaller, no matter how much ash fell from it like snow.

"I'm sure it sounds fascinating, dear. What are they, some sort of conjurers?"

"No, no, they tell stories. Write them down, I mean." Marya grabbed at her tea to buy a moment's thought. Buyanites had an

insatiable lust for information about the human world, but anything
Marya told them became a daring new fashion, spreading like gossip. She had to be careful. "A playwright writes a story that other
people act out. They memorize the story and pretend that they are
the heroines and villains of it. A poet writes one that rhymes, like a
song." Marya grinned suddenly. She shut her eyes and recited, the
words coming back to her like old friends:

> *There, weeping, a tsarevna lies, locked in a cell.*
> *And Master Grey Wolf serves her very well.*
> *There, in her mortar, sweeping beneath the skies,*
> *the demon Baba Yaga flies.*
> *There Tsar Koschei,*
> *he wastes away,*
> *poring over his pale gold.*

The waiter tucked his cloth under an arm and applauded vigorously. Lebedeva clapped her hands. "Oh, superb! It's about us! How
gratifying to be so recognized."

Encouraged, Marya hurried on. "A novelist writes a long kind of
story, with . . . a lot of smaller stories in it, and motifs, and symbols,
and sometimes things in the story really happened, and sometimes
they didn't."

The waiter wrinkled his lovely nose. "Why would you tell a story
about something that didn't really happen? At least the poetry was
straightforward, manful. Not concerned with idle fancies, just a
respectable census report!"

Marya slurped at her soup thoughtfully. "I suppose because it's
boring to keep telling stories where people just get born and grow
up and get married and die. So they add strange things in, to make
it more interesting when a person is born, more satisfying when
they get married, sadder when they die."

Lebedeva snapped her fingers. "It's like lying!" she exclaimed. "Well, we understand that, of course! The bigger the lie, the happier the liar."

"Yes, a little like lying. But . . ." Marya leaned in close to them conspiratorially. She couldn't help it—she enjoyed being an expert, an acknowledged authority. Watching her opinions become fact. And as she lived and ate and slept in Buyan, she learned better to explain things so that her comrades could understand them. "But you know, a wizard with black hair and a thick mustache put a curse on Moscow, and Petrograd, too, so that no one would be able to tell the truth without lying. If a novelist wrote a true story about how things really happened, no one would believe him, and he might even be punished for spreading propaganda. But if he wrote a book full of lies about things that could never really happen, with only a few true things hidden in it, well, he would be hailed as a hero of the People, given a seat at a writers' cafe, served wine and ukha, and not have to pay for any of it. He'd get a salaried summer on the dacha, and be feted. Even given a medal by the wizard with the thick mustache."

The waiter whistled. "That's a good curse. I should like to shake that wizard's hand and buy him a vodka or two."

"Someone ought to write a novel about me," said Lebedeva loftily. "I shouldn't care if they lied to make it more interesting, as long as they were good lies, full of kisses and daring escapes and the occasional act of barbarism. I can't abide a poor liar."

"For a while," said Marya Morevna, "I thought I might like to be a writer. I walked to school in the mornings and read poetry and wondered if I could be like the men and women in the reserved tea shops. If there was a story in me, somewhere deep, sleeping, waiting to wake up."

"I doubt it." Madame Lebedeva sniffed. "Your lying really needs work. Perhaps it's because you're so far from Petrograd. Curses haven't much sticking power, geographically speaking. Honesty is *such* a nasty habit, dear. Like biting your nails."

Just then, the round window of the cafe, fashioned from the lens of a whale's eye, shook with a quiet tremor.

"It's possible you chose an unfortunate poem to recite, my love," said Madame Lebedeva, finally allowing herself a single, decadent slurp of her pale green soup. Her eyes slid closed in exquisite satisfaction. The waiter hurried off, suddenly quite interested in a table far across the room.

Outside, a black car approached. Its long nose sloped and curved like a merciless beak; its fenders hunched up as round as eggs. Like clever eyes, the windows narrowed. It was both like and unlike Volchya-Yagoda, the car who had borne Marya to Buyan. This one seemed wholly larger, more careful, more luxurious, more serious.

Below it, four yellow chicken legs loped gracefully on the road where wheels ought to have been, their black claws scrabbling at the hard snow.

Setting her silver spoon aside, Madame Lebedeva extinguished her cigarette on her plate, then retrieved it with a flourish, whole and unsmoked, tucking it into her hat.

"Much as you know I adore you, devotchka, there is about to be far too much excitement in here for my poor little heart. I believe I shall adjourn myself to the cigar room and snuffle out their oldest yaks blood. To settle my stomach."

Lebedeva left in a flurry of feathers and pale, swinging hair—she did everything in a flurry. Marya Morevna blinked twice and glanced nervously at the car again, its chicken legs shuffling back and forth on the icy cobbles. Her own stomach quavered—her body had learned to feel it deep in the guts when something strange was about to happen. This was useful, but uncomfortable. Marya kept her hands steady.

The cafe fell abruptly silent—a complete, profound silence, with no tinkle of plate or dropped cup to blemish it. The skin of the walls prickled in gooseflesh as a broad-breasted woman with a nose like an axe blade strode into the place, her throat swallowed up in a black fur coat, her white hair strangled back into a savagely tight chignon. She looked to her left, then her right; then her eyes fell on Marya Morevna like an old, fat crow settling on a branch. She seated herself with the confidence of a landlord; three waiters hurried to bring her tea, vodka, golden kvass in a fresh jar. A fourth appeared, a rusalka, his hair dripping wet, bearing a whole goose on a golden tray. The woman tore off a leg and bit into it, licking the juice from her slightly fuzzy chin. The waiter was obliged to stand, a piece of furniture hoisting the goose for her further enjoyment.

"So you're her," growled the old woman, grinning with her mouth full. She had all her teeth, and they were sharp, leonine, yellow.

"I'm not sure what you mean," said Marya Morevna softly. The old woman crackled with potency; Marya's stomach felt it like a blow. The crone tapped the table with the goose's leg bone.

"Kid, let's skip this pantomime where you pretend you're not rutting with my brother up in that gauche tower of his—come off it! Does everything have to be black? He's an affected old bull, I'll tell you that for free. Anyway, I have no patience for innocent girls, unless they have apples in their mouths and are on speaking terms with my soup pot."

Marya tried to smile politely, as though they were having a pleasant conversation about the weather. But she gripped her teacup so tight the handle left red moon-shapes in her palms. Her face flushed and the old woman rolled her jaundiced eyes.

"Oh, quit that, Yelena! Blushing is for virgins and Christians!"

"My name is not Yelena."

The old woman paused and crooked one eyebrow, whose scraggly hairs had grown so long she'd braided them neatly along her brow bone. Her voice changed timbre, rising to an interested tenor. "Forgive me. I just assumed. My brother has a"—she stirred her tea with the fatty end of the goose bone—"*fetish* for girls named Yelena, you see. Almost a monomania. Occasionally, a Vasilisa will sneak in there, just to keep things spiced. So it's an easy mistake. What is your name, my child?"

"Marya Morevna. And there aren't any others. There have never been."

The crone tossed her goose bone over one shoulder. The waiter, still silent and dutiful behind her, caught it with a deft hand. She leaned over the table, her fur coat sloshing into the vodka, and plunked her face down in her hands.

"Well, isn't that just *fascinating*," she breathed. "The devil take lunch! Let your old baba take you on an . . . expedition. It'll be good for you! Morally fortifying, like having a good stare at a graveyard. A body needs a good *memento mori* to flush out the humors."

The crone seized Marya Morevna by the arm and shoved her out of the restaurant. She paid for nothing.

Marya was no fool. She could add two and two and two and come up with six—which is to say, add *old grandmother* and *chicken legs* and *terrified waitstaff* and come up with Baba Yaga. No magician outranked Baba Yaga. Her seat at the magicians' cafe was sacrosanct, to say the least.

Outside, snow floated down a lacy path, so thick it obscured even the Chernosvyat, hunched dark and impregnable on the hill. Baba Yaga gave a bleating cry and leapt up into the air, her skinny legs scissoring beneath her. She landed hard on Marya's shoulders, digging her heels into the girl's armpits.

"Mush, girl! Mush!" she yelped. "A wife must be a good mount, eh?"

Marya's knees trembled, but when she felt the snap of a goathide whip on her back, she stumbled ahead, running through the snow. Baba Yaga's car snorted to life and hopped along behind her, nipping at her heels with its front bumper.

"That way, not-Yelena!" Baba Yaga hollered into the storm. Marya groaned like an old nag, and ran.

Marya's mouth dripped saliva like an overworked horse. She rounded the snow-swept corner into a half-sheltered alley, her breathing shallow, rough, and fast. Baba Yaga hauled on her hair to stop her at the threshold of the door and vaulted off. Marya gasped with relief, the hot weight finally vanished from her back. She bent over, her heart wheezing, sweat pouring off of her, crawling in her scalp. A horse-bone door cut into the side of a blood-brown boar-skin building. Rubbish and smashed glass carpeted the thin street. The car honked happily, shuffling its chicken legs.

"In you go, and in I go," chuffed Baba Yaga, her breath fogging. "And stay close—I want to see if you cry."

They shouldered through the horse-femur door together. It towered over them both. Within, a yawning factory floor opened up below an iron balcony. They peered over the railing, the screws and bolts groaning with the leaden weight of Baba Yaga. Below, dozens upon dozens of girls worked away at looms the size of army trucks, their fingers flashing in and out of strands of linen, their shuttles racing their hands. Most of the women were blond, their hair braided in a tidy crown around their heads. Only a few dark ones, like Marya, dotted the sea of pale gold. They wore identical blackberry-colored uniforms. The old woman beamed like a holiday morning.

"Every one of those pretty little things is named Yelena. Oh— I'm sorry. *That* one is Vasilisa. And that one. And that plump one in the corner . . . and the tall one with her dolly still in her pocket. How sweet."

Marya wiped her sodden brow. Her calves burned thickly. "What are they doing?" she panted.

"Oh, this is a wartime facility. Didn't you know? Doesn't your lover tell you just *everything*? They're weaving armies. Noon and midnight, and no days off for good behavior. See? There, one is coming off the line just now."

Directly below them, one of the looms and one of the Yelenas were finishing off the helmet on a soldier. He was as flat as paper, but perfect, his uniform crisp, his eyes serenely shut, his rifle at the ready. The shuttle scooted back and forth, weaving in the last of his helmet's spike. When it was done, the Yelena opened up the leg of his trousers and blew hard into it, first the right, then the left. The soldier inflated, his nose popping into shape, muscles plumping in his thighs. He sat up stiffly and, with much creaking of new stitches, marched to the rear of the room, where the blocking baths awaited.

"They're not alive, see," explained Baba Yaga. "Well, not *properly* alive. Not alive like a frog or my car. It's all so Viy can't pull his old trick of killing our folk like he's getting paid per pint, then turning around and lining them up in his own formations. When you stab one of these poor bastards, they just unravel. Good trick, yes? Can't say my brother's not clever."

"Comrade Yaga—"

Baba Yaga whirled on her, the tails of her fur coat whipping around. "Don't you call me *comrade*, little girl. We aren't equals and we aren't friends. *Chairman* Yaga. That comrade nonsense is just a hook by which the low pull down the high. And then what do you get? Everyone rolling around in the same shit, like pigs."

Marya fought to keep her voice strong and deep. She would not show fear in front of this wolf of a woman. "Chairman Yaga. Why did you bring me here?"

Baba Yaga grinned, showing all her teeth. Her black fur coat had heads on it, Marya suddenly noticed, three of them—slit-eyed minks, their muzzles frozen in a triplicate of snarling. "To show you your future, *Comrade* Morevna! Koschei, my insatiable brother, abducted all those girls—from Moscow, from Petrograd, from Novgorod, from Minsk. Spirited them from their cozy little homes, barreled them through the snow, telling them what to eat, how to kiss, when to speak, bathing them when they fell sick, just so they'd love him and need him—oh, my brother does yearn to be needed! He needs so much himself, you see. And then, well, what always happens with husbands? A few of them he got bored of; some of them betrayed him, stealing his death or running off with preverbal bogatyrs with necks like hams. And then *they* steal his death. Oh, the vixens! They were shameless. Anyway, it doesn't matter. My brother always ends up dead in the end. Oh, the funerals I've had to attend! And flowers and gifts for each of them! I'm half-bankrupt with his theatrics. It never takes, though. That's what *deathless* means. It's only his death that dies. Koschei goes on and on. None of those milk-assed girls down there understood it, even though he practically wears a letter of intent on his chest. They snatch up his death and break it open and stomp on it like the curs they are, but what can you do? A dog is a dog. She only knows how to bite and eat. But most of them, Marya—my, what a black, soft name! I could lie in it all day—most of them couldn't get by me to begin with. Family is a thorny, vicious business, and Koschei can't marry without my say-so. Those stupid ox-wives weren't fit to sweep my floor! They couldn't even fire an arrow through the eye of a needle! What good is a wife who can't, I ask you? I've done him a thousand favors." Baba Yaga reached into her coat and pulled out a cigarillo. She chomped on its end and spat, rolling it over between her lips. "So there they sit. They don't get any older—the elderly make terrible workers, I ought to know.

Never like to do half a day's work when I can do none, myself. And they don't die. That Yelena there—with the mole on her neck!—she's been here, oh, since the days of Knyaz Oleg. Lenochka!" Chairman Yaga called down, and blew the seamstress a smoky kiss. The girl did not look up from the rifle she wove. "I'm sure we've got room in here for you somewhere, Marya! After all, what kind of babushka would I be if I left even one of my babies out in the cold?"

Marya's eyes blurred with tears. She felt dizzy; another step and she'd topple over the edge of the balcony. All of them? All of them had loved Koschei, slept in his huts? Snuggled with vintovniks? Learned to be cold?

"He said there were no others, not ever. He said I misheard Volchya-Yagoda, and I was his only love." But more than the lie she had been told, Marya's heart could not absorb the ugliness of her lover keeping these girls prisoner, year after year, like a treasure hoard.

"Husbands lie, Masha. I should know; I've eaten my share. That's lesson number one. Lesson number two: among the topics about which a husband is most likely to lie are money, drink, black eyes, political affiliation, and women who squatted on his lap before and after your sweet self."

Marya covered her face in her hands. She could not bear to look at the Yelenas and Vasilisas. To think of them wrapped up in mustard plasters, or opening their mouths to receive bread and roe. And worse, never going home, never looking up from work that could never, never be done.

"Hounds and hearthstones, girl, haven't you ever heard a story about Koschei? He's only got the one. Act One, Scene One: pretty girl. Act One, Scene Two: pretty girl gone!"

"I didn't think it *meant* anything." *I thought the stories were about me, somehow. That I was a heroine. That the magic was for me.* "They don't even know what writers are, here!"

Baba Yaga softened, as much as she could soften. Her braided eyebrows creased together gently. "Doesn't mean we don't know what stories are. Doesn't mean we don't walk in them, every second. Chyerti—that's us, demons and devils, small and big—are compulsive. We obsess. It's our nature. We turn on a track, around and around; we march in step; we act out the same tales, over and over, the same sets of motions, while time piles up like yarn under a wheel. We like patterns. They're comforting. Sometimes little things change—a car instead of a house, a girl not named Yelena. But it's no different, not really. Not ever." Baba Yaga pressed the back of her withered hand to Marya's cheek. "That's how you get deathless, volchitsa. Walk the same tale over and over, until you wear a groove in the world, until even if you vanished, the tale would keep turning, keep playing, like a phonograph, and you'd have to get up again, even with a bullet through your eye, to play your part and say your lines."

Marya's tears trickled off her cheeks and dripped through the iron balcony grate. One splashed upon a Vasilisa's red hair. She did not move, even a little. *Oh, I will do something, something,* Marya thought with a fury like a fever. *When I am Tsaritsa I will break all these machines and I will set them free.* "If you're here to decide if I can marry, why have you waited so long? I've been here nearly a year. I've believed him for a year!"

Baba Yaga withdrew her hand. Stamping out her cigarillo on the balcony rail, she straightened her back.

"Lenin died," she said curtly. "He's better at it than my brother. His death stuck to him. What should I have done? I went to dance on his coffin. I owed him at least that. No one saw me, of course. After all these years, I'm nimble enough to step under the wind. The horns played and the dirges sang and I danced on his ugly glass coffin—like Snow White, the bald devil! I wonder, if I kissed him, would he wake up?"

"I could have an order made up, if you like," said Chairman Yaga, marching back down Skorohodnaya Road on her own steam. She stopped short, sniffing the air with long, snorting breaths like a hound. Baba Yaga snuck around the side of a darkened, quiet distillery. "Aha! Thought you could hide, did you?" she cried, kicking a massive storage barrel of new vodka. Snow crusted its iron bands. She petted it fondly. "I have a nice brass stamp, big enough to bash heads. But I believe it's all more or less standard. Three tasks, completed on schedule, and you can put on a nice white dress and blush to your heart's content. Well, I doubt he'll let you wear white. But you get the idea. And if you fail, I get to crunch your green bones between my teeth—snick, snick!"

"I thought you punished girls by putting them to work in that factory."

Baba Yaga tapped at the vodka barrel like a safecracker. "That's the privilege of a Yelena. You, I want to eat. Family shares alike, you know. My brother gets to taste you. Why should I be left out? You've been eating like a tsarevna for a year! Look at those buttocks, those meaty arms! I could get a Lenten feast out of you, and half a New Year roast."

Marya Morevna stood in the cold, hands shoved deep in her woolen pockets. The wind buffeted her fur hat. "Isn't it the groom who's supposed to get firebird feathers and rings from the bottom of the sea to prove his worthiness to the bride?"

Baba Yaga laid her head on its side, as if considering which answer would be most amusing. "Women must cast off the chains of oppression, my little suckling calf. Besides, that sort of thing really only works if you don't let the groom have his way with your womb for a year before the wedding. Once you do, you can't get grooms to carry out the hearth-ash, let alone mess about with fire-birds. Appalling creatures, if you ask me. Nervous bags of burning excrement—and have you ever seen one eat? You'll get nothing but blisters and a kick in the mouth for the trouble. And that goes for husbands and firebirds both."

Marya allowed herself a smug smile. She hadn't a scratch from her firebird.

"But the Yelenas," she whispered. "I can't bear to think of them. There must be a mistake. I have to talk to him. I have to—" Maybe it was all nothing, or the old witch was lying just to upset her, and she would laugh with Koschei about it in the morning.

"What, hear him explain? Grovel? I can understand wanting him to crawl. I'm sure he's made you do enough of that, and what have you done to deserve it? Had pretty breasts and memorized a bit of poetry? Listen, devotchka. A baba knows. Just tell yourself a story that'll satisfy you and pretend he told it. Save you a bowlful of trouble."

"I thought you didn't want him to marry."

"I don't give two teats whether he marries or not. But I won't tol-erate his bringing hang-jaw, lackwit brats into the family." Chairman Yaga crooked her finger at the oak vat. Her long, warped fingernail sparked as she cut a tiny, neat hole in the side of the thing, then tipped her head to slurp the vodka spurting out. Liquor splashed onto her dry tongue as she lapped and slurped away. Finally, the crone wiped her mouth with her sleeve and traced her finger the other way, sewing up the hole. "And you have to admit, I've a devil of a habit for being right. Which of those brats *didn't* pounce on the first potato-gobbling cretin that passed her way? Which of them *didn't* plot against Koschei? He's been hurt, my brother, so often. I only want what's best for him. Tell yourself that, if it helps you smile when he kisses you. And you'd better smile. I've been married seventeen times, Marya Morevna. Do you have any idea how much I know about men? And women! Don't look so shocked— after an eon or two of being a wife you'll want one of your own, too. Fiendishly convenient things, wives. Better than cows. They'll love you for beating them, and work 'til they die."

"I'm not like that."

"We'll see. Anyway, what I know about marriage could fill the sky on a starless night. I don't get to give the tests because I buttered up the right kommissar. I give them because I know. A wife must terrify, she must have a stronger arm than a boyar, and she must know how to rule. That's all that matters, in the end. Who is to rule. And if you can't, *tscha*! You've no business with a ring."

Marya lifted her chin. "And if I don't want one?"

"You wanted one this morning. What's changed? That he had a herd of girlfriends before you? Surely you didn't think deathless meant dickless. Those are nice girls! Hoarding virginity is a criminal act, like hoarding food. Besides, don't forget the part where I eat your bones if you fail. Better married than rendered into girl-broth and maiden-cutlets."

10

The Raskovnik

What's it look like?" said Naganya, polishing her long walnut legs with viscous oil. She poured the golden stuff onto her skin and giggled as it tickled, trickling into the gunmetal works in the hollows of her knees. She adjusted the bony sighting over her right eye.

"How should I know? I've never heard of it." Masha threw herself disconsolately onto the little velvet chair perched near her cosmetics table. The sun knocked at the windows, turning the red curtains into flames. She never used the cosmetics, though Lebedeva was forever coaxing her to learn the arcane rites of powder and rouge crème. Still, they were there, in small black pots like fell unguents, untouched, but waiting.

Naganya shrugged. "Oh, well, I've *heard* of it. Some hairy little herb that unlocks all locks, supposedly. But that's not the fun part. The sport of it is, you find raskovnik by locking an old lady up in iron leg shackles and making her walk across a field at the dark of the moon. Wherever her chains fall off—poof! Raskovnik. Never seen the stuff, though. It's murder to keep fresh—lilies last longer in a vase full of dust."

"I have to bring it to Chairman Yaga by tomorrow, or she'll have me in her soup pot. She's already looking through her cabinets for recipes." Chairman Yaga had made sure she could not see Koschei, kept him busy and closeted, so that she could do nothing but obey the vicious, ancient witch's whims. "Do you think we could get Lebedeva to do it? She's a bit old."

The vintovnik laughed, the greased metal of her jaw clicking like a gun firing on empty rounds. "I shall tell her you said so next time she pinches my cheeks and fusses with my hair. No good, though: has to be an old human lady. Scarcity drives desire, you know. We haven't had any proper old grandmothers here in a kingfisher's year."

"Then what am I to do? I don't want to be soup." *And if I cannot get the crown, I cannot get the Yelenas free.*

"And you want to marry Koschei. To be worthy."

Marya Morevna frowned into her chest. "I should go thrash those dogs of his and toss his death off a cliff, that's what I should do. Nasha, you didn't see those women! He ought to be scrambling to prove he's worthy of *me!*"

Nasha squirmed. Her great dark eyes creased with worry. "But I did see them. I did. When they lived in this room. When they met Chairman Yaga. And I met the other men, too."

"What other men?"

"The Ivans. Wherever there is a Yelena or a Vasilisa, there is an Ivan. Surely Babushka told you. About the bogatyrs? They aren't too bright, usually, but bless me if they aren't a handsome species.

They're always the youngest of three sons. They're always the honest type, dumb as toenails but big in the trousers. And the Yelenas, they always fall in love and run off. I remember one Ivan came with a wolf, a huge grey monster of a beast. The wolf did all the work, tricking Koschei into telling them where his death was, telling Ivan what to say so that Yelena the Bright would swoon in her seat for him, even though he was a youngest son with no inheritance and mud under his nails. The two of them rode off astride the wolf when it was all said and done. They left Koschei bleeding in the snow. When they'd safely gone, he picked himself up and washed the blood off. He stood watching the road for a long time, like he thought she might come back. But what can you do? Gone means gone. He didn't come out of the Chernosvyat for weeks. Chairman Yaga won't even say the name Ivan anymore, she hates them so. If she meets one on the street—snick, snick! She eats him up on the spot, and belches like a grain commissioner, so everyone will know she isn't sorry."

"You knew them? You slept curled up with them and you know where they are? But you don't try to rescue them?"

Naganya scowled. "Chyerti don't go in for rescuing. If you eat rotten fish, you're bound to get sick. If you're a faithless spittoon of a woman, you end up in the factory. It's only common sense. And besides, people being miserable is natural. Just like it's natural for an imp to enjoy them being miserable. As a system, it works terrifically well."

Marya picked at her nails. She knew the answer before she said it. "And if I end up there, you won't come for me, either?"

Naganya the vintovnik looked away, her oily hair falling into her face.

"Well," said Marya softly. "If I ever meet a man named Ivan I shall eat his heart before he can wish me a good morning."

Nasha grinned, eager to skate over such uncomfortable subjects.

"That's on account of how you're one of us, Mashenka! Spleen and sleeping, marrow and mind. Now, there's raskovnik to dig up, and not much time."

"If we need a human, how can we ever get back to a city without Volchya-Yagoda and an armful of weeks to spare?"

"There's border places. Places where the birches are thinner than paper, and you can tear through. Places where the Tsar of Life and the Tsar of Death fought so hard that their territories lie crushed right up to each other, on either side of a pebble, in the leaves and root of a turnip, on a cat's tail and his tongue."

"I should try to see him again, before we go. Baba Yaga can't keep me out if he hears my voice. Surely he will wrap me up in his arms and tell me—"

"Don't, Masha." Naganya fidgeted. "The war is going badly."

"The war is always going badly."

Marya and Naganya took a young horse, green and fleet and hungry, and trotted down Skorohodnaya Road in the evening light, the vintovnik tucked in front of Marya herself, clutching the saddle horn with her wooden hands. Twilight drifted lazily, taking its time bringing down a violet-pink haze. The last rays of sun winked on their stallion's ears.

"I make horses nervous," Naganya fretted. The safety in her cheek cocked and uncocked sharply, echoing down the road. "Surely this one will rear and drop me! And then roll over on top of us both!"

"I chose a young one, who has not yet heard that you sometimes shoot people. It will be all right." The horse snorted; snow bleated from his nose.

Naganya twisted in her seat as the road dwindled behind them and the wood rose up, dark and excited, icy and rustling. She grabbed her friend by the chin. "Marya, listen like your ears are bottomless! Border places are dangerous. Very disreputable things live there. You must be careful or Koschei will smelt me for losing you. If you see anyone you know, or someone with a silver star on their breast, you mustn't talk to them, not even to curse them or ask their names. You mustn't get off the horse. If your foot touches the ground, I won't be able to help you. Even the enemy's pebbles bite and are fierce. I shall find the old lady for you. I shall push her across the field."

"Isn't that cheating?"

"*Tfu!* She *expects* you to cheat! Masha, whom I love: These tasks do not test your strength or your wiliness; they test your ability to cheat, which is the truest measure of a devil. They are designed to be impossible if you play fair. What should you do instead? Walk into no-man's-land unprotected and be lost forever?"

"Is that what the others did? Did you tell the Yelenas these things?"

"*Yes!* And they refused to listen because they were innocent maidens without a lie in their hearts or a smear on their souls. Don't be innocent, Marya. Innocent means stupid. Follow your friend, who is a goblin and knows better, and we'll have raskovnik salad before dawn."

But if I am not innocent, are there lies in my heart? Smears on my soul? Am I a devil? What does it mean, to be one of them? Marya resolved to sort it all out when she had a moment to think through it, when Baba Yaga's soup pot was not dangling over her head.

The forest deepened, the birches filling with crows, the underbrush with red, pointed hedgehog eyes. Overhead, violet seeped out of the sky and black crept up until only the sharp, cutting stars sliced through the night. Naganya's body warmed against her own; she worked the trigger in her throat gently to keep her oils from freezing. Finally, the wood opened up into a wide glade where the

snow flowed even and smooth as water. A dozen houses glowed
and smoked and did the sorts of things village houses do in the dark
of winter. Naganya whooped, her cry echoing through the owls
like one of their own. An old woman crept out of one of the smallest houses and into the snow. Once she had passed the ring of
light cast by all those windows, she squatted in the field, the hissing of her urine loud in the silent evening.

"We've luck like a mushroom hunter tonight, Marya! Look at
her, all fat and full of juice!" Naganya hopped lightly off the horse,
neither sinking in the snow nor leaving tracks, but dancing on it
like a mayfly on a lake.

"Why is it safe for you and not for me?" whispered Marya Morevna.

"Because you're still a girl." The vintovnik grinned. "Girls have
to obey rules. Chyerti break them."

The rifle imp scampered off through the snow. Marya nudged
her horse along to keep her friend in sight.

"Pssst, babushka!" Nasha hissed. "Old lazy slattern! How many
babies have you got off your man, hm? Spend your life with your
legs open, do you? Just leaves room for the devil to slip in!"

The old woman started and looked around her—right at
Naganya—but saw nothing.

"Shame on you, baba! Haven't even got the decency to get up to
witchcraft in your old age! Just lie about, why don't you? Screech
at brats got from half your neighbors. *Plump my pillows! Feed me
cherries!*"

The old woman shivered, peering hard into the dark.

"Babushka! Put your ankles together for once! What if Christ
comes back tonight and the first things he sees are your saggy old
bones pissing in the snow like a horse? Straight back to paradise
with him, on the double quick, that's what!"

The woman leapt up, drawing her knees together with a dry

knocking sound. Naganya dove down and clapped her irons on the old lady's legs, giggling.

"Marya," came a soft voice. But Marya reminded herself not to speak to anyone, and stared straight ahead.

"March, Comrade Lazybones!" cried the vintovnik. She boxed one of her own ears, stamped her foot, and shot three bullets out of her mouth with the soft *psht psht psht* of a silencer. The shots landed all around the old grandmother but did not hurt her, only made her leap forward like a spooked cow. "Faster! Faster! The police are after you! Run! You remember how to hike up your skirts!"

The woman bawled and stumbled, her ankles tangling up in the manacles. "Don't fall or I shall have you arrested for wasting your life on babies and borscht!"

"Marya," said the voice again. Marya squeezed her eyes shut. *I will not answer,* she thought frantically.

Naganya nipped at her human's heels, spitting silenced bullets and whacking at her toes with bayonets Marya had not known she hid under her arms.

"Don't cry, you wrinkly old camel! Just think of the stories you'll have to tell all the other spitting beasts! The devil chased you through the snow! You'll be Queen Camel, prize pisser!"

"Marya Morevna, look at me."

Marya could not help it. She looked down. A beautiful young woman stood below her horse, her blond hair gathered up in an elegant ballerina's bun. She wore a thick white fur coat, the kind a man gives to his mistress. On her chest glimmered a splattering of light, as though someone had thrown a bucket of molten silver onto her. It glowed like a watery star.

"Svetlana Tikhonovna!" Marya gasped.

"Yes, it is me," the woman said. "Come down and hug me, my darling. I was one-twelfth your mother, after all."

Svetlana held out her arms. The star on her breast rippled.

"I'm not supposed to." But she felt her eyes burning with tears. She had not known how much she wished to see a human face, a motherly face.

"The Marya I know didn't care much for *supposed to*. You stole my hairbrush, after all, and ran off in the middle of the night like an ungrateful brat. But I give without bitterness, as a mother should."

"How can you be here, Svetlana? This is the other side of the world." Marya's fingers ached to brush her icy cheek, to say, *What of my birth mother? What of my father? Any word of my sisters? And I am not a brat.*

"So true, so true! Well, the tale of it is, I died a few months after you left. I couldn't help it, I was so hungry. When the police came to question my husband about his club memberships, I spat at them and told them they ought to be shamed, to be so fat, in their big apartments, while my babies and I didn't remember what meat tasted like! You can't say that sort of thing. I knew that. I think I was just tired of being alive. It's no good, these days, being alive."

"I like it," whispered Marya.

"That's because you don't live in Leningrad. Can you believe it? It's Leningrad now that the old dragon is dead. They keep changing the name. Mark me, in twenty years they'll call it Lemon Popsicle and shoot people who laugh when they say it. Life is nice when there's cucumber soup and eye powder the color of scallions and a samovar piping away on every table. I forgot how nice, until I came to the Country of Death, where Viy is Tsar and the ghosts of the meals the living eat make all our larders groan. Come down, Masha. I'll give you a candy."

"I'm afraid. I don't want to go back. I don't want to be hungry. I don't want to be ordinary and ignored. And I certainly don't want to be dead. My home is in Buyan, in the Country of Life."

"Your home is *Leningrad*," Svetlana Tikhonovna snarled. "You've only forgotten it."

"I haven't! But you can leave your home and find someplace new. People do it all the time. Why can't I?"

Svetlana Tikhonovna shrugged as if it didn't matter to her in the least. "Come and kiss my cheeks, devotchka, and I will tell you how beautiful you've grown up to be. What have the living to fear from the dead?"

Naganya whooped from the far corner of the field, where the woman had stopped, her manacles springing off with a clang. The old grandmother set off at a dead run back to her house, and the vintovnik danced, the shackles jangling in her hand.

Marya shook her head. She felt as if a silver fog clung to her head, making her dull and drowsy. "Svieta, you do not mean to kiss me, really."

Svetlana Tikhonovna cackled and leapt at her, clawing and grasping at her leg. Folk spiraled up out of the snow like smoke, men and women and children, all with the silver splatter of death on their chests, all hungry and showing their teeth.

"Come down, come down!" they wept. "We only want to love you, and embrace you! You are so warm! Why should our enemy have all your kisses?"

A hundred cold fingers pulled at Marya, and no rider can stay on their horse with such hands on their skin. She toppled and fell into the mass of them, snow and vapor puffing up around her. As one they fell on her, weeping all the while. They did not bite her or claw her, but kissed her, over and over, their lips on her flesh. With every kiss she felt colder and colder, thinner and thinner, as though the night wind might blow her away. Svetlana Tikhonovna lay against her, her full, frosted lips closing over the mouth of Marya Morevna.

"Come down," the ballerina whispered in her frigid ear. "I will teach you to dance so perfectly as to stop a hundred hearts with every step."

Marya moaned beneath the shades. She tried to think, to fill her heart with living, hot things, to remember that she was alive and not sunk in the earth under the weight of all these ghosts.

"Tea," she whispered faintly. "Raspberry jam still in the pot, ovens, soup with dill, pickle broth." The shades recoiled, their teeth reflecting moonlight, silver and flat. Marya struggled to lift her head. "Peppers on my plate and running in the cold and dumplings boiling in an iron pot and Lebedeva's powders and Zemya's curse words and gusli playing as fast as fingers can pluck!" she continued, her voice stronger, lower, almost growling. The ghosts glowered resentfully at her.

Svetlana Tikhonovna grimaced.

"You were always a vicious child," she spat.

"A firebird in my net! A rifle in my fist! Mustard plasters and birch switches and blini crisping in my pan!" she screamed, and the citizens of Viy's country threw up their hands, wandering back into the forest.

Marya shakily pulled herself back onto the young horse, who, to his credit, had not spooked or run, but munched on weeds buried in the snow and thought nothing of the whole business. Naganya stood on the other side of his barrel flank, squinting up at Marya.

"Don't be too pleased with yourself," she said. "Imagine! You could have just listened to me in the first place—how novel that would have been! A first, in the annals of Buyan!"

Naganya held up her dark hand. In her palm was a flower, its blazing orange petals as thick as cow tongues, covered with bristling white fur, its leaves sharp and shredded, its stem studded with wicked thorns.

"Remember this when you are queen," said the vintovnik

solemnly. "That I went into the dark for you, and scared an old woman half to death."

Chairman Yaga sat at her monumental desk in the rear of the magicians' cafe, its wood black and glossy as enamel. She turned over the raskovnik in her hands, peering at it with a jeweler's glass.

"Well, it's a runt," she conceded.

"You didn't ask for a bouquet," Marya snapped. Dark circles rimmed her eyes; her fingers had gone pale and bloodless. Every inch of her ached, worn out, run down, exhausted.

"True, true. I'll remember that, for the next girl."

Marya said nothing, staring straight ahead, but her cheeks burned.

"What have we said about blushing, devotchka?" Baba Yaga pinched her thick nose. "Goats and gangrene, girl, I can't stand the smell of your youth!"

"Wait a while. It'll go away."

"Oh ho! Now we're sniping at our betters, are we? Listen, soon-to-be-soup. In marriage, the highest virtue is humility. If you're humble, they'll never see you coming!" Baba Yaga slapped the table to emphasize her point. As if by coincidence her fingers found a glass of vodka there, and she knocked it back in a gulp. "Whenever I get married, I always wear a caul ripped off of twin calves. Makes me young, makes me beautiful like a dollop of butter, makes me blush and tug my braids and pray in churches and bow down, humble as manure. The boys can't resist it! They come panting with their cocks on a silk leash, their balls painted gold for my pleasure. I give them a night on my knees, just like they like, sweet and obedient and dumb as a thumbnail, confused by their mysterious bodies, oh my, so much stronger than mine! Then they wake up and—ha! There is Baba Yaga in their beds, extra warts, teeth like spikes, and the soup pot already red on the hearth. It's a good trick. You should see their faces!"

"I'm not like that."

"We'll see. There is no such thing as a good wife or a good husband. Only ones who bide their time."

11

White Gold, Black Gold

You see why I need you," said Marya Morevna, sitting down on the forest moss next to Zemlehyed, who, for his part, seemed uninterested, burrowing his attention instead in a crown of violets and plump rosehips he had braided together. He held out his thumb and squinted at it, his stony tongue sticking out of his mouth with the ferocity of his concentration. Finally, he threaded three scarlet nightshade mushrooms into the crown and squinted at it again.

"Don't," he said brusquely.

"Zmey Gorinich," she repeated. "That's a dragon. Quite a step up from shrubbery. I haven't the first idea how to fight a dragon, let alone get his treasure to Chairman Yaga while I stay Marya Morevna, daughter of twelve mothers, and not

Roasted, daughter of Scorched. She wants his white gold and his black gold—and to be honest, I want nothing. I want to sleep."

"Snipe him," gruffed Zemlehyed. "Rat-a-tat, between his eyes. Chew dragon-steak, be happy. Bother Naganya." The leshy peeled a strip of birch bark from a nearby tree and twined it deftly through the violets—more deftly than Marya ever thought his thick, bark-covered hands could manage.

"Are you angry with me, Zemya?"

The leshy cracked an acorn between his granite teeth and spat the cap into the grass.

Marya tried again. "Naganya isn't half strong enough to wrestle a dragon, and shooting him seems convenient, except that killing such a beast would hand Viy an aerial bombing platform. With three heads."

"Strong enough. She slumbers near to you."

Marya looked down at the moss. Ants wandered toward some distant battle or wheat-seed orgy. Leshiyi were so delicate in their etiquette. She doubted he cared who slept in her bed—leshiyi mated by cross-pollination. He cared, she guessed, because he believed that the strongest of them should guard Marya in her sleep, and Marya had chosen Naganya because she held the—clearly mistaken—belief that the vintovnik could beat him, if it came to fists and grappling. Zemlehyed pouted and tucked a sprig of bright rowan berries into the crown.

"Naganya's mouth is strong," Marya said carefully. "But her arm is young. Yours is old, and hard, and I choose it." Besides, grappling was never Naganya's style.

Zemlehyed smiled broadly. His rocky eyes prickled moisture like raindrops.

"Morevna chooses!" he beamed. "And chooses best. Zemlehyed knows where Zmey Gorinich nests. Nasha knows nothing but how to make holes. Gorinich sleeps on top of bones. On top of gold. Zemya would like such a bed, but *tfu*. He makes do."

The leshy, his moss-hair trailing down in several green braids, held up his forest diadem. He reached down without looking and pulled up a clutch of winter onions, sticking them in so that their green stems fell like a veil from the back of the crown. Zemlehyed reached up and placed it on Marya's head. It matched her rosy trousers, her black-violet boots.

"He will help you, if you build him a promise."

"Anything, Zemya."

The leshy smirked, stroking his fir-needle mustache. "A kiss, for Zemlehyed, on his lips. He won't tell."

Marya Morevna laughed. Even devotees of cross-pollination must occasionally be curious, she reasoned. No more harm than in kissing a tree or a rock. And besides, Koschei had kissed all those Yelenas. Or probably had. Who could tell the truth? Marya felt defiance boil up in her chest. She did not care. She would kiss whom she liked. "All right, Zem. A kiss."

Without warning, the leshy shot up into the air, somersaulted, and came down hard on the mossy loam, digging furiously. His fists flew at the earth; his teeth gnashed and tore; his feet kicked like a diver plunging into deep water. Clumps flew; Zemlehyed disappeared into his hole. After a moment, his fingers, knuckles ringed with lacy mushrooms, popped back up.

"Morevna! Bustle! Faster than you is still too slow."

Marya took the leshy's rough hand and he hauled her, headfirst, underground.

Marya flipped in her descent and landed neatly on her feet in quite another forest, full of stubby scrub trees and tall lilac flowers. Golden-orange mountains rose on all sides, closing them in.

Zemlehyed hung from the branches of one of the taller trees, kicking his short legs back and forth in delight. He wiggled the top of his head out of a crack in the branch and fell—thump, bash!—onto the needle-strewn ground.

But the forest imp bounced up, and when he righted himself, he was a handsome man in a dark green soldier's uniform with red piping, his cap sparkling gold. He had a twisted, thorny black beard and muscled arms like pine trunks. Zemlehyed laid his finger aside his nose.

"You cannot tell," he said, his voice suddenly very much changed. "They mustn't know."

Marya Morevna gaped. She could not make her mouth close. All that time, and her friend was . . . what? She could not even say. A man. And a beautiful one. "Why not? Zem! Even Lebedeva would have to admit you're handsome!"

"Forests have secrets," he said gently. "It's practically what they're for. To hide things. To separate one world from another. You might not think it, but I love Lebed, and Nasha, with all my muddy heart. But as long as they think I'm stupid I can keep stealing from their stashes and they'll never suspect. Lebedeva would never think for a moment that I would want her night cream, or Naganya's holster-blouse. But I have them, and they are mine, and I will not give them back, no."

"Why *would* you want them?"

Zemlehyed shrugged. "It's in my nature. I hoard. It's in their nature, too, which is why Lebedeva has more night creams than nights, and Nasha collects tin cans. Zmey Gorinich, he is like this as well. But I think it is also in your nature."

Marya blinked. "I don't think so. What have I collected?"

Zemlehyed smiled in a lopsided way, as though he did not quite know how to use his face.

"Us."

The leshy led her through a field of spiky yellow blossoms fuzzy with pollen, heavy with buzzing bees. Puffy white cotton plants waved around them like tiny clouds. The sun pressed its hands to their shoulders, hurrying them along. The mountains, streaked with snow, rose strange and thin around them, as though a starving man slept under the earth, his ribs poking through the stone. They followed a deep blue river that ran deliriously through the meadow, fish splashing as though no spearman could dream of happening by. In the distance, at last, just as the sun was getting red and tired, Marya saw a great furry yurt in the dry grass. Thick, curly fleeces covered its roof; long poles stood tight together, curving in a round sweep. A ram pelt hid the door.

Zemlehyed did not knock. He pushed the pelt aside and ducked into the hut, squeezing his enormous frame into the doorway. Marya followed him into the warm yurt-shadows, where a bald man with round glasses sat at his desk, dwarfed by mountains of paperwork.

"Do you have an appointment?" he roared, a flush traveling all the way from his scalp to his brows in a long red wave.

"We seek Zmey Gorinich," said Marya, her voice firm.

"You are tiny," the man concluded. "Zmey Gorinich does not exist for the use of the tiny. Only the big does he notice! As big as he is!"

"I am big." Zemlehyed shrugged.

"Not very, compared to Zmey Gorinich!" bellowed the man, his head going red again.

"We did not come to compare ourselves to Zmey Gorinich," said Marya sweetly, measuring the mood of the man in glasses. He grabbed at a sheaf of paper at the bottom of the pile and yanked expertly, pulling it free without disturbing the rest. He set to scribbling in the file. "How could we compete with three heads, a tail like a mountain range, and the breath to burn empires down?"

The man in glasses looked up exasperatedly. "Look, you criminals, I don't have three heads. I never had three heads! This is what comes of letting writers have free rein, and not bridling them to the righteous labor of the Party the moment they learn to slap an accusative case around. I am *Comrade* Gorinich, and I have *one* head."

"I am not a criminal," said Marya Morevna. Zemlehyed did not protest for his own honest status, being a goblin and in spirit a criminal, even if no warrants bore his name.

"Of course you are," snapped Comrade Gorinich. "Everyone is a criminal! We are beset on all sides by antirevolutionary forces. Naturally, then, humans fall into three categories: the criminal, the not-yet-criminal, and the not-yet-caught." Comrade Gorinich gestured at them with an enormous fountain pen. "Even the man who is all his life vigilant, who keeps his mind and body so clean that he never has a single antirevolutionary thought—even *that man* is a criminal! He should have been effortlessly pure! If he had to fight so hard to hew to Comrade Stalin's vision, then obviously, he was a criminal all along!"

"I thought you were a dragon," sighed Marya, sitting down in a small chair. She still longed for the best heights of magic, to see dragons and mermaids, to see the naked world. Not this, which made her think only of home, and how her own warrant might at least read *runaway*. Zemlehyed stood calmly behind her, at attention.

Comrade Gorinich pounded his files with both fists. "I *am* a dragon! Look around! What do you see, eh? This is my bed of bones! Look how I crunch them!"

Marya quirked her eyebrow, which seemed to enrage him even further. Soon she thought his head would fly right off. She shrugged. "I don't see any bones."

"Your criminal nature blinds you! Look!" He snatched up a file in his hand. "Comrade Yevgeny Leonidovich Kryukov! Convicted of anti-Stalinist organization on Tuesday the twenty-fourth! I had him shot on my lunch break! Bones! Comrade Nadezhda Alexandrovna Roginskaya! Convicted of concealing her fugitive, criminal cousins from me! Arrested on Thursday, shot on Friday before dinner! Bones!" He held an enormous file up above his head. "The village of Bandura, in Ukraine! Refused to collectivize! Too bad—either way they starve to death! Bones!" The bald man leaned over his desk, caressing the papers. "*Three hundred and sixty-seven* separate anti-Bolshevik spies convicted of the murder of Sergei Mironovich Kirov! Or will be, as soon as we can manage to have Kirov shot in Leningrad! Bones! Bones! Bones!" Gorinich clutched the papers in his fists, quite beside himself. "I sleep with my orders of execution stuffed into my mattress. It is good for my back!"

Marya watched him, horror searing through her, sour and cold. "Why do you do this, Comrade Gorinich?" she said softly.

"It is the least I can do! Here, in the hinterlands, the Party does not have it so easy. People are so attached to their yaks and their children. But I, I understand the east. I have been here longer than the dirt! My mother was a great dragon. She lived in Lake Baikal, snorting storms, spitting floods, diving down to the bottom of the lake to bite the floorboards of the world. My father—you will not believe it, I know!—my father was Genghis Khan, and so great a heart had he that alone of all creatures in heaven and earth he was strong enough to force himself on my gargantuan mother, laughing all the while. My egg rode with the Golden Horde. I nursed at the villages they burned, the bodies full of arrows! I am full of easterners! So I know them, toe and pate. And they know me. They know if they go against the Party, they go against Comrade Gorinich, and Gorinich has always been their comrade, their bedmate, their dinner guest, their funeral master."

He adjusted his glasses and mopped his brow with a red kerchief. "I am a conduit. Moscow, she sends me meat and bones, and I send her rich, soft cotton, rich, soft petroleum. Tribute. It's an old, honorable system."

"What do you care if the Party has interests in the east?" Marya said, remaining as calm as she could, for calmness seemed to upset him, and the upset beast is careless. "I am only curious. It seems to me, in the old days, Gorinich did not work for the Tsars."

"Pah! Why should I? I am a Khan by birthright! The Tsars could offer me nothing I did not have. Dilettantes, the whole painted lot of them. But now! The Party deals in *bulk*, in *industrial quantities*. They are like me. Gluttons. They hoard. The Party lines my bed with luxurious femurs, sternums, ribs! Without the Party to tell folk it's all for their own good, I wouldn't sleep half so well."

Comrade Gorinich suddenly clapped one hand over his eye and stretched his neck toward them like a turtle.

"What did you say your name was, criminal girl?" he said sharply.

"Marya Morevna." *Runaway,* she thought. *That's all he can say against me. And occasionally rough with her friends, but only because they let her.*

Gorinich riffled through his papers, lifting files, his tongue flicking in and out of his mouth. "What have we here?" he cried triumphantly. "I knew it, I did! What do I forget? Nothing and no one! Comrade Marya Morevna! Convicted of gross desertion at Leningrad in 1942! Bones! Bones! And that makes you *my* bones, and that makes you my tribute. What say I shoot you now and get it over with? Why wait? Time is communal, Marya Morevna, the most purely communal of all commodities. It belongs to us all equally. So why hoard it?"

Marya squared her shoulders and laid one ankle over her knee. She could not, could never show a dragon, even one in glasses, that he had frightened her. If it spooks a horse, it will spook a snake. A Khan respects only strength. Even so, she wanted to be back in her red room, warm, with supper ready.

She leveled a stare at him. "If it belongs to us all equally, then I will take and enjoy my share, thank you."

"Feh." Gorinich snorted, dropping the black file back onto his desk. He scribbled in it. "Then you eat up my day and shit out only more paperwork. Now I must note that you were here, that you declined to be shot, that you breathed a cup of air, that you disturbed a tablespoon of dust. You left skin flakes and three strands of hair in exchange. I'm really very busy."

"If you will give us what we've come for, we will happily go," said Zemlehyed simply.

"And what is that?"

"Your gold," said Marya. "I don't think I need much. A coin. One white, one black."

Comrade Gorinich leaned back in his chair, folding huge, meaty red hands behind his bald head. "You, my young criminal, are an idiot."

Zemlehyed took off his officer's cap and cradled it in his muscled, oak-root arms. His wild black hair stuck out in licks and corkscrews. "Gorinchik." He grinned. "Say no. I would love you to say no."

"I don't say no. I don't say yes. I say you're an idiot with balls for brains, you hulking leshy rock. Oh, I can see the moss on your bones! Who fools Zmey Gorinich? Nothing and no one! What do you think you're doing out here? You and me, boy, we can dress ourselves up as men, we can conjugate all our verbs perfectly, and they still won't love us. She'll never want you smearing her tits with mud and shooting wet leaves into her. My father was more like us than any human since, and he had it right: Take them if you want them, keep the children, and eat your fill of the world. The best humans will ever give us is tribute. You ask your Koschei.

He knows better than anyone. It's *them* who've no souls and no hearts. Who makes Zmey Gorinich's bed? Not him!"

"I have a soul," said Marya Morevna, and the golden faces of the Yelenas crowded her mind. "I have a heart. I don't sleep on anyone's bones."

Comrade Gorinich leered. "You're young yet. Give it time."

"You were slurping bones clean long before the Party wrote them down for you," Marya snapped. "Don't you go drawing lines between chyerti and humans. You are hungry; we are hungry. What's the difference?"

"The *difference* is, the whole world is yours, but you keep pushing us out! It's not enough to have the cities and the churches, have to have the farms, too. Not enough to have the farms, have to have the forests. Not enough to have the forests, have to have the snow, every flake, every crystal! And now you come demanding my gold, too, as if you have the first idea what a dragon's treasure is, what it means. Well, I have you beat, Marya Morevna. You are already dead. But me? Zmey Gorinich survives everything. I can be a Mongol if I must. I can be Chinese, if that's the thing to be. And I can be a good Party man without breaking a sweat. At the end of it all, come looking, and still you'll find Gorinich swimming the ashes, sunning his belly on your skulls!"

Zemlehyed put his cap back on and straightened it. Then, he walked quietly out the door, letting the goatskin flap fall behind him.

"What is he doing?"

"Go find out for yourself," said Marya, though she had no idea.

"I can't, imbecile. What, you think a dragon can turn into a man? I'm too big for that! A man's flesh is no more than a sock to me. You are so deep in my coils I can already taste you. That chair you sit in, that is also me. This desk is me, this floor, this yurt.

Even a few of the flowers outside. My scales, my tongue, my crest, my stomach. I can't walk outside myself."

Comrade Gorinich took off his glasses and folded them delicately. He opened his mouth horribly wide, all his flat teeth showing. Wider and wider his mouth gaped, until it fell back over his skull like a hood. Marya bolted for the door, but the air around her swelled and darkened, coils she could not see before shimmering into sight around her, as high as walls and higher, squeezing around her, vising her in. Marya tried to beat against the lizard flesh closing her up, but the coils had pinned her arms already. They reeked of rotting flesh and old marrow. She gulped for breath, her chest shallow and frantic, her head only just protruding from a nest of serpent loops the color of underground caverns, black and blue and silver. She could not see the face of Zmey Gorinich, if he had one, only his inexorably tightening body. Even Marya's tears were strangled away.

"Comrade Gorinich," she whispered hoarsely, her voice squeezed away, her heartbeat jangling in her ears. "You will have me, soon enough. Your file said so, and files do not lie. You will have me for your bed of bones, and sleep on me forever. But your file does not say *Comrade Marya Morevna, eaten by a Kazakh dragon in 1926!* There will be discrepancies, Zmey Gorinich! And paperwork! Let me go. You will not have to wait long." Then Marya Morevna shut her eyes. She leaned as far forward as she could, and kissed, very gently, the snake-flesh closing around her face.

The coils flushed scalding hot, and Marya truly thought for a moment that she might die there. A tiny flame went up on her cheek, just below her eye. Her lashes began to sizzle—and then the coils were gone. She stood in a cotton field outside the yurt, bent double, chasing her breath. Marya slapped her face to put out the flame.

"Masha!" cried Zemlehyed, farther up the meadow, at the riverbank. "Are you all right?"

"She's bitter and not worth eating!" bellowed a voice from within the yurt.

Marya ran to the leshy, who had taken off his olive jacket and was sweating in his undershirt.

"Where did you go, Zemya? He might have choked me. He might have killed me."

Zemlehyed wiped his forehead with one massive fist. "I am diverting this river, Marya Morevna. I am coaxing it to run into that horrid yurt, and wash him away. When he is gone, we shall be able to rifle through the wreckage for coins, white ones and black ones. It was his babbling about the Khans that gave me the idea. We did this sort of thing when they were underfoot."

Zemya bent by the riverbank, his huge knees popping loudly in the blue air. He gathered up a mound of earth in his arms, so much earth that great, long bones and boulders came up with it, so much that behind the mass no leshy could be seen, and flung it away from him. It exploded against a hillock in a shower of dust and broken rock. Zemlehyed winked at Marya and hopped into the hole he had made, already filling with river water. He leaned his shoulder against one side of the earthen hole and shoved, the cords of his neck taut as guitar strings. He burst through the soil and kept shoving, so fast and so far that Marya immediately lost sight of him amidst the black dirt and the river rushing to fill up the path he had made for it. By the time he reached the yurt, the river could not be stopped. He leapt up out of the foam and roaring water as the current swept over Comrade Gorinich, carrying him along with it to join another stream farther down the hill. The screeching of Zmey Gorinich echoed in the valley, but so did the laughter of Zemlehyed, who spat after him.

Marya walked back to the place the yurt had occupied, her hair drenched with spray, her scalded face throbbing. When she reached the place the yurt had recently occupied, the river had calmed somewhat, and Zemya was picking through the grass, looking for gold.

"There's nothing here, Zemya," sighed Marya. "Not even bones. Look, everywhere there is nothing but cotton plants!"

Marya laid her head on one side. She scrambled over to a clutch of cotton, pale wisps blowing lightly in the hot wind. She snapped off one of the fluffy white heads. She knew it, she knew the riddle, and triumph made her scalp tingle.

"Oh, Zemya! I see it now. Do you see it? White gold. Comrade Gorinich was right to laugh at us, begging for coins." She turned the blossom over in her hand. "And the black must be—"

"Oil," finished Zemlehyed.

Marya frowned. "But I have no equipment to fish up oil from the earth. Perhaps there are barrels somewhere. Perhaps there is a drill, in the hills."

Zemlehyed grinned again, his beard glittering with sweat and river water. He drew up one ponderous arm and, with a yell, brought it crashing down against the earth. It gave way, and the leshy sank into the ground up to his shoulders. His face creased as though he were groping in a barrel for herring. Finally, with a cry of strain, he pulled his fist back up again. It overflowed with black ichor, thick, reeking. Zemya sat down heavily, panting, pollen spinning about his head.

And in the dimming, bleeding light, Marya Morevna knelt at his side, put her hands on his broad cheeks, and kissed the leshy just as the first star came on in the sky. It was a real kiss, a deep one, and she meant it.

When she pulled away, Zemlehyed's craggy face was wet with tears.

"Remember this when you are queen," he whispered hoarsely. "I moved the earth and the water for you."

––––––

Chairman Yaga crooked her braided eyebrow at the lump of black muck and the cotton flower on her desk. The magicians' cafe bustled and buzzed beyond her door. She stuck her finger in the oil and licked it experimentally.

"Low-grade." She snorted.

Marya said nothing. Yaga would accept it.

"Look at you, all full of yourself, thinking two out of three makes you a somebody! *Tscha*, you are still *nobody*. The last is hardest— that's the rule—and you'll never pull it off."

"I will, though."

"Have you decided that you forgive Koschei his girlfriends, then?"

Marya chewed the inside of her cheek. "It is better," she said slowly, only realizing she told the truth as she said it, "to store up all one's advantages before one moves. I will have your blessing in my holster before I say one word to him, Chairman Yaga."

Yaga lit up a cigarillo, blowing a fat ring at her bookshelf. "I see my extremely expensive games are not a complete waste. And you're at least a bit interesting now, with that fancy scar to remember me by." Comrade Gorinich's burning skin had left its mark under her eye, a diamond-shaped blister that nearly cut her lower lid in half. Even when it healed, she would look as though she were weeping gunpowder, weeping wounds. "But it doesn't matter. Having a brain like a potato and a sweet little civilized cunt that minds its own business, you've no hope of besting my last."

Chairman Yaga gestured toward the window with her cigarillo. "You see my friend out there?"

Marya looked, expecting the car with chicken legs to be there, hooting at stray cats. But outside, in the thick snow and shadows of the endless winter evening, sat a great marble mortar, red as slaughter, bigger than a horse, its pestle slowly grinding around the bowl.

"Ride him. Take him all the way to the northern borders of Buyan, to the spot where the fern flowers grow. There is a cave there, in the cliffside, and in the cave, a chest. Bring me what you find there. My mortar, he won't make it easy. But you will learn to master him, break him, make him obey you." Yaga sighed, blowing smoke. "Or you won't. I can't teach you about mastery, kid; you either have it or you don't. And if you don't, well, you might as well climb into a stove now—your husband will burn you up to keep himself warm, sooner or later." Baba Yaga beckoned to Marya and patted her lap. Under her black fur she wore a leather apron like a butcher or a blacksmith.

Marya recoiled. "I don't want to sit on your lap. I'm not a child."

"The littlest fly on a lump of goat shit interests me more than what you want."

Marya grimaced, crossed the room, and sat, gingerly, clenching her jaw, on Chairman Yaga's lap. The crone cupped her face like her own grandmother.

"If you think my brother is any different, girl, then there's no help for you. He'll burn you down like wax if you let him. You'll think it's love, while he dines on your heart. And maybe it will be. But he's so hungry, he'll eat you all in one sitting, and you'll be in his belly, and what will you do then? Hear me say it, because I know. I ate all of my husbands. First I ate their love, then their will, then their despair, and then I made pies out of their bodies—and those bodies were so dear to me! But marriage is war, and you do what you must to survive—because only one of you will."

Marya swallowed hard. "I'm not like that," she whispered.

"We'll see. When you're flying along in a mortar and pestle with the moon screaming in your ear, and you look so much like me no man could tell us apart, we'll see what you're like. Only one thing matters, almost-soup: Who is to rule."

12

Red Compels

No," said Madame Lebedeva, dipping her finger into a pot of powder the color of amber. It matched both her teapot and her tea. With a deft movement she swept it over one eyelid and inspected her work in the tall, iron-rimmed mirror of her vanity. A gauzy white skirt fluttered at her ankles; a severe blouse gathered its lace around her throat, pinned by her cameo. Her snowy hair rippled in smooth finger-curls, drawn up into a cascading mass of feathers and pearls. The image on her cameo also had such curls, such feathers and pearls.

"What do you mean, *no*?" said Marya. Her friend's denial stung—for all her haughtiness, Lebedeva refused her so little.

"I mean I don't do that sort of thing."

"What sort of thing?"

Lebedeva sighed and put down her pink cake-icing rouge with the loud smack of metal against enamel.

"What do you think, Masha? The sort of thing where you come to me with some kind of impossible task oddly suited to my particular talents that simply *must* be completed and *Oh, Lebed, darling, help me in my hour of need!* I don't do that. I don't drink the ocean so you can fetch a ring from the bottom of it, I don't stay awake for three days to glimpse a snotty little tsarevna traipsing off to who-knows-where, and I certainly don't mess about with a mortar that never troubled me."

Madame Lebedeva perused her armory of lipstick and snapped one up decisively, the color of a peony seen through layers of ice.

"What's eating you? Naganya and Zemlehyed came with me; they helped me. If I fail, Chairman Yaga will have me in her pot."

"Naganya and Zemlehyed are your companions, Marya."

Marya warmed a little with embarrassment. She began to feel she had behaved poorly, somehow. "And what are you?"

The pale lady turned incredulously from her mirror. "I am Inna Affanasievna Lebedeva! I am a vila and a magician and I am not your servant, Marya Morevna! What have you done for me except refuse my advances and mock my concerns because they are not your concerns, because you think cosmetics and fashion and society frivolous? What regard have you shown me but to decline my offers of badly needed instruction and allow your other friends to tread on my pride? When have I come to you saying, *Masha, help me curse this cattle, help me woo that shepherd for my amusement!* I keep to my affairs, which are not your affairs!"

And Marya Morevna *knew* she had behaved poorly, and was deathly sorry. She could not bear for a beautiful blond girl to speak harshly to her; it pained her in her throat, where a red scarf once lay. "Oh, Lebed! I did not mean to insult you!"

The vila sighed, pinching her cheeks until they got pink and bright. "That is your nature. You may not be a Yelena, but you are a kind of cousin to them. And your sort does not treat my sort well. So no, I will not help you ride the mortar. I certainly don't wish you eaten, darling; it isn't that. But I have my pride. Some days, Masha, when I have not made a cikavac and the cafe turns me away at the door; when shepherds shriek and show me the sign of the cross; when Naganya sleeps in your bed and my lover has left me for a bitch rusalka who is only going to drown him, and it serves him right; it's all I have. And you laugh at me because I try to teach you about lipstick."

"Well, you must admit, when placed alongside the threat of becoming soup, lipstick is rather silly."

Madame Lebedeva stared at Marya until Marya felt her cheeks burn and her black blister flare painfully.

"Do you think I am a fool, Masha? All this time, and you speak to me as though I were a flighty pinprick of a girl. I am a magician! Did you never think, even once, that I loved lipstick and rouge for more than their color alone? I am a student of their lore, and it is arcane and hermetic beyond the dreams of alchemists. Did you never wonder why I gave you so many pots, so many creams, so much perfume?" Lebedeva's eyes shone. "Masha, listen to me. Cosmetics are an extension of the will. Why do you think all men paint themselves when they go to fight? When I paint my eyes to match my soup, it is not because I have nothing better to do than worry over trifles. It says, *I belong here, and you will not deny me.* When I streak my lips red as foxgloves, I say, *Come here, male. I am your mate, and you will not deny me.* When I pinch my cheeks and dust them with mother-of-pearl, I say, *Death, keep off, I am your enemy, and you will not deny me.* I say these things, and *the world listens,* Masha. Because my magic is as strong as an arm. I am *never* denied."

Marya's unpainted lips parted in surprise.

"I did not know."

"You did not *ask*."

"Please help me, Inna Affanasievna." Marya took the vila's pale, soft hands in hers. "Please."

"Every once in a while, my darling sister, you must do something for yourself."

Marya looked at Madame Lebedeva—her deep amber eyelids, her pale lips, her frosted cheeks. She could hardly stand the beauty of her friend. It dazzled her. She did not think she could deny Madame Lebedeva, either.

"Will you paint me then, for this task? Will you make up my face, as you have so often asked to do?"

Madame Lebedeva frowned. Her pearly lips turned downward, and she seemed a space older.

"No, Mashenka. I will not. It would only be an extension of my will, and it is yours that is at issue. But I will say to you: Blue is for cruel bargains; green is for daring what you oughtn't; violet is for brute force. I will say to you: Coral coaxes; pink insists; red compels. I will say to you: You are dear to me as attar of roses. Please do not get eaten."

Madame Lebedeva leaned forward on her little gold stool and kissed Marya on both cheeks, eyelashes gently fluttering against Marya's temples. She smelled like rain falling through honeysuckles, and when she drew away, her kisses remained on Marya's skin, little twin circles of pink, almost invisible.

"Remember this when you are queen," she breathed. "I told you my secrets."

A bashful winter's noontime showed only its modest ankle before slipping into darkness again. Marya walked along Skorohodnaya Road, kicking clumps of ice. *Mastery,* she thought. *I know nothing of that. Who was master when Koschei fed me and silenced me? Not I.* An explosion of laughter spilled out of a tavern with eaves of black braids that hung down the corners like bellpulls. Marya stopped and stroked the building's wall: pale, smooth skin, too hairless to be anything but a girl's. The building shivered with the attention. *And yet, I chose to be silent, to eat what he fed me. And he shook when he touched me. I made him weak enough to shake. What does any of it mean?*

Marya stopped and turned up her face to the stars, which sparkled like the points of knives. She turned up the collar of her long coat; the wound below her eye pulsed in the cold. She thought of the year that had turned since she had come to Buyan, how she had trembled when she first saw the Chernosvyat, the fountains of warm blood even now gurgling behind her, Naganya's fearful clicking laugh. Nineteen forty-two, she thought. *At Leningrad.* It was the *at* that made her shudder. Not *in* Leningrad. *At* Leningrad. *At least I shall die at home. But did he really say I would die? He said* gross desertion. *I will be a deserter. Same as a runaway, really. And what is home? Buyan is home. Leningrad is so far; 1942 is so far. Why would I ever go back?*

"Volchya-Yagoda," she whispered, reaching into the wind for something familiar, something huge and kind.

"Yes, Marya," said the voice of the horse, beside her in a moment as though he had always been there, breathing against her shoulder. He glowed milky in the night.

"I wondered, if I wanted you, if you would come."

"I would not call it a rule. But I have very good ears, and I am fast."

Marya turned and put her arms around the horse's long neck. He did not smell of horse, but of exhaust and metal.

"Promise me, Volchya. Promise that you will never take me back to Leningrad. If I do not go back, I cannot die there."

"Did someone say you were going to die?"

Marya's brow furrowed. "Well, no, not exactly. He said convicted. But convicted usually means died."

"Perhaps it will not be so bad."

"Volchya, you must swear it. What do horses swear on?"

"Nothing." Volchya spoke with a strange accent, his brassy deep voice pinched and contorted. "Horses are godless. There is only the rider, and the whip. But I promise."

"Take me home, Volchya."

The bone-pale horse crouched down and wriggled within Marya's embrace so that she found herself swept up onto his back before she could breathe twice. She could feel his oily blood churning hot and heavy beneath her. He turned toward the Chernosvyat, a dark blot against the dark sky. In the torchlight, the shadows of his bones moved under his thin skin.

"Why do you let me ride you? Are you more tame than Chairman Yaga's mortar?"

Volchya-Yagoda snorted. "That thing is a dish. It has no mouth, no teeth. You cannot call something living if it has no mouth. Many things in Buyan are mixed-up and backwards—mossy rocks and guns that speak, birds that turn into men and buildings like youths—but you will notice that everything living has a mouth. Mouths bite and swallow; they talk; they taste. They kiss. A mouth is the main tool for living. The mortar is like a very vicious spaniel. It is alive in some sense, but you wouldn't set it a place at dinner." His hoofbeats echoed in the darkness. "As for why I let you ride me, ah, what a terrible science, riding and being ridden! Which is the servant: the one who bears his mistress, or the one who combs and brushes her mount? It is simple, Marya Morevna. You served me when first we met. You polished my skin and gave me new shoes. You slept against my flank. Service buys service. In my four hearts, service is the only possible expression of love. I serve Koschei. But if you had not run your hand along my fetlock, I would never have served you." Volchya-Yagoda turned his gaunt head to nip at her. It hurt, but she took it as it was meant, gently, with affection. "But that will not work with the mortar, you know. It is a kitchen beast. You could not make yourself so low as to serve it, not if you crawled on your belly. And Yaga's tests never measure the length of your humility. It wants force, Marya. It wants you to be bigger than it is. It wants a mistress, and it is accustomed to one who is ancient and strong, whose thighs can crush it between them, whose iron hips drive it home. You will never manage it."

"Everyone is so sure I cannot do it."

"Oh, Marya, of course you can't! Even after a year with us you are gentle and kind yet! A little wilder, perhaps, more keen to bite and be bitten, to steal and fight, but how warm you are still. How willing to do as you are told. That is no girl to ride the mortar. You do not have it in you. Come, I will take you to the north wall. You can fetch her bauble, and no one will be wiser."

Marya shook her head. "She needs only to ask the mortar and I will be caught."

"I told you, it has no mouth to betray you."

Marya frowned deeply. She wanted it to be that easy. To be helped along. So much nicer to be helped along. But Madame Lebedeva's voice sounded in her: *Every once in a while, my darling sister, you must do something for yourself.*

"The task is not the bauble, it is the mortar," she sighed finally. "Take me to my tower, Volchya. That's all. I must find the way myself."

They rode in silence for a long while. Skorohodnaya Road stretched out like a black ribbon, the great pendant of the moon sliding down its center.

"Volchya-Yagoda, may I ask you a last thing?"

The great horse sighed. "You want answers like oats in a feed-bag, Marya."

"I have spoken with domoviye and leshy and Zmey Gorinich himself, and all of them call themselves loyal; they love the Party like a mother. They recite back to me the slogans of my childhood, and their eyes shine with fierceness. And yet Koschei lives in his great palace and Lebedeva hoards her night creams and her cameos and prizes her patronymic. Little folk scramble to wear badges of belonging on their breasts, to agitate and join up, but big folk live as they always have, like dragons, like Tsars. How can this be?"

Volchya-Yagoda considered. "Is it not so in your world?"

"I suppose. But such things upset people. We hold demonstrations and civil wars when inequities are discovered."

The stallion snorted, and his breath curled in the cold. "Marya Morevna, we are better at this than you are. We can hold two terrible ideas at once in our hearts. Never have your folk delighted us more, been more like family. For a devil, hypocrisy is a parlor game, like charades. Such fun, and when the evening is done we shall be holding our bellies to keep from dying of laughter."

Marya did not light her lamps. Her eyes moved fondly over her red room, turned black by the moon and shadows. She trailed her hands over her things: a brocade chair, the curtained bed all full of silky, bristling furs, her silver writing desk, a firebird's flaming quill, burning dimly as it slept. Somewhere, a beast missed that feather. Marya regretted suddenly that she had never written anything at that desk, not even a letter home, to her sisters at their marriage-hearths. Not even a poem. Her fingers, hunting and purposeful though her heart drooped hopelessly, found her vanity and its tall mirror, the pots and boxes and brushes Lebedeva had given her on every holiday with calligraphed cards abjuring her to enter the world of grown women and all their secret privileges.

Marya Morevna sat at her mirror, as lightly as in dreams. Her hands fluttered over the array of cosmetics as though they played a harpsichord. The pots brimmed with colors that made her heart swim, creamy, untouched swirls of oxblood and peacock indigo and a pink like a kitten's paw.

I shall be red as slaughter, as the stone of the mortar, she thought. She collected her memories of Lebedeva's toilet like cards in her heart: how she had done it, the strokes of her pale hands, the order in which the vila had painted her face. First the powder, like snow, swept over her cheeks and brow with a heavy puff of ram fleece. Then to line her eyes. Marya chose a tiny carved pot of gold pigment, like an icon, a saint's eyes. Each of her lashes she lined in silver, the wetness of it cool and slippery on her skin. Then she took up a thin boar's-hair brush and dipped it in crimson, carnelian dust. Under her brow bone she drew a long red line, and over her lids she drew a darker scarlet still, like the blood that pools at the bottom of a heart. *Red compels.* She pinched her cheeks and rubbed a shiny ruby-bronze cream into them. The lips came last— the mouth that Volchya-Yagoda said was the tool of the living. She found among the forest of lipsticks a fearful autumnal shade, like fire, like dying leaves.

Marya looked at herself in the glass, still herself but girded, made more terrible, older. She had not managed it all flawlessly, as Lebedeva would have done. Her face was a little wild, a little ragged, the lines around her eyes wobbling, the colors too bright, unblended, unsubtle, as if an old woman's weak eyes and shaking fingers had drawn them. Marya raised up her hands and folded her long black hair into a savagely tight chignon, so tight the pins that held it drew tiny drops of blood from her scalp. In the night, with the moon so high and quiet all around her, she knew the rest like a poem recited. Laughing with Naganya in the sunlight, she could never have thought of it. But the night, close around and heavy, guided her steps, her choices. She went to her closet and drew out a leather apron she'd gotten in summer, when Zemya had decided her arms were too skinny and taught her to beat out fireplace pokers from bubbling iron. It was so heavy, its straps weighting her down, digging into her neck, her waist. *Oh, I will be sorry,* she thought as she pulled on her thickest, blackest fur and closed it over the apron. Into her pockets she gathered the dry duck bones of last night's supper, still resting on their ivory tray. Onto her throat went a daub of resinous myrrh and a splash of vodka from a crystal bottle.

Marya Morevna did not want to look in her mirror again. She feared what waited in the glass. But she crept up on herself, and dragged up her eyes to see. How broad her chest, suddenly; how dark and squared her shoulders. How the fur brushed her pale chin; how severe her hair and dark lips looked!

"I am Marya Morevna, daughter of twelve mothers, and I will not be denied," she whispered to the girl in the mirror.

Far below, on the snowy street, the red mortar waited, impatient, steaming in the winter night.

It snuffled the black air and purred in its odd way: The black pestle ground slowly, with satisfaction, around the bowl of the mortar. *Ah! There is the smell of old bones and embalming spices that is my mistress!* It jumped up, thrilling to her nearness, stamping deep circles in the snow. *Ah! There is the black coat and flapping leather apron that is my mistress!* The mortar began to spin with anticipation. *Ah! There is the bloody mouth, fresh from a husband, and that means my mistress!*

But the mortar hopped fretfully back and forth, out of reach. It smelled youth, too, under the old bones and spilled liquor, and the dark figure did not seem big enough, and her hair was black where it should have been white.

The dark, fur-swaddled figure walked up to the uncertain mortar. Without a moment's hesitation, she snarled and slapped the mortar hard across its belly.

"Let me up, you ugly teacup!" she growled, pitching her voice low and rough.

The mortar exulted. *There is the rough hand and cruel words that my mistress owns!* It tipped forward onto its face, abject, so that its beloved witch Yaga could climb in.

But as soon as it scooped her up, the mortar knew it had accepted an impostor. *My mistress weighs more than three bakers who gobble their own bread! Out, out, tiny liar!*

Marya's feet slipped and skidded in the concave bowl, scrabbling for purchase. The mortar spun and lurched, trying to spill her out. It bucked, reared. It launched up into the air, flipped itself and slammed sharply down in the snow three times—but still Marya clung to the pestle, gritting her teeth, clawing at the smooth stone with her fingernails until they snapped and bled. When the mortar had gotten itself right side up again, she straddled the pestle between her legs like a broomstick, her knees knocking gently into the smooth grooves where Baba Yaga's knees were accustomed to resting. The stone seethed, hot as a stove bottom, pulsing as though blood moved through it. Marya Morevna drove into it with her knees, her bones grinding painfully down against it, but still the mortar protested, trying to bounce hard enough to bash her head into its sides.

Marya wrapped one arm around the pestle, her thighs squeezing the trunk of it, and dug in her pocket. Hauling out a dried duck leg, she rolled it against the bowl of the mortar, to give the beast the scent of fatty, rich fowl, and then flung it down Skorohodnaya as hard as she could. The mortar leapt, ravenous, and hopped after it, up into the air and down again, leaving a trail of wide, deep stampings in the snow behind it, like an endless ellipsis.

Between her legs, the pestle rattled and shuddered, whipping her around the bowl. Pain flared white and black everywhere she slammed into stone, and then again, when her bruises got bruised.

"North, trash heap!" she hissed at the mortar, broadening her voice, shredding it. The mortar paused, confused again by her voice, which would never be as broad or shredded as its owner's. Marya Morevna breathed deep, the stabbing cold flowing through her. *I am not so stupid that I do not listen to you, Chairman Yaga! I know what this is about!* She bore down on the pestle, letting it press lasciviously against her, its pulsating heat suffusing through her legs, her belly. She ground her bones against the thing, circling her hips, pushing at it, coaxing. She opened her legs wider, until it felt like a part of her, a stone Marya jutting out awkwardly from her body, swollen and wild. She swiveled herself so that the pestle pointed north and thrust forward. The mortar spun once more, in joy, thrilling to her touch—this was right, this was what it knew!— and bolted north, through the dark and the ice.

The wind cut right through her, lifting her chest out toward the starry trees. A kind of awful pleasure sliced through her: the pine air and the freezing moonlight; the warm, leaping pestle beneath her; and the soft pocking sounds of the mortar stamping the snow. All the small beasts of the forest shrank away from the road and the screaming laughter of Marya Morevna as the starlight whipped her red cheeks. She rode the mortar and pestle like a savage thing, ripping through the night.

The northern boundary of Buyan flows over a hilly, snowbound country. The earth there has never yet seen the sun. All year the

ice crowds close around the three or four grass seeds that val-
iantly pray for the coming of light. Once, the leshiyi built a wall
through the winter, so that the northern sea would know it was
forbidden here. But like all stones touched by leshiyi, the wall
sighed and dreamed and wished for more than it had, and all the
while, silently grew. Now, only an archaeologist might be able to
guess that the purple-black cliff with a dozen goats gnawing at
its roof was once a wall, could see the old, vague shapes of bricks
in the foot of the cliff. Could pick out the crack of a cavern,
where the wall's watchtower was once kept, from which alarms
once rang down the valleys, rung by some mossy, granite-heavy
soul.

The mortar, no archaeologist, but afflicted with a kind of dumb
sympathy for the old wall, stone to stone, brought Marya Morevna
right to the cavern, little more than a slit in the rock, like the thin
triangle of darkness between the pages of a book left facedown on
a white table. The mortar stomped three times in the snow and
tipped forward, spilling Marya out into the tamped circle of firm
snow in the midst of soft, hushed drifts. The pestle rolled around
the bowl, purring, begging for approval. Marya thought of kissing
it, but knew Chairman Yaga would not grace her beast so. She gave
it another hard smack instead. The mortar snapped back upright,
spinning in rapture.

Snowflakes blew into the crevice; three winds skipped in, howl-
ing hollow and hoarse. Marya Morevna's black fur glittered, nearly
white with clumps of ice. She ducked into the cave mouth, her
skin still flushed from the riding, her breath steaming in the stony
closet. The ceiling drooped low, stalagmites like drops of spittle
teetering above her head as the floor sloped down, down, into the
dark. *How can I find a chest in all this blackness?* Marya despaired,
her hands groping in front of her, clutching at shadows.

"Haroo, Grandmother!" growled someone invisible, somewhere

beyond Marya's grasp. "Why do you stumble about so? Are you drunk again?"

"Gahvoo!" another raspy voice howled. "Someday you'll sprout gills and learn to breathe vodka. And then we will miss you!"

"Guff, guff," grumbled a third. "I shall light you a match on my teeth." A phosphor-flash sparked, turning the cave walls green and white.

Four dogs panted amiably before Marya, their paws huge and bony in the ghostlight: a proud wolf slowly beating her thick tail against the cave floor; a starved racing hound licking his chops; a haughty lapdog, his curled fur fringing his face like a little mane; and a fat spotted sheepdog, her chin resting on two pillars of congealed saliva like long, thick teeth. Marya sucked in her breath. Behind them sat a glass chest, frosted over, glittering.

"Rup, rup!" yipped the lapdog. "You're looking very fine tonight, Grandmother! Why, you've hardly any warts at all! Bathing in blood again, I'll warrant. Virgins or capitalists this time?"

Marya could feel her eyeliner sticky around her lashes, her hair half-loose from its bun. *I must look frightful—but then, frightful is what they expect. What they want.*

"Virgins," she snarled. The fat sheepdog leaned forward on her pillars of spit, which wobbled like jelly.

"Guff, guff! Your voice is so strong and loud, Grandmother!" she whined. "Last time you visited, you sounded like you'd swallowed six knives! How'd you get it so sweet?"

Marya bit her lip. "I, er, I drank up a songbird's soul," she barked. "Just cracked open her little chest and sucked the song right up, like marrow through a bone!" After a moment, she added, "As if it's any of your business!"

"Haroo, Grandmother," howled the wolf, her eyes round and cunning. "Your skin is so soft and smooth! Last time you visited, you looked like a crumpled page! You had more spots than a toad-stool! How did you get it so supple?"

"Comrade Stalin's wife is nursing!" Marya hissed, warming to her pantomime. She spat onto the floor of the cave for good measure. "I snuck into her room in the night and squeezed her teats out into a tub until I could swim in her milk and rub it into my skin like night cream! Tired out that old cow so she could hardly walk in the morning!" After a moment, she added, "You mangy old bitch!"

"Gah-voo," huffed the racing hound, his ribs showing like the strings of a balalaika. "Your scent is so delicious, Grandmother! Last time you visited, you smelled like death and tooth rot!" The hound inhaled deeply. "Now I smell orange blossoms and fresh blood under a bouquet of old duck bones and myrrh. How did you get yourself so clean?"

Marya squeezed her fists hard in her pockets. She spun out her lie like thread. "I found an old perfume peddler traveling to Odessa with his wagon. After I rode him through the forest, I snatched up all his little bottles and smashed them against my forehead, one for every gulp of vodka in his stash!" After a moment, she added, "He died! I killed him!"

The dogs looked dubious. The pillars of saliva jiggled as water dripped on them from the stone ceiling. Finally, the wolf shrugged her furry shoulders.

"Haroo, Grandmother. What brings you to our house tonight? If you are hungry, we have a nice blood soup boiling, if Bitter here hasn't lapped it all up."

The racing hound reached up and bit the wolf's ear. "What have I said about using my name? No one is supposed to know!"

The wolf rolled her yellow eyes, turned bone-bright by the phosphorescent light. "It's our grandmother, Bitter. She knows our names. Besides, she would never harm our Papa! Unless he really deserved to be hurt; then she would."

"Well, *Bile*," groused the hound, "don't tell means don't tell. Even a last-born pup knows that."

"Rup, rup! I shan't ever tell *my* name," yapped the lapdog, licking his paws. "That way, when Papa comes to praise us, he will know I was good and the rest of you were naughty, wicked *curs*, and pat me on the head and give me biscuits."

The sheepdog laughed, the rumbling of her swollen chest shaking the pillars of spit. Her jowls sloughed over their edges. "She's our babushka, Blood, you ungrateful, toadying poodle! See if she brings you New Year's presents!" The lapdog squeaked in indignation at the sound of his name. The sheepdog looked up at Marya in frank, canine adoration. "Will you let me ride with you again this year? How I remember the wind in my cheeks!"

"Haroo, Brumal, you kiss-up! She called you a drunken hag, Grandmother. I heard her, not a week ago," crooned the wolf confidentially.

"And I said she wouldn't be angry! Would you, Grandmother? I was singing a dinner song in your honor! *Drunken hag* rhymes with *hearts in a bag*!"

"You and your songs!" giggled the lapdog, Blood. "Star of the Moscow stage, you are!"

Brumal leapt off her saliva-pillars and tackled Blood with a snarl.

Marya watched them fight. She could not believe her luck—all their names, cast into her lap like dolls. But if these were Koschei's dogs, then Koschei's death rested in that shining glass chest. Chairman Yaga clearly meant for her to steal it and return to the Chernosvyat triumphant, only to be shown up as a faithless Yelena who meant only to destroy him. And yet, if she did not return with it, Yaga would devour her, and none of her innocence would matter.

Her belly churned. The dogs wrestled at her feet, blood dripping from both of their throats.

"Blood," she whispered, holding out her hands. "Brumal, peace."

The two dogs froze, the whites of their eyes showing. They turned to look at her, betrayal sparkling in their gaze, and fell down dead, Blood curled into rigor on Brumal's enormous, spotted chest.

The regal wolf leapt at her, slavering.

"You are no Grandmother!" she spat.

"Bile, Bitter!" Marya shouted fearfully—and the wolf fell dead out of the air, thumping onto the cave floor with a crackle of bones. The racing hound died quietly, lying in a tight ball, minding his own business, as though he had always expected to die this way.

The chest gleamed softly, ringed in dead dogs. Marya knelt and worked its slippery clasp. The lid sprang open with a jingle of broken ice.

Inside lay an egg, wrapped up in black silk. A simple hen's egg, brown and round, its crown spattered with freckles.

13

The Tsar of Life and the Tsar of Death

Marya Morevna wanted to run across the throne room to Koschei, to lay her head in his lap, to tell him everything that she had suffered, to hear him reassure her with some obvious explanation of the girls in the factory which did not include the word *Yelena*. But he sat heavily on his throne of onyx and bone, his chin thrust into his hands. He did not look at her. The same maps and papers cluttered his great table, and Koschei scowled so deeply the walls curved away from him, desperate to escape his displeasure. He did not even flinch when the tall black door banged open and Baba Yaga stomped in, her cigarillo leaving blue trails like battle flags behind her. She strode up to Koschei's chair, her coat flaring, and kissed him wetly on the lips, her wide mouth hungrily devouring him. Koschei turned up his face and returned her kiss. Marya was too racked to gasp or cry out. Her eyes simply filled with tears, and she wanted to disappear.

"Don't look so shocked, soup!" laughed Chairman Yaga, smacking her lips. "This one was my husband, oh, centuries back! My ninth, I think. Only fair that I rumple your mount a bit: My mortar is half in a swoon with your riding it so hard, rubbing another mistress' musk on its pestle so that the poor beast gets all confused!"

"You said he was your brother," Marya said numbly, her face burning. Her chest sank, kicked in by the sight of them.

"Chyerti, kid. Demons. What should we care? When you live forever, sooner or later you try everything, just to see. Didn't work out, though, all the same." Yaga caressed Koschei's cheek tenderly with the back of her hand. "The only one I couldn't eat." Koschei smiled wanly. The crone jumped off the black dais and marched up to Marya, her breath dank and old in her face. She looked over Marya's coat, her leather apron, her makeup. "I get to give the tests because I know what it takes to be married to a snake. I do know what I'm talking about." She pursed her cracked lips. "I just *love* your coat, Marya."

"I passed your tests, Chairman Yaga."

"Oh? Well, then, let's see it!"

Marya pulled the egg from where she had kept it, close to her breast, warm and safe. Koschei hissed, sucking his breath through his teeth.

"I told you, Brother. Just like the others. She'll be the death of you."

Chairman Yaga turned the egg over in her calloused hand, cracked it open, and slurped up the insides, her teeth shining with yellow yolk.

Marya cried out, agonized. Was that his death? It looked like an egg. "No! You can't! I did everything you asked me!"

Baba Yaga sucked her tongue. "She's right! Have her if you still want her, Kostya. I give my blessing with both hands. She's a sneaking, lying, dog-murdering thief, and she looks just like me! I'll even dower the bitch." The old woman sat with a satisfied plop at the map-strewn desk, putting out her cigarillo on a sketch of the countryside.

Hot tears fell down Marya's face. "I didn't know where she'd send me. I didn't know the dogs would be there—"

"But once you got there you killed them all and took the egg," pointed out Baba Yaga. "Knowing exactly what you did. My poor, bereaved brother raised those dogs from pups."

"Koschei, say something!" Marya pleaded. "Why don't you speak to me?"

"What should I say?" Koschei said softly, his voice dark and grinding. "It should be clear that the egg was not my death, since my sister has made lunch of it. Why would I ever have told you where I hid it? Of course you would go after it. You can't help it. Tell a girl something is a secret and nothing will stop her from ferreting it out."

"You lied to me." And she meant it all. The egg, the Yelenas. The insult to her girlhood. Everything.

Koschei's face betrayed no expression at all. "With good reason, as you can see."

"You cannot condemn me for betrayal—a betrayal connived by her, contrived by her!—if you lied to me yourself, and about more than the egg."

Koschei cocked his head to one side curiously, like a black bird. He rose and crossed the room to her, taking her face in his long fingers. He gripped her jaw tightly. "Have I condemned you, Marya Morevna? Have I called you faithless?"

Marya wept bitterly, an unlovely, shattered kind of crying that strained at the bones of her face. When tears slipped over her scar, they sizzled and burned. "You left me alone to do all those awful things myself without seeing you, without talking to you. I saw the factory, but I couldn't see you to ask how you could keep those girls, what you would do with me if I disobeyed."

Koschei studied her, his black eyes roving. "Of course I left you alone. Wedding preparations are the province of the bride. Should I have shepherded you like a father, so that anything you did would not be your own deed, but mine? I have no need to prove myself worthy of myself."

Marya jerked her chin free. "But what have I to prove? It should be *you* wrapped up in Zmey Gorinich's coils, proving that you are not a monster, that you are worthy of *me*!"

"Have I not proven it? Have I not taken you out of your starving city and fed you, clothed you in fine things, taught you how to listen and how to speak, brought you to a place where you are a mistress, a tsarevna adored and worshipped, made love to, your skin dusted with jewels? Did I not dower myself? Did I not come to you on my knees with a kingdom in my hand? And as for *those girls,* they belong to me, and that *should* terrify you. It should cow you and keep you gibbering and silent at my feet, like a beaten dog who knows what's coming to her. Yet you still shout at me and rip your face from my hands and call me unworthy. You come to me dressed like my sister, with my death in your coat. No matter that it is not my death. You thought it was. Why do you do these things, even knowing that those girls sew away at my armies through this very hour?" Koschei wrapped his arms around her and drew her close. Marya shut her eyes against him, her lover, her death, her life. But she was afraid, too, of all of the things he could be. "I will tell you why. Because you are a demon, like me. And you do not care very much if other girls have suffered, because you want only what you want. You will kill dogs, and hound old women in the forest, and betray any soul if it means having what you desire, and that makes you wicked, and that makes you a sinner, and that makes you my wife."

No. I do care. I will get what I desire by all the tricks I know, and what those girls in the factory desire, too. You are mostly right, my love. But still wrong. She could say none of it, but she saved it in her chest, where it did not need to be spoken.

Baba Yaga chewed off the tip of her thumbnail and spat it at them. "She kissed the leshy, you know. And not a nice kiss, either. She used her tongue and tasted his mud."

Koschei pushed Marya away to stare at her coldly. "Is this true?"

"Yes." She felt no shame on this score.

Koschei smiled. His pale lips sought hers, crushing her into a kiss like dying. She tasted sweetness there, as though he still kissed her with honey and sugar on his tongue. When he pulled away, his eyes shone.

"I don't care, Marya Morevna. Kiss him. Take him to your bed, and the vila, too, for all it matters to me. Do you understand me, wife? *There need never be any rules between us.* Let us be greedy together; let us hoard. Let us hit each other with birch branches and lock each other in dungeons; let us drink each other's blood in the night and betray each other in the sun. Let us lie and lust and take hundreds of lovers; let us dance until snow melts beneath us. Let us steal and eat until we grow fat and roll in the pleasures of life, clutching each other for purchase. Only leave me my death—let me hold this one thing sacred and unmolested and secret—and I will serve you a meal of myself, served on a platter of all the world's bounty. Only do not leave me, swear that you will never leave me, and no empress will stand higher. Forget the girls in the factory. Be selfish and cruel and think nothing of them. I am selfish. I am cruel. My mate cannot be less than I. I will have you in my hoard, Marya Morevna, my black mirror."

Marya trembled. She felt something shake free inside her and drift away like ash. She reached up to him and gripped his jaw in her hand, digging her nails into his cold flesh. She would make her gambit; it was all she could do. "If you want me, Koschei Bessmertny, tell me where your death is. Between us there must be no lies. To the world we may lie and go stalking with claws out, but not to each other. It is only fair: You know where *my* death is, at the point of your knife or between strangling fingers or in a glass of poison. Show me that you can rest in my hand like a chick, small and weak and knowing that I could crush you if I wished it, but that I will not, will never. You owe me this, on the bodies of all those Yelenas, all those Vasilisas—and you owe me their bodies, too."

Koschei said nothing for a long while. His face floated above her, impassive, unmovable.

"Don't do it, Brother," sighed Baba Yaga.

"A butcher in Tashkent guards my death," he said finally. "I left it in his care when I came for you. It sits in the eye of a needle, which sits inside an egg, which sits inside a hen, which sits inside a cat, which sits inside a goose, which sits inside a dog, which sits inside a doe, which sits inside a cow, and the cow lives with the butcher, very beloved of him and his children. His sons ride upon the cow who contains my death and slap its rump."

Marya kissed him hard, as if to drag out the truth, and the fringe of her black coat brushed against his chin.

Chairman Yaga sat back in her chair. She lit a new cigar, and spat.

"I guess some people would call those vows," she grumbled, but the crone smiled, showing her brown teeth, still stained with golden yolk. "Weddings give me gas."

A cold wind began to seethe through the windowless room. It picked up speed, circling like a racing horse, whirling around and around, riffling through maps and papers, prickling skin, blowing hard and fast until it screamed by Marya Morevna and Koschei and Baba Yaga alike, snatching at their clothes, their hair, stealing their breath. Koschei raised his arms to shield his new wife. Baba Yaga rolled her eyes.

"Shit," she said succinctly, and the wind stopped short, leaving a white silence in its place.

And someone stood in the room who had not stood there before. The man's black hair fell all the way to the floor. He wore a grey priest's cassock, and his chest glowed with a splatter of silver light, like a star. His eyelids were so long that they covered his body like a priest's stole, their lashes brushing the floor. He held out his hands, stretching his long, colorless fingers toward them.

"My congratulations on your nuptials, Brother," the man rasped. His voice sounded far away, heard through three sheets of glass. "I would have brought gifts, if I had been invited. Cattle. And cease-fires." He smoothed his eyelids like lapels.

"But you weren't invited, Viy," snapped Baba Yaga. "Because you make a terrible guest. Putting out all the fires and wasting the dancing girls to skeletons when everyone else is trying to have a good ogle. Why would anyone invite you?"

"Because I attend all weddings, Night," purred Viy. "Death stands behind every bride, every groom. Even as they say their vows, the flowers are rotting in her crown, his teeth are rotting in his head. Cancers they will not notice for thirty years grow slowly, already, in their stomachs. Her beauty browns at the edges as the ring slides up her finger. His strength saps, infinitesimally, as he kisses her. If you listen in the church, you can hear my clock tick softly, as they tock together toward the grave. I hold their hands as they stride proudly down the very short road to dotage and death. It's all so sweet, it makes me cry. Let me kiss your bride on both cheeks, Life. Let me feel her hot blood slowly cool against my eyelids."

"She is not for you, my brother," said Koschei.

"Oh? Have you removed her death, too, then? I remember when you did yours—feh, what a mess!" Beneath his eyelids Marya could see the orbs of Viy's eyes turn to her. "Of course he hasn't. Has he, child? I can see your death blossoming like a mushroom on your chest." Marya's hand rose to her chest, groping for the invisible death's-head there. Viy extended his fingers toward her, slowly, as if moving through water. A pinprick stung between her breasts—it did not hurt, exactly, but it anchored her, wholly, so that she knew Viy could move her wherever he liked. He had caught her by her heart, or her death, or both, and she wavered as he wove his ghastly fingers through the dark air. Marya had never even thought to ask for her own death to be gouged out. Not so clever, after all. She fought to hold still, to resist, but her torso writhed and shuddered. Viy dropped his hand and shook his ponderous head. The sting faded. "Don't take it personally. Never for anyone else does our brother take out his scalpel. Only he lives forever. Everyone else, one way or another, is for me. Can only be for me. And Life, that old tyrant, he knows my land is fertile now. So many white flowers. So many dead since '17. So many more of us than of you. Soon there will be nowhere you can walk where my folk do not flow over and around you, do not drink of your sweat, do not swallow your heat. So maybe I will still attend your wedding, eh, girl? Maybe it will be me standing by your wraith at a silver altar, putting a stone ring on the shade of your finger, suckling at the ghost of your virginity. I could fight on the field of your belly. We could split you like a province, between him and me."

Baba Yaga scratched her braided eyebrow. "So, how did you manage to break the treaty, Viy? You aren't allowed in Buyan and you know it. There's doors and dogs between you and us. These little family gatherings are so awkward! Three of us in a room! That hasn't happened since . . . hm, I make it since the fall of Constantinople. We went to so much trouble to keep your carcass out. It hurts our feelings when you ignore our wishes like this. Of course, oldest children are always stuffed full of their own snot."

Viy looked at her with a strange expression—something, Marya thought, like love and care. "And what of your carcass, Night? I'll have it too, before the century turns. We'll all be together, one family, with one head." The edges of Viy's smile vanished beneath his eyelids. "The raskovnik," he hissed with vicious satisfaction, "unlocks all locks. How considerate of our Marya to go and fetch it for us! No fool like a new bride, the old tales say. And it was not so hard a thing to send my soldiers following her stinking, beating, hollering heart across the border, then pull her off her horse so she might not see us snuffling where her vintovnik snuffled. The doors of the Country of Life lie open, and even now my comrades are streaming in like water to celebrate your wedding and leave our gifts at your doorstep. I do hope you like them. After all, Marya Morevna, we are family now."

Viy bowed courteously, his long eyelids wrinkling. Before anyone could take another breath, he bent over at the waist until he folded up into a great white albatross and flapped slowly out of the door and down the long black stairs. Marya tore away from her new husband and after the Tsar of Death, chasing the pale, gleaming tail feathers of the bird until he burst through the huge, carved gate of the Chernosvyat and wheeled up into the grey morning sky, cawing a lonely, doleful cry.

Skorohodnaya Road stretched out before her, streaked with silver like spilled paint. Wherever the silver lay it wriggled, eating into the stone until it boiled. Infantrymen with silver-plashed chests marched through the houses, bashing in windows with the butts of their rifles, calling inside with their faraway voices, bayoneting the taverns until the walls bled. From everywhere came the sound of glass shattering.

And leaning against the rear wall of the magicians' cafe, piled up with pale flowers and ribbons as though they were meant to be presents, rested Zemlehyed, mud trickling from a gash in his stony head, and Naganya, her iron jaw stove in, and Madame Lebedeva, a neat bullet hole blooming over her heart. She had painted her eyes red, of course, to match. Their dark stares tilted towards the dawn, but saw nothing.

PART 3

Ivanushka

You enter here, in helmet and greatcoat,
Chasing after her, without a mask.
You, Ivanushka of the old tales,
What ails you today?
So much bitterness in your every word
So much darkness in your love
And why does this stream of blood
Disturb the petal of your cheek?

—Anna Akhmatova

14

All These Dead

In the autumn, when the woodsmoke hung golden and thick and the snow tested the wind with white fingers, a young officer walked alone down a long, thin road, smoking a long, thin cigarette. He enjoyed his cigarette, sucking smoke with relish, taking his time. Tobacco was precious, one of his few privileges as an officer. It was like smoking gold. Little shivers of delight ran down his spine as the cold sun hit his smoke, splitting into paradisiacal rays. His boots crunched on the frosted dirt of the road, and that too, he enjoyed: the crisp, bright sound of his own steps through the broad-leafed forest, the warmth of his woolen coat and fur cap, the meeting of cigarette and frozen dirt and yellow leaves and Ivan Nikolayevich, for whom the morning proceeded exceedingly well.

Ivan had already tasted not only tobacco but butter that day. The memory of his knife scraping over fried bread and leaving a trail of glistening salted cream still thrilled him. He had begun to think butter a prize from some mythical tale, like a firebird's feather. But even now his blood beat faster recalling the slip of grease on his bread. His bones felt strong, his legs big enough to take three rivers in one stride. Just last Saturday, during his mandatory volunteer labor, he had picked more apples than any of the city boys, those brainy students with glasses and sloppy hair. The pleasant hum of his muscles and the taste of his one stolen apple, hard and sweet and sour, still hung around him like a bright, beery haze. What to do with this surplus of good feeling and big legs? Ivan Nikolayevich had taken up the jewel of his lunch break and gone for a walk in the larch forest beyond the fences of his camp.

And so Ivan strode expansively through the first falling leaves, taking tiny gulps of his cigarette to make it last. But the sweetness of cigarettes is, in part, that they spend themselves so fast. The young officer, with regret, but a chest full of richness, stomped out the last tiny nub of it into the frost.

A few feet away, under a bright scaffolding of golden leaves, Ivan Nikolayevich saw a man's hand. The fingers had gone grey and bluish. The hand still clutched a scrap of last night's snow. Ivan did not move, but followed the hand with his eyes, up to the wrist, the forearm, the shoulder, and finally the face of the dead man, lying in the forest, his eyes shallow and staring, his mouth open as though he had forgotten what he meant to say. He was not Russian—Ivan could be certain of that. The man wore a spangled, scarlet scarf around his head, and a row of steel earrings in his left ear, which had been half sawed off. His clothes glittered with ornament; his boots shone, a strange buttery green leather. Further, he still clung to his rifle, even in death, and Ivan Nikolayevich knew well that Russian dead never kept their rifles long. Ivan knew he ought to return to his camp at once and report the dead foreigner in the woods. Instead he took a few steps in his threadbare boots and prodded the corpse with his toe.

Maybe those boots will fit me, thought Ivan Nikolayevich. He could already feel their softness on his sore feet. Russian dead do not keep their boots long, either. *I've a dog's luck today! Butter, a good smoke, and new boots!* But beyond the dead man lay another upturned hand, a woman's, spattered with blood. Ivan shivered and shoved his hands deep in his pockets. Best to leave them. He could never explain the color to his comrades, anyway. But still, he inched forward, peering around a slim birch to see the face of the dead girl, her cheek well pecked by birds, one eye gone. She wore a wild scarf, too, yellow as the leaves, and on her forehead twisted two small horns, like a baby goat's. Ivan hissed through his teeth and made the sign of the cross. It was a bad habit, crossing yourself, but like biting fingernails, hard to break.

As if they were bread crumbs, he followed the dead deeper into the wood. Sometimes a cluster of them lay fallen in a circle, back to back, having perished defending themselves. Sometimes they had died alone. Sometimes they had horns, like the woman in the yellow scarf. Sometimes they had tails. Sometimes they looked not very different from Ivan himself. Here and there the frozen ground glittered: splashes of something awful, like silver paint. There were so many of them. Ivan began to feel sick, and he regretted his precious butter. But he did not stop. How could there have been such a battle so near to his camp without one of the sentries raising the alarm for rifle fire? The wind kicked at the flaps of his grey coat. He longed for another cigarette to comfort himself.

Finally, the wood opened out onto a deep, stony valley clouded with brown leaves. Ivan Nikolayevich's horror escaped his lips—he cried out, and fell to his knees. Thousands of dead littered the earth, their hands upturned, their eyes blind and flat, their beautiful clothes flapping in the breeze. A shrike cawed bitterly overhead, swooping in to yank on an eyelid, shaking his little black head to rip it free. Great gouts of the silver paint soaked the ground. Many of the fighters' chests were sprayed with it. It had no smell. None of the dead smelled. Up on the next ridge of the valley a black tent stood, long, thin flags in red and white and gold snapping stiffly under low clouds.

Ivan shouted into the wind, "If any man remains alive here, let him answer! Who slew this great army?"

One soldier, near to him, coughed, blowing bubbles of blood from the corners of his mouth. Ivan Nikolayevich rushed to him, gave him water from his own flask. But the water just ran over his face, wetting it darkly, like silk. The soldier drew a ragged breath, and threads popped free in the corners of his lips. Ivan recoiled.

"All these dead belong to Marya Morevna, the queen from beyond the sea."

And then the soldier died, with that name on his threadbare lips.

Ivan stumbled up toward the black tent, tripping over bodies, clutching his hat to his head. He knuckled tears from his eyes, moving like a mountain climber over their scarves, their spangles, their perfect boots. *Don't look down. Don't look down.*

No guards flanked the tent. Ivan Nikolayevich started as a silver-white thing moved in the corner of his eye. When he turned toward it, he saw only more dead, only more leaves. The tent shuddered.

"Screeeach," croaked something neither the tent nor a soldier. Ivan whirled. It lumbered over the broken flotsam, teetering here and there over a crooked elbow, a twisted leg. Ivan could not tell if it was a man or a woman—its dark, hairy shoulders hunched up, hiding its head, and it creaked when it moved, like a weather vane. Ivan desperately longed to run, to move his strong legs, to take three rivers in a stride. Instead, he waited, his heart half-faint, until the thing stepped over a bony corpse and pulled up its head from deep in its chest.

It had a woman's face, so perfectly young and beautiful that Ivan Nikolayevich hurt with the force of her gaze, his skin prickling to life. Her exquisite eyebrows arched over fierce blue-violet eyes, and her lips parted like a bride waiting to be kissed. But her dark hair snarled and matted like a bear's, and she wore no clothes but bedraggled feathers, more like fur than down, hanging in clumps all the way from her huge, square, skeletal shoulders to her lizard-yellow, three-toed feet—a bird's talons, clawing at the frozen ground.

"I've a dog's luck today," she barked, spittle flying. "Butter, a good smoke, and new boots!" The bird-woman chuckled as though she had made a quality joke. When her lovely mouth opened, Ivan could see that she had only three teeth, sunk in rickety white gums. She arched her back; her shoulders opened up into half-denuded wings. She flapped them twice, three times before settling, folding them down against her back. Ivan crossed himself again.

"Please, boy. What is that? You're supposed to be through with God. Threw up your hands and called Him a lot of dirty names, what? Threw bricks through His windows! Personally, I have nothing against opiates or masses, but you had Him there. It's a fair charge." The bird-woman opened her mouth wide and *screeeached* again.

"You're a devil!" cried Ivan Nikolayevich.

"Well spotted."

Ivan tried to breathe more slowly. The cold sliced up his mouth. "God doesn't exist only so long as devils also don't exist," he whispered. "Otherwise, the whole game is up."

She lifted one leg, then put it down and lifted the other, rocking back and forth.

"Then up it goes, Ivan Nikolayevich."

"How do you know my name?"

"Do you know, every time I have spoken to a human, I have been asked that? It's almost a comfort. Almost endearing, how you look at me all big-eyed like that. I am the Gamayun, boy. I know everyone's names. Of course, even if I didn't, you're always named Ivan Nikolayevich. It's cheating, I admit. Not too much better than pulling an egg out of your ear."

Ivan did not believe in God. Not really, the way he believed in breakfast, in butter, in cigarettes. Unlucky enough to have been born before the Revolution, he had been baptized and was prone to unfortunate lapses such as crossing himself. But Ivan knew that religious dogma served only to oppress the workers. He was proud of his clean mind, his modern thinking, which was free of all those holy, hollow promises.

Ivan Nikolayevich did not believe in God, but he did believe in the Gamayun. His mother had stopped reading the Bible to him as a good mother should, but she had never stopped telling stories around the stove, when winter hunkered down in the dark. Ivan could not remember her saying, *Our Father who art in Heaven.* But he recalled with a piercing clarity her face lit by the pitch-pine firelight as she whispered, *The Gamayun eats from the bowl of the past and the present and the future, the bowl in which my Ivanushka is a baby, and a strong boy, and an old man with grandchildren. Here she comes, looking like a bird, but she is not a bird—creak, creak, creak!*

"You know me, eh?" The Gamayun grinned. "Good. I know people in high places, see. I have assurances from the government. If Christ returned on a golden cloud, they'd arrest him on the spot, but me they leave alone. Revolutions can only go so far."

Ivan's palms stuck together in his fists, clammy, cold. How

could he put this in his daily report? "Who is in that tent, Gama-yun?"

"Go in and find out. You will eventually anyway. It can't un-happen before it happens. And then it will all start, like an engine, going and going 'til there's nothing left to burn."

"I don't understand," he whispered.

The Gamayun waddled toward him, her head bobbing over her massive wing-shoulders. She crouched on the belly of a dead sol-dier, her weight cracking ribs, her claws gripping clumps of his wine-colored shirt. "Sit down, Ivan Nikolayevich. I am going to tell you everything that will ever happen to you. Come on, then, find your knees—there you are, that's how they bend." The Gamayun's beautiful face peered out of the wreckage of her bird's body. Her neck stretched out long and sinuously, like a swan's, but thick, ropy with sinew.

Ivan sat down in the grass, carefully avoiding offense to some poor dead creature.

"Why would you do such a terrible thing?" Ivan asked.

"Because I have to make sure things happen the way they hap-pen."

"But they must, mustn't they?"

The Gamayun laid her head to one side. Her eyes shone. "Oh, Ivanushka, not by themselves, they don't. Think of when your mother told you stories by the stove. You had heard those stories a hundred times. Jack always climbed the beanstalk. Dobrynya Ni-kitich always went to the Saracen Mountains. Finist the Falcon always married the merchant's daughter. You knew how they ended. But you still wanted to hear your mother tell them, with her gentle voice and her fearful imitation of a growling wolf. If she told them differently, they would not happen the way they have already happened. But still, she must *tell* them for the story to continue. For it to happen the way it always happens. It is like that with me. I know all the stories. The boyars always shave their beards. The Church always splits. Ukraine always withers in a poison wind. But I still want to hear the world tell them the way only it can tell them. I want to quiver when the world imitates a wolf. It still has to *happen* for it to happen. You have already gone into that tent. You have already made off with her. You have already lost her. You could tell your tale differently this time, I suppose. But you won't. Your name will always be Ivan Nikolayevich. You will always go into that tent. You will see her scar, below her eye, and wonder where she got it. You will always be amazed at how one woman can have so much black hair. You will always fall in love, and it will always be like having your throat cut, just that fast. You will always run away with her. You will always lose her. You will always be a fool. You will always be dead, in a city of ice, snow falling into your ear. You have already done all of this and will do it again. I am only here to make sure it happens."

"You frighten me." And indeed, he was shaking, all over, every cell vibrating with the presence of the Gamayun, with the pressure of her words, so heavy, like a storm coming that he could feel in his knees, in his chest.

"Yes," she said simply.

"I don't understand. I want to understand."

"You will. Before the end. You will. You always do."

"Then why do things happen the way they happen? If I understand it I can change it. Is it your fault? Do you stop me from changing it?" The Gamayun had to tell the truth. Ivan knew that; he remembered it from every tale. And so he could not find any part of himself with the capability to disbelieve her.

"They happen because Life consumes everything and Death never sleeps, and between them the world moves. Winter becomes spring. And every once in a while, they act out a strange, sad little pantomime, just to see if anyone has won yet. If the world still moves as it used to." The Gamayun ruffled her ragged feathers and glanced up at Ivan under her eyelashes. "Like a passion play. Like a sacrifice. It is certainly not my fault."

Ivan looked towards the black tent. "I could run home, back to my camp. I could resume my watch and say nothing, ever, of this."

The Gamayun arched one perfect eyebrow. "Go, then, Ivanushka. Run. Believe me, she isn't worth it."

Clouds riffled through Ivan Nikolayevich's hair. He frowned and thought of how much he had loved the cigarette of this morning. Of his dog's luck. If he ran, he would still die, sometime. It was 1939. People died all the time. He would still die, but he would die not knowing who was in the black tent. He would wonder about it constantly, like a cut on the inside of his mouth he could never stop worrying with his tongue. Whenever he died, wherever he died, it would be the last thing he thought of: the flapping of the black silk, and how it sounded like whispering.

Ivan had not moved.

"Dobrynya Nikitich always goes to the Saracen Mountains," said the Gamayun softly. Then she tucked her head under her shoulders and disappeared between two blinks.

15

Dominion

Marya Morevna bent over her desk, her hair bound up in a braid around her head, her marshal's uniform mud-stiff. *The war is going badly.*

The war is always going badly.

She passed a hand over her eyes. A year and more now, that she had needed glasses. *Look,* those glasses said from her desk. *Look how much you are not like the others. You grow older and your eyes wear out. In case you could ever mistake yourself for belonging.* Marya supposed this was why no one asked after stolen fairy tale girls. What embarrassments they turn out to be. They grow tempers; they join the army; they need glasses. Who wants them?

Marya tapped her silver telegraph. Telephones did not agree with her countrymen. She did not know why and neither did they, but

their noses bled when they tried to speak into the receivers. Their
ears, too, but not so much. Tap-tap-tick-tap. *It is over. No one is
left. I am coming home.*

She felt a man in her tent suddenly, like a bolt sliding into place.
The warmth of him beat against her back, golden, innocent. He
smelled like cigarettes and hot bread and male skin. She had gotten good at smelling as everything wore on; she smelled as a wolf
smells, now. Marya Morevna did not turn to look at him, but she
knew him, how big he seemed in the tent, big as the whole sun.
Not now, oh, not now. She almost threw up—and that was how she
knew how far she had gone. Once, magic made her feel hot and
sick all at once. Now humans did it, twisting her stomach until
she longed to rip it out and have done with her whole body.

"I assume," she said, her throat thick, "your name is Ivan Nikolayevich." She wanted to accuse him, to have him arrested and
brought up on charges of being Ivan, to see him hung for it. How
often had Koschei and Yaga told her this day would come, warned
of it like a cholera outbreak in the next village, extolled its inevita-
bility. How she had always laughed.

"Yes." And she heard his voice for the first time, soft and deep
as summer mud. She heard as a wolf hears.

"And naturally, you are the youngest of three sons."

"I . . . I am."

"And you are the honest one? Your older brothers, they are
wicked and false, and your poor father could never tell the difference?" Marya tasted the bitterness in her voice, like a tannic tea
brewed from everything unfair, puckering her mouth.

"My brothers died. In Ukraine, in the famine. I could not say if
they would have grown up to be wicked or false."

Marya paused, her hand floating over a map of the gnarled, twisting borderland between Buyan and the Siberian city of Irkutsk.

"I could call in my men. I could have you killed. For no reason but that your name is Ivan and I wish it. I should kill you myself. A bullet is not so bad."

His voice rolled over her again, rich and alive, Russian and familiar. "Please don't."

"She said you'd come and I swore to eat your heart. You can't break oaths to the dead."

"Who said?" asked Ivan Nikolayevich.

"An old friend. It doesn't matter."

"Who are those soldiers there? For what did they die?"

"For the war. For me. I don't know."

"What war? There is a treaty. We are safe from Germany."

Marya laughed harshly. She rubbed her aching eyes again. What a word to hear, now, in this place. "I had forgotten there was such a thing as Germany. We fight for Koschei, against Viy. For Life, against Death. Some of those soldiers are ours. And once they die, they go over to Viy, conscripted. We bleed souls to him. The ones with silver on their chests, they are Viy's dead, his ghosts, whom we have killed. But we don't know where they go. They do not come over to *our* side. They leave corpses, like the living. But they're just gone. Maybe there's another army, invisible, even more invisible than ghosts, fighting over things we don't know and can't see, and they fill the ranks there. But we don't know. And what can you do? Died means died. Even for them."

"How is it possible to kill a ghost? And will you please look at me?" Marya could hear it in his voice: *Crazy girl. You're a crazy girl.* Her ears burned.

"Same way you kill anything else. A bullet works fine. Bayonets, too. A good strangling never goes wrong. And no. I will not look at you. I will never look at you." *And I'm not crazy. How dare you think such a thing, how dare you come here, how dare you live?*

"You are Marya Morevna," Ivan said. "The queen from beyond the sea."

"Do they still call me that? It's so strange. I'm too young to re-member when there was a sea here."

"Are you a demon? Do you have horns? Wings?"

Marya thought for a long while. *Who do you belong to, little girl? Why are you out here in the deep, dark wood?*

"I am Koschei's wife," she answered finally. "And I am a woman. I do not have horns."

She could feel Ivan breathing, as though the tent expanded and contracted to fill him and drain him and fill him again. "I think I have intruded," he said softly. "I only wanted to have a cigarette and a walk. I do not understand what is happening here. I under-stand my camp, and my comrades, and that we will each have broth and a turnip tonight. I am looking forward to it. I like tur-nips. They taste a little buttery, and they are so hot when they first come out of the pot. I can be satisfied with turnips all my days, I think. I do not need to know about the kind of girl who would marry Koschei the Deathless."

Marya's knees ached. *Have I ever been so tired? Tired as an old saddle.* She realized that she still worked the telegraph beneath her cold fingers. Tap-tap-tick-tap. Automatic, like a charlatan me-dium channeling the little lost tsarevich.

"Do you know we tell stories about you?" she said, staring at the telegraph knob under her hand. "You are a monster, an ogre. We laugh about you. *Be good to your girl, Koschei, or an Ivan will come and whisk her away!* That's what they like best, Ivans. To seduce Kos-chei's wives. It is their number one hobby. Somehow, I forgot that there really are boys named Ivan."

"I am not seducing you!"

"You are, though," said Marya, and she heard her own voice fill up with familiarity, with longing. She almost turned. She almost called him Vanya, Ivanushka, as though they were already lovers. Her hip already moved toward him a little, as though her whole self meant to fix him with a gentle expression and forgive him, in the beginning, so that she would not have to, later. She could not explain it, the pull of him, like Viy pulling at her breasts with his pinprick sting. The dead Tsar had caught her by the death and spun her around. Ivan, oh, just his voice, had caught her by the life. "You are. Just by lifting the flap of my tent, you are. Just by being warm and alive and near me. After this long day, and all of Viy's cavalry sweeping over my battalion like water. I lost two colonels today. Two colonels and a major and so many horses. So many girls. And tomorrow I will wake up and pin up the front of my uniform and look them all in the eye, my comrades, the very same, only they'll have silver stars shining on their chests and they'll want to cut out my liver. And into all that you come, so hot and young and innocent. You smell like a human. I can smell your heart. It's like a rich meal, set out just for me. And I should know by now: Rich meals laid out as if by magic, in the wood, unlooked-for—those are seductions. And even though I know you are an Ivan and you exist to make me betray my husband, I still want to kiss you. To feel the life in you seize on the life in me. Raw and fresh and new. And you—you have not even seen my face, but I can feel the shock of your desire in my shoulder blades. The shape of me, the size of me—already you will not leave this tent without me."

"Yes," breathed Ivan.

"Yet you insist on your innocence."

"I only found you by accident. I followed a trail of bodies."

"Then maybe I am seducing you, too."

"It's a grisly kind of bride gift," Ivan said, and did not laugh.

"Maybe every soldier I killed fell in just a certain way, to lead you out of your world and to me. Maybe my body did it without my knowing, the strokes of my sword, the shots of my rifle." Had she? Marya felt as though all her limbs were connected by thin threads, and a wind would blow her apart. Who was she to know what those disconnected limbs wanted, what they did when she was not looking? "But it's not so bad as you think. Most of the soldiers are just empty, cloth, with a little breath in them, a thimbleful of blood. It troubles no one when they are torn. Well. No one that matters. But some, yes. Some are grisly. Some were alive."

Marya gasped as Ivan placed his hand on her waist. She had not heard him move toward her. Had not been on guard. And what had he looked like before he came into her tent? Had he fallen from a tree? Had he been a crow, a robin, a sparrow? No. Not him. He had been a man, out there and in here. There was no bird in him. Ivan did not circle her waist with his arm, was not possessive. He just rested his palm against the curve of her, hesitant. The nearness of him crushed her, like being held by the sun. His gravity pulled at her ears; his breath blossomed against her neck. He whispered, unseen, as close as a ghost, and she could not understand why he was saying this to her, not at first. But the sound of him speaking, the vibrations of his words against the bottom of her skull, moved in her like soldiers, staking territory, gaining ground.

"When I was a boy," he said, "my grandfather died. My mother was very close to him, and for a year we visited his grave every day. But I was a boy, restless, so I wandered away from her. Her grief was a closed house, and it made me afraid. I learned to read from the gravestones, sounding out each letter in the long grass. One in particular struck me. A little one, no bigger than a schoolbook. *Dorshmaii Velichko,* it said. 1891–1900. Underneath it said: *For death hath no dominion over her.* I didn't know what *dominion* meant. But I imagined Dorshmaii over and over, with black hair or blond hair, taller than me, not so tall as me. A long braid, or short hair like a boy. She would be my friend and read gravestones with me. She would be haughty and shun me and I would love her anyway. I would reveal my loyalty to her quietly; I would declare my love in loud songs and promises. I thought of her all the time, and those words: *Death hath no dominion over her.* And then one day when my mother went to see grandfather and I went to see Dorshmaii, there was an old woman standing near her grave with a brown scarf over her head. One of her stockings had fallen down. The old woman had set up a table among the tombs and she was setting it with food: bread and relishes and dumplings and big green grapes and little chocolate candies and an old samovar full of tea. She set places at the table like someone was coming to eat with her. But she didn't eat. She turned around like she knew I was there and held out her arms to me. 'Eat,' she said. 'Eat.' I was shy. I didn't know the woman. 'Please,' she said. 'My son died in the war. He was all I had in the world. That is him, there. Vitaliy. My Vitaliy. I will never see him again. There is a hole in me like a bullet. I want to feed everyone who is not my son, to keep them living. I want no one to have holes in them. I have no one anymore whose mother I can be. Eat, eat. Here are some blintzes, sweet boy; here is cheese pastry. Eat. Be fat. Be alive.' And I ate her food while the rainclouds drifted in. I have never eaten anything sweeter. I left grapes on Dorshmaii's grave, and I never went back. The day after I ate the old woman's bread and cheese, my mother finished her grieving, and took me to the park instead. I never went back."

Marya shut her eyes. She thought of a hut in a dark wood; a heavy table. "Why are you telling me this?"

Ivan Nikolayevich leaned his head against her hair. "What I am saying is, in this graveyard, I would like to feed you, so that you will not have holes in you like bullets. Sit at my table, Marya Morevna. Let me be a mother to you. Be fat. Be alive."

And Marya turned. She saw a young man, but not so young, with a broad, sun-reddened face and dark gold hair, like a coin that has often changed hands. His eyes were tea-colored and crinkled at the edges, and this made them look kind. She clenched her jaw to show him that she was not kind, would never be.

Around his arm he wore a red band, an old scarf, knotted like a ludicrous sort of knight's favor. Marya touched it with her finger-tips gently. She thought for a moment it might go up in flames. That it might vanish rather than allow her touch. *A person, but not of the People.* But it stayed soft and bright in her hand.

"You are so hard, Marya Morevna. You could cut me. Why are you so hard?"

"Because I joined the army and all my friends died."

And then she burst into tears, her first tears since that awful night-wedding. She rested, just for a moment, her burning fore-head against the chest of Ivan Nikolayevich.

16

The Constant Sorrow of the Dead

During the Great War, the Tsar of Death came closest to victory. His great strength has always been in numbers, and in patience. Death can always afford to wait.

It was in those lightless years that the Tsaritsa of Salt was killed.

In the Land of Death, Viy grew rich. The treasuries of death filled up with burnt grain and apples, with starved cattle and blighted potatoes. The cafes of the dead filled up with patrons drinking spilled coffee and reading banned books. Souls were relieved to come to Viy's country, for they were not shot at there, nor did they get dysentery, nor did any of their friends suffer. Viy made his country as like the living world as he could, even to building film houses where *silvery images of the war showed, so that the dead might be grateful and not wish to return to life. For this is the constant sorrow of the dead, that though they drink and eat and dream much as they did before, they know they are dead, and yearn desperately to live again, to feel blood inside them once more, to remember who they were. For the memory of the dead is short, and thought by thought they lose all sense of their former lives until they drift from place to place as shades, their eyes hollow. After a time, they believe they are alive again.*

So it was that Viy sent his chief boyars among his people to announce that if any among them would serve in his army, he would send them home when their terms of service ended. Home, to Life, to hearth and blood and labor. He lied, and they knew he lied, but the dead can live for a long while on such a diet. No longer would the Tsar of Death be content to wither corn on the stalk or slowly rot men with infections. He would attack the source of all he hated, the Tsar of Life. After all, why should he dine on the ashes of living feasts? Why should he be held in less esteem than his brother? Why shouldn't the Empire of Death surpass any earthly power?

And they tore the streets of Buyan piece from piece. The territory of Death advanced one inch each day; the territory of Life retreated. But the next day the territory of Life would advance, and Death retreat. While Viy's ranks filled up with human dead from the French front and the German lowlands, he would not lie still. To walk down Skorohodnaya Road was a heedless hurtling through patches of dark and light. That cobblestone might belong to the enemy, and to touch it with one toe called their dogs. Soon Buyan became a country of dancers, leaping and turning and crawling to remain in their own country and not slip, putting just a fingernail, just a strand of hair, into Viy's territory.

In those days the Tsaritsa of Salt called herself neutral. She would not take part. She worried and wept over the cities of the human world, where she made her home and took in morality plays and entertained pigeons in her pale parlor. But even there the Country of Death showed through in patches: Men and women would fall dead in the streets, having sunk their foot, all unknowing, into that invisible and depthless world. The Tsaritsa of Salt defended the cities as best she could, laying the endless salt of her body over the snowy holes where Death bled through. Each time she saw an old grandmother tottering, her eyes rolling back in her head, the Tsaritsa of Salt threw herself toward the babushka to catch her, give her salted bread, and set her aright. Soon the Tsar of Death hated her more even than the Tsar of Life and sent his chief boyars, all of who had mouths like crocodiles and wings hung with jangling knives, to cut her to pieces and scatter the pieces throughout Russia, so that she would never repair.

It is not easy to kill a Tsaritsa. But Viy was bold, and his boyars hewed her arm from leg from neck, and threw down her salt-crystal kokoshnik from a great height, so that it shattered. Without her, the cities began to starve and joined Viy in great sheaves, not only souls but opera houses shelled to dust, and apartments exploded one unit from the next, and factories obliterated by gasoline.

It is said that Viy married the left arm of the Tsaritsa of Salt to finally silence her completely, and that it rests, fingers rigid with grief and rage, on a throne of knucklebones in the heart of the Country of Death.

"Do you understand?" Marya looked up from Likho's black book and stared intently at Ivan, searching for signs of disbelief. If he didn't believe her, then she would not love him. *Crazy girl. You're a crazy girl. Why would you say things like that?* Silently, she willed him not to believe her, to make this easier.

"Koschei is the Tsar of Life and you are married to him. And that's why you lead his armies."

"Yes, but it's the part about the sinkholes you ought to listen to. If I'm going to take you home you must listen to me, and do exactly as I say."

Ivan kissed her instead. *Oh,* thought Marya, *I will not survive this. Why do men come knocking at my door? Why do they take their hats off and look at me with big deer eyes and bare their necks? If they stayed home and gave their kitchen tables such stares, I might have a little peace.*

"We have to travel through Viy's country to get back to Buyan. It is not far, but you must step just as I step, and breathe just as I breathe, and speak only as I speak. Everything is contested ground now. If you picked up a single leaf in this forest, it would have a dead side and a living side. You may see people you once loved, once knew. You cannot speak to them, or they will pull you close and never let go. You cannot even look at them. If they wear a splash of silver on their chests, you must turn your face away."

"What about my camp? They will worry about me. I will be classified as missing, or dead."

Marya gave him a withering look. She could not care about his little camp. Leningrad was far enough away. The war would not have reached there yet. It would be beautiful there; the lime trees would be just flowering. Violinists would play something sweet and nostalgic in a cafe Marya would just barely remember. She could stop. Just stop. And sleep. *Get me away from this war, human. Why are you being so slow about it?* "You know, when I was in your position, Koschei said 'get your things and come with me.' And I didn't make such a fuss about it."

Ivan blanched a little. He coughed. "Well, Marya, when someone says that to you these days, it's not so nice. Usually . . . usually it means 'you're coming to my camp.'"

"Then you should be glad to leave your camp, if it is such an awful place."

"Kiss me again, Marya, and I'll go anywhere."

She did. It felt like firing her rifle, and watching a firebird fall out of the sky. *Who would I have been,* she thought, as his mouth warmed hers, *if I had never seen the birds? If I had never been sick with magic? Would I have loved a man like this, so simple and easy and young?*

After ten years, Marya Morevna could see the markings of the Country of Death. It left a stamp, like a customs officer, on every part of the world it touched. Sometimes the stamp looked like a shadow with pinpricks of silver in it, like stars. Sometimes it looked like ripples of water reflected on the bottom of a pier. Sometimes, when she had to pass through their strongholds, it looked like an imperial seal with a three-headed bear raising six paws in rage. It was always better not to look, though, to look only at the Country of Life as it wound its slender path through Viy's territory, the marks of Buyan, a kind of thin winter sunlight, the smells of things baking, of everything green.

"Marya," Ivan hissed as they walked back and back, toward her home, toward her husband. "Someone is following us."

"I told you not to speak. I know. They're . . . they're always following me, Ivan. Always."

Marya did not have to turn around. They would surely smile at her, their eyes lighting with hope like gaslights, their silvery chests blazing. A little man with a head like a stone, a girl with a rifle scope where one eye should be, and a lady with swan feathers in her hair. Always. She could smell Lebedeva's perfume, violets and orange-water.

"I told you. You may see people you once loved. You cannot speak to them, or they will pull you close and never let go. It would be like leaping into Death's country with both feet. I cannot talk to them, not ever." Marya's head swam. She had never spoken of them, her dead friends, and how they hounded her, how they wanted her still; Koschei did not sympathize. *I love you,* he said. *I did not die. Is that not enough? Can you not befriend some other soul in Buyan?* "I cannot touch them. Military service is not meant to be easy."

Marya Morevna slid forward on her right foot, crossing three large, flat stones without lifting it. She picked up her left foot over the same stones and brought her legs together. Ivan mimicked her. She followed the path she knew, stepping only on every seventh patch of dirt, only every third fallen leaf. She got on her belly to squeeze under a hoary, mushroom-clotted tree trunk rather than stepping over it. She did not look behind her, or to either side. She moved like a snake moves, and carefully breathed only every second breath. But at last they came to the place Marya feared, where there was no safe path marked with shadows or ripples or seals. There was only a black patch in the mountains, utterly without light. Far in the distance, like a painting, the evening hills opened up again, violet with mist and the last spoonfuls of sunlight. Marya Morevna reached behind her. Ivan took her hand tightly in his, and she could feel his fear like sweat. His fear made her stronger; she could be brave for both of them. Together they stepped into the black field.

Their footfalls echoed as though they walked through an invisible city street, though beneath their feet they felt only soft loam. Little bursts of sound floated by: rough tavern braying; the shattering of heavy things; pottery and wood; a fiddle, played low and fast. Marya's eyes widened in the dark. *I am safe,* she told herself. *I have passage. I have always had passage. They will not reach for me.*

"Ivan Nikolayevich," a little voice called, full of joy and recognition.

"Don't turn your head," Marya hissed. "Keep walking. Keep with me."

"Ivan Nikolayevich, it's me!" the voice rang out again.

"If you look, it will be your death and you will never kiss me or smoke a cigarette or taste butter again," Marya warned through clenched teeth. Her jaw ached from clenching—every part of her closed up, bound tight.

"Ivanushka, it's Dorshmaii. Come and hug me at last!"

And Marya felt him turn, pulling her with him.

The voice belonged to a young girl with pale braids done up in the old style, like two teardrops hanging from her head. She had on a lace dress and her smile looked like a photograph: pristine, practiced, frozen. She held out her arms.

"Oh, Ivanushka, I have waited so long! How loyal you were at my grave. How sweet were the grapes you left me! Ivan, come and kiss me! I dreamed of you kissing me while all the worms were knocking at my coffin."

Ivan's broad face lit like a lantern. "Dorshmaii! Oh! You are blond, after all! And kind."

"So kind!" the silvery girl agreed, her braids bobbing as she nodded. "Everyone here says so. I always share my ashes!"

Ivan Nikolayevich drew back a little. Marya tried to pull him away, but he was big and stubborn and he would see this through. *More fool you.* Marya gave up. *I warned you.* "What do you mean?" he said uncertainly.

Dorshmaii Velichko took a cigarette out of the sash of her dress and put it into her mouth. It had all been smoked. The cigarette was a long column of ash. But she breathed in happily, and the ash slowly turned white again, until it was whole. She held it out to Ivan.

"You can have it, now. I know you like them. I saved it for you."

"Don't you dare," snapped Marya.

Ivan did not reach for it. Dorshmaii shrugged and dropped it, grinding it into the ground with her dainty foot. "It's no good to me now. All used up. Oh, but *you* are not used up, Ivan! You are so warm and bright I can hardly look at you! Thick and full of juice, that's you! Like a green grape! Come and share my bed, like you always wanted. And I know you wanted to, even then, you wicked little thing."

Ivan stared at her. His hand in Marya's went slack, and she could feel him flow towards the girl like water pouring from one glass to another.

"Dorshmaii," Marya said, without raising her voice. She had hoped he would be strong enough on his own, that she would not have to use her authority. She was ready to lay it down, so ready. "He is under my shield."

The girl in the lace dress looked from Ivan to her and back again. "I don't think your shield extends to playthings, little Tsaritsa. Let me have him. I'll ride him to Georgia and back before morning. He'll bleed from my spurs. Then you can have him back."

Marya reached for the pale, intricately carved rifle slung over her back. She loved her rifle. There was no other like it. She had found it in Naganya's house, so long ago. The vintovnik had whittled it out of the bones of the firebird they had killed on their hunt, the last time they were all together, meaning it to be a wedding present. Marya Morevna brought it to bear on the ghost and adjusted the sighting.

"Don't!" cried Ivan.

"Oh!" Dorshmaii breathed. "It's so beautiful! I can see the flames still! Oh, Marya Morevna, you have no right to a weapon like that! Give it to me! See, the bird opens its mouth to me; it wants to be mine!"

Marya fired. One of the girl's teardrop-shaped braids dropped off.

"Oh, I hate you," Dorshmaii spat. "I had him first. It's not fair!"

Blood seeped from the stem of her braid, yellowish and thick. A clump of black, dripping earth struck the ghost between the eyes, and she screeched in indignation. Ivan whirled to see who had thrown it.

"Stop looking, Ivan! I told you to listen to me! You can't look at them!" But Marya, unable to let him go or lose him to the dark, was looking, too, as a little man with a beard of pale, frosty moss and hands like broken stones gathered up another handful of earth and tested it in his hand. A silver splash stained his chest. He looked only once at Marya, and big tears welled up in his eyes, falling like rain.

"Run, Ivan," Marya whispered.

He did. And behind them, the dark spasmed, as if in grief.

When they reached the light, Marya seized him close to her, spun around three times, laid her finger on the side of her nose, and disappeared.

17

A Pain Where My Death Once Lay

We're home," Marya sighed. "This is home."

But Ivan went white and trembled in his long grey coat. He looked at the blood fountains gurgling and spraying. He looked at the braids lying along the eaves, the chapels with their skin doors and bone crosses, the gate of antler and skulls. He looked at the black domes of the Chernosvyat looming before them, all shadows.

"This is hell," he whispered. Marya saw his hand twitch, longing to cross himself, keeping his fingers still for her sake alone—and she liked that, that in his horror he still wished to please her.

"No, no, it's not like that. It's the Country of Life. It's all living, see? The blood and the skin and the bone and the fur. It's all alive. Nothing is dead here, nothing. It's beautiful."

But Ivan was shaking his golden head. "At least in Leningrad we build *over* the bones."

Marya Morevna laughed. She wanted to brush his hair from his eyes. "Of course you are from Leningrad," she said. It would not be temptation if he came from Moscow, or Minsk, or Irkutsk. Only a boy from her home could come bearing an old red scarf and scratch at her core. He had been built for her, like a perfect machine.

"I don't want to stay here!" he cried. "This is the devil's country!"

"Of course it is," said a deep voice, familiar to Marya as her own bed. "And you should go home immediately."

Koschei the Deathless swept Marya into his arms. She smiled—a frank, open smile, unguarded and bright as winter. She kissed him, and where their mouths joined, drops of their blood spontaneously welled and mingled, so deeply did their bodies interlock.

"Have you brought a toy?" Koschei said curiously, setting his wife down, his long black cassock whipping in the heavy Buyan wind. "Is he for me as well?"

Marya watched his face carefully. If she played it right, if she managed it, no one would be hurt. "He found me, at Irkutsk, after the battle. He is from Leningrad."

Koschei the Deathless grinned enormously, his black hair lifting a little, blowing in the wind. "Oh, my Marya has grown up and started stealing humans for herself! I am proud."

"It isn't like that." But wasn't it? Hadn't she appeared to him like a bird-husband, out of nowhere, and dragged him out of the world?

Koschei turned to the young officer. "Oh? What do you think, young man? Is it like that?"

Ivan was somewhat beside himself. He could not stop staring at the fountain of blood, how the sun turned it half-black.

"Is he mute? Does he have a name?"

Marya faltered and cast down her eyes. She could not say it, could not begin to bring herself to say the name Ivan in the presence of her husband. But he guessed it. He saw it caught in her mouth like a fish hook. They had been married a long time. Koschei's black eyes flared fury; his jaw clenched, just like hers. *What mirrors we are, set to face each other, reflecting desire.*

"You would not do that to me, would you, Masha? Tell me he is Dmitri Grigorovich. Tell me he is Leonid Belyayev. Tell me his name is Priapus and you could not resist him. But my wife would not bring an Ivan into my house; she would not stab me so, through the neck."

"I thought there were no rules between us," Marya answered softly, somewhat embarrassed to discuss it in front of Ivan himself, who was no part of their marriage, and should not hear its private arrangements.

Koschei blinked twice and straightened his back, crow-hunched with resentment.

"Of course you are right, wife. I have forgotten myself. What is a name? Nothing and no one. I am a silly old man." His smile froze on his perfect face, the youthful curve of his jaw, his eyes not even a little wrinkled with age. He remained utterly the man who had appeared on Marya's doorstep with stars in his hair. "You must bring your friend to dinner, and we will discuss our options, with regard to the war."

The Tsar of Life turned on one shining black heel and strode toward his palace. Over his shoulder he called, "Oh, have a care not to walk on the right side of the road. We lost it while you were gone."

Marya brought her hand to her mouth. She had not seen it. How could she have missed it? A long black strip ran down Skorohodnaya Road. In the darkness, silver pricked like stars.

———

Koschei served them himself: pheasant on a black platter; diamond goblets of colorless wine; two loaves of bread, one dark and one pale; pears poached in a fragrant sauce Marya did not recognize. A mound of shining butter rested in front of Ivan's seat with a small golden knife sunk into it. Marya wore a long black dress, its silk bodice scooping well below her neckline, its gems winking. Koschei loved it specially, and she wished to make peace. *You look like a winter night,* he had told her when he had given it to her. *I could sleep inside the cold of you.* She tried not to look at either of the men.

"Eat," Koschei said tonelessly. "You will need strength for the road."

Ivan folded his hands in his lap. "I . . . I don't think I ought to eat your food, Comrade," he said shakily.

Koschei sneered at him. "Why not? You have already supped at my table, tasted my wife. I can smell it on both of you, like perfume so sweet it sickens."

Marya put down her fork. "Why are you doing this, Koschei? I have had lovers before. You have, too. Remember Marina? The rusalka? She and I swam together every morning. We raced the salmon. You called us your little sharks."

The Tsar of Life held his knife so tightly Marya could see his knucklebones bulging. "Were any of them called Ivan? Were any of them human boys all sticky with their own innocence? I know you. I know you because you are like me, as much like me as two spoons nested in each other." Her husband leaned close to her, the candlelight sparking in his dark, shaggy hair. "When you steal them, they mean so much more, Marousha. Trust me. I know. What did I do wrong? Was I boring? Did I ignore you? Did I not give you enough pretty dresses? Enough emeralds? I'm sure I have more, somewhere."

Marya lifted her hand and laid it on her husband's cheek. With a blinking quickness, she drove her nails deep into his face. "Don't you dare speak to me like that. I have worn nothing but blood and death for years. I have fought all your battles for you, just as you asked me. I have learned all the tricks you said I must learn. I have learned not to cry when I strangle a man. I have learned to lay my finger aside my nose and disappear. I have learned to watch everything die. I am not a little girl anymore, dazzled by your magic. It is my magic, now, too. And if I have watched all my soldiers die in front of me, if I have only been saved by my rifle and my own hands, if I have drunk more blood than water for weeks, then I take the human boy who stumbled into my tent and hold him between my legs until I stop screaming, you will *not* punish me for it. Are we not chyerti? Are we not devils? I will not even *hear* your punishment, old man."

Koschei grabbed her hand, dragging her by her wrist from her chair and into his lap. The dishes clattered and spilled pears onto the floor. Blood streaked her palm where his nails scratched her, and he kissed it, kissed her thumb, her ring finger, until his chin was smeared red. "How I adore you, Marya. How well I chose. Scold me; deny me. Tell me you want what you want and damn me forever. But don't leave me."

Marya studied him, searching his face, so dear, unchanging, unchangeable. Ivan reached for her hand under the table, but she had forgotten him. She felt his fingers no more than a napkin folded across her skin. Koschei loomed so great in her vision, all shadows. He filled her up, her whole world, a moon obliterating the light of any other star. She thatched her fingers into his hair like a ram's wool. "Take my death away," she said. "Cut it away. Cut it up, lock it in a duck's eye. Behind four dogs. Make me like you, as if we are two spoons. Then I will never leave you." Koschei gently took her hand from his head and laid it in her lap. "Would it not be better for your war-mistress to be as deathless as you? I am not safe because of a treaty. Viy's fear of you is no shield, not really. I am naked and far from you most of the year. Open my bones and scoop out my death. Bury it at the center of the earth. I deserve so much. You know what I deserve."

"You have asked me this before. I cannot."

"You took my will."

"So all seductions go. One will presented to another, wrapped in a bow. The question is always who is to take and who is to give. I took first, that's all. You will take last. I am better at such games than you, but students wax in their talents, always, always. Your death you cannot give me by opening your pretty mouth and tasting roe. And I will not take it."

"Yet you demand my loyalty, my whole heart, my marrow."

"Those things are mine. You don't understand, Masha. You have never understood. You are my treasure, my pale gold, the heart of my heart. You lie at the bottom of my being and gnaw upon my roots. But you are not one of us. No matter how like us you become. You were not with us when the world was so young, so easily misled. When there was only one star in the sky. You cannot know what we know. You are not built as we are built. You've learned so much, you have, and I am so proud of you. But you . . ." Koschei laid his hand on the black silk of her sternum. "You are still made of meat, and gristle, and bone."

She searched his eyes, without depth, without end. How she loved him, still, forever. He was the source of that hot, sickening, gorgeous magic, and he poured it into her like wine. "What are you made of?" she asked, her bitter anger softening. *Perhaps I can stand this war for you a little longer. If I can keep you by me, and Ivan, too. No rules, not ever.*

"Not meat," Koschei said gently. "Not even blood." He took up her fingers again, passing them over his lips so that their bloody stains left smears there. "I put on blood for you like a cosmetic, just like I put on this face, and this body all full of leanness and litheness. It is to please you, only to please you, my human girl, my volchitsa. Didn't you know? Didn't you guess? But it's no good, Masha. You carry your death in every cell of you. Every tiny mote in your body is dying, faster than sleight of hand. You are always dying, every second. How could I take that out of you? My death is not so diffuse. I have only one. You have millions. Not even my sister, my darling sister whom you know so well, not even Yaga asks me to take her death. Do you know why?"

Marya Morevna kept silent. She could think of only one thing; her whole mind clutched it: *What do you look like without your face? Who are you, husband? I will see it. I will.*

"Because she knows how I did it to myself. You would not think it of her, that she could be tender. But we were so young then, and there is a kind of understanding between brothers and sisters. A history shared. I will not tell you, my love. You are what you are and I think you might try it, just to show me you could. I will say it was something like how you came here with me, and something like letting a wolf eat my liver every day for a thousand years, and something like slowly suffocating in a gas the color of jaundice, and something like dying every second, to avoid ever dying. There is still a place in me, Masha, where my death once lay. I have a pain there, the way some men feel their legs long after they've been cut off at the knee. It is my pain, and I cannot share it. I would not, even if I could. I will age with you, if it will please you. I will match you, wrinkle for wrinkle, grey hair for grey hair, creak for creak, tumor for tumor. You will be so beautiful when you are old."

"Death hath no dominion," said Ivan, and both Marya and Koschei turned to stare at the young man as if he had appeared out of nowhere. Marya's attention was a cat's attention, now. Whatever she wanted most held her utterly, so that she abandoned emphatically anything other than the object of her fixation. And then something new would appear and she clapped it with the same impenetrable stare. She knew herself, how she had slowly, over years, become a cat, a wolf, a snake, anything but a girl. How she had wrung out her girlhood like a death. And now Ivan sat there, studiously not eating his bread smeared thickly with butter, waiting for her attention, her regard, but she could forget him in a moment if Koschei pulled her towards him like a little moon, and she knew it, and she felt herself splitting and tearing between them, her human heart, her demon heart.

"Well said," Koschei allowed him, generosity coating his words. "Please, boy, eat. I promise, no one will appear and cackle at you that you must now stay here six months of the year. You must be starving for a glistening bit of meat."

Ivan stared at the butter, how it shone. "You said this was the devil's country."

"So I did. Then I must be the devil. And she the devil's bride. Aren't you lucky, to have fallen in with such exciting people?"

Marya tried to help him. She remembered when this was hard. "He's only teasing you, Ivan."

Koschei snarled suddenly, his lips drawing back from sharp and suddenly yellowish, blackened teeth. He threw his goblet against the wall. It did not shatter, but thudded heavily to the floor.

"Not that name," he growled. "Not in my house. Call him something else, if you insist on dragging home strays."

Marya rose from his lap, her loose hair falling towards his face like a leash. He would deny her, no matter what he said. She did not feel a pain where his denial sat, not anymore. In fact, Marya did not feel much of anything besides want, an endless want that coiled in her, that lashed out for Koschei, for wine and goose and melon, for the hilt of her bone rifle. The want survived any fight, with her fists, with her guns. It was a wolf, tenacious. It had swallowed up Ivan Nikolayevich. She could not remember, now, ever having felt happy or sad. Only hungry. Only empty, and greedy, and insatiable. It was as though she had never taken off that leather apron, that black fur coat, that terrible red paint.

Koschei kept her hand, tight in his cold fist.

"Don't leave me," he said helplessly. "No rules but that rule. Don't leave me."

Koschei the Deathless allowed Ivan to sleep in Marya's house. He liked to show magnanimity. He liked to be expansive, so long as he didn't really have to share in the end. Thus Marya was not surprised when he caught her by a length of hair and drew her back to him once Ivan's golden head had disappeared down the hall of the Chernosvyat. He wound her hair in his hand, running his thumb over it.

"All my onyxes, my agates, my obsidian. All my black treasures in this one strand," Koschei murmured. "How long your hair has grown. You could strangle a man in it."

Marya took her hair from his fist and lifted it, heavy as a rope, twisting it around his neck, bringing his face close to hers. He smelled like barley and old trees. But then, maybe he smelled that way only because it pleased her. Marya Morevna shivered in her husband's arms. He pressed his forehead to hers, shutting his long-lashed eyes.

"You *should* go with him," Koschei whispered harshly, "when he asks you. You should go, and have his babies and kiss their wounds and teach them to read."

"You don't mean that." The air between them was thick, knotted.

"I don't mean it." He pushed her back, away from the black feast table, against a long, broad wall all covered in silver tapestries showing peacocks and apples and archangels with long teeth. Save for the long chains hanging from the eyes of one peacock's tail. "I don't mean it. Stay with me forever, forever, until you die, and then, still, I will keep your bones and clutch them to my breast." He lifted one of her arms and clapped it into the chain. Marya knew those chains. She owned them, had tamed them. Though she wanted to speak plainly, calmly, her heart leapt as the locks caught. Her breath found itself. She searched his eyes, ducking her head to catch his gaze.

"Koschei, it's me. Your Masha, your Marousha. What do I want with wounded babies?"

He bound up her other arm against the silver brocade, and Marya hung there, helpless. But her blood and her wanting lashed themselves, and of all the times she had hung against Koschei's wall, she knew that this time she was not helpless at all. His fear wrote itself on every familiar angle of his face.

"But if you go with him, you will not be safe. Viy will not always respect our treaties. The accords only keep you alive—they do not keep you happy, or unmaimed, or those you love anything near safe. I bargained for you, not for any other. If you leave me, he will come for you one day with silver shears, and you will fall. If he were not a coward and bound by me, he would have done it already."

"You do not need to send me away for my own good like a child. I chose to fight, and I still choose it." But as she said it Marya Morevna knew she lied. She wanted an end to war. An end to cold and blackness and half the road gone silver with death.

Koschei went to an armoire and took out a long birch branch, white and thin.

"I meant to give you a life of greed and plenty," he said, moving the branch over the tops of her breasts. "I wanted to keep you innocent, so that I would always have your purity to eat, every

breakfast and every supper. You *can* be innocent again. It's not
true, what they say, that you can never get it back. You can. It's
only that most folk cannot be bothered." Koschei the Deathless
hooked his fingers into the glittering neckline of her dress and
tore it with deliberation, down to the hem. Tiny gems clattered to
the floor. Marya shut her eyes; her body arched toward him, the
little striped animal that it had become, desperate and starving,
always. This, this kept her here. Alive, aflame. At the end of fighting this wall, this man, these chains woke her heart again.

"You should go with him. He will ask tonight, I think. I would
ask tonight. There is a reason they all leave me for Ivans. I can
never be an Ivan. I can never roll with you in the sun like a mind-
less golden pup. I am too old for it, for warmth and simplicity. I
burn, I freeze; I am never warm. I am rigid; I forgot softness because it did not serve me." He brought the branch down against
her breasts, and the sear of it tore a cry from her. She felt her skin
rising up into a scarlet welt, the molten fire of the pain showing
on her flesh. *Yes, I am still alive,* she thought. "When I say forever,"
Koschei whispered, "I mean until the black death of the world. An
Ivan means just the present moment, the flickering light of it, in a
green field, his mouth on yours. He means the stretching of that
moment. But forever isn't bright; it isn't like that. Forever is cold
and hard and final." He lashed her again, across her stomach, and
she smiled, arching her back to receive the next blow on her hip
bones, the seeping fire of it churning, unbearable. For a moment
Marya *did* remember being happy and sad, the pleasure of roe and
pickled melons, the night in the bathhouse when she was so ill.
Koschei brought down the branch again and again on her belly,
and she understood. That belly, which could bear children for an
Ivan but never for him, that made her different than him, that
made her human, not chyerti.

Tears streamed down Marya Morevna's face. She chased after

her breath, caught it, calmed it, and Koschei paused, his head hung low as an old wolf.

"Koschei, Koschei," she whispered. "What would I have been if I had never seen the birds? I am no one; I am nothing. I am a blank paper on which you and your magic wrote a girl. Just the kind of girl you wanted, all hungry and hurt and needing. A machine for loving you. Nothing in me was not made by you. I was six when the rook came—six! That's my whole life that you've bent in your hands. What could I have grown up to be? What kind of human woman, what kind of simple, happy thing? If I had never been broken on a bird's wing. If I had never seen the world naked. I want to be myself again. I want to be six. I want to stop knowing everything I know. Ivan looks like the life that you stole from me."

And the Tsar of Life roared with agony, shaking his head from side to side like a bull. He struck the wall with his fist, and black dust crumbled from the crater it made. He bit the long neck of Marya Morevna, but she did not bleed. Her skin had hardened, become strong, become impenetrable. And she could not help thinking, *How many times have you played this scene, old man? It's new and raw for me, but not for you, no.*

"If I go with him," she said, her voice low and shaking with the thing she did not want to say but had to, "will you put me in the factory with the Yelenas?" But what she truly asked him was forgiveness, some forgiveness for her greatest failure, that she had done nothing for the Yelenas, that the war had distracted her and she had failed, had been faithless, had abandoned them because her friends were dead and her goodness broken.

Koschei dropped the branch quietly and put his hands over his face. For a moment, Marya thought he wept. But then he snarled and bellowed and leapt on her with such a ferocity she thought he might bite her in half. He tore at his own clothes and pushed her legs apart until her hips groaned, entering her with no gentleness, but as a king enters an enemy hall. He climbed her body and clawed at it, and Marya shook violently, in pleasure, in pain, in fear of him, in adoration.

"Yes," he growled, "yes, I will put you there and turn out the light in your eyes and come to stare at you for centuries, to pore over you, because you are mine, my treasure, my hoard, and I cannot keep you and I cannot let you go."

He thrust against her over and over, his growls echoing. At the last moment, crying out into her like a broken thing, Marya saw his face wither for a moment, becoming impossibly old, old as stone, his hair white, his eyes sunken into a bleached skull, only his teeth remaining, sharp and cruel and ready.

18

What We Carry Between Us

Once, two years, two months, and two days after her wedding day, after three funerals with brown, green, and white coffins, after the battle of the Chernosvyat, in which Marya was wounded in the left thigh and the whole of the north tower withered, died, and sprang up silver in Viy's possession, Marya Morevna had gone to visit the factory. She crept through the streets of Buyan at night and looked neither at the dead fishmongers sitting on their morbid stoop, smoking and drinking dust from crystal glasses, nor at the tavern she had once loved, now washed in silver, full of ghosts singing revolutionaries' songs. They were part of the other Buyan now, and she could not bear to listen, even if it were at all safe to let one eye slip sideways, to look into the windows of the dead city.

Marya remembered the way. The path burned in her memory, phosphor popping and hissing. How much easier, with a straight back free of a cackling rider. The bone door, the sound of clicking looms within. The moon moved in the sky like a railway car, and the young bride slipped inside, onto the great iron balcony she had shared with Baba Yaga in another lifetime, when she did not know the color of a dead man's blood. Green globes lit the place: the broad, tiled floor; the long, thin windows; the stacks of finished cloth snipers and infantry and cavalry officers with organdy horses in the corners. Even in the dregs of the night, brightness touched the head of every Yelena, dozens of them, heads bent to leaping shuttles, hurtling looms. Marya climbed down the iron staircase, her heart in her throat. No one marked her. No one looked up. She could not see a foreman, though every few moments, small breaths interrupted the clacking of the machines as a girl blew into one of the cloth soldiers and the cloth soldier took his or her first breath, which was really that poor Yelena's breath, traveling from cuff to mouth.

Marya Morevna crouched down at the side of one of the women. Her hair, brown as good walnuts, was braided into a circle at the nape of her slender neck, and her fingers moved so fast, so terribly fast! She already had half a girl's torso finished, her darned arm clutching a sniper's rifle. The Yelena—or was she a rare Vasilisa? Marya could not be sure—did not turn her head. Her eyes were filmed with milky gold, her irises invisible, and she never blinked, not once.

"Yelena," Marya whispered. "*Is* your name Yelena?"

The girl kept weaving, her fingers flashing like fish darting under water. Marya touched her arm. Her skin was warm. "Yelena?"

The milky gold caul over her eyes swirled and shifted, but the girl did not speak.

"Oh, please wake up. Please!" Impulsively, having not the smallest idea why, Marya rose a little and kissed the girl on the temple. Marya's lips pressed on the girl's warm, soft skin, her fine, downy wisps of hair. Wasn't that how you woke up a sleeping princess? "Please wake up," Marya whispered again.

But the girl did not. She froze, threads frazzling and sliding out of their pattern. She folded her hands in her lap but did not look up or speak, and the gold film did not thin.

"Yelena? Can you hear me? Is anyone left inside you? I'm so afraid, Yelena. Did he love you? Did you leave him? Did he chain you against the silver tapestries? Did you like his kisses? Were you happy here? Did you know a boy named Ivan? Do you want to go home? How long was it, between the time when you were happy, and the time when you wanted to kill him?" Marya swallowed hard. "He told me to forget you, to be selfish, to be cruel, to be a demon. But I dream about you, and in my dreams you carry water for Baba Yaga, and have a firebird hanging in a golden cage, and Koschei loves you as much as he loves me."

The girl stared at her folded hands.

"What if I said, *Go, Yelena, I will not sound the alarm. Run, get out, fly!*"

The girl did not move.

"Yelena, Yelena, you're the only ones like me in all the world. What will happen to me? What has happened to you? To all of you? Yelena, every spring I march out with all these soldiers, and when I touch their shoulders, I think of you, all of you. I can't help it. And it strikes such awful fear in me, because I seem to see terror and uncertainty in their woven eyes, and they are not meant to be alive. But they cry out when they are shot, as if they were alive, and I shiver. Speak to me, Yelena. Or Vasilisa—is it Vasilisa? I feel my heart draining from me, every day, in every cold tent, in every inch of half-dead earth where blood spills like thread. I am so afraid, Vasilisa. I fear the war is going badly."

But the weaver did not look up, and all around them the machines whirred on, without a care for either of them. Marya wiped her tears and stood up. Her knee popped and creaked, having been bashed in during the first battle of Skorohodnaya Road, one they had won, but barely, oh, just barely.

The weaver, Yelena or Vasilisa, turned her head slowly, without moving the rest of her body. She stared blindly at Marya's stomach, at the height where her face had been a moment before.

"The war is always going badly," the girl said, and picked up her shuttle once more.

Marya Morevna pulled at the girl's arm. She hauled as hard as she could, but it was like pulling stone. She went from girl to girl, pleading, crying, her face hot and shamed, forgetting, for once, all about herself, knowing only that one had spoken, and so they must all be alive. But no Yelena budged, and no Vasilisa spoke again, and none of them would go with her, even when she fell into a heap in the center of the whirring factory's floor, hopeless and defeated.

"Is he a vampire?" asked Ivan Nikolayevich, sitting uncomfortably in the red sea of her bed, unconcernedly naked, ignoring the black nightshirt Koschei had provided.

"What an odd thing to say," said Marya, standing by her mirror. She watched herself as she brushed out her long, ruined hair with long strokes of a boar's bristle brush—one which called no strange old woman, which brought no fate to bear. The boar's hair passed through Marya Morevna's hair, glistening. She liked her body, liked looking at it, even—especially—scored with the tiger stripes of welts across her naked heavy breasts, her belly. She did not have a girl's body anymore; her hips were a lion's hips, her chest strong and muscled, her legs trained to leap and run and kneel to fire.

Scars marked her skin like constellations, leading all the way up to the first, Zmey Gorinich's mark, which still stood on her cheek like a streak of black paint.

"He licked the blood on your hand," Ivan said. "And he is old, and pale, and his teeth are like tusks. I know he looks young, but he's not, really. Sitting next to him is like sitting next to some impossibly ancient statue in a museum. So I think it's a logical question, really."

"He is the Tsar of Life, and blood is life. So is soup and vodka and baths and fucking. But I don't think he's a vampire. At least, not the kind you bury upside down at crossroads."

Ivan frowned and ran a broad brown hand through his hair. "You keep calling him that. The Tsar of Life."

"That's what he is." *And am I the Tsaritsa of Life, then?* half her heart asked. The other half answered, *Not even for a moment were you ever queen.*

"But it's a certain kind of life, isn't it?" Ivan leaned forward, his sunburned head catching the candlelight. He looked like a wonderful dog, huge and hearty, who had found a bone. "It's . . . mushroom-life. The pale, rooty kind that grows in blackness. I'll bet in all your years here he has never given you a fresh apple to eat. Everything he loves is preserved, salted . . . *pickled*. I suppose it's alive, but it's kept alive, forever, in a glass bell. And he is, too. A pickled husband, that's what you have."

Marya turned from the mirror, scowling. "And you are fresh, is that it? Right off the tree? But then you will brown, and turn mealy, and there will be worms in you, someday. Koschei will never wilt."

Ivan shrugged bashfully. "I would not presume."

"Of course you will. You presume already."

"You are a human woman," he said quietly. "You do not belong here, with all this blood, all this pickling. And their brine is seeping into you, bit by bit. You can even disappear like they can. And who knows what else!"

"Well." Marya laughed gently. "I can't really, not like they can. I'm not very good at it. I can only do it in certain places, where the boundaries are quite thin. We had to walk to the place where I spun around and carried you off, remember? I do not know so many of those places. Territory changes too fast to keep the maps up-to-date. But you could probably do it, too, in the thin places. If you practiced. It isn't hard."

"I don't *want* to do it." Ivan Nikolayevich began to roll a cigarette. Without her asking, a bronze tray had quietly appeared, set neatly with papers and crisp, curling tobacco. Ivan thought the stuff hers, but Marya knew better—Koschei had inserted himself here, between them, even when he was gone.

"Why not?" She shrugged. "It's fun. It feels good."

"Not to me. *You* feel good, and sunlight on wheat, and fresh butter and eggs and cigarettes like these, which I roll myself, just as I like them. Magic feels like stripping off my skin and putting it on again, backwards."

Marya put down her brush and crawled onto the bed, reveling in the feeling of stalking him, catlike, hungry. Of knowing more than he did. It was how Koschei felt, she guessed. All the time.

"Well," she purred, "I like all of those things, too. I don't want to choose between them. Koschei doesn't make me choose."

"Yes," Ivan said softly, stroking her face with his hand. "He does. It's only that he makes stripping off your skin taste like fresh butter and feel like sunlight on wheat."

Marya frowned. If he would only ask her, if he would only behave like a bird, like a man in black, she would find all this so much easier. "Ivan, you do not understand us. A marriage is a private thing. It has its own wild laws, and secret histories, and savage acts, and what passes between married people is incomprehensible to outsiders. We look terrible to you, and severe, and you see our blood flying, but what we carry between us is hard-won, and we made it just as we wished it to be, just the color, just the shape."

Ivan kissed her, hesitantly, sweetly, as a boy kisses a girl on the schoolyard. Her mouth flowed with warmth.

"Look how you kiss me, Marya Morevna," he whispered, "while you tell me what marriage is!"

"It is selfish to hoard resources, Ivan Nikolayevich, when we might share, each according to need. Why can I not have both? Both of you, Leningrad and Buyan, pickled and fresh, man and bird?"

He kissed her again, deeper, and the taste of him in her mouth was bright, brighter than blood.

"What do *we* carry between us, then, Masha?"

"Nothing," she breathed. What he dared, to call her Masha so soon! "Yet."

Marya Morevna gripped his shoulders in her hands and pushed him down beneath her. She clamped his narrow hips between her lion-thighs and kissed him with all the biting and possessing she had learned, with everything she had to give to a kiss. Her hair swept over his face, a black curtain, hiding all light, plunging him inescapably into her.

Ivan clapped his hand to the back of her neck, moving under her, arching his back to press closer. He moaned under her, his coin-colored lashes so long, like a girl's.

"Come with me, back to Leningrad," he whispered. "Come back." *There. There, he has asked. And I must choose. War before me, and behind, a woman I do not know, the woman I could have been, a human woman, whole and hot.*

And in the depths of herself, Marya felt her old house on Gorokhovaya Street, on Kommissarskaya Street, on Dzerzhinskaya Street, unfold and creak and beckon, and the sounds of the

Neva gurgle greenly. Things she had not allowed herself to remember came pouring out of Ivan's kisses, out of his skin, out of
his seed. She smelled the sea. *But 1942 is not so far off now,* she
thought desperately, his warmth suffusing her whipped belly. *Not
so far.*

And the heart of Ivan Nikolayevich broke inside the body of
Marya Morevna, and the pieces of him lodged deep in her bones,
and through the window, the stars watched.

Later, after they had shared water and a few slices of ruby meat,
Marya saw the red scarf Ivan Nikolayevich had had knotted around
his arm peeking out from beneath his jacket. She bent and touched
its tip, which protruded like a tongue.

Ivan smiled a little. "It's my Young Pioneers scarf. I don't know
why I still carry it. I just like it. It made me feel safe when I was
young. Made me feel good, as though I could not be harmed, because I was so good, because I belonged."

He looked at her for a long moment, his warm tea-colored eyes
darkened by candlelight until they were almost black, like Koschei's. But Ivan's gaze held her in a circle of heat and quiet night
truths. Marya said nothing; held her breath. And then he did it,
and she thought her body would shake itself apart. Ivan Nikolayevich untied the scarf from his coat and hung it around Marya
Morevna's naked neck, lifting her long hair over its cloth, so that
the tails hung down over her breasts, covering them in scarlet like
bloody tears.

Marya woke in the bottomless well before dawn, her eyes snapping
open in the dark. She sat up straight, Ivan a pleasant warm heap
beside her, insensate. A silvery white woman sat at her vanity, her

long, pale fingers touching the pots, one by one. Her white hair hung loose to her waist. She wore a cameo, a perfect carving of a woman with long pale hair and a silver star on her breast.

"Mashenka, my darling," Madame Lebedeva sighed. "How I miss you. How I wish you would talk to me."

The vila turned, and the silver star on her chest cast sinuous shadows on the ceiling. Her eyelids were painted a lighter color than Marya had ever seen.

"I won't hurt you," the ghost said softly. "I won't. All these years, and you still don't know I would never drag you after me, not ever. It is the terrible hour when anything may be said. I have waited for this hour. Speak one word to me, Masha. Acknowledge me. I love you. Once you are dead, shame sloughs off like an old shirt. It costs nothing to be plain about such things. I love you. Do you not love me?"

Marya's eyelids slid heavily closed again—but she forced them open. And she did look, intently, at her old friend. She could hardly bear her face. She wanted to run to her and be held, but no, no, never again. Never. She would not mean to drag Marya off, but it would happen anyway, like gravity, like falling a long way. She did not want to speak. But the weight of those years spent not looking behind her, not noticing the silver footsteps at her back, oh, that weight sat heavy in her lap.

"I love you, Lebed," Marya Morevna said finally, and wept, slowly, without sound, without tears. She had dried up, utterly.

"It's not so bad, my darling. Being dead. It's like being alive, only colder. Things taste less. They feel less. You forget, little by little, who you were. There isn't much love, but there is a lot of vodka, and reminiscing. It's rather like a university reunion, but the cakes and tarts are made of dust. And there is always a war on. But there was always a war on before, too, wasn't there? And the sight of warm things just makes you furious, angrier than I ever thought I could be. I have no warm things of my own, you see. I want them so. And I cannot remember things so well. As though I am getting old—but I cannot ever get any older. Still, I am glad you spoke to me before I forgot you."

"I thought if I didn't look at you, any of you, you would go away, and I wouldn't have to remember."

"Someday, we will go away. Or maybe we'll forget who you are but still cling to you because of habit, and all we will know is that we have always clung to this girl with black hair, whoever she is." Madame Lebedeva touched the mirror, looking at herself as though she were a very beautiful stranger. A wet, silver stain spread out from her fingertip over the glass like frost forming.

"Did it hurt?" Marya whispered. "When you died?"

"I don't remember. I was bringing your veil—really, how could you get married without a veil, Masha? It's shameful. I was bringing it and someone shot me. I thought I had tripped over something for a moment, and then the assassin took me in his arms—oh, how silver they gleamed!—and put his mouth to my wound. He suckled like a babe, and I thought, *I will never suckle anyone, not ever*—and then I died. It was like pulling on a rope as hard as you can and then suddenly it jerks free and you fall, because you were straining so hard that you couldn't help going over the edge. I put flowers on my body. I was so fond of it. And, you know, during the struggle for the Chernosvyat, a phosphor-shell hit the old magicians' cafe. Now it's in our country, and I can eat there whenever I like. Dust soup, dust dumplings. Little tartlets of ash." Lebedeva pointed at Marya suddenly; her voice sharpened. "You ought to go with Ivan, Masha. Listen to your friend. She is still a magician. She still knows things."

"It will break Koschei's heart." She had decided to stay. She had decided to go. In her sleep she had decided a thousand times. Her dreams were split in half.

"Eh. It's been broken before. And it isn't a heart. You have to look out for yourself. Soon enough my lord will decide he has had enough of your rifle and come to feast on you, treaty or no treaty. Why should you not have some peace before then? Leningrad in 1940—such a quiet place. You could be happy."

"I hardly know this boy." Marya drank in the sight of her friend, and a dull ache began between her breasts. She must stop speaking to Lebedeva; she must stop—but she could not.

"You hardly knew Koschei. Abduction is a marvelous ice-breaker."

Marya Morevna passed her hand over her eyes. "Lebed, why? Why would I ever leave Buyan? This is my home."

"Because this is how it happens. How he dies. How he always dies. The only way he can die. Dying is a part of his marriages, no less than lovemaking. He wouldn't know what to do if you didn't kill him at some point."

"I will never kill him! Even if I go, even if I leave, I wouldn't *kill* him!"

"We shall see. But you will go. Because you are still somewhat young and you need the sun on your face, the high Leningrad sun, to redden your cheeks. Go, and sleep easy, and do not think about how many men will die today."

"Koschei would stop me." But would he? Perhaps he would simply find another girl. Perhaps it would start all over again, only without Marya Morevna, and she could steal some measure of respite.

"He's too proud for that. Think he ever stopped the others?"

"I am not like the others."

"Oh, but Masha, can't you see? You are. An Ivan has come. That is like saying, *Midnight has struck. It is time for bed, little one.* You cannot have both. In war you must always choose sides. One or the other. Silver or black. Human or demon. If you try to be a bridge laid down between them, they will tear you in half."

Marya spread her hands; only Lebedeva could hear her fear, the wounds she had hidden in her jaw, in the space Koschei had made when he took her will. "Lebed, how can I live in that world? I am hardly human. I was only a child—how can I find the girl I was before I knew what magic was? That world will not love me. It will kick me and slap me in the snow, and take my scarf, and leave me ashamed and bleeding."

"You will live as you live in any world," Madame Lebedeva said. She reached out her hand as if to grasp Marya's, as if to press it to her cheek, then closed her fingers, as if Marya's hand were in hers. "With difficulty, and grief."

And slowly, with the infinite care of a woman dressing for the theatre, Madame Lebedeva stretched her long, elegant neck—so far, so far!—her breasts fluffing into feathers, her slender legs tucking up beneath her, until she was a swan, a black band across her eyes. She hopped onto the windowsill and flew away into the aching, raw night.

19

Three Sisters

And so Marya Morevna stole the human boy with gold hair, pulling him down the icy, dawn-darkened streets lined with yawning silver echoes. They kept to the left side; they did not look back. Ivan Nikolayevich rode behind her on a horse with red ears and small hooves, who was not of Volchya-Yagoda's get, but rather his sinister-slantwise nephew, as horses count such things. The horse was possessed of no mechanical leanings whatsoever, only a horse who loved his mistress and thrilled, deep in the memories of his slantwise cells, to be used as an instrument of abduction. Marya, for her part, wondered, as her teeth took cold from the wind, if there could ever be love without this running in the night, this fleeing, this hurtling into dark lands; without the fear that someone, mother or father or husband, might reach out a sorrowful hand to pull her back. Ivan held her around the waist as their horse careened into the forest, heedless of bough or stone. He said nothing. She could think of nothing to say. She had taken him, and what can you say to a taken thing? Her bones jangled in the saddle. Her knee creaked. The old blister below her eye throbbed.

But no hand unhorsed them. No black guard flew through the yellow larches to yank her backwards by the hair. The morning sun pointed redly at them, accusing, righteous. Under its disapproving stare they rode, through the day, into the afternoon. Through the afternoon, and into the night. The stars drew a map of heaven onto the black above.

Finally, the horse with red ears wheezed, spat, and fell to his knees in the snowy shadows of a forest clearing. They had stopped at a great estate, firelight glowing and glimmering in every crys-talline window with the cozy wintertime carelessness of the very rich. Stables it surely had, and hay. The horse had led them well. A great glass door stood ever so invitingly ajar. Marya's eyes swam with the whipping of wind and snow. She peered in, afraid to en-ter, certain Koschei had set this up for her, to rack her with guilt, to make her remember all those soft, quiet little houses on the road to Buyan. To place himself in their bed, like tobacco appear-ing noiselessly on a table.

But they were alone. The horse nosed peaceably in the snow. No sound, not even owls, broke the blackness. And so Marya helped Ivan—saddle-sore and shivering in the bitter, rigid cold—across the threshold.

The foyer of the dacha flowed around them, its deep malachite floor speckled with brown jasper, its candelabras all ruby and am-ethyst. And in the center of the shining floor sat a great egg of blue enamel, crisscrossed with gold leafing and studded with diamonds like nail-heads. Atop the egg perched a middle-aged woman, her

224 CATHERYNNE M. VALENTE

fair hair clapped back like a hay-roll in autumn. She peered at two silver knitting needles over her glasses, where half a child's crimson stocking hung, growing slowly, inch by inch.

Marya's heart spun in surprise.

"Olga!" she cried out. "How is this possible? How can you have come to be here, so deep in the forest? How can I have found you in all the expanse of the world? It is your sister, Masha!" Marya might have wept, but her tears froze within her, so tired and afraid and stiff was she, so afraid that she was being tricked, that the woman would slide off the egg and bounce up something else, something awful, something accusing.

The woman looked up, and her face shone, all porcelain and pink. She filled like a wineskin with the sight of her sister, and, tucking her knitting under one thick arm, leapt down from her egg and kissed Marya all over her face before turning to Ivan and kissing him very chastely on the cheeks. "Marya! Oh, my darling sister!" she exclaimed, and she smelled so like Olga that it could not have been a trick. "So much time has passed! Look at you, grown as a bear! Ah! When did we stop being children?"

Marya longed to raise up her arms and have Olga lift her and twirl her as she used to, when they were young together in the house on Gorokhovaya Street.

"Olya, are you happy? Are you well?"

"Oh, very well! And with my sixth daughter on the way!" She patted the jeweled egg fondly. "This sort of thing is what comes of marrying a bird." She winked. "But then, you always knew he was a bird, didn't you? And you didn't tell me. Wicked girl. But what about you? Are you happy? Are you well?"

"I am tired," said Marya Morevna. "Olya, this is Ivan Nikolayevich. He is not a bird."

Ivan bowed to Marya's oldest sister.

Olga daintily pushed her glasses up onto her nose. "Oh, I know who he is. Think lieutenants don't talk, do you? Gossip is like gold in these parts. Just look at my sister, run off, a scandal, and at her age! I'll have you know I've been faithful to Gratch since he first took my arm, and I've fourteen precious little chicks to show for it!"

"So many!" Ivan whistled.

Olga narrowed her lovely eyes at him. "Haven't you heard there's a war on?" She scowled. "We must all do our part."

"I've told Marya. We've a pact with Germany. War does not even dream of Russia. Your sister will be safe in Leningrad."

"*Tfu!*" Olga spat. "That's what you know." She turned her broad back to him and embraced Marya Morevna once more. "But you must stay the night, refresh your poor horse—what a skinny beast!— eat from my board, drink from my cabinet. You are my sister. What belongs to me belongs to you, even if you are a wicked Delilah with a double ration of men. What is a little bad behavior, among family?"

And so Olga led them to her long ebony table set with bread and pickled peppers and smoked fish, dumplings and beets in vinegar and brown kasha, mushrooms and thick beef tongue and blini topped with little black spoonfuls of caviar and cream. Cold vodka sweated in a crystal decanter. Goose stew bubbled over the hearth. At the head of the table sat a man in a fine black smoking jacket. His head was a glossy-feathered rook, and he snapped cruelly at Marya when she pulled out her chair. Olga kissed his beak and drew him away with her, crooning and chirping to him in the soft, secret language of the wed.

For a moment, left alone, neither Marya nor Ivan moved to eat. Marya's head hurt. Was it the same food she had eaten so long ago, a child, a nothing, a hungry little wolf? She could not remember. Ivan reached for the vodka with his strong red hand.

"Wait . . . ," she whispered faintly. "Wait . . . volchik." The word thrilled her, rolled off her tongue like something forbidden. Ivan withdrew his fingers. He obeyed her; he trusted her. Marya licked her dry lips. The shape of things moved in her mind. A heat rose in her cheeks. She could hardly speak, so big hung the words in her heart. "Do not speak any more tonight, Ivan Nikolayevich. Instead, listen to me, and do as I say." Ivan blinked uncertainly and started to protest. Marya clapped a finger over his mouth. She took her hand away. He did not speak. *Oh, this is a big thing,* she thought. *How enormous it feels in me. I did not understand before.* "Now." Her voice quavered a little. She made it firm. "Taste the caviar first." Marya Morevna cut a thick slab of bread and smeared it with white butter, then spread glistening red roe over it. She held it out to him, and like a child, he ate from her hand. She watched him, distant, a queen on a high chair, but so close to him, so bound to her stolen beauty. "Now, sip your vodka, and then bite one of the peppers—see how the vinegar and the vodka war with one another? This is a rare thing. A winter thing." Marya's throat thickened. She spoke around tears. "You can taste summer in this mixture, summer boiled down and soaked in brine. Because that *is* life, Ivan. Jars on a shelf, bright colors under glass, saved up against the winter, against starving."

Ivan sighed heavily and put down his glass.

"This is stupid, Marya. I am hungry. Let a man eat in peace."

He fell to his fish with a passion, and the spell broke messily at her feet. Marya Morevna stared at him, her jaw tightening until she thought her teeth might crack.

When the dawn lit the great house, Marya and Ivan Nikolayevich found Olga once more atop her rich egg, knitting like a humming-bird, too fast to see.

"Masha, my own, my littlest sister," the matron called down. "Take this with you."

She bit off her yarn in her teeth and tossed the red ball to Marya, who caught it and squeezed it like fruit at the market. The yarn was softer than any wool, expertly spun, thick.

"It will always lead you back, to your country, to your home. I make all my children's stockings with the stuff, so they will know how to come home to their mother." Olga climbed down the cobalt side of the egg and held out her arms to her sister. When Marya stepped into them, Olga lifted her up and twirled her around. Marya laughed despite herself, as she always had.

"Tell our mother I love her, when you get to Leningrad," Olga said, and kissed Marya on both cheeks. Olga smelled like coins and mothering, and Marya Morevna held her tight.

Thus they traveled, into the dawn, into the afternoon. Through the dusk, and into the night. The stars stitched intricate patterns onto the dark hoop above. Still, no pale knife flashed out of the forest to pierce Marya's heart, nor lift Ivan Nikolayevich's head from his shoulders.

Finally, the horse with red ears fell to his knees in a meadow full of spiky, sharp herbs that poked up out of the snow, ringed with birch trees like bones. A smaller house stood in a clearing of hard ice and snow so cold their boots squeaked when they stepped upon it. Half the windows glowed with firelight; horse-breath steamed from half the stables. A great wooden door stood ever-so-invitingly ajar. Marya's eyes ached. She wanted to close them forever. Instead, she helped Ivan Nikolayevich, his knees shaking from the long ride, across the threshold.

The foyer of the house lay around them, its deep maplewood floor dotted with handsome squares of ash, its candelabras all bone and antler, a hunter's trophies. And in the center of the shining floor sat a great egg, its warm, freckled brown shell crisscrossed with rose-colored ribbons. Atop the egg sat a sly, ruddy woman, her grey eyes snapping at every fascinating thing. She peered at a basket of apples on her lap over the rims of a pair of glasses, and sliced each one in seven pieces, for pies and tarts and dumplings.

Marya's heart reeled in surprise. She searched her stomach: Is this magic? Is it chyerti work? But she could not tell. She felt nothing.

"Tatiana!" she cried out. "How is this possible? How can you have come to live here, so far into the wild? How can I have found you, after all that has passed? It is your sister, Masha!" Marya might have wept, but her tears had wrung dry with weariness within her, so long and fast had she flown.

The woman looked up and her face shone, all brown and crimson. She filled like a silk balloon with the sight of her sister. Tucking her knife under one strong arm, she leapt down from her egg and kissed Marya all over her face before turning to Ivan and kissing him, not very chastely at all, on the cheeks. "Marya! Oh, my dearest sister!" she exclaimed. "So much time has passed! Look at you, grown as a goat! Ah! When did we all go blind?" Tatiana tapped her sister's glasses, tucked into her breast pocket, yet just the same as her own.

Marya longed for Tatiana to rub her head and fuss with her hair as she used to, when they were young together in the house on Gorokhovaya Street.

"Tanya, are you happy? Are you well?"

"Oh, very well! And with my fourth son on the way!" She patted the brown egg fondly. "Marry a bird, wake up in a nest." She winked. "But then, you always knew he was a bird, didn't you? And you didn't tell me. Clever girl. But how goes it with you? Are you happy? Are you well?"

"I am tired," said Marya Morevna. "Tanya, this is Ivan Nikolayevich. He is not a bird."

Ivan bowed to Marya's second-oldest sister.

Tatiana bemusedly pushed her glasses up onto her nose. "Oh, I know who he is. Think lieutenants don't get around, do you? Gossip is like cups of sugar in these parts. Just look at my sister, a fallen woman, a heartbreaker, and at her age! I'm so proud of you. I'll have you know I've had twice as many lovers as Zuyok since he first took my maidenhead, and I've nine sly little chicks to show for it!"

"So many!" Ivan whistled.

Tatiana widened her lively eyes at him. "Haven't you heard? We've cast off the oppressive hierarchies of the old world." She grinned. "We must all do our parts for modernity."

"Life is hard enough, I think, without modernity," Ivan sighed.

"*Tfu!*" Tatiana spat. "That's what you know." But she turned her shapely back to him and embraced Marya Morevna once more. "Of course you must stay the night, refresh your poor horse—what a loyal beast!—eat from my board, drink from my cabinet. You are my sister. What belongs to me belongs to you, even if you are a notorious slattern. We are family; we take after each other!"

And so Tatiana led them to her long walnut table set with roast swan, vereniki stuffed with sweet pork and apples, pickled melons, cakes piled with cream and pastry. At the head of the table sat a man in a fine brown smoking jacket. His head was a thick-feathered plover, and he snapped suggestively at Marya when she pulled out Ivan's chair. Tatiana swatted his wing and coaxed him away with her, warbling and clicking to him in the bright, squabbling language of the well-matched.

Ivan devoured the sweet pork and gulped deep red wine.

"The vineyards that gave us this wine also provide the wine for Comrade Stalin's table," Marya said with a solemn, blank expression. "Someone told me once that even when children starve for the sake of righteousness, Papas always have wine at their table."

She sipped the wine herself. "When I was young, it seemed far too sweet. I savored bitterness, the spice of those who have lived long and wildly. Perhaps you, too, should learn to prefer it. After all, when all else is gone, still you may have it." Marya Morevna drained the glass. "Now, even this candied syrup tastes bitter to my tongue," she sighed.

When the dawn pinched the great house's brown cheeks, Marya and Ivan Nikolayevich found Tatiana once more atop her ribboned egg, slicing apples like a woodsman, too fast to see.

"Masha, my own, my littlest sister," the plover's wife called down. "Take this with you."

She tossed an apple to Marya, its red ball spinning in the air. It was firm and bright as a gem.

"No matter how much you eat, so long as you leave the core, in the morning it will be whole again. I make all my children's suppers with the stuff, so they will know their mother looks after them, and thinks of the future." Tatiana climbed down the smooth side of her egg and held out her arms to her sister. When Marya stepped into them, Tatiana stroked her head and fussed with her curls. Marya laughed despite herself, as she always had.

"Tell our mother I love her, when you get to Leningrad," Tatiana said, and kissed Marya on both cheeks. Tanya smelled like bread and loving, and Marya Morevna held her tight.

Thus they traveled, into the dawn, into the afternoon, across thrice nine kingdoms, the whole of the world between the Country of Life and Leningrad. Through the twilight, and into midnight. The stars wrote strange names onto the dark papers above. Still,

Welcome to North Bay Public Library!
You have the following items:

1. Marvin K. Mooney, will you
   please go now! /Seuss, Dr., pseud
   Barcode: 33874003670238 Due:
   Nov 14, 2016 11:59 PM

2. Twins in the park /Weiss, Ellen
   Barcode: 33874000979814 Due:
   Nov 14, 2016 11:59 PM

3. Puppy Mudge has a
   snack/Rylant, Cynthia.
   Barcode: 33874000980226 Due:
   Nov 14, 2016 11:59 PM

4. Waiting is not easy!/Willems, Mo
   Barcode: 33874004605241 Due:
   Nov 14, 2016 11:59 PM

5. Deathless /Valente, Catherynne
   M.
   Barcode: 33874004279450 Due:
   Nov 14, 2016 11:59 PM

> Cost of buying these items:
> $111.00
> Cost of using the library:
> Priceless!

no woven soldiers appeared to seize Marya Morevna, or to shoot Ivan Nikolayevich with rough woolen rifles.

Finally, the horse with red ears fell to his knees in a stony pass smeared with ice, where no flower or tree showed itself. A humble hut stood in a circle of sharp rocks, protected on all sides. One of the windows glowed with firelight; horse-breath steamed from one age-blackened barn. A small iron door stood ajar, as though daring, rather than inviting them. Marya's fingers throbbed with cold. She helped Ivan, who was coughing hoarsely, his skin flushed and fevered, across the threshold.

The single room of the house lay around them, its hard earthen floor dotted with studs of ice, its candles all tallow, thick and long as arms. And in the center of the compact floor sat a great egg, its shining steel shell studded with iron bolts. Atop the egg sat a slim, gentle young woman, her blush quicker than shadows passing. She peered over a pair of glasses at a basket of keys in her lap, and sorted them, the iron from the copper from the brass, for smelting.

Marya's heart sang in delight. She had hoped, she had hoped, after the others.

"Anna!" she cried out. "How is this possible? How can you have come to hide here, so high in the mountains? It is your sister, Masha!" And Marya wept, her tears warm and free and glad.

The woman looked up, and her face shone, all pale and bright. She filled like a pail of water with the sight of her sister. Tucking a ring of keys under one slender arm, she leapt down from her egg and kissed Marya all over her face before turning to Ivan and kissing him coldly on the cheeks. "Marya! Oh, my dearest sister!" she exclaimed. "So much time has passed! Look at you, grown as a wolf! Ah! When did we grow so serious?"

Marya longed for Anna to seize her up and dance with her, as she used to when they were young together in the house on Gorokho-vaya Street.

"Anyushka, are you happy? Are you well?"

"Oh, very well! And with my second daughter on the way!" She patted the steel egg fondly. "A wife and her husband must be in complete agreement." She winked. "But then, you always knew he was a bird, didn't you? And you didn't tell me. Traitorous girl. But what of yourself? Are you happy? Are you well?"

"I am tired," said Marya Morevna. "Anya, this is Ivan Niko-layevich. He is not a bird."

Ivan bowed to Marya's third-oldest sister.

Anna angrily pushed her glasses up onto her nose. "Oh, I know who he is. Think lieutenants do not inform on each other, do you? Gossip is like ration cards in these parts. Just look at my sister, disloyal, a criminal, at her age! I'll have you know I have lived with virtue since Zhulan took my conscience, and I've two upright little chicks to show for it!"

"So few!" Ivan whistled.

Anna slitted her plain eyes at him. "Haven't you heard? It is wicked to have more than your neighbors possess." She grinned. "We must all do our parts for the Party."

"Of course," said Ivan.

"*Tfu!*" Anna spat. "That's what you know, both of you." But she turned her elegant back to him and embraced Marya Morevna once more. "But you must stay the night, refresh your poor horse—what an earnest beast! But your prisoner looks sick. He would throw up anything you fed him. You are my sister. What belongs to me belongs to you, even if you are an exile. We are family. But you mustn't tell anyone I harbored you."

And so Anna led them outside, through the silver ice to a little bathhouse, hardly bigger than one of Olga's closets. A man in a threadbare grey coat exited the banya with a puff of steam. His head was a lean shrike's, and he would not look at Marya as he passed her by. Anna smiled at him, her face lighting like an oil lamp, took his wing and walked back towards the house, croaking and cawing to him in the strident, ordered language of the incorruptible.

Marya Morevna refused to let Ivan speak. This time she made her will iron, flexing it, testing it. Ivan submitted to her, and there was gratitude in his submission. *You are spoiled,* she thought. *All that rich food and you have kept it all in your belly, enjoyed every bite. But you are sick now, and must yield.* She seated him in the bathhouse. On a little paint-scraped table rested a mug of vodka.

Marya stood very still. She felt as though she were two women: one old and one young; one innocent and one knowing, strange, keen. Marya undressed Ivan Nikolayevich, and her hands seemed to move twice for each motion, to unbutton his shirt now, and to unbutton her own then. His eyes rolled and his red brow sweated. He nearly called out her name, but remembered to be silent, and she kissed him for it. Marya Morevna rubbed his skin with her long, hard fingers. Her golden boy nearly fell asleep sitting up, calmed by her hands and her soft, sad little singing, melodies half-remembered, about biting wolves and uncareful girls. Soon both sweat and tears rolled down Marya's face, and she wished Koschei were with her to show her how to tend to this sick human, the care of whose body was now inexplicably hers. But gone is gone. There could be no more Koschei. Only Marya remained.

"Drink, Ivanushka." She clucked gently, like a mother, and put the mug to his lips. "Your lungs want vodka." Obediently, he drank, and coughed, and drank once more.

Marya Morevna sank his clammy feet in her sister's shallow tub. She held a handful of water to his nose and ordered him to breathe it in. Ivan spluttered, and gagged, but did it anyway, so accustomed was he now to her voice, her command. Finally, she made him stand. She reached into the foggy corner of the banya, knowing with all of her marrow that a long white birch branch would rest there.

But Ivan had drifted away into his fever, and slept curled on the floor of the banya like a hound.

Marya let go of the birch branch slowly. She watched him in the dark without a sound.

When the dawn roused the humble hut's household to work, Marya and Ivan Nikolayevich found Anna once more atop her steel egg, sorting keys like an engine, too fast to see.

"Masha, my own, my littlest sister," the shrike's wife called down. "Take this with you."

She tossed a key to Marya, with brass teeth. It glowed dimly in her hand, catching the sun.

"It is the key to our old house, on Gorokhovaya Street. But of course it is Dzerzhinskaya Street now. One of us should still live there. One of us should be young again." Anna climbed down the grey side of her egg and held out her arms to her sister. When Marya stepped into them, Anna pressed her face to her sister's breast, took up her hand, and began to dance with her, a gentle, slow circle around the little hut. Marya laughed despite herself, as she always had. She remembered, as if through a glass, having laughed like that, a lifetime ago. She kissed Anna's forehead with passion.

"When our mother died," Anna said, "the Housing Ministry sent the keys to me. I was the only one they could find. We keep our registrations current." Then Anna kissed Marya on both cheeks. She smelled like iron and strength, and Marya Morevna held her tight.

PART 4

There Are No Firebirds in Leningrad

And always in the frigid, prewar air,
The lascivious, menacing darkness
There lived a kind of future clanging . . .
But then, you could hear it only softly, muffled,
It could scarcely cloud the soul
And it drowned in the snowdrifts along the Neva.
As in a mirror of appalling night,
A man thrashes like a devil
And does not want to recognize himself,
Along the legendary embankment
The real—not the calendar—
Twentieth Century draws close.

—ANNA AKHMATOVA

20

Two Husbands
Come to Dzerzhinskaya Street

In a long, thin house on a long, thin street, a woman in a pale blue dress sat by a long, thin window, waiting for her punishment.

Neither fell nor fiery did it come. For one year, one month, and one day, it did not come. And forgiveness did not, either.

It was late spring when Marya Morevna slid her brass key into the lock of the house on Dzerzhinskaya Street, feeling it slide, too, between her own ribs, and open her like a reliquary full of old, nameless bones. The house stood empty. All the curtains—green-and-gold, cobalt-and-silver, red-and-white—had been yanked from their rods. Spiders' webs made a palimpsest on the walls, endless generations of spiders weaving spider-tales into silk. The house seemed so much smaller than it had, darker, an old, hunched beast past its use. A hole had opened up in the roof, dripping rain and plum blossoms into the room which had once belonged to Marya and her parents. The downstairs stove stood silent and cold, full of old ash no one had taken out. Vacant room opened up into vacant room.

"The Dyachenkos lived in this room," she said to no one. To Ivan Nikolayevich, she supposed, his hand proprietary on her back. It was all wrong. She was supposed to have found warmth here, like Ivan's warmth. Life, and living. "They had four boys, all blond. I don't remember their names. The father ate this awful pickle soup every night. The place just reeked of dill. And here—oh, the Blodniek girls! Oh, they were so beautiful. Their hair! How I wanted hair like that. Shiny and straight as wood. They used to read." She turned to Ivan, her eyes hollow. "They used to read this fashion magazine. They each had their hour with it, every day. They memorized hemlines, and color palettes. Little Lebedevas! And oh, there, there the Malashenkos tied bunches of flowers to sell, and Svetlana Tikhonovna brushed her hair. Oh, why is no one living here? This was a good house! I had twelve mothers in this house, twelve fathers. I ate such sweet fish in this house."

And Marya Morevna fell to her knees before the great brick stove in the empty kitchen. She did not cry, but her face grew redder and redder with the pain of her not crying.

"Zvonok," she whispered to the floor. "Zvonok, come out."

Finally, she curled up on the broken tile and went to sleep, like a ragged feral cat who has finally found shelter from the rain.

Ivan Nikolayevich went to the ministry that evening to ask them to pardon his disappearance from his camp posting with a long tale of illness and good service among the Buryatskaya province villages. He opened and shut the door with a kiss to Marya's cheek that felt as alien to her as a tattoo pricked there. Kisses crushed, pulverized, obliterated, bit—they did not peck. They did not smack and then vanish in a second. The scent of new lime leaves and forsythia blew in after him to fill the space. Marya Morevna watched him go down the street. The blue-and-lavender evening threw sashes around him, and he passed by young men in black caps who leaned against the linden trees, playing guitars. Marya shut her eyes. When she opened them again, the guitars still twanged under the first faint stars and Ivan Nikolayevich had disappeared around a corner. She suddenly felt afraid to leave the house. What awful place waited out there, whose fountains spouted dead, tasteless water, whose tall houses had no names, no skin, no hair? This house, she knew. It stayed within her as it had always been, the architecture of her girlhood. The wood held the oils of her skin deep in its grain; the windows still bore the imprint—long gone, invisible—of her tiny nose. A ghost of the Marya without magic, the little girl who was not broken, not a soldier, not a wife. But Leningrad, Leningrad was a stranger. It did not even share a name with the city where she had been born.

The plumbing creaked to life, spitting brown chemical resentment into the sink. Marya waited, watching the baleful dragon-faucet spew its venom into the drain. It did not run clear, really, but it ran tepid, the color of weak tea. After a moment's consideration, Marya Morevna took off her boots and placed them deliberately by the stove, where she had once shrunk to the size of a rolling pin. She rolled up the legs of her black trousers and slopped water onto the kitchen floor with cupped hands, having no bucket, kneeling to scrub with an oily rag and a few old newspapers she found stuffed into the stove. *Vicious Spies and Killers Under the Mask of Academic Physicians!* the newsprint said, and she crushed it into the floor until the ink ran with water and filth. Her creaky knee complained, popping against the tile, but gradually, she uncovered a single bleached and faded rose, the pattern she remembered in the once-tidy kitchen. *I want to see those roses!* Papa Blodniek had hollered at his daughters.

"What I would not give for one Blodniek sister to kiss me now, and light the stove with me," Marya whispered. She scrubbed until her back wept and convulsed, giving up. She had been stabbed there, near her kidney, the night they lost the candlemakers' district, and Koschei had howled at the sight of her blood, so like a wolf that the wolves in the wood had taken up the chorus. Marya lay flat on her stomach, waiting for her muscles to unclench and let her rise. The cool tile kissed her face. Outside, through the broken window, she heard a young girl laugh, a cream-colored, strawberry-ice kind of laugh. Her lover sang to her: *We'll meet again in Lvov, my love and I . . .*

A rough, ringing voice chided her. "Not an hour in Leningrad and he's got you scrubbing floors."

Marya smiled against the wet floor. She squeezed her eyes shut, relief lancing through her chest.

"Zvonok, oh Zvonya, I thought you'd gone."

She turned her head and the domovaya stood there, her blond mustache ragged and full of split ends, her vest buttons mostly missing, patches on her brick-colored trousers. "Not that I don't appreciate it," Zvonok said. "It's been so long since anyone cared about the floor. A cat could give up a grudge since this house has heard a holler to *shut the door, the winter's coming in!* But then, the winter came in, didn't it? It did, it did." The domovaya nodded to herself.

"But it's a fine house. Why would no one live here? And what about the Domovoi Komityet, all your friends?"

"Gone, with the families. Only I stay with the house. It's my house. I married the old bastard. I'm stuck. A lesson some girls haven't learned, exactly." Zvonok sat down, cross-legged, near Marya's nose. "Well, you know, Svetlana Tikhonovna died. A bad business, that. And her boys, well, they had no one to get meat for them, and they went begging one day and never came back. It happens to little ones. I like to think they fell into the Neva, the monsters. They stuffed up the mouse holes with their old socks. I needed those holes! And then the Abramov twins caught something, and pretty soon everyone had it, and there was a line outside the bathroom like at the cabbage shop, and then they didn't bother with the bathroom anymore. And then the municipal hygiene authority just started carrying them all out, one by one by one. Some flat dead. Some not. Your mother was one of the last. And with them, their domoviye crawled out, clutching their stomachs, pulling their mustaches. We can't get dysentery, you know, but we feel it when our family hurts." Zvonok tugged her own mustache and looked at the clean rose on the floor. "I felt it when you caught that bullet in your shoulder. And the bayonet in your back. Such a lot of bother I suffer for you. Anyway, the Housing Committee tried to assign new tenants, but I didn't want them." The domovaya spat—carefully avoiding the clean patch Marya had opened up. "No, I didn't! Fat and lazy, nothing but toadies and drunks! They put the Baghirlis—all eight of them—in your old room upstairs. And then the Grusovs showed up. Husband and wife, rat and ratitsa! They informed on their last household, so they got the rest of the house all to themselves! And no children between them! That bitch's ferrety old womb would suffocate a babe, I'm sure. Well, Zvonok has opinions, and her opinions are this: to smoking hell with the lot of them. I broke things and rattled rafters until they ran off. Funny how no one's asked for an assignment here since! Ha!" The imp slapped her knee.

Marya Morevna laughed a little, though it made her back hurt. "Oh, Zvonok, I have missed you."

"Well, I can't say you've moved up in the world. I saw that lug you brought in. Smells like an informant to me. Smells like a *Grusov*."

"I don't think so." But then, she had not asked. She knew nothing about him, except the taste of his mouth. What else didn't she know? Everything, everything.

"Bet Papa Koschei didn't have you on your knees in filth sopping up his kitchen. Bet you had a kokoshnik all of sapphires and a striped cat on your lap."

"Not exactly." But gems there had been, and no weak pecking kisses. Perhaps she had been wrong. Perhaps hasty. But she could not think that, not yet; she had to try. *Because what's back there? The war and blood and silver splashes like stars.*

"Well, after Viy came, sure. I felt that too, even so far off from you. But before that. Before, it was good, yes? Sturgeon eggs every night? Copper bathtubs?"

Marya smiled again. Her hair slid off her back. "Yes, it was good, Zvonya. Before the war."

"Well, I will tell you something, Masha, my girl. You should have stayed put. I understand the need to ride a new horse every now and then—you think I haven't gone and taken a good look at the wallpaper in another house every century or two? But you don't trade a tiger for a fat little kitten, you know what I mean? It'll just piss on your floor and ignore you when it's not biting you for fish you don't have."

"When I saw him I thought I could curl up inside him and go to sleep and never wake up."

"Men are no good for that, Masha. They'll always want you working, when you're not softening their fall into bed at the end of the day."

"I wanted to be alive again. I wanted to be someone else."

Zvonok stood up, brushing off her red trousers. She put her hands on her hips.

"Well, I hope lying on that floor like a broken dog is everything you hoped it would be." She shrugged. Then the domovaya hopped

up onto one foot, spun around three times, took a deep breath—
and stopped. She squinted at Marya for a moment and reached
into her vest pocket, pulling out something tiny and white. It grew
bigger and bigger until Zvonok could hardly manage it herself.
She let it fall onto the tile: a china teacup, with cherries on the
handle, cracked in many places.

Zvonok jumped through the hoop of the handle, and vanished.

"Masha!" came the voice of Ivan Nikolayevich, booming through
the house along with a bluster of last year's leaves.

Marya Morevna started awake. She pushed herself up off the
kitchen floor, her bones crackling their displeasure, her back still
shaky, but it had released its awful grip. She brushed her black
jacket clean—it was still too cold to take it off, and she had nothing else but her marshal's uniform, which Ivan had said she should
not wear on the street.

"I have good news, Masha!" Ivan called. His golden head appeared in the kitchen door, and his smile upon seeing her lit the
room like a stove.

Behind him, a young woman with a long braid followed shyly,
carrying a sleeping baby in her arms.

"The Housing Committee was so grateful to have someone
willing to live in this damned old place, they've only asked that we
share with one other family. Isn't that extraordinary? Just think of
the space! Marya Morevna, may I present Kseniya Yefremovna
Ozernaya and her daughter, Sofiya. Comrade Kseniya is a nursing
student, so we shall be very glad of her, I'm sure. Mashenka, did you
try to clean the floor by yourself? With no soap or bucket? You see
what an industrious wife I have, Kseniya!" Ivan was babbling. He
was nervous; she could see it. Fear sluicing through him, that they
should be found out. She was not his wife. Marya pitied him his

244 CATHERYNNE M. VALENTE

need for no one to know it. Who could care? She thought of the Grusovs, and shuddered. What else did she not know about him? But she did not care. She only wanted him to take her to a bed and make her feel warm again, make her feel the sun on her insides.

But all she said was, "Good evening, Comrade Ozernaya."

"Good evening, Marya Morevna," said the young woman, and her dark eyes filled with such warmth and hope.

How lonely she must be, Marya thought.

"Where is the child's father?" she said curiously, and not without coldness. She did not sniff at the propriety of it, but it was interesting.

"He died," the young woman said bitterly. "Men die. It's practically what they're for."

Ivan Nikolayevich cleared his throat. "Well, there will be plenty of time for sharing personal histories. Would you prefer the upstairs or the downstairs, Kseniya Yefremovna?"

"Please," Marya hurried, before the girl could answer. "Take the downstairs. It is nearer the stove. For the infant." *And upstairs is home,* she added silently.

"Thank you. We find a way to be comfortable wherever we land. But this is certainly . . . better. I bathe frequently."

Ivan beamed at them. "Will you excuse us, Comrade Ozernaya? I wish to have a word with my wife."

"Of course."

Marya snorted softly. *How odd you are, Ivanushka, kicking her out of the room you just gave her.*

Kseniya Yefremovna ducked into the parlor where the Malashenkos had once squabbled over rouge creams. Where Svetlana Tikhonovna had posted all her playbills. *The Pharaoh's Daughter. Giselle. Spyashaya Krasavitsa.*

Ivan Nikolayevich crushed Marya to him in a rush. He buried his face in her hair.

"Masha," he breathed, "do not look at this house. Do not look at the dead stove, the hole in the roof. I will make this place whole for you, your childhood home, and then you will know that you chose well, in choosing me. You will see how well I serve you."

Marya Morevna sighed against his shoulder. She breathed his scent. *Yes, like that. More like that. Tell me all the ways in which this was the only choice.*

"Take me upstairs," she whispered.

He did. And as they passed out of the kitchen, Marya noticed that a puddle of water, perfectly round, rippled in the place where the young girl with her braid and her baby had been standing.

So it went. The Housing Committee sent men to repair the roof, and Ivan grinned widely at Marya, as if to say, *Look how I command men, too.* With harsh blue soap and lye they burned the filth and any lingering sickness away from the kitchen floor. All the roses bloomed on the tiles—though they were never to be pink again, but faint and brown. Ivan carried out bucket after bucket of ash from the stove, and oh, how Marya wept when she saw the burnt corner of a magazine in the grey coals, the scorched tip of a lady's feathered hat. All four of them gathered in the kitchen to light the clean stove for the first time. Baby Sofiya clapped her chubby hands, and they all blew on the little flame until it caught. Soot and smoke and the smell of sawdust and pine needles filled the house, but it was warm. Kseniya made them all a sweet ukha that night, with salted mackerel she had been saving for an occasion and green, redolent dill from the old window garden, now overgrown and thick with new sprouts.

They were allotted furniture and food cards according to Ivan Nikolayevich's new civic position in the Cheka, the Extraordinary Commission. Marya laughed when he said those words to her.

"But that doesn't mean anything, Ivanushka! What's extraordinary about it?"

"It's like a kind of policeman, Masha. A sheriff."

But she never could keep it straight. All the letters, the acronyms, the codes, the colors, changing like musical chairs, every week, every month. Games demons play. It meant nothing to her, except in a charming sort of way, as it had when Naganya wanted to play at interrogation, while the rest of them wanted chess.

Ivan bought her three dresses and two suits with trousers, one black, and one brown. She never wore the dresses. They hung on the empty curtain rod—red, white, and yellow—and kept the sun out. Many days Marya, Kseniya, and the baby walked together to the market to get potatoes and bread, cabbage and onions. Sometimes there was fish. Sometimes there was not. If all the stars aligned, there might be beef, but it would certainly have run out by the time they got to the head of the line. Kseniya Yefremovna and Marya would joke about the riches that the people ahead of them would already have snapped up.

"Those who get here at three o'clock get bananas!"

"Old widow Ipatiev gobbles up all the chocolate. See how brown her teeth are!"

And Marya thought, *I sound just like a Leningrader. Imagine it.*

And at night, in a narrow bed in her old room, Marya Morevna would hold Ivan tight inside her, demanding his obedience to her, demanding that his soul be ripped out and emptied into her. Only then did she feel whole and rooted—but she did not feel like herself. Sister of Anna and Tatiana and Olga. Daughter of twelve mothers. Young Pioneer. Six years old and birdless, birdless.

Marya began to stalk the house as she had long ago, restless, uneasy. She paced. Reading, thinking, speaking. Her sleep came in brief, spontaneous concussions; at night she kept her eyes peeled like an owl's. She was afraid to dream, afraid, still, to leave the house. Every time she looked out the long, thin windows onto the cherry tree where her sisters' husbands had ever so briefly alighted, she thought she might see Buyan again, all crimson, all bone, all radiant, whole, no silver to be seen. Or worse, to see Viy's colorless country seeping through the seams of Leningrad, too. She did not know whether she longed to see these things, or feared to. Her body still tensed in every moment, ready to take up her rifle again (hidden now under her bed, with Ivan above it, as though he, too, might spark and fire in her hands) and run with all those men behind her, all those woven men with their soft, soundless shoes. At the raucous, talkative bursts of boys and girls passing below the windows on their way to Nevsky Prospekt, to ice cream and films and cafes, she jumped in her skin, ready to leap on them and bite out their throats.

The house had definitely shrunk; that she knew. Where once she had counted, endlessly, the five steps to walk from the vanished cobalt-and-silver curtain to the disappeared green-and-gold curtain, it now took three. But then, maybe her strides were longer. *There are so few of us now,* she thought, and left a shoe for Zvonok that night. Ivan, endlessly vexed by her bottomless appetite for shoes, called her mad, a wolf. She winced. That night, while he slept, she suddenly sprang upon him and bit his cheek savagely. She was not mad, not a wolf, not anymore. He looked at her with such shock, such wounded surprise. She kissed away the blood and roused his body to her, her fingers and her lips. He protested, his hands plunged already in her hair. *I have to report early in the morning, Masha!*

Do you think I came through the living and dead worlds to be a Party mistress? I am your loyalty; I am your kommissar.

And he yielded to her, always.

It was because she could not sleep that Marya Morevna discovered Kseniya Yefremovna's peculiar habits. In the long, impenetrable night of January, the queen from beyond the sea crept downstairs to put her freezing feet against the stove, meaning to walk on her softest toes and wake neither the earnest nursing student nor her little one. The child had a dark mess of tangled hair now, and babbled an unending stream punctuated by *mamochka, Sofiya, milk, fishes!* Sofiya had just learned to walk, and terrorized them all with her headlong rushes down the hallways, across the parlor. But Marya found them both wide-awake in the starless hours of night, waiting for a great kettle to steam on the great brick stove.

"Good evening, Marya Morevna!" Kseniya whispered. "What is the matter?" The baby waved her fat arms senselessly.

"Nothing, Ksyusha, I am only cold. The old roof still lets in a draft. May I sit by the stove?"

Kseniya Yefremovna frowned. "Of course. Nothing belongs to me that does not belong to all." Marya heard, too, the other half of her words: *but I wish you wouldn't.*

Marya huddled with them next to the baking brick of the stove. Warmth sopped through her, dull and sleepy. She put her finger into baby Sofiya's hand.

"She squeezes well. Maybe she will grow up to be a soldier."

Kseniya stared at her. Marya never said the right thing, especially around the child.

"Have you begun teaching her words?" she tried again.

"Yes, she's very clever."

As if recognizing her cue, Sofiya threw her hands up and squawked, "Water!" And giggled riotously.

"Yes, rybka, my little fish! It's time for water." Kseniya twisted her hands.

"We are modest," she added, awkwardly.

"I shall turn my eyes if it will help. I am chilled, still. But why are you bathing at this time of night? You'll chase your death in your sleep."

The young nurse sighed heavily, untwisting her long braid and loosening her dark hair, slightly damp. "I have . . . a condition. My daughter has it, too. We become . . . ill, when our skin dries out. Our hair. It is especially dangerous at night. Pillows drink up so much water. For myself I wouldn't even get out the kettle, but my little fish can't bear the faucet."

Marya Morevna laid her head on her shoulder, watching the nursing student with a crow's interest. Rusalka were like that, she knew from long experience. They fall down dead if they dry out. In Buyan, the rusalki kept a great glass-ceilinged natatorium full of clear blue pools and hot saunas, so they could stay in the city overnight. At home, in their lakes, they never worried—a quick swim and they shone, sang, drowned their lovers with abandon and cheer. But too far from the green, grassy depths of mountain waters, they fell prey to a wide variety of arcane personal rituals, all of them necessary to keep a rusalka alive from day to day.

"I knew someone once, who had a condition like yours," Marya said slowly. She could not be sure; she did not dare call the young woman out.

Kseniya Yefremovna fixed her with a deep, unwavering gaze. "I am not surprised that you did, Comrade Morevna."

In the silence of the kitchen, broken only by the settling of blackened wood chips in the stove, Marya helped Kseniya to fill a little tub and sink her long hair into it. She stroked the young woman's curls, making sure every strand got soaked through. Impulsively, she kissed the young woman's damp forehead.

In the morning, they did not speak of it.

———

Was she happy? Did she think of Koschei? She saw herself from a long way off, moving as though through water. Little things brought her singing down into herself again: the smell of cherries rotting on the ground outside her window; the crackle of the radio, which always startled her; the sharp sear of the vinegar Kseniya used to preserve half the eggs, mushrooms, and cabbage that she brought in from the market. Kseniya was better at being alive than Marya. Marya accepted that difference, and only once a day, at dusk, did she look beyond her friend's moist shoulder, expecting to see Naganya clicking her jaw disapprovingly in the corner. But she saw nothing; they hadn't followed her, or were content to remain unseen. Marya did not know which she preferred.

And then, Ivan, always Ivan, the motion of him within her, the ways in which she could force him to bend to her will, the getting of small items, a comb, a cup of water. She clung to him, for if she clung to him, then leaving Buyan could be right, could be right forever. He did not speak of his work. She did not ask him what he did when he left her. Ivan Nikolayevich did not seem to have much of an idea what to do with her, now that she had come to Leningrad, done as he asked. *I can get you a job, Mashenka. Wouldn't you like to work? Wouldn't you like to have comrades?* But she would not like that. She wanted only to rest and to read her old, rain-swollen books, turning the pages carefully, so carefully.

"Ivanushka," she asked one night as the jingling street sounds played below the window. "Would you perform tasks for me, if I asked?"

"What do you mean?"

"Would you . . . get me a firebird's feather, or fetch a ring from the bottom of the sea, or steal gold from a dragon?"

Ivan pursed his lips. "Those sorts of things are so old-fashioned, Masha. They are part of your old life, and the old life of Russia, too. We have no need of them now. The Revolution swept all the dark corners of the world away. Yes, remnants still lurk in the hinterlands—Koschei, a Gamayun or two. But they are irrelevant. The old world left its dirty, broken toys lying about. But soon enough we'll have everything tidy. Besides, there are no firebirds in Lenin-grad."

Marya Morevna turned her back to him, and he kissed her shoulder blades.

The main thing was the tiredness, which swaddled her and stayed. The main thing was the ruin of her house, like film laid on top of other film, so that she could look at a wall and see not only the wall but Svetlana Tikhonovna and her mother arguing over laundry in front of it, and Zemlehyed pawing at it, and the skin of a Buyan wall, so far from her. Everywhere her vision doubled and trebled, and her head sagged with the weight of it. Everything kept occurring all at once, each thing on top of the last.

Was she happy? Did she think of Koschei?

She thought of mushrooms, and vinegar, and old wounds.

At last, after a year had come gone in the house on Dzerzhinskaya Street, Marya sat on her bed by the long, thin window. She looked up at the red dress hanging there. It had a deep neckline, and a full skirt. A young woman's dress.

"What is thirty-three?" she said to the empty house. "A crypt?"

And so she put on the dress, and let her black hair fall down to her waist. She took some of Kseniya's lipstick—she would not mind, not with so many classes this term. Marya had gotten better at applying it, and her mouth shone neatly. Marya Morevna walked down the stairs and put her palm to the knob of the great cherry-wood door. She would go down to the river, and have an ice cream of her own, and someone would dance with her at a piano hall, without even knowing her name. Outside, she could smell the summer acacia, blooming early this year, in the long half-golden dusk that passed for night in Leningrad's June. A young man played a violin a little ways off, singing boldly: We'*ll meet again in Lvov, my love and I . . .*

Marya Morevna turned the knob and opened her door onto the city. She stood there in her bright red dress, and her face drained of blood. A man looked down at her, for he was quite tall. He wore a black coat, though the evening's warm wind blew through his curly dark hair, so like a ram's. Slowly, without taking his eyes from hers, the man in the black coat knelt before her.

"I have come for the girl in the window," he said, and his eyes filled with tears.

21

This House Has No Basement

I vanushka, you must make me a promise.
Anything, wife.

A pure kind of light fell like cold hammer-blows on Dzerzhinskaya Street the next day. Morning passed, but the light kept its quality. Waxen, hard, merciless. A young woman with a pale blue band around her hat knocked crisply at the great cherrywood door. She had never been a bird—not a rook, nor a shrike, nor a plover, nor an owl. Her crisp features matched the morning, pitiless and sharp. She knocked again.

———

Ivanushka, no matter how strange it seems, you must obey me.
Always, wife.

The man in the black coat held up one hand to her, as if he could not believe she was real. "I look at you, Masha, and it is like drinking cold water. I look at you and it is like my throat being cut."

"Get off your knees." Her chest hurt. She felt old, and the wind off the river smelled sweet, but impossible.

"I do not tolerate a world emptied of you. I have tried. For a year I have called every black tree Marya Morevna; I have looked for your face in the patterns of the ice. In the dark, I have pored over the loss of you like pale gold."

"Everyone endures hard things." *I endure them. There was never any choice because it is hard here and hard there. Hardness everywhere.*

"I refuse," he whispered

"No one can refuse."

"Is life here so filled with bliss?"

Marya Morevna sank to her knees, her dress spreading out over the threshold like a pool of blood. She pressed her forehead to Koschei's.

"What about the war?"

"The war is going badly."

Ivanushka, this is my house, whatever the papers say.
Yes.

"My name is Ushanka," said the woman with the blue hatband, smoothing her crisp brown skirt as she seated herself, "and certain irregularities have come to light which I must ask you to make regular, Comrade Morevna. Answer my questions, and you may go about your afternoon as you please. Stroll by the river, make rolls."

Marya sat lightly in a threadbare green chair, wishing she were elsewhere, longing to spring away like a deer. But Ivan Nikolayevich had said that if anyone came asking questions, she had to answer; it was not about wanting or not wanting. "All right."

"I work with your husband; did you know that?"

"No. We do not discuss his work."

"Ah! What a balm is the conduct of a good citizen. Still, I keep returning to these irregularities."

"Oh?" Marya did not move any part of her face. She was better at interrogation games than this woman could ever be.

"Well, surely you admit the *oddness* of a man appearing out of nowhere, after a long absence from duty, and suddenly having a wife where he had none before." Ushanka's smile stretched very wide, very frank, as if they were old friends.

Marya willed her fingers not to fidget. She stared straight ahead. "Surely soldiers often meet women in foreign parts."

"Are you a foreigner, then? Your Russian is excellent." Her pen scratched against her notepad.

"No, no. I was born here, in Leningrad. Before the Revolution, of course."

"Of course. Allow me to ask an obvious question, Comrade Morevna. Forgive me for insulting your intelligence, but it is only my job. Are you, in fact, married to Comrade Ivan Nikolayevich Geroyev?"

Ivanushka, if you break this promise it will be like breaking a very old crystal glass. Nothing will be able to be put right again.
  I understand.

"Come back with me," insisted Koschei. "Hide inside me, as you did before. I will pile such jewels on your lap. Viy can burn this world, if I have you. Already the Chernosvyat is his. Already my country hoists a silver flag. Come with me. I will take out my death and smash it under a hammer and Viy can have us and in his silver country I will fuck you until the end of the world."

Marya brushed his nose with hers, two affectionate beasts.

Koschei the Deathless shut his dark eyes. "I can take you anyway, if you say no."

"I know you can." She felt his words in the basement of her belly.

"But I will not. It would be sweeter to pay him back with the same currency."

"I do not wish to be dragged back and forth between the two of you like a bone between two dogs. You promise the same things, and neither of you delivers."

Ivanushka, it will be difficult for you to keep this promise. You will have to build the keeping of it like a chimney.

Tell me what I must do.

Ushanka leaned forward, putting her notepad aside. She had a long, Byzantine nose with a bump in the middle of it. "We already know, Comrade Morevna. There will be no punishment if you simply admit what is already a matter of public record. It is too late for Geroyev, but no blame need attach to you for this incident."

Marya blinked. "What is it you think you know?"

Ushanka shrugged luxuriously. "Who is to say what I know?

Maybe I know something now that I will not know when I leave. It all depends on you, Comrade."

The queen beyond the sea tried to remember how Naganya liked to play this game. *No, no, Masha! You can't avoid my eyes like that! Then I'll know you're lying! You're doing it wrong! Now, tell me you're innocent, and I'll pretend to pull out your thumbnail.*

"I assure you that whatever you think I have done, I am innocent of it."

"Do you now?" Ushanka tapped an unlit cigarette on her knee. "I am absolutely certain you're right. Do you mind?" Marya Morevna demurred, but the young officer flicked a brass lighter anyway, waving around the terminus of her cigarette. "Which is why you and I can be so convivial. We are just having a conversation in the afternoon, as ladies will. A cup of tea, a cigarette? All these little niceties, and no lies between us. Now, Comrade Geroyev reports that he met you in the vicinity of Irkutsk, near the Mongolian border. Is that correct?"

"That sounds right." She had no idea. Geography was fungible, fluid, unreliable.

"And what brought you to such a distant city, when you say you were born in Leningrad, in this very house? And why have you no traveling papers? No identification? You see, I know you, Comrade Morevna—or is it Geroyev? I notice you did not answer my previous question. Silence, is of course, its own answer, and I will not embarrass you further by repeating myself. You see how quickly we progress!"

Marya smiled faintly.

"Something amusing?"

"You remind me of an old friend, that's all."

Ivanushka, I know you will break your promise.
  I will not.

"Take it," sighed Koschei.

It weighed so heavy in her hand: a black egg, embossed in silver, studded with cold diamonds.

"You rolled this over my back. To soak up my nightmares." Marya stared at it, how it caught the light.

"It is my death. Oh, my volchitsa, don't you see? I have always been in your power. I have always been helpless."

"What about the butcher in Tashkent?"

The corners of Koschei's mouth quirked. "He sends his regards."

Marya turned the egg over in her hands. The diamonds pricked her; blood welled. Down in the dark of her, a door opened. She stood, her eyes blank, imperious, as strange as he had once been. She knew, finally. What she could become.

"Come with me, Koschei."

Ivanushka, do not go down into the basement of this house.
Do not open the door. Do not peer into the lock.
  Is that all?

"Comrade Morevna, allow me to show my cards. When something is amiss in the life of a citizen, it is as though he walks around all day with his shirt inside out. To the casual observer, all may seem normal, but in truth, the natural order of things has been upset. Even if he wears a coat, even if for all the world he appears the picture of a man, something within him is backwards. I

suggest that during his disappearance Comrade Geroyev associ-
ated with antirevolutionary elements, and continues their work
even in the depths of Leningrad."

Marya laughed out loud. "Is that what you think?"

"Either that or you yourself are a spy, having attached yourself
like a lamprey to a good man, and harbor even now—in the attic?
in the basement?—seditious persons of great interest to myself
and those whom I represent. Tell me, Comrade. What would I
find if I looked in your basement right this very moment?"

Ushanka extinguished her cigarette on the windowsill.

Ivanushka, for you, this house has no basement.
I promise, wife.

The basement of the house on Dzerzhinskaya Street stank of
shadow and disuse. Old jars of onions cured into mothballs grew
veils of cobwebs, sharing space with a rusted typewriter, a box of
nails, a dressmaker's form, and three jugs of home-brewed beer
long ago overfermented and burst, even their spilt foam calcified,
crumbling. Koschei wrapped his long arms around Marya's waist,
pressing his cheek to her hair. She squeezed the black egg in her
palm; he moaned into her scalp. She tucked his death into her
dress, between her breasts, where it touched her heart.

"Stand against the wall, Koschei."

Without a word he obeyed her. In the jetsam, Marya Morevna
found, as if by magnetism or divining, what she wanted: a coil of
moldy rope. She stood against Koschei, so much taller than she,
her hips moving against him out of old memory. She lifted one of
his hands, knotted the rope around it, and looped the rest through
an iron ring that once held a hook for the curing of meat.

Koschei the Deathless regarded her knotwork. "That will not hold me. It is a joke. I could breathe on it and it would crumble."

"What proof would it be if you couldn't get out?" said Marya softly, and kissed his pale mouth in the dark, all her child's worship of him seething feverishly back into her. *I need this. I need it. You will not deny me.* She lifted his other graceful hand and bound it, too, pulleying his arms up above his head.

He hung there, tears streaking down his face.

"I love you, Marya."

She laid a finger over his lips.

"There is no need for you to speak, Kostya. There is only one question: Who is to rule? And that is never answered with words. You will not move. You will not try to loosen my knots. You will suffer for me, as I suffered for you. Then I will know that your submission to me is total, and true. That you are worthy of me." Marya Morevna took Koschei's face in her hands and pressed her forehead to his. "We are going to do something extraordinary together, you and I," she whispered. "Do you remember when you said that to me, so long ago? Do you know what it is we are doing? I will tell you, so that later, you cannot say I deceived you. I am taking my will out of you, and I am taking yours with it. Out of the eye of a needle, hidden inside an egg, hidden inside a hen, hidden inside a goose, hidden inside a deer. When we are finished you will give your will to me, and I will keep it safe for you." She smiled, her eyes serenely shut. "I learned very well how to give up my will to my lover. I was a savant, you might say. You, however, are a novice. Less than a novice. And, like a good novice, you must swallow your pride."

Marya drew away, her eyes shining, her blood singing. Then, she turned and walked up the staircase, her red dress trailing behind her on the black steps. She shut the door behind her, and turned the key.

Thank you, Ivanushka. How good you are to me.
That is all I want in the world, to be good to you.

Marya's eyes sparkled with sudden interest, even delight.

"Isn't this fun?" she said, a grin starting on one side of her face and traveling the slow road to the other. It was a game, always a game. And when you were done playing, when you got bored, you just called it off, and went to hunt mushrooms by moonlight.

"Pardon me?" Comrade Ushanka recoiled.

"I do like games. You play so well! Almost like it's all real." Like the acronyms and colors and committees were real, which is to say not at all. All toys; all amusing; all tiresome, eventually.

Ushanka spluttered, clutching her notepad. "I assure you, Comrade—"

"Come play again tomorrow, will you? It's been so *dull*! I feel as though we are friends already! How wonderful, to have friends again." *Get out, get out, get out,* Marya's body hissed, but she kept up her smile.

"I am not finished, Comrade Morevna!"

"Now, now, Ushanochka, it's almost lunch, and nothing is so important it can interfere with lunch!"

Ushanka stopped spluttering. She put down her pen and pad. She folded her hands over them and grinned down wolfishly.

"Yes, Comrade Morevna," she whispered. "It is fun." And she walked calmly to the door, her hand steady and sure on the knob.

When the woman had gone, Marya put her hand to her throat, her heart hammering horribly, sweat prickling in the fine hair of her temples. She watched Ushanka go, down the long, thin street. A loose thread dangled from the hem of her skirt, catching the sunlight.

22

Each of Them Uncatchable

Marya Morevna carried her secret like a child. Her heart grew fat with it, for secrets are the favorite food of the heart. Her life bent in half, and the seam of her life was the floor of the house on Dzerzhinskaya Street, separating her world into upstairs and downstairs, into day and night, into Ivan and Koschei, into gold and bone.

"I swear March has come three times already this year, Kseniya Yefremovna," she said in the morning, putting on her kettle, watching her tea disperse in the water like paint, hushing Sofiya, slicing sausage into a pan. Marya put her hand over her heart, to keep the secret in. Kseniya laughed and said the snow loved Leningrad too well to ever let it go before June. They talked like two young women with young women's cares, and little Sofiya banged a wooden spoon on the table, hollering *mamochka, mamochka* like a whip-poor-will's song.

When Kseniya went to classes, Marya Morevna would take up her iron keys and open the door to the basement. Her secret would swirl up toward her out of the dark, and her heart would lead her down.

"You look older today," she whispered, and pressed her whole body to that of Koschei the Deathless, bound to the wall.

"I have always been old. It is only that you want to see my oldness now."

"If I kissed you, would you become young again?"

"I will always be old."

And the kisses she had of Koschei in the dank, moldering cellar were the sweetest kisses of her life, so sweet her teeth hurt. She lay against him, or struck him with her fists and accused him of taking her girlhood, or took his body as she pleased. Sometimes, when she lifted her hands against him, he smiled so beatifically she thought he had died. But his excitement promised that he had not, and where his seed spilled on the cellar floor, strange blue plants grew. When they opened into flowers, dust trickled out, and the flowers died again. When she questioned this, and why sometimes he had wrinkles now, and sharp teeth, and long, protruding bones, Koschei the Deathless answered, "When do you feel most alive, Marya, but when you are closest to death? That is where I live. That is what my body is made of."

And she rested her head on his chest, so that her long black hair covered his nakedness like a cassock. She whispered, "I think we're finally married, you and I."

When Ivan returned from his work, he, too, often looked older. He ate his cutlets and bread silently, with a sullen kind of savagery, and with a sullen kind of savagery he wrapped Marya up in his body, and kissed all of the skin she had, and cursed her for not having more. These kisses, too, were sweet, so sweet her head spun, and she hurtled between them like a trolley car, up and down, up and down. Marya Morevna carried her smile in her pocket, close to her skin, so no one could steal it. In her mind she pored over her secret, her hoard, as though it were gold. If she went to the market, she sped home to unbutton her winter coat and her blouse and press her breasts to Koschei's lips in the cellar. If Ivan was delayed, she paced and stomped, so that he would hear her pacing and run home to her—but also so Koschei below would know whom she waited for. In those days, of every meat she ate only the tenderest parts.

"Do you like it, Kostya? Hanging here, in the dark, waiting for me?" she asked Koschei the Deathless one day as the square of light from the one tiny cellar window traveled slowly across the floor.

"Yes," Koschei whispered, his eyes rolling back as she kissed his throat and stroked his chest like a favorite cat. "It is new."

"Losing the war, that's new, too, isn't it?"

"Everything is new, volchitsa. There was a revolution, or hadn't you heard?"

To Ivan, she gave exactly seventy kisses each night, and no two kisses the same. She said to him, "Do you remember where I lived before? That we were at war? That I was a soldier?"

Ivan yawned. "All that was so long ago, Mashenka. Like a dream. In fact, some days, I think it was a dream. I'm amazed you remember it at all."

"I can't forget things. They stick to me."

"And what is sticking to you tonight?"

"If there is war here, I think the war there will end. The ghosts will eat everything because the bellies of ghosts want the whole world, just to fill one tiny corner."

Ivan turned on his side beside her, the long, broad lines of him leonine and sated. "I have told you. The war is just so much foreign peacockery. German business. It's nothing to do with us."

In April, the melt held for an entire week. Festivals hummed in the Haymarket, and Kseniya Yefremovna insisted on taking the baby, and Marya, too, to see the balloons.

"Mamochka!" cried Sofiya. "So many!" And she clutched at the sky with her little hands.

As the spring sun wheezed and panted in the sky, they strolled back down the boulevards, each of the women with fried dumplings overflowing with bloody cherries in hand.

"What is that?" said Marya Morevna suddenly. She meant the black house on Decembrists Street that rose up between two everyday apartment buildings.

Kseniya Yefremovna answered her. "It is a house they painted with all sorts of things from fairy tales, so that it would be wonderful and people would bring their children to see it, just as we brought Sofiya today. You can see there a firebird on the door, and Master Grey Wolf on the chimney, and Ivan the Fool scampering over the walls, with Yelena the Bright in his arms, and Baba Yaga running after them, brandishing her spoon. And that's a leshy, creeping in the garden, and a vila and vodyanoy and a domovoi with a red cap. And there—they've put a rusalka near the kitchen window." Kseniya turned to Marya. "And Koschei the Deathless is there, too, near the cellar. You can see him, painted on the foundation stones."

Marya put her hand over her heart.

"Isn't it strange and marvelous, the things people will believe?" said the nursing student.

"Yes," said Marya shakily, and stared at the house, its colors, how everyone painted there seemed to be running, running, chasing each other forever, each of them uncatchable, in a long, chained ring. Tears blurred in her eyes. *Where am I painted? Was I never part of them, those tales, that magic?*

"What I mean to say, of course," said Kseniya softly, "is that I will not go down into the basement. You do not even need to ask me to promise."

Between them, they traded silence for a long while. The sun complained of arthritis, cracking its bones against the bare linden branches. Marya wanted to have a friend again, and sometimes she felt it was so. A living friend, with red cheeks.

"Why do you want to be a nurse, Kseniya Yefremovna?"

"It is better than being a rusalka," Kseniya said, shrugging. Marya wondered at the deliberation with which her friend dropped the word between them. "Why should I not want something better?" she went on. "Doesn't everyone? Don't you? The old order, it is good for the old. A farmer wants his son to be afraid of beautiful women, so that he will not leave home too soon, so he tells a story about how one drowned his brother's cousin's friend in a lake, not because he was a pig who deserved to be drowned, but because beautiful women are bad, and also witches. And it doesn't matter that she didn't ask to be beautiful, or to be born in a lake, or to live forever, or to not know how men breathe until they stop doing it. Well, I do not want to be beautiful, or a woman, or anything. I want to know how men breathe. I want my daughter to be in the Young Pioneers, and grow up to be something important, like a writer or an immunologist, to grow up not even knowing what a rusalka is, because then I will know her world does not in any way resemble one in which farmers tell their sons how bad beautiful women are."

"Sofa will be good," said the child solemnly, and patted her own head.

It so happened that a shipment of peaches arrived from Georgia not long after that. Ivan, Marya, Kseniya, and the baby sat at the kitchen table near the brick stove, which still crackled and glowed away—for the melt had not stayed, but had given up its maidenhood to another snowstorm, and another after that. They all stared at the slightly overripe peaches, their fuzz, their green leaves still jutting out from the stems. The peaches looked like summer to each of them, like summer and sunlight and rain.

"It is because I arrested a man skimming from his workers that we have these peaches before anyone else in Leningrad," said Ivan Nikolayevich.

"Why would they give them to you?" asked Marya Morevna, turning one over in her hands.

"Because I am good at arresting. It is an art, you know. The trick is to arrest them before they have done anything wrong. That's the best thing for everyone."

Marya looked at him out of the corner of her eye. What a disturbing creature a man is. "What I mean is: Even with the investigation into your affairs, they're giving you peaches?"

Ivan's voice rose sharply. "What investigation? Has someone been to the house?"

"Comrade Ushanka, who works with you. She asked how we met." She had guessed he did not know. Comrade Ushanka had a secret, too, and Marya knew it, though she could not guess what it was. Like knows like.

Ivan relaxed, rolling his head over his shoulders to pop the bones. "Well, that's a relief. You're mistaken, Masha. There is no Ushanka in my office. Nor in any other office in the city. It is my business to know. I think your brain wants work. Perhaps you have had enough time lying about idly, hm?"

Kseniya bit into her peach, and the juice sprayed up in a sugary stream. The sound of her bite cut their conversation in two. All of them fell to the golden peaches, and soon they had slurped them up, every one. The pits lay strewn across the table like hard red bullets.

Save the one peach Marya Morevna closed up in her skirt. She brought it to Koschei in the basement, when all the house slept. She showed him her breasts and fed him one piece of peach for every lie he confessed to her.

I told you I didn't care that you kissed the leshy.

I told you a shield lay between you and Viy.

I told you there were no rules.

I told you there was a difference between your world and mine.

I told you I couldn't die.

And on that day, as Marya Morevna walked back up the steps into her other life, a glint of silver caught her eye. She dug in the black dust of the cellar, her fingernails pulling up chunks of the earthen floor until she had it: Svetlana Tikhonovna's old hairbrush, boar's bristles still stiff, silver still bright. And as she held it up in her hands, half-frozen muck crumbling from her fingers, the shadows hanging in the basement stitched themselves one to the other until old widow Likho stood there, just the same as Marya remembered, her black spine bent flat by the ceiling. She rubbed her long fingers over her knuckles and peered at Koschei with a smirk.

"Brother, girls are no good for you, you know that," she said, her voice dragging across the floor as it always had.

"I hang here of my own will," Koschei said. "She will release me of hers."

"I wouldn't," cackled Likho. "Never, never."

"You are meant to be elsewhere, are you not, Sister? Carrying out my program, my orders, are you not? Did I not make provisions for my absence, and were you not one of them?" Koschei's eyes flared hatred at her; the air between them arced and bent.

"Oh, but I *had* to come! I had to come and watch! I can hardly think of worse luck, you know. Worse timing. *Tscha!* Of all the cities, Marya, of all the years! It brings tears to these old eyes. My spleen is so proud. You follow in your old teacher's footsteps after all."

Likho reached out her long, skeletal hand and pinched Marya's cheek, her smile stretching all the way around her face. Marya recoiled. She did not understand. She did not want to. Her place had been invaded, her secret meant only to hold two. She wanted to crush Likho down into that black hound and kick her.

From somewhere far off, the sound of an air raid siren wound up and spooled out over the city, and the street, and the cellar.

23

A War Story Is a Black Space

Look, I am holding up my two hands, and between them is Leningrad. I am holding up my two hands and between them is a black space where Marya Morevna is not speaking. She would like to, because she thinks a story is like a treasure, and can belong to only one dragon. But I make her share; I will not let her have the whole thing. I have this power. I will not let her speak because I love her, and when you love someone you do not make them tell war stories. A war story is a black space. On the one side is before and on the other side is after, and what is inside belongs only to the dead. Besides, what happened between the two hands I am holding up is squeezed between the pages of the books of the dead, which are written on my hands, because I died in that space where Marya Morevna is not speaking. And now it is all clear, and now you understand.

For storytelling, a domovaya is always better than a human because she will not try to make a miserable thing less miserable so that a boy sitting at his grandmother's knee can nod and say, *The war was very terrible, wasn't it, Babushka? But it is all right because some people lived and went on to be good and have children.* I spit on that boy because he thinks only of his own interest, which is that he should be born. Miserable means miserable. What can you do? You live through it, or you die. Living is best, but if you can't live, well, life is like that, sometimes. So now I stop everything, and I say it is time for the dead to talk with the dead, and Zvonok has the floor, if there is a floor left to have.

For a long time nothing changed, except that Ivan the Fool and Yelena the Bright finally escaped Baba Yaga because the black house on which they were painted was hit with a shell and burned down. That is an excellent strategy for escaping her, really, and maybe the only one, if you are a Fool. But the house burned down and red clouds fell like curtains over the whole city, not from the house of fairy tales, but from the granaries, where so much bread and butter and sugar burned up that later babushkas made cakes out of the scorched earth. Everything smelled like burning grease. When the red clouds that were like curtains lifted, Leningrad began to perform something very dreadful, but no one noticed yet.

It took a whole day for the house of fairy tales to burn. People came out to take turns looking at it.

Marya Morevna did not take a turn at looking. She took a turn at staring out the window, which she is very good at. Guns make horrible sounds, like a punching in the sky, and I heard the sound of the guns go through Marya and leave her burning down, like the house. She looked out the window because she was afraid that Leningrad was going to start dying, like Buyan did, and she was right, but she was also wrong. Like I told you, nothing had changed yet, except that we could all hear the guns, all the time—first sirens, then guns, and then no sirens anymore because there were so many guns the sirens could not keep up.

The houses of Leningrad inventoried themselves on the double. They said, *How long?* And their larders said to their cellars, *Not long.*

Papers fell from the sky between snowflakes. They clogged the chimneys, and in the street young girls would pick them up and start crying, uncontrollably, like someone turned on a switch in them and jammed it so that it could never be turned off again. The papers said, *Women of Leningrad, go to the baths. Put on your white dresses. Eat funeral dishes. Lie down in your coffins and prepare for death. We will turn the sky blue with bombs.*

Marya never cried. There was a switch in her, too, and it was also jammed.

Ivan Nikolayevich punched his rage like dough. It rose up and he hollered all day. "Marya, you have no papers! How can I get you a ration card? What devil can you be that you have no identification? I was a fool, a fool to take you into my house. You will make a criminal of me!"

"This is *my* house," said Marya Morevna quietly.

They were both wrong. It is *my* house. But I let them fight over it because he is a fool and she is a devil like me, and what is the world but a boxing ring where fools and devils put up their fists?

A ration card says, *This much life we have allotted you.* It says, *This much death we can keep from your door. But no more.* It says, *In Leningrad there is only so much life to go around.* It says, *The only thing not rationed in Leningrad is death.*

But he got her a full set of papers, didn't he? And don't think I didn't see the marriage certificate in the pile. The ink was still wet when he brought them home and threw them at her. Marya, when I said I would choose another for you, he was not what I meant.

"You have made me a forger," he spat at her. "You have made me a malfeasant. Every time you eat your bread you should think, *I owe this to Ivan Nikolayevich, who overlooks my wickedness.*"

Marya Morevna listened to him with only one of her ears. *In both marriage and war you must cut up the things people say like a cake, and eat only what you can stomach,* she said to me later. Look who is so wise now, I said, and she answered, *To have two husbands, I must be four times as clever.*

Of course I knew about the basement. Nothing can happen in the corners of my corners that I do not know about. I creep as I have always crept, through the walls, the floors, in the spaces where my comrades used to meet as we raised glasses of our best paint thinner to the Revolution, our Revolution. I saw every kiss on every floor. Some of them were good kisses. Some were so-so. I've seen a lot of kissing, so I am a good judge. You might think a domovaya knows only about her own house. But a city is only a lot of houses put together, so don't be closed-minded.

For an example, Marya Morevna left the house every morning and came home exhausted every night. Kseniya went with her, and Sofiya, toddling like a furry baby pig in a coat too big for her. Ivan came home angry to the dark house with no pancakes cooking, only a bit of slimy juniper brandy in a dirty cup. But the houses all knew where the women went, and not just the women of my house. They got pails full up of whitewash, and painted over every number they could find, every address, every street sign. Leningrad had no names anymore, like an infant city who does not know what she will look like when she grows up. They did this in case the Germans came crawling in, which the Germans are good at, having lots of practice at behaving like animals. Better that they should get lost, and we should not. I approved of this. The labyrinth is, after all, a devil's trick. Devils know only good tricks.

For a while, the bread was bread and the butter was butter.

I believe that Marya Morevna saw him come first, for Marya saw as a devil sees. I heard her cry out of the left side of her mouth as she sat by the window—and all of us saw General Frost step over the Neva. All of us held our breath and snapped our fingers to keep off his eye. His shoes were straw and rags; his beard was all hard snow. He had no hat, but his skull had chilblains, and his great blue-black hands held the double chain of his dogs, December and January. How they bite, with those teeth! Old Zvonok does not make up stories to frighten you. Ask anyone, and you will be told that Russia's greatest military man is General Frost. He whips our enemies with ice and freezes their guns in their paws and sends out his dogs. On the breast of General Frost hang more medals than icicles. Should you ever be so lonely and un-lucky as to be a soldier in Russia—may some unbusy god preserve and keep you!—you may see him. Hold your left hand over your right eye, put a lump of snow in your mouth, and crouch in a trench all night without sleeping, and you may spy him wandering through the drifts, laying his hand on German heads and turning their helmets to death masks.

But, alas for us, General Frost was blinded in his youth. An oily rag he wears over his useless eyes, and the old man is just as happy to gobble up Russian souls as the Hun, as anyone else. It makes no difference to his big stomach. He blunders, the old god does, and his dogs get off the leash, yapping away into the dark.

No one could get out. Nothing could get in. Winter's bitch dogs got hold of the ration cards, and shook them until they broke in half, and then in half again.

What does a domovaya eat, you ask? Sure as sin she doesn't line up at the bread store for her crusts, equally divided two million ways? No. I eat ash, and embers, and the sweet, hot stuff of the stove. When everyone finally puts their sleep together, I make my ash-pies and my ember-cutlets and eat until my lips get all smeary with fire. When I was young, and only courting an apartment or two, I could not believe humans ate the fuel and not the fire. Who cares about cakes? I had no use for meat, except to keep the fire hot. But when you are old and married you learn to tolerate unbalanced foreign customs. So what I am saying is that at first it was not so bad for me. At the end of the bread there was ash enough. I thought, *Tscha! Zvonok can live through this!*

But still, the papers kept falling. They made drifts, like snow in the streets. *Beat the Kommissars. Their mugs beg to be smashed in. Just wait till the full moon! Bayonets in the earth. Surrender.* At least the Germans hire good writers, yes? But no one cried over the messages anymore. They reached up their hands to catch the papers before they fell and got wet, to use for fuel.

I had three conversations before the New Year which were all the same conversation. I will tell you about them.

The first one was with Kseniya Yefremovna, whom I could never startle, no matter how I tried. I stood on the stove bricks and got my feet warm while she fried some flour in fish oil for Sofiya. Hard to remember now, that in the beginning of it all we still had real flour, and real fish oil!

Why don't you get out, eh, rusalka? I said to Kseniya Yefremovna. Why do you hang around like you're one of them? Marya throws herself into the pot with these others, and who knows why crazy women do what crazy women do, but why don't you go hop in Lake Lagoda and wait it all out?

Because it is not my lake, Comrade Zvonok, Kseniya Yefremovna said to me. *I would bounce off the surface just like a skipping stone.*

Then go to your lake, I said. I am smarter than all of them sealed in a jar together.

Instead of answering, Kseniya Yefremovna picked up an ember with her bare fingers. She held it up to her eye; her wet fingers popped and steamed, and then she handed it down to me. I chewed it while Sofiya chewed her pancake and the snow came down outside. The charcoal squeaked on my teeth.

I am not a rusalka anymore.

I spat to show her what I thought of that.

I am a Leningrader now. And so is Sofiya, and we will survive because of our strong backs, not because once, before the war, we were rusalki. No one is now what they were before the war.

To the furnace with her. I don't care. What are tenants? Temporary. Might as well mourn cheese.

When General Frost had a foothold in every house, and the pipes froze like sausages, and Marya Morevna chopped a hole in the river every morning to lug water back to the house for soup—but also, secretly, for Kseniya's and Sofiya's hair—I marched down into the basement on account of the very witless situation going on down there. I did not like to see my Papa Koschei like that, with his moldy rope over his head and wearing three layers of Ivan Nikolayevich's coats for warmth.

Papa, I said to my Papa, why do you not burst out of this place and take Marya Morevna with you? Even the pupils of her eyes are skin and bones. Can you not see it?

I see it, domovaya, my Papa said to me.

And do you see your brother the Tsar of Water outside, stomping on the streets, setting his dogs on old women? For so General Frost's family calls him, on formal occasions.

I see him. But I bound myself. I used her as a chain. I cannot unbind myself. I cannot use her as a key.

Well, what a lazy husband you turned out to be, old cock-wit! Zvonok learned boldness from a boiler, and does not always profit from it.

I am not Koschei the Deathless anymore.

I spat to show him what I thought of that.

After love, no one is what they were before.

When the bread was only half bread, because the other half was birch bark, and the butter half butter, because the other half was linseed oil, I went to Marya Morevna, who every day stared at the gun under her bed like it was a cross.

I could go to the front and fight, said my girl to me. *Then I would get a double ration. But what of my two husbands, then?*

Why should the wolf worry about the safety of the sheep? I said to my girl. If my hand were bigger I would whap you one. Grab Koschei by the horns and hang the rest of us!

I cannot leave Ivan Nikolayevich. Or Kseniya or baby Sofiya. Or you.

If you want to kill yourself, do not use us as your knife.

I think I could make a kind of biscuit out of paint, and turpentine, for frying, said my Marya, and scraped some paint off the wall with her fingernail.

I spat to show her what I thought of that.

When you are this hungry, you cannot even remember who you used to be, she whispered. *Who you might have been, if not for the hunger.*

That night, she burned all the books in the attic for heat. She carried them down, one by one, because December ate up her strength. She lit them in the stove while they all huddled around and put out their hands. Last one in was the Pushkin, and she cried, but without tears, because you cannot have tears without bread.

"I will remember these books for you," said Ivan Nikolayevich, because he did love her, even if it was beef-love: stupid and tough and overcooked. "I will recite them to you whenever you want to read."

I ate the ashes, slowly, to make them last. I put out my hands with the rest of them. Outside, the wind and the guns went on and on.

After the pipes, the lights went off, like a throat being cut. Ah, I felt it in my shins! My poor house, his bowels frozen, his heart beating only every other beat! I coughed blood when the electricity went black.

Marya Morevna did a secret thing. I will tell you about it. Every morning when the dark kicked up dark outside the windows, she sat down at the table and pulled out an apple from the pocket of her coat. She cut it in half. Half she gave to Ivan Nikolayevich before he went to work at the arrest factory; half she gave to Kseniya Yefremovna, who gave half of that to Sofiya. Every morning the apple burned so bright in her skinny white hands. Redder than red. She kept a few slivers of the core, like chicken bones, and before the stars could get all the way around the sky, the apple would swell up again, just as whole as before. Made Zvonok wish she ate apples, it did. Marya never said anything. They ate it like people used to eat communion. Not chewing. Letting it melt. She just held out the halves like the halves of a heart, and even when little Sofiya started forgetting her words, even half-blind in her frozen cradle, she still reached out for her bit of apple at that hour of the morning.

That is not the secret thing. I saw that every day. The secret thing I saw only once. After the apple, when they finally let her alone, Marya went down to the basement. My Papa got skinny, too, but of course, of all of us, he couldn't die from ugly and starving. He looked at her, and oh, if a house had ever looked at me like that, even bound up on the wall like poultry, I'd have never spoken to a human in all my days. Marya started sniffing and shaking, and her face broke up into pieces. Her shoulders fell, like when she was little and her mother was in a punishing mood. She was crying, not out of her eyes but out of her hungry bones.

Papa Koschei closed his eyes. A wound opened up on his neck just like a kiss. Redder than red. No knife, no anything. Blood dribbled out; and down in the basement, with me hiding under the staircase, Marya Morevna put her mouth on Koschei and drank like a baby, worse than a baby, her face all smeared with it. She kept on with her dry, shuddering crying the whole time.

Finally, the bread wasn't bread at all and the butter wasn't butter, because the bread was cottonseed cake and paper and dust, and the butter was wallpaper paste, and you still had to hold up a ration card to get a scrap of the stuff. Dust cakes, dust tarts, dust bread that didn't even rise. Nobody had anything to burn because if you could burn it, you could eat it, and a fire does a dead man no service. So no embers for a poor domovaya, and her house also sick. Still, I thought, *Tscha! Zvonok can live through this*. I will tell you how we made soup in those days: Hold a ration card over a pot of boiling water for thirty minutes, so that the shadow of the card falls on the broth. Then eat it up, and don't you dare spill a drop.

Once, Ivan Nikolayevich came home in his leather coat. The leather coat meant he had been busy arresting people. He went up to his bed and found Marya Morevna on it. Both of them were just sticks, sticks from old trees. He wrapped her up in his arms and their bones knocked together. He petted her hair like a cat. Long pieces of it came away in his hand. Ivan would not tell her what was wrong, but I knew because I could put my ear to the roof and hear the other houses say, *There is meat in the Haymarket,*

*and it is for sale. A fat old woman sells it. She wears a leather apron
and a black fur coat; her cart has strange wheels, like claws. She has
cutlets, dozens, dozens. For pearls she sells it, for watches, for rubles, for
boots. Where did she get it all? Only a fool questions good meat.*

Send a boy back to me with some, I told the domovoi I know in
Maklin Prospekt.

You do not want this meat, he said to me.

I said back, Sofiya must have meat now or she will die, and this
house cannot bear even one death or they will all start in on it.

So a boy arrived with two cutlets, for which I left a diamond
necklace I swiped from Svetlana Tikhonovna years back. The boy
didn't like it one bit, but he took the necklace and left the meat.
Kseniya Yefremovna shook her head.

I know what this is.

So do I. You're not human. What difference does it make?

You cannot argue good sense. She fried it in a pan, and the
house smelled very rich with it. Sofiya ate it all, every scrap, and
paid us back with a small laugh. Fair trade, thought the both of us,
and I had an ember out of it all. That was the night Ivan Nikolayevich wore his leather coat.

What could I do? Miserable means miserable.

When Sofiya died, Kseniya Yefremovna and Marya Morevna
wrapped her in sheets and put her on her little yellow sled. They
pulled her onto the road, and each of them left their hearts on the
doorstep. Everyone else was pulling sleds, too. There were more
sleds than snow. Sometimes, a wife would pull her husband to the
cemetery, frozen as a pipe, and she'd die pulling him, so neither of
them got where they were going, but they both did. Because of the
ice nothing smelled, but everywhere stopped sleds grew mounds

of snow like hair. I sat on Sofiya's tummy as they pulled. A house makes a family, and they were mine. My last family.

Nobody talked. They breathed into their scarves and lugged and lugged. But no one was left to bury anyone else, so people just left the sleds in a pile by the cemetery gate. That's where we left Sofiya, with Kseniya lying over her like a flower, with snow piling up on her hair. I said them a domovoi's mass, but no one heard me because grief is louder than praying.

By the window that night, Marya Morevna said to me, *I think I have finally found my home, for everyone I love is here.*

Close up your head; your brain is getting loose.

Koschei is below me, and Ivan above. And out in the snow, everything has gone silver, and there is Madame Lebedeva making jelly with her lipstick, and Zemlehyed minding the linden trees, and Naganya down on the frozen river, pouring gasoline into her mouth so her trigger does not freeze. And you, and Kseniya Yefremovna, and little Sofiya. We are all together, at last.

I looked out the window where she had looked for months stitched back to back. And there in the dark glowed silver wounds in the street where another Leningrad bled through: another Neva, another Dzerzhinskaya Street, all splashed with silver. And there walked a woman with swan feathers in her hair, vanishing around a corner; and there walked a short, fat creature with dead leaves on his head; and there walked a woman like a gun. And there walked Kseniya, too, her chest stained and shimmering, holding baby Sofiya's hand as the child jumped and tried to catch the silver balloons drifting just out of her reach.

Mamochka, she cried. *So many!*

In the middle of them all came walking like a kommissar a man with eyelids so long they brushed the snow out of his path, wearing a silver brocade and a silver crown. And as we watched, the

Tsar of Death lifted up his eyelids like skirts and began to dance in the streets of Leningrad.

The shoulder blades of Marya Morevna touched behind her back, and the knees of Ivan Nikolayevich banged together in front of his belly. Icicles grew inside the house. Together they pulled down the wallpaper to get at the paste, and then they boiled the wallpaper to make bread. They were all mouth and bone, and their eyes slipped gears whenever they tried to meet. They ate their bread with paisley and flowers on the crust, and smeared paste on it like butter. Bread had never been bread, and butter had never been butter. They could not remember such things.

"The Germans have printed invitations to a gala ball at the Hotel Astoria," Ivan Nikolayevich whispered, as though anyone but me might overhear him. "They will serve whole pigs, and a hundred thousand potatoes, and a cake that weighs five hundred pounds. I have seen the invitation myself. Embossed in gold ink, with a red ribbon. They say, 'Leningrad is empty. We are only waiting for the crows to tidy things up a bit before the party.'"

I don't believe you, said my Marya. She is so stubborn her heart has an argument with her head every time it wants to beat. I know. I raised her, I did.

When you are hungry, a whisper is a shout. "Whore! I will let them have you, and they will roast you on a spit with their suckling pig. What do you keep in the basement?"

You promised, Ivanushka.

"Fuck your promises. You are keeping food from me down there, I know it. Devil bitch. Kulak goat-wife."

You promised, Ivanushka.

"Promises to the devil's woman are no promises! No court would hold me! You are hoarding food, and you put a spell on me, in Irkutsk! Why else would I want a sack like you?"

I hid behind the stove. Marriage bears few witnesses.

You are going to break your promise. I understand. And I hold my hands over the ears of my heart, so that I will not hate you.

When you are hungry, a step is a shove. Ivan hobbled to the basement door, and, well, he was a fool. Hasn't he always been? You can't blame a fool for his thick head. Why else was he born, but to blunder and buffoon and once a year make a black-haired girl laugh? Look, I am holding up my two hands, and between them is the old, dear house on Dzerzhinskaya Street, and between them is Marya Morevna and her husband, mad with hunger like a cow, and between them is Koschei the Deathless looking up from the darkness. He is smiling down there, and his smile has two edges.

"Who's down there?" Ivan said, though he knew already.

I am so thirsty, Comrade.

"Who is it?" Ivan peered down, his eyes searching for pickled eggs, for cherry preserves, for a jug of beer, for every good thing a cellar might have.

I am so hungry, Comrade.

And Ivan went down because he was a fool, and because it could not be only Koschei she kept from him. All winter he had tortured himself with dreams of the food she was hiding, and it must be there, it must, or else he was worse than a fool.

Will you not give me a little water, Ivan Nikolayevich? Koschei said.

Ivan's dry body could not weep, so he borrowed on the tears of his future, so that Koschei could see his grief, and there could be no confusion.

"Why can't you leave us alone? Get out, get out, old man; leave us in peace."

I would be glad to, only I am so weak. No one should relent just because my Papa smiles.

So the fool loosened Koschei's ropes, and gave him water from a filthy, half-frozen puddle. Marya Morevna watched it all from the top of the stairs, and her black hair hung all around her; and I was there, so I saw him roar up toward her, and I can tell you now that she looked at the two of them with crow's eyes and said, *Yes, Kostya. Take me. Take me.*

And then we were left alone together, Ivan Nikolayevich and I, in the frozen, dank cellar.

I spat to show him what I thought of that.

Old Zvonok died because her house died. That's what married means.

They'd all left us already, all of them, some more than once, and if a domovaya ever showed her tears, it wasn't me. What else can you say? Everyone died. Kseniya Yefremovna died. Sofiya Artyomovna died. Even Ivan Nikolayevich died, by spring. Only Zvonok was left, and then not her, either. A German shell hit us and left the house on our right and the house on our left still standing. Well, that's what happens to things you love.

I walk in the other Leningrad now. The silver one, the one with teeth. The one Marya and I saw out of the window on the coldest night of winter.

And here, in the other house on the other Dzerzhinskaya Street, Kseniya Yefremovna still makes soup out of ration-card shadows, but now it tastes thick, and marrowy, and sweet. And I drink it down with the rest of them and it runs into my mustache instead of into my mouth, but my soul is drunk and sated.

PART 5

Birds of Joy and Sorrow

Will you not say to me once more
That word which conquers death
And answers the riddle of my life?

—Anna Akhmatova

24

Nine Shades of Gold

Marya's black book lies open on the floor of the cellar where she no longer stands. Very slowly, mold grows in the spine, crawling out over the words, reading softly, greenly, to itself.

A ptarmigan lays a speckled, tea-colored egg; a moorhen leaves behind her a white egg spattered with red, as if with blood. By the egg, you may guess at the bird.

The Tsar of Birds, despite being a Tsar and not a Tsaritsa, is not wholly eggless. Speckled with jewels are his eggs, copper and chartreuse and turquoise, enameled in jet, painted with scenes of dancing girls and sunsets behind churches. And from this, child, you may guess that Alkonost is a bird of impossibly many colors, possessing a soul so rich and fecund that he cannot help lay eggs. Anything which passes through him emerges streaked with grace. Alkonost's long tail lashes and whips, possessing feathers of indigo, fuchsia, and nine shades of gold. His broad, downy chest flashes six hues of white; his talons shine green, his claws pearl. Above his bird's body, his human face floats beardless and exquisite, his hair bright as coins beneath his crown. All these things you could tell from his egg, if you could but see it.

Once, Alkonost hatched a daughter. He named her Gamayun. Like her father, she saw the future and the past projected onto her eyelids like two film reels running together. Like her father, she preferred to be alone, the company of her own eggs being preferable to that of her extended family. Together, father and daughter chose the meditations and quietude of the sky over the worries of the earth. They knew how it would all come out already, you see.

Once, because it is not possible to possess so many colors and also a hard heart, Alkonost pitied his brother, the Tsar of Life.

"You are so fragile, Brother, and often in despair. At any moment, Death might take you."

"Tscha!" said the Tsar of Life. "Life is like that."

Alkonost, his azure tail feathers waving in the wind, embraced his brother with infinite succor and love, which he had learned from the clouds, which they had learned from the sun. His glittering wings opened around the Tsar of Life like the doors of a church, and when Alkonost withdrew his wingspan, they lay together in his nest, which rests so high in the mountains that the air turns to light and the light turns to air. The Tsar of Birds thatched his nest from the braids of firstborn daughters, and its softness knows no equal. Into these ropes of gold and black and red and brown the great bird laid his brother and fed him like a chick, retching his own sweet meals into the mouth of the Tsar of Life.

Much time passed, and secret things only brothers may speak of. And all the while Alkonost tended an egg in secret, holding it beneath the feathers that covered his ankles. The egg began from his pity for the Tsar of Life. It swelled with each passing day. And each day the Tsar of Life cried out in agony, clutching his chest.

"Brother," he wept, "my heart is being cut in two. I cannot bear it."

"Tscha!" said the Tsar of Birds. "Life is like that."

As the egg neared its time, Alkonost could conceal it no further. It shone huge and black in the light that was air and the air that was light, studded with cold, colorless diamonds. Alkonost did not love it, for it bore more of his brother's countenance than his own. When it hatched, the two brothers peered over the shattered, starry rim of the shell to see what waited inside the thing that they had made together. Once they had seen it, they agreed to seal up the egg again and conceal it beneath their hearts, never to let it be found, to the extent of both their powers. A ptarmigan could not seal up a hatched egg. Alkonost can.

The voice of the Tsar of Birds is so sweet that should he wish it, anyone hearing him would forget the whole of her life, even her name. Of course, she must wish it. But should Alkonost speak with the smallest kindness, the littlest mercy, the richness of his voice would sweep away any sorrow in any heart, and leave there instead only the perfect world *that might have been, if only the world had not invented hearts in the first place. For this reason, some folk stuff their ears with wax. Some seek out the bird of heaven all their days, praying to be drowned in him. Each of these cannot comprehend what drives the other. How can you want to lose yourself, your history, your name? How can you run from the voice of God? But of course, no amount of seeking will find Alkonost, and no amount of hiding will avoid him.*

Life is like that.

25

Gross Desertion

t the end of a long, thin road lies the village of Yaichka. Pale gold larch trees close it in as tightly as a wall, and in the autumn, the mist touches the ground only on Sundays. Much rich-smelling smoke from well-made chimneys and aged, crisp wood rises up to the very clear night stars, which look like nails in a strong, black roof. Wolves howl in the forest, but are never seen. Thick, new straw is piled high on every roof; green onion shoots poke out of every kitchen garden. Yaichka possesses several fields whose soil forgives all offenses; four horses; ten head of cattle; two hens and a rooster for every family; three sheep (one pregnant); a solitary goat who has a passion for onion shoots; and a small river, so small it forgot its own name, but which neverthe- less allows for Yaichka to possess one mill. A liking for meat keeps these numbers pleasantly accurate. Rain comes only when every-one has shut their doors as tight as they can; snow falls only after each man has chopped all the logs he needs.

No one ever leaves Yaichka—what is out there to want? And no one ever visits from out of town. In the village they have a saying, *Yaichka possesses many things, but the forest possesses Yaichka.*

Among the other things Yaichka possesses is a short, wide house where Marya Morevna lives with her husband. She has al-ways lived here, and never anywhere else. One other thing Yaichka owns is the secret sight of Marya lying naked in the summer for-est, drying her black curls in the sun. On Thursdays and Mon-days she briefly touches the ring of iron keys hanging over her hearth, but cannot remember what they might unlock. Then she takes out one of the four horses—her favorite, a dapple grey named Volchya—and gallops into the larch forest so fast her heart flies out ahead of her. With her rifle on her back and her best red scarf knotted around her shoulders, she hunts in the depths of the shad-ows, crouching, chasing, firing—and on Thursdays and Mondays her peals of laughter are the Yaichka's church bells. She returns with deer or rabbits, pheasant or goose, sometimes, mysteriously, a wolf flopped over Volchya's broad back, one of those who howls but is not seen. Marya Morevna shares her meat with her village. No one likes wolf soup much, but they do not complain. Marya does not complain when her hens forget to give her eggs. Life is like that.

Marya Morevna's husband, Koschei Bessmertny, is so hand-some that he could lend a cup of his beauty to every man in Yaichka and still charm the bark from his dogs. Wheat falls into loaves at his feet, but also at the feet of his friends, and all of Yaichka is friends with Koschei Bessmertny. When he bends to pull beets out of the earth, he sings a little song with four lines of five words each, and the last word of the song is *wife*. When his cow catches pregnant, he offers the calf to the family with the fewest cows, and the milking heifer to the family with the most children. Of the goat he says nothing, and lets him go on his onion-hunting way. Sometimes, in a certain light, he seems to recall to Marya someone she used to know, and could almost remember: a kind of golden cast to his black hair, a way he had of laughing, like a hound baying.

Once, Marya Morevna woke and saw someone working the fields before Yaichka had washed the dreams from its eyes. The someone wore a bright coat of many colors, and cut grain with an enormous pair of shears.

"Who is that?" she asked of her husband.

"Do not look at him, volchitsa," said the handsome Koschei. "Let him take his share."

Marya Morevna thought no more of it, kissed both of her husband's sunburned cheeks, and rode into the wood after two fat beavers with tails like pancakes. When she returned to Koschei Bessmertny in the evening, being held by him was like being held by the sun, and together they relished the pale god of the butter on their bread.

On Marya's left-hand side lives Vladimir Ilyich and his wife Nadya Konstantinovna, whose hens have such good memories they never forget an egg. Nadya's scowl is so severe even winter leaves her well enough alone. Vladimir has gone bald and needs glasses, but he broke his comb over his knee and made his peace with God long ago. Around that time old Vova fell asleep with his new glasses on and was visited by a dream involving an army of red ants and an army of white ants. Somehow this led him to gather together the four Yaichkans who owned horses and devise the system of horse-shares which provides both for Marya's hunting expeditions and for the equitable tilling of Yaichka's several fields.

In his youth, a smaller Vladimir encountered a beautiful jackdaw with a red blaze on her chest. The bird snapped savagely at him, and ever since then the boy has possessed a gift for convincing people of strange things. Once, he declared to his neighbors that the tall, beautiful roses that climbed the walls of his house grew unjustly, so that they received both theirs and the lilacs' share of the rain. The roses were corrupt, he said, and both Aleksandr Fyodorovich and Grigory Yevseevich listened sympathetically over cups of sweet myod. The roses are vicious by their nature, Nadya agreed, and scowled so fiercely that the myod spilled immediately, in order to absolve itself of any involvement. Vladimir Ilyich tried to encourage the lilacs to take the rain for themselves, going so far as to hang buckets from his eaves and distribute the water himself, sprinkling it evenly among the flowers with his long, thin fingers. But this did not suffice.

"What is to be done?" he demanded. "What is to be done?"

And one morning the village of Yaichka woke, and the heads of Vova's roses had all been hacked off at the neck.

Vladimir and Nadya have two sons under their roof, Josef and Leon. They dream boys' dreams: of getting a slice of their father's fortune, of girls, of growing big mustaches. Several jokes concerning the brothers buzz through Yaichka, for one never hugged the other without making his hands into fists. Josef has chased Leon into the woods many times, red in the face, bellowing for his brother never to return. But of course, around dinner, Lyova slinks back, and Josef embraces him as if nothing was amiss. Leon, for his part, scowls in his room and breaks his toys to show them who their master is. After the incident with Vladimir's roses, Josef stomped upon all the flowers of the garden—lilac, rose, peony, daisy, and even his mother's flowerless savories, mint and dill and thyme. He stood in the middle of all his destruction, panting, his dark eyes wild as a kicked horse, looking to his father for praise.

"You are my favorite son," said Vladimir Ilyich to Josef, which is all the boy ever wished to hear. "And so I forgive you for the flowers."

This made the child smile, but did not really shine up his disposition. One spring day, as fine as a cake, the boy marched straight up to the very kindly Sergei Mironovich and shot him with finger pistols: *pow, pow!* The two stared at each other in the muddy, fragrant road of Yaichka, as if remembering something that happened long ago.

"Lyova did it!" cried Josef, frightened by Sergei's silence, and ran off to hit his brother soundly. So it goes with Josef. Every village has one.

On Marya's right-hand side lives Georgy Konstantinovich, who sits out on his steps and plays his birchwood gusli so prettily that the moon faints away from love, and whose wife Galina Ivanova has a lamb's modesty. Everything in Georgy's house proceeds with perfect precision. Even the eggs boil when he says so, and not a moment sooner. The bees in his garden sup only at the flowers he likes best. When the wolves in the forest howl, Georgy wakes up and stands watch with his daughters all in a line, their rifles on their shoulders, and it cannot be disproven that this is why wolves are heard but not seen. Georgy is more modest, even, than his wife. He would never say that he saves Yaichka each night with his strong antiwolf posture, but his neighbors say it for him, and bring to him and his girls hot tea and slices of pie wrapped in muslin when the cold snaps. Georgy herds the cows as well, for they recognize his authority, and proceed in formation into their pen without argument.

Now, just down the way lives Nikolai Aleksandrovich and his long-haired wife Aleksandra Fedorovna. Before their open door play their four beautiful daughters—Olga, Tatiana, Maria, and Anastasia—and their sickly young son, Aleksey, who sits in the shade of a poplar and reads while his sisters kick pine cones between them on the green. Nikolai himself is a bit dim and distracted, but his mustache is thick, and he means very well, even if his garden half dies every winter for lack of water, even if his cow screams to be milked every so often, and he does not hear her. Vladimir Ilyich once tried to discuss his doctrine of roses and lilacs with Nikolai, who gave him a cup of kvass and listened intently. The sun passed behind a cloud. But Nikolai Aleksandrovich only laughed and sent old Vova on his way, his sympathies being rather with the roses. Aleksandra, her apron embroidered with a moth's delicacy, her arms muscled from arguing with sheep, once told Marya Morevna that her husband was visited by the same dream as his neighbor, of the white ants and the red, and had wept in his sleep for weeks. She kisses Nikolai's knuckles, where dreams live, until he quiets, but then she herself cannot sleep, and watches the stars spell out the words of a long poem from the warmth of her bed.

Many more folk bustle and quarrel and clap their hands over their ears in Yaichka. That is what villages are like. All day long, this or that grandmother could tell tales that stretch on like taffy concerning Vova's plans for the distribution of the pregnant sheep's lamb, or Josef's somewhat more worrying plans for the goat, and they wouldn't have even begun to recount the rumors of Aleksandra's infidelity with a certain monk, let alone remember to name half the folk in Yaichka. That is what grandmothers are like. Cows moan in the grass; hens flutter when the rooster happens by; the earth turns blackly, wetly under plows; and for a while, just a little while, everything shines and nothing is the matter, anywhere, ever.

Yaichka has always been here, and never anywhere else. It has always possessed these people; their four horses; ten head of cattle;

two hens and a rooster for every family; three sheep (one pregnant); the small and nameless river and its mill, owned by everyone and worked on a biweekly schedule designed by you-know-who;
the solitary goat who would stop eating up everyone's onions if he
knew what's good for him; and several fields whose deep, dark soil
forgives everything done to it.

26

What Will We Call Her?

In the house of Marya Morevna, even the windows laugh. Long after the winter hearth has gone dark, the bodies of Marya and her husband glow. He is so alive in her that his skin tastes like an apple tree, full of sap and juice. *The warmth of him*, she thinks, *the warmth!*

"Oh, volchitsa," he whispers to her, his belly brimming with soup and good bread, "I've a dog's luck! Butter in the barrel, a good smoke after supper, and you, my bootlace girl, drawn up so tight to me!"

"When you said that just now, I almost thought you were some-one else," sighs Marya. But Koschei is always himself, perfectly so, whole and bright.

And he sets on her like the sun, and all her teeth show when she smiles. Each day she looks at the iron keys hanging by their door, and tries to think: *Where have I seen those before? When have I had a thing I needed to lock?* And each day, unless it is Sunday and the mist is down and all of Yaichka staying in, she shakes her head to gather it and strides out onto the long, thin road. Each morning, Marya Morevna thinks that she has never been so full, and each evening she is fuller still. Her black curls shine as if seen underwater.

On Wednesdays, Ushanka visits, her friend whom those old grandmothers most likely forgot to name, since she is the kind of girl who shows only half of her face at a time. No one knows her surname, but that's all right. Surnames go politely unmentioned in Yaichka. Marya Morevna always makes sure she has a leg of rabbit and fresh bread with a little bowl of honey set out, and Wednesday is her day with the silver samovar that makes the rounds of all the houses, just like a horse.

"And how is your husband?" says Ushanka, a beautiful blue ribbon fluttering from the scalloped edge of her lace hat. Ushanka makes lace like a spider, and gives her shawls freely to the women of Yaichka. Just yesterday, gentle Galka pulled one up around her shoulders, feeling a draft.

"He feels sure the new calf will be a heifer, and so go to Aleksandr Fyodorovich. I've discussed the prospect of juniper-cheese with Natasha."

"How lovely for all of us. And you, Masha? Are you well? Do the ladies visit when I am not about? Do the men let you drink with them when you're thirsty?"

Marya Morevna puts her chin in her hands. "I believe I have never been so well, Ushanochka. I am so well that my glass fills before I think to be thirsty. To be certain, I am sad when the moon is thin. I remember friends long gone, and how one of them painted her eyes to match her soup, and how one slept curled next to me, and another kissed me, just once, by a river. I remember one with wet hair, and her baby. I wish they could drink from full glasses, too. I wish they could see the new lamb when it comes. But the moon waxes, and my sadness dries up. Life is like that, of course."

"Of course." And Ushanka puts her hand on Marya's, for they have shared tea more often than tears. Her skin is like cloth. "The sweetness of it all is sharpest when placed alongside sorrow, close as knife and fork. But it is my job to interrogate your happiness, to prod its corners, to make sure it holds. When a sadness chews at the bottom of your heart, it's as though you walk all day with your dress on backwards, the buttons facing the forest, the collar facing the village. To everyone else, all may seem normal, but my eyes are so keen."

Marya Morevna poured tea, coppery and steaming. "I have sometimes wished for a child," she confessed. "But when I ask Koschei about it, even while he tells me he loves me with a bear's love, he says, 'Can we not wait a little longer? Just a little longer.' Isn't that strange?"

Ushanka shows only half of her face, and that half grows very thoughtful, but says nothing.

"I saw the bird again while hunting this rabbit," says Marya brightly, picking at the gleaming bone. "So terribly bright it could have been on fire! I think it's a male. His feathers shine golden, and bronze, and scarlet, and blue—such flames!—and the air around him bends into oily waves. His song echoes like Georgy's playing. A firebird, just like in the old stories. I shall catch it, Ushanka, if I have to ride all the way through the forest and come out the other side."

"What other side?" says Ushanka, showing the other half of her face. "You've been listening to Josef's silly insinuations. There is

only Yaichka, and you, and I, and Sasha's juniper-cheese, and rabbit with bread on Wednesdays."

That afternoon, Marya Morevna goes to the well after Yaichka
has shaken off the dust of the day and sees someone working the
fields. The someone wears a bright hat of many colors, and cuts
grain with an enormous pair of shears.

"Who is that?" she asks of her husband, just returning, his
hands all bloody with the afterbirth of the new calf.

"Do not look at him, volchitsa," says the handsome Koschei.
"Let him take his share."

Aleksandra Fedorovna—who ought to know, having five of her
own—once told Marya that a woman knows it when the night
passes and leaves her with a child.

"They tap you, Masha. Like a root."

"Oh, I don't believe you, Sasha! How can you feel such a tiny
thing?"

The beautiful Aleksandra shrugged. "When you are cut, you feel
it, even if the cut is tiny. Such a thing is a child, a wound within."

When the perverse moon pries through their windows, spying
round the curtains, Marya does not feel it, but her handsome husband does. Koschei Bessmertny winds his red limbs in hers, as
young as young, and shatters inside her, the shards of him floating
free in her body, until one, sharp-edged and cruel, lodges in her
and will not be moved, stubborn thing. In the guttering stove-
light he lays his head on her belly.

"And death shall have no dominion over her," he whispers, and
kisses her navel.

"What a thing to say!" Marya moves her fingers in his shaggy hair. "Someone else said that to me, once, so long ago I cannot remember. Sometimes you seem to me to be two men: my Kostya and another I cannot quite recall, all squeezed into one body."

Koschei looks up at her. The whites of his eyes show. "Nothing wants to die," he says faintly, and Marya Morevna does not understand, because she has seen so few dark things.

"What will we call her?" Koschei says, and smiles the best smile he has learned, so golden and hot that Marya thinks of the bird in the forest, the one that eludes her still, and turns the air to oil.

"Who?"

"Our daughter, who already knows your name."

Koschei Bessmertny will not sleep for nine months. He gives all his sleep to his daughter. It is her due.

Does magic number among the things Yaichka possesses, along with the river without a name and the pregnant sheep? One day, the old man Grigory Yefimovich decided to settle the question once and for all. He tells all the children he was once a priest, but everyone knows there is nothing before or after Yaichka, or alongside it, or underneath it, and only stars above it, so old Grisha seems mysterious and wise to them indeed. Nevertheless, all the folk of Yaichka entertain him, for he tells wonderful stories, knows how to deliver babies, and tugs on his beard when he lies, and thus can be relied upon utterly, so long as he leaves his beard alone. "I saw a star in his hair," whispered little Olga Nikolayevna, Aleksandra's daughter, and she was generally believed.

To settle the question of Yaichkan magic, Grisha took Aleksandra Fedorovna, whose hair was like gold wire, to the exact place where the larch forest meets the edge of Sergei Mironovich's medicinal garden. He stood with one boot in the wood and one boot in the village—magicians know the import of such stances, and Grisha certainly knew the import of knowing what a magician should know.

"Now, Sasha, watch me eat this mushroom with silver spots on it, which you and all your children know has a terrible poison."

Aleksandra watched carefully. Grigory Yefimovich chewed it up. Nothing ill seemed to happen. His limbs did not seize up; his tongue did not turn purple.

"Do you see?" said Grisha.

"I see," said Sasha.

"Now, watch me hang myself from the larch. Give me your apron to throttle myself."

Aleksandra watched carefully. Grigory wound the apron around his neck and hung himself from the tree. Nothing ill seemed to happen. He smiled pleasantly and swung back and forth for a while. His eyeballs did not burst; he did not sputter a final confession while choking.

"Do you see?" said Grisha.

"I see," said Sasha.

"Now, you must shoot me, for the final proof." And the old not-really-a-priest produced a small pistol—which, if Aleksandra had thought about it, was entirely the most magical thing to happen that afternoon, as no one in Yaichka had ever produced a pistol before.

Aleksandra shot carefully. Her bullet entered his heart exactly as every bullet dreams of doing. Blood seeped out of Grisha's shirt, which he had gotten from Galina Ivanova in exchange for a tale about a great warrior who defended a city against soldiers with faces like rats. Galina had nightmares for weeks, and called it a good trade. But then, Grigory Yefimovich smiled and showed Aleksandra that his breast was whole, with the same scraggly hairs still on it as had been before. He took the pistol back and no one ever saw it again. Sasha did not tell anyone that Grisha had ever had it, or that she herself now knew what a pistol was, and had fired it as easily as rolling out dough for vereniki.

"I will tell you the magic of Yaichka, Sasha. Death has forgotten Yaichka, and knows nothing of it."

"Surely not. Everything dies. The cows, the sheep. Marya shoots her deer."

"Can you remember any *person* dying?"

Aleksandra was silent for a long while. The sky got blue and depthless. "I seem to, in my heart. In a part of my heart locked up behind the farthest, smallest room of my heart. Under that lock is a place with a dirt floor where it is always winter. There I seem to think that someone has died, and no one helped them. Then I weep so bitterly that horrible flowers grow from my tears."

Grigory Yefimovich put his long, rough arms around Aleksandra Fedorovna, whom he had loved secretly since he was young. She knew it, of course, and because of both of them knowing a thing like that, they treated each other with a very tender kindness.

"Never mind, Sasha," said Grisha. "It was only a trick I can do. Don't cry."

On Fridays, Marya Morevna goes to the fields to cut grain. In Yaichka, the grain always sighs to be cut. Even six months along, she does not shirk, but takes up a short scythe, its handle well worn by all the hands of Yaichka, all those oils, all that skin. The sun polishes the tips of the trees and turns Marya's black hair blue. Up she raises the scythe and down again, and the blade knocks back the golden stalks, and the solitary goat bleats ecstasy as he discovers a patch of wild onion no one will scold him for devouring; and up sings the scythe and down again, and lovely little Anastasia Nikolayevna drops a stitch in her knitting, and Volchya the dapple grey deliberately throws a shoe so that Marya will have to tend to him later, because he is that sort of beast; and the grain falls in a pile, a cairn, and six mice that Yaichka does not know it possesses wash each other's ears with pink tongues; and up she swings her blade and down she swings it low, and without knowing why, the women of Yaichka go to the exact place where the well-tilled field whose soil forgives them all meets Nadya Konstantinovna's radishes, and they watch Marya without understanding why it is they came to watch a pregnant woman with a belly like a bow drawn back all the way, her scythe raised like a sword, slicing down again and again, and the clean sweat dampening her hair as the sun sings a little song with four lines of five words each, and the last word of the song is *death*.

It is Thursday, and Marya is too big around to ride Volchya into the larch forest. She walks instead, her long red woolen dress trailing behind her, her black hair almost as long as her dress, her rifle strapped to her back. The leaves pose at the exact moment before they should fall, but do not. Tiny birds like scraps of bark fly up in whorls behind her. The smell of the forest pricks at her cheeks, brightening them, kissing them. She holds her belly with her right arm—she is sure that Mars in all its mountains could not be so huge as she.

"If I could talk to you, Daughter, I would say, We made you when our eyes were at their darkest, when the solitary goat was full of onion, and the moon looked just like an egg. I would say, Who will you be when you are grown? I would say, What will we call you?"

Behind a copse of seven birches, a thing rustles. The leaves crisp and spark under the feet of the thing, and smoke wisps up. A streak of orange winks out of the birch trunks, and Marya cannot run, really, but she can hold still as a house. Inside her, her daughter moves, pushes her tiny hand against her mother, her tiny foot against the eggshell of her world. *I want it, Mama,* the hand says. *The beautiful bird,* the foot says. One step forward, through the leaves, then another, and there it shines: the bird's long, long tail, shaming any peacock ever born, dragging along the forest floor like a red dress burning.

Marya Morevna hoists her rifle. She loves her rifle. Someone made a present of it to her, though she cannot remember who, or when. It is warm from her hands. The bird rears up, flapping his wings, sending sparks into the air, smoke, and the bird is burning, burning, so white and gold Marya sees spots dancing around her eyes. Her daughter stretches out her tiny arms inside her. *Mama,* the arms say, *the light!* When she fires, the child in her belly surges downward, as though she means to be born right now, right this very moment.

In all of Yaichka, no one can beat the firing arm of Marya Morevna. The bullet collides with the firebird like a child leaping up into her papa's arms when he comes home after a long journey. The bird stumbles backwards against the birches, trapped by their trunks. He lifts up his eyes to the sky and Marya clutches her belly; but there are tears floating like naphtha in the firebird's eyes, there is a song in his mouth like blood; and the sound hurts her, pulls at her, plucks the bones of her ribs like gusli strings. The tips of his wings blaze like blue gaslights. *Allee, allai!* the bird ululates; Marya hears a beckoning in it, like a calling to prayer. *Allee, allai!*

Mama, the light! Marya steps into the ring of the firebird's flames. He does not burn her, nor is he wounded, no more than Grisha was wounded by Sasha's pistol. His eyes grow huge, crimson, spinning; his wings fold around her, drawing her close in, his tears dripping wax on her head, but he does not burn her any more than she killed him, and together they fall to the forest floor in each other's arms—*allee, allai!*

"What does it mean?" whispers Marya in the embrace of the firebird. He smells of burning bread, and butter, and sugar, boiling down into the earth.

"It means I forgive you," he sings to her, "for the last time you killed me, and this time, too, and forever and forever, until death."

Inside the body of Marya Morevna, her daughter grows very quiet, and listens to the sound of the firebird's impossible, enormous heart beating slowly, sounding so much like her mother's, so much like her own.

Marya Morevna returns to Yaichka empty-handed, but that is all right. Shame is for other villages, other women. There is still so much, even without firebird soup. She says nothing of the bird in the forest, and no one asks. On Monday, Marya Morevna caught two beavers (and their tails) as well as a young boar with one broken tusk. Tonight, with the help of her handsome husband and Nikolai Aleksandrovich (whose mustache sweats prettily), she lugs their great wedding table out into the middle of the village, where the red leaves of autumn already skip and blow, bright and sharp as stars. She boils a stew of onions and potatoes and mushrooms with glistening lumps of those pancake-tails floating in the broth. She roasts the pig over a great fire. Georgy Konstantinovich brings fish he caught yesterday through stealth and planning; Grigory Yevseevich brings a basket of apples redder than the leaves. Vladimir and Nadya Konstantinovna contributed a store of honey smelling faintly of their long-vanished roses. Nikolai brought vodka from his own still, just as clear as rain. The children run around the table, pelting each other with leaves, their laughter rising up to the sky like smoke. Little Anastasia and Aleksey dance together to Georgy's gusli, and Josef pinches all of them savagely under the table.

Around the great table all the people of Yaichka rise and hold up their glasses.

"Nastrovye!" cry Georgy and Aleksandr; cry Grigory and Sergei; cry Josef and Leon; cries Koschei Bessmertny; cry all four of Aleksandra's beautiful daughters and their brother, too; cry Grisha and Sasha; cry Nikolai and Vladimir. The setting sun shines through their glasses.

"To life," they say, and crash their glasses together, laughing, as wolves howl distantly from the forest, but never show themselves.

And Marya cries out, too. She clutches her great belly as her child protests the hunt and the lugging of the table and the drinking without her. The child sears through her, ready at last to be born, right now, right this very moment. Marya Morevna falls to her knees, her hair spreading out around her, as black as if it has been burnt.

27

The Sound of Remembering

In Yaichka, they say a child draws her first breath through her ears, her second through her eyes, and her third through her mouth. This is why it sometimes takes a moment for a baby to cry. The first breath is for the mother, the second breath is for God, and the third breath is for the father. The breath through the mouth brings the most pleasure, and we forget immediately that we ever knew how to breathe any other way. When a child in Yaichka cries, his mother will pick him up and hoist him on her hip and laugh and say, *Look at my little bearlet, breathing through his eyes again!* And the child stops his crying because he likes to be called a bearlet.

Marya and Koschei's daughter takes her first breath through her ears, like any other child. The breath makes a tiny whistling sound, too high for even dogs to hear.

Then she grows up.

It happens so fast even the cabinets turn their heads twice. Marya Morevna puts her child to her breast; she latches just as perfectly as any child has ever done, and with one long drink, the baby takes all the milk of her youth into her belly and stands up seventeen years old, naked, with her mother's blood still sticky in her black hair.

Koschei Bessmertny smiles so sadly Marya puts her hand over her heart as though a bullet had bit her there.

"But you have been happy here," he says softly. "You have been happy here with me?"

"Kostya, why are you so sad?" says Marya, and she is perplexed, but not upset, for a daughter grown up so fast is strange and a little tragic, but not less strange than a firebird. "Help me name our girl!"

Koschei looks long at his child. The girl takes her second breath, through her eyes. It makes no sound at all. "She has a name already, volchitsa, my love, my terrible wolf. She is my death. And I love her abjectly, as a father must."

Death, their daughter, who will never learn to speak, who will never need to speak, holds out her bloody arms, streaked white and silver with fluid.

"I always die at the end," he whispers, and he is afraid now, his hands shaking. "It is always like this. It is never easy."

The iron keys on the wall bead blood as though they are sweating. Marya stretches out her hands, and she is a mirror of her daughter, but she does not know whom she wishes to catch, only that she wishes to catch someone, anyone, to be anchored, to be connected, to be not abandoned.

But Koschei the Deathless steps into his daughter's embrace and holds her, gently, tenderly, proudly, for a moment, smoothing her wet hair with his hand before kissing her forehead as perfectly as any father has ever done. She opens her mouth and takes her third breath, wholly, fully, through her mouth, the last trickles of the water of her mother's womb spilling from her lips. The force of her third breath drags Koschei's eyelids down, down, down, until they droop, and fall like scrolls unfurling to the floor; and he is become his brother, the Tsar of Death, for a tiny silver moment no larger than the prick of a pin. He lifts his eyelids with one arm to see Marya Morevna one last time, lifting them over his daughter's shoulders; and beneath the lids and lashes there is only light, more and endless light, silver as water, pouring out of him; and suddenly they are both gone and there is a bird in the room, a bird both like and unlike Marya's firebird; and Marya's belly is flat and firm as though she were never full of daughter, and she is not in bed, but standing in a corner of her house in Yaichka, in the dark, and all is grey and cold except the bird, the bird staring at her with a human face.

"Sit down, Marya Morevna," says the bird, and his voice is like Georgy's gusli. "I am going to tell you everything that ever happened to you. Come on, then, find your knees."

Marya sits without knowing if a chair will catch her. But of course one does; this is Yaichka, where she cannot fall. Her face thins and hollows even as she stares at the bird, his feathers of indigo, fuchsia, and nine shades of gold, so bright in the freezing black house, so bright beside her drained body.

"Do you know where you are, Mashenka?" The bird cocks his head, his exquisitely beautiful face tender, his sorrowful eyes like an icon.

Marya Morevna stares dully out the window. The grass there freezes slightly at the tips of the blades.

"Do you remember when Koschei gave you his egg? How black it was, how silver?"

Marya Morevna puts her head in her hands. Her hair shrivels up. Her tears freeze slightly, falling to the floor with tiny shatterings.

The Tsar of Birds shakes his coppery green chest feathers. Beneath his wings human arms reach out to her, their fingers slender, perfect, soft as down. He lifts her cheeks up and kisses her, his mouth the color of blood, hers the color of ash, and in his kiss her gentle tears become harsh sobs, her whole body racked with them, her bones stretching to let more darkness in. Her lips peel back from her chattering teeth, and even they grieve, but still he kisses her, kisses her until she is screaming.

"I remember, I remember," Marya weeps, and Alkonost wraps his flawless arms around her, and his turquoise-and-golden wings around them both. In the dark, she disappears into his iridescent embrace.

"I laid that egg, Masha, poor child. Every egg must be laid; otherwise they cannot live. I laid Koschei's egg long ago, far away, up high in the air, and when we saw what was in it we swore to each other never to open it again. But brothers are built for breaking promises. Do you know what was in it?"

"His death."

Alkonost strokes her hair with his human hand. "Well, yes, obviously. But an egg has a rooster and a hen both. The way a child has her mother's impressive nose, her father's sloping eyes; the way you could spend your whole life watching a person, picking out the parts of her which owe to her mother, the parts which are copied from her father. Our egg had a death from him, a beautiful death, compact, perfect, terrible. From me it had Yaichka. You have lived all this time within my egg, Marya, within my world. Oh, I know! How can you believe me? So many people, so many seasons, and the forest, and the firebird flashing between the birches! Even I did not understand it at first. I am a bird of prophecy, but no future I have ever seen contains Yaichka, hanging in it like a jewel. The trouble with prophecy is that it is alive. Like a small bear. It can get angry, frustrated, hungry. It can lick and bite and claw; it can be dear; it can be vicious. No one prophesies. You can only pursue prophecy. So perhaps my little bear was playing a trick on me, yes? I pored over this egg long after my brother left me to pursue war and girls, which are his particular obsessions. I pored over it and tried to understand what Koschei and I had made together. Do you know, Masha, how revelation comes? Like death. So sudden, though you knew all along it must occur. A revelation is always the end of something. It might even be cause for grief."

The Tsar of Birds kisses Marya's forehead, clucks over her like a mother.

"You told him to take you away, do you remember?"

Inside her heart, Leningrad opens up from a single, almost vanished point, growing bigger and colder and whiter, and a hunger begins in Marya, a hunger barely remembered, that chews at her like a worm and will not be satisfied. She groans against Alkonost, a groan so heavy, like iron crumpling. The warmth of his heart radiates out like a star in her arms.

"Yes, that is the sound of remembering," sighs Alkonost, and his plumes flush violet. "Koschei brought you to me. You were so near death that ghosts crowded around you, weeping silver tears, waiting for you with such smiles. You humans, you know, whoever built you sewed irony into your sinews. Sometimes, when a person has starved nearly to nothing, feeding them will hurt them worse than starving did, and push them the rest of the way over into dead. My brother wanted to show you his houses again, and feed you sweet things, and put into your ashen mouth a slice of thick bread with roe shining on it like rubies. He wanted to sink you in steaming water, and brush your hair, and make you well. But he could not. You were too far gone. So instead he and I held you between us and I fed you, I fed you like a chick. I chewed up clouds and starlight and the rind of the moon and vomited them back into you, the most wholesome food we have known since the youth of the world—it could not hurt you, not ever. And you opened your eyes. And I, more fool me, nuzzled you as I would a chick, and whispered nonsense in your ear, as chicks love to hear: *Allee, allai!* I should have known, but the little bear of prophecy was wicked that day. I spoke, and my speaking swept everything from your heart, and you vanished like a record skipping, and where you had been was the egg. The ghosts wailed for the loss of you, and my brother wailed, too. With his nails he clawed open the egg to climb after you, and I was suddenly alone in my nest with all abandoning me. And I understood, like revelation, like death. The place in the egg, Yaichka, is a very elaborate place, a place to hide a death from its owner, and also to lead him to it. It is a perfect world, a world which could not survive outside the jeweled egg of Alkonost and Koschei, no matter how many permutations of this story the world might cycle through. (For of course you know the world tries on this story over and over, trying to make it work out differently, trying to make it perfect as an egg.) The world that is left behind when you forget what sorrow looks like, and death, too. A prophetic world that can never come true."

The Tsar of Birds wipes Marya's tears, but more replace them, and his feathers darken with salt.

"Mashenka, his death was hidden in the depths of Yaichka, and you were the path to it, as life is always the path to death. Here, he could be yours, he could be whole, both Koschei and Ivan, devil and man, powerful and weak, dark and gold. You could be the girl you might have been, if you had never seen the birds. If you had never had your scarf stolen. And if he did not want to die, all he had to do was never touch you once, never get on you the child he cannot have in the real world, for he is the Tsar of Life, and death always looks like a child—the end and only purpose of an animal body. But of course it ended as it always ends. Life is like that.

Who in a perfect world does not demand their lover, forever de-lighted? Oh, Marya Morevna! Do you know how the church-folk call me, me and my daughter Gamayun, when they paint us on their ceilings? They call us archangels, and say that we live in heaven, where no vine of sorrow or memory grows. That is where I sent you, not to heaven—*tscha!* I know nothing of that place. But to a place like the ceiling of a church."

"Why didn't he take me out again, to Buyan, where he could still be deathless?"

Alkonost sighed, and his sigh moved the strands of her hair like a winter wind. "Buyan is gone, Marya. Didn't you know? The war is over."

"Is that why the iron key bleeds?" Marya whispered, hiding her face in his feathers. If only she could stay there in his wings and forget again. Again and again.

"No, child. Those are the keys to your own house, and they bleed because in that house Ivan is dying, and he is alone."

28

I Saw a Rook in the Ruins

Marya Morevna spun like a spool; she had the peculiar feeling of a huge hand pressing down on the crown of her skull, of her ribs being squeezed as they had so long ago, when a domovoi showed her the world behind the stove. She felt herself shrink down, fold up, all the golden light of Yaichka going out within her like luchina, the lit coal at the tip of a pine needle when no candle can be found. Her legs sucked in again, skinnier than branches; her arms hung down weak and light; her tongue so thirsty, so terribly thirsty and thick in her mouth. And she feared she would never be big again, never full, never warm. She hung in the dark like that, small, skinny, ragged. She put her shoulder to the dark, pushing, pushing, pushing as she had when Koschei's death had been born.

Mama, the light!

The dark gave; Marya Morevna stepped out from behind the old stove into her kitchen. Snow sifted down off of the bricks—a shell had taken out half the roof, and flakes drifted down from splintered rafters. The rose tiles lay burst and shattered over the floor like broken dishes. Ice coated the iron pans in blue; pipes had burst and wet everything—the cabinets, the table, the chair where Sofiya used to sit. Marya's knees nearly buckled as the memory of Sofiya cracked open inside her. The table was still set for someone to eat. Snow filled all the bowls like soup.

"Ivan?" Marya called softly. She felt as though she had not used her voice in years. How does one measure the time spent inside an egg? "Ivanushka?"

Wind answered, blowing blackly through the rooms. The house was boarded up with silence. Marya crept up the stairs, afraid to find him, a skeleton still wondering where his wife had gone. "Oh, Ivanushka, where are you?"

The roof upstairs had held, but their bed was frosted in silver, furry with ice. The linens lay wrecked in forlorn hillocks and heaps. Frozen dust speckled the bedknobs. Finally, Marya whispered, "Zvonok?"

And the domovaya tugged at Marya Morevna's trousers. Marya looked down, her black hair spilling over her shoulder like a curious shadow. Her friend stood there, stooped almost in half, her beautiful golden hair straggled and grey, her mustache falling out, her clothes torn and tattered. She wore no shoes, her toes chilblained and sore. Zvonok's cheeks stood out like knives; her eyes flared yellow, starveling and feral.

"He's there," growled Zvonok, her voice scratched and ugly with disuse. Marya knew hers sounded much the same. The domovaya pointed to the frosted bed, and Marya saw how the hillocks were shaped something like a man.

"Zvonok, what's happened to you?"

"The house is sick, so I am sick. All the houses are sick. Everyone is dying. The winter will never end."

Marya shut her eyes. "What year is it? How long have I been gone?"

"Nineteen forty-two. It is February. If such things still existed, it would be the end of Lent now. But of course they don't, even though we fasted so well this year. So well we could be mistaken for pious. I think that's funny. Isn't it funny? Last week a man held a concert at Glinka Hall. Snow fell in through the broken roof the whole time, piling up on the oboist's head. The air raid sirens played, too. We all listened from the roofs. Like cats. But not like cats. There are no cats left in Leningrad. Ivan said, *If only we could eat violin music.* I kissed his thumbnail. He said he was glad of me. Then he crawled into that bed, and I don't know if he's dead or not, but I will be, soon, I think. I wonder how Comrade Chainik has fared? Old Chairman Venik? I would like to think they are fat, still. I remember what it was like to be fat. Wonderful, it was. You could roll them down the hall like marbles. Those were days I wish I could eat now, but remembering is like eating, don't you think? Gobble up the past to keep warm. I hope it was warm, where you were."

Marya Morevna lay down on the frozen floor of the house on Dzerzhinskaya Street, the house on Gorokhovaya Street. Zvonok crept into the crook of her neck, near her ear, where the blood flows so close to the skin, where warmth stays when it is gone from everywhere else. She kissed her there, and held her arms wide to embrace the whole of Marya's face.

"Where were you?" the domovaya whispered. "Where did you go?"

And then she vanished, arms outspread, melting away like vapor. Marya stood up, her mind expecting her Yaichkan body to respond, young and full and strong. But her Leningrad body answered, creaking, wizened, brittle. She limped to the bed, not wanting to see what lay beneath the frosted covers, to pull back the blankets and find herself too late for anything, useless to both her husbands, in the end.

"Ivanushka, are you alive? Are you awake?"

From under the linens, a moan, tapering into a rattling breath, then a cough. "Leave me alone, Zvonok. Don't, not today. Don't pretend to be her."

"It is me, Ivanushka, it is me. Come out; look."

A hand rose out of the bed: blackened around the fingernails, fingers shrunken into claws with huge knuckles, grey as the frost. It could not be Ivan's, not Ivan, always so warm, always so big. His eyes peered up at her, sunken and old, the same starveling, feral flame in them that the domovaya had. He was so thin, so thin she could not imagine how he still lived. But somehow, Marya Morevna felt that she saw him naked for the first time, the intimacy of his bones showing through his skin, his helplessness. He was beautiful, still. She felt as though she looked at him from a long way off, through a telescope, at the bottom of a well. *Bounce up,* she thought. Bounce up and become Ivan again.

"Oh," he rasped, "oh."

"I do not know if I ought to say I am sorry," Marya said, putting her hand gingerly on his head, on his matted hair. "It seems too small a thing to say."

"I will say it," Ivan whispered. "I was harsh with you. You did not make me a criminal. I should not have said such a thing. In fact, when I forged our wedding certificate, I was so happy to write your name beside mine, so happy to hold in my hands evidence of us, something to carry between us, this falsified document which told the truth even while it lied. I'm sorry, Masha. I should not have said half again the things I said."

"Hush, Ivanushka. It doesn't matter." It didn't. She had said cruel things in both her marriages. She had never begrudged him his share of barbed words. Marya lifted him into her arms—he weighed so little, so little, and if her muscles were shrunken and battered, still they remembered Yaichka, still they remembered being strong. In her grey arms she wrapped her grey boy, and the snow fell outside without sound, and no one talked on the streets or played guitars, and no one came to any door looking for any girl in any window. Leningrad lay so empty, as empty as an old bed.

"Masha, do you know, I tried so hard to find you!" Ivan coughed, and Marya wiped his mouth a little, but her hand only opened up the pink sores there.

"Don't speak, my love. Talking isn't worth the strain." *And I cannot bear to hear how loyal you were. Do not tell me.*

Ivan rasped; his throat rattled like stones in a jar. "Talking is the only thing I can do! I cannot take you in my arms, or kiss you, or make love to you as one should to a wife who has returned after a long journey. I cannot make you understand that I forgive you, that I know you loved both he and I, the way a mother can love two sons. And no one should be judged for loving more than they ought, only for loving not enough, which was my crime. After all, I took you from him to begin with, so I cannot begrudge him taking you from me—" Marya Morevna tried to protest, to absolve him or herself or both. But he looked at her with eyes leached of color and tried to lift his hand to hush her. "Oh, don't interrupt, Masha! If I stop I shall never start again. I know I did not take you and he did not take you. I thought that for a long while, but you chose me, and then you chose him, and choosing is hard—one choice is never the end of the story. Gamayun told me this was all a story, and I had to be sure to love you, or else it would not work out as it should. He needn't have worried: In the space of one heartbeat to another I loved you and I was lost to you, like one of

those dead soldiers made of cloth. And I have had such a long
time to think about it, Marya! Such a long time to lie in the basement in the ropes that held him and wish that they had held me,
because that would have meant you wanted me enough to keep me
secret, the way I wanted you, and kept you secret." Ivan rested his
ashen hand on her arm. It was so dry, so light. She could feel his
bones, as she had once felt Koschei's bones beneath his skin. "But
do you know, after you disappeared—I had forgotten you could do
that—and after they cut the rations again, and then again, I
thought, *Why did she stay so long?* And that was comforting, because you must have stayed for me. Don't answer. I don't want to
be corrected. But do you know, I looked for you? All over the city,
over thrice nine districts, thrice nine prospekts. I asked everyone
for news of you. I went to Maklin Prospekt, to Decembrists Street,
where that house you liked used to stand, the one with all the
paintings on it? It burned down, did you know?"

"Yes, I knew."

"Zvonok cried when she saw it. But I went to that house and I
saw bits of the paintings in the rubble: golden like a girl's hair, like
chicken legs; and red like a firebird; and green, where the coat of
Ivan the Fool once was. And I laughed because of course I am Ivan
the Fool, of course I am. Only a fool is so innocent as to think he
can measure up to a woman's first love, can measure up to deathless.
You know, it's like when the Tsar was killed. I think maybe Russia
had two husbands, too, and one was rich and one was poor, one old
and one young, and the poor husband shot the rich husband in the
chest, and all his daughters, too. He was braver than I am."

Ivan shut his eyes. His brow furrowed as though he might like
to cry, but had no strength for it. "I went to the house on Decembrists Street, and I saw a rook in the ruins, just as black as if he'd
been burnt himself. I looked at the rook and he looked at me, and
I thought I had never seen such a big bird, so fat, such a sheen on

him, like a duke among rooks. Even before we ate all the birds we could shoot, I had never seen one with such a sharp glance for me. My stomach said, *I'll have that bird.* But my heart said, *There are few enough fat and beautiful things left in this city.* And you were not there, not in the rubble, not in the snow. I walked home, but as I walked the rook followed me, hopping from stoop to stoop, flying down the dead power lines, his sharp glance bouncing off the roof tiles and down and down to me. When I turned back onto Dzerzhinskaya Street and touched the door of our own house, the rook flapped his wings and spoke to me from the branch of the cherry tree.

"'Give me something of hers,' he squawked. 'And I will help you.'

"All I could think of was the red dress I bought you so long ago. It hung in the closet; it still held your shape. I pressed my face into it, but your smell had gone. I fed it, inch by inch, out the window, and the rook took it with his curved beak.

"'Forget her forever, that is my help,' he squawked. 'But if you cannot, let me keep the dress. She is my family. I will look on it and remember her. It would not be the first time some good has come from remembering.'

"I did not want to, Masha, but I gave him the dress. He turned up his black throat to the sky and choked it down until the fluttering red sash disappeared into his mouth. Then he flew away."

Ivan stroked Marya's arm thoughtfully. His skin rasped against her; they were both wrung down to nothing. Well matched, finally. "Still, I looked for you. All over the city, over thrice nine districts, thrice nine prospekts. I asked even the corpses for news of you. I went to the Haymarket, where we heard of that awful woman selling pies, do you remember? She is gone now. Other people sell the same horrible pink pies, and their faces are so heavy and full—heavier and fuller than mine, anyway—and I don't want to tell you if I bought their meat. Don't ask me. But I went to the Haymarket and I saw the pie-sellers, and the boot-sellers, and the bread-sellers. They wanted six hundred rubles for a hunk of bread that was mostly sawdust. Today it's probably a thousand. Still, I wanted that sawdust bread. My mouth moved as if I were already eating it. A few months ago barkers hollered in the Haymarket, and people brought strands of pearls to trade for bread. Now everyone stands still and lets the snow pile up on their shoulders and they are so quiet. Either you can buy it or you can't. They haven't the strength to haggle.

"I saw a plover in the market, just as brown as if he'd been baked out of sawdust himself. I looked at the plover and he looked at me, and I thought I had never seen such a big bird, so fat, such a sheen on his white chest, like a baron among plovers. Even before we ate all the birds we could catch, I had never seen one with such a keen gaze for me. My stomach said, *I'll have that bird.* But my heart said, *There are few enough keen and shining things left in this city.* And you were not there, not in the market, not in the ice. I walked home, but as I walked the plover followed me, hopping from stoop to stoop, flying down the dead power lines, his keen gaze bouncing off the roof tiles and down and down to me. When I turned back onto Dzerzhinskaya Street and touched the door of our own house, the plover flapped his wings and spoke to me from the branch of the cherry tree.

"'Give me something of hers,' he squawked. 'And I will help you.'

"All I could think of was the silver hairbrush you loved so well, so long ago. It sat in a drawer in your dresser; it still held a few strands of your dear black hair. I brushed it through my own hair, so that our curls could take comfort in one another. I passed it out the window, and the rook took it with his short beak. The weight of it nearly toppled him.

"'Forget her forever, that is my help,' he squawked. 'But if you cannot, let me keep the brush. She is my family. I will look on it and dream of her. It would not be the first time some good has come from dreaming.'

"I did not want to, Masha. But I gave him the brush. He turned up his white throat to the sky and opened his beak so wide! He choked it down until the carved handle disappeared into his mouth. Then he flew away."

Ivan moved his eyes over Marya's face, memorizing it. She memorized his in turn, both as it had been and as it was now, for in her memory she would be honest. "Still, I looked for you. All over the city, over thrice nine districts, thrice nine prospekts. I asked even the stray ordnance for news of you, squatting huge and grey and stubborn in the streets. I went to the Hermitage, where the statues of giants hold up the roof—do you remember? Their elbows are all full of bullet holes now. Still, they look so strong, and beautiful, standing there in the snow, carrying their burden, their knuckles frozen over. I admire them. I thought, *If only I could be like them.*

"I saw a shrike on the big toe of one of the statues, his cheek just as red as if he'd been shot himself. I looked at the shrike and he looked at me, and I thought I had never seen such a big bird, so fat, such a sheen on his black wing, like a prince among shrikes. Even before we ate all the birds we could shoot, I had never seen one with such an ardent eye. My stomach said, *I'll have that bird.* But my heart said, *There are few enough ardent things left in this city.* And you were not there, not below the statues, not in the dark. I walked home, but as I walked the shrike followed me, hopping from stoop to stoop, flying down the dead power lines, his ardent eye following the snow, down and down to me. When I turned back onto Dzerzhinskaya Street and touched the door of our own house, the shrike flapped his wings and spoke to me from the branch of the cherry tree.

"'Give me something of hers,' he squawked. 'And I will help you.'

"All I could think of was your rifle. Forgive me. It lay where you left it, under our bed. It still held the marks of your hands; the bone gone brown where you used to hold it, so often, so well. I would imagine you, when you were younger, gaily shooting things, not because you were hungry for them, but because you could. I cradled it in my own arms.

"'It is all I have left of her,' I said. 'When it is gone, she will be gone.'

"The shrike said nothing.

"What could I do? I passed it out the window and the shrike took it with his sharp beak. The size of it nearly pulled him from the branch.

"'Forget her forever, that is my help,' he squawked. 'But if you cannot, let me keep the rifle. She is my family. I will look on it and mourn her. It would not be the first time some good has come from mourning.'

"I did not want to, Masha. I had nothing else to give the bird. But I gave him the rifle. He turned up his red throat to the sky and opened his beak so wide! He choked it down until the butt disappeared into his mouth. Then he flew away.

"I sat in the dark house without you, without Kseniya Yefremovna, without little Sofiya babbling about fishes and balloons. I cried so hard that day I thought my spine would crack. And then Zvonok was sitting beside me, patting my knee. The little domovaya said she'd known you all your life, and that you were wicked and had left her, too, but also that you would come back, probably. *Wicked creatures never stay away for long,* she said. And we began going up onto the roof, taking our posts there to watch the German line and report any movement. We did our best, even though it is colder on the roof than anywhere I have ever been.

"And once, when our watch was done, the domovaya came to

me, and she had grown big, and grown long black hair, and she said, *What is the point of suffering more than you must?* And she kissed me . . . and I don't want to talk about that now; don't ask me. You left me; she stayed. But the next day, I sat on the roof, squinting out at the edge of the city, and a rook flew up onto the gutters, just as fat and black as a rain cloud.

"'The dress has lost its color,' he squawked. 'There is a pain growing in Marya Morevna.'

"And he coughed, and retched, and the dress came up out of his mouth, colorless, not even grey, a dress like spittle. He spat it out onto the roof and leapt back into the snowy air.

"And you can guess it, Masha, of course you can. The next day it was the plover, so brown, so like bread I could have eaten him, and I would never be sorry.

"'The brush has tarnished,' he squawked. 'There is a grief growing in Marya Morevna.'

"And he coughed, and retched, and the brush came up out of his mouth, black with tarnish, not even a little silver showing. He spat it out onto the roof and leapt back into the snowy air.

"Of course you know what I will say next, Marousha. You know this is a story, and you know how stories transpire. The shrike came last, so red, so red. I could hear music playing, somewhere far-off, violins and oboes—but that's mad, who would play their violin in Leningrad? Why would anyone bother?

"'The rifle fired itself, and killed a passing owl,' the shrike squawked. 'There is a death growing in Marya Morevna.'

"And he coughed, and he retched, and worse, for a rifle falling out of a bird's mouth is an ugly thing. It clattered onto the roof, but I caught it before it tumbled off. The shrike looked at me with such pity. And he leapt back into the air, snow already on his wings.

"And then you came. You are here. My Marya, all whole and alive and come back for me. That was my whole soul gone out into the telling of all that has passed. But I have your dress and your brush and your rifle, just where you left them, in the closet, in the dresser, under the bed. Where is your pain, Marya Morevna? Where is your grief? Where is your death?"

Marya held him close to her and wrapped him in her hair to keep him warm. And she told him all she could think to tell, of Yaichka, and her hunting of the firebird, and how she had given birth to a child called death, and the radiant bird who had held her, just as she held Ivan Nikolayevich now. "I do wish you had not kept the brush," she sighed.

"Birds are such trouble," Ivan said, and for a moment he seemed to want to speak again. But he only coughed, and shivered. Tears spilled out of Marya's eyes and splashed onto his cheeks.

"If this were really a story, Ivanushka, I could heal you with the Water of Life, and you would stand up and dance with me, and then we would find a table set with all sorts of food and the city would wake up from an endless sleep, and what shouting and singing we would hear, coming up from the streets like steam!"

"*Tscha!*" hacked Ivan, his cough catching in his throat and unspooling into threads of spittle and phlegm. "Life is not like that."

"Don't worry," Marya whispered, kissing his forehead. "My old bones will follow yours soon enough."

"Wife, you could sow wheat in the rock of Dzerzhinskaya Street, wait for it to grow, reap it, thresh it, grind it into flour, bake it into bread, and eat the bread and share it round, and even then, you could not catch me."

And then Ivan died in her arms, his last breath spiraling up to the ceiling like cigarette smoke.

Marya Morevna put on her colorless dress and dragged her rifle out from under her marriage bed. *To two husbands I brought death with a woman's face,* she thought, and stumbled out onto the slush-bound, ice-packed length of Dzerzhinskaya Street. A pack of men in furred coats and hats ran by, their boots stamping shapes in the snow like ellipses. Marya stared at their tracks mutely, her tears chafed into freezing.

"Hey, old woman!" cried one of the men, his own black rifle cocked over his shoulder. "Can you shoot?"

Marya stirred and met his eye. He gestured at the beautiful bone rifle in her hands. "Well?" he demanded.

"Yes," she said finally, and her breath broke into pieces, carried off by the wind.

PART 6

Someone Ought to Be

A voice came. It called consolingly:
"Come here,
Leave your deaf and sinful country.
Leave Russia forever.
The blood from your hands I will wash
The black shame from your heart I will release
I will soothe the pain of defeats and insults
With the balm of a new name."
But calmly, with cool blood,
I clenched my ears with my fist . . .

—Anna Akhmatova

29

Every One Written on Your Belly

The major-general watched Tkachuk, the crippled boy, run across the shorn wheat of Mikhaylovka, tripping, limping away from them. Beside her, the staff sergeant sighed.

"You always let them go. It defies the purpose of arresting them to begin with."

"What do I want with a dead child, Comrade Ushanka?" said Marya Morevna, passing a hand over her eyes. She was so tired these days. Even her blood could not be bothered with redness. It was all too much work.

"I do not serve your personal issues, Morevna. I serve the People, and the People will have crimes against their body answered. You fought at Leningrad. So did I. Why should he be spared?"

"Someone ought to be." *And it will not be me. I have survived, but I have not been spared.*

The major-general slid her hand into the pocket of her uniform. She drew out, as casually as a handkerchief, a ball of red yarn. Marya Morevna could not think why she had waited so long to do this. Perhaps it had just hurt too much before. Perhaps she thought by staying she could be called loyal. She could be forgiven.

The major-general set her ball of yarn down on the dusty earth, the cut wheat, the flecks of ash, and pushed it gently. It rocked back and forth, and then rolled swiftly forward, off into the east, threading a path between stunted trees and dried-up vines. The two women folded up their tribunal table into a long black car with neither chicken legs nor an empty driver's seat, but simply a car, with a petulant engine and a phlegmatic muffler. Marya Morevna shifted the thing into gear, following the yarn as it unspooled toward the dusk.

In this way they traveled across thrice nine kingdoms, the whole of the world. Ushanka insisted they make the stops they had been assigned, no matter how much Marya did not care, did not even want to look at the starving deserters they were supposed to be shooting. Besides, who was she to judge them?

"I am a deserter myself," she confessed to her sergeant one night, in a barracks near Irkutsk. "Nineteen forty-two, Leningrad. Just like an old friend of mine promised I would be. If your precious records were any good you'd know that."

"I do know that, Morevna," whispered Ushanka in her long, thin bed. "But you came back. You may think I have the heart of a rat, but I believe that the coming back makes up the difference."

And so they went. They followed the red yarn, an idiosyncrasy which Marya marveled at Ushanka never questioning, even once.

She knew nothing of the sergeant, who no longer wore a blue ribbon. But she had suspicions. *We shot all the colors in the war,* the
officer liked to joke, but Marya did not laugh. She never laughed,
really, but especially not at Ushanka's jokes. Between them they
carried little but their mutual suspicions, and never, never did they
discuss the strange coincidence of their having met before the war.
But the coincidence occupied space at their table, ate its own ration of bread and wine and grinned at Marya's discomfort.

On and on the yarn spun.

Sometime in July they passed through a tangle of underbrush:
snarls of blackberry, broken larch branches, ferns like old oars.
They got out of the car to clear a path, for the yarn ran right underneath the deadfall. Marya sweated under her cap as she tugged
at the limbs and grasses and glimpsed, here and there, the bleached,
sun-stripped skulls of some small creatures—voles or hedgehogs,
rabbits, perhaps. A bit of antler; a bit of horn. Something about
it disturbed Marya, made her hackles rise. She frowned deeply
and shut herself back into the car, her hands white on the wheel.
Ushanka climbed in beside her, wiping her hands on her skirt,
smiling her secretive little smile.

Beyond the wreckage wall a village sprawled out before them.
Not much of a village—but then, none of them were much of anything. Not Mikhaylovka, not Schirokoye, or Baburka, or whatever
this miserable place was called. A broad road ran down the middle of
it, dividing one row of houses from the other. Marya saw a tavern—
there was always a tavern. A butcher's shop, a dressmaker. The road
seemed to lead to a fairly large building in the distance, painted
black, half ruined by storm and years. An old munitions factory,
perhaps. Or some reclaimed estate, from the days when estates could
be borne.

The red yarn finally spooled itself out. The frayed end lay at

Marya's feet, caked in dust. It pointed at the broken black build-ing. Marya's heart roused itself like an old wolf, nosing at the air, at a familiar scent.

"Will you have a drink with me, Comrade Ushanka? I believe I am thirsty," she said at last. She felt strangely at home here. The village tickled at her, like a cough in her throat. She wanted a drink and a rest, and to put off whatever tribunal Ushanka would insist on performing. The other officer nodded, her expression as severe as ever.

The tavern stood empty; tables and chairs collected a custom of dust. Three bottles of unidentifiable liquor reflected the sunlight behind the bar, and an old poster, faded and stained, warned, *Elect WORKERS to the Soviet! Do Not Elect Shamans or Rich Men!* Marya touched it, and the light on her hand reminded her of something, though she could not say what. Everything in her old life was hard to grasp now, like catching fish as they swim by—so fast, so fast!

"Can I help you, Comrade?" the bartender growled affably.

He was remarkably short and fat, not quite able to see over the bar he tended. He looked as though he had not brushed his hair in years; it tumbled down around his ears in dark tangles, and he sported a big beard, all over his cheeks like moss growing on a stone.

"Zemlehyed!" Marya cried. Her memory plunged into cold wa-ter; it seized a fish. She put her hand over her heart to keep it in her chest. *It worked, it worked; oh, Olga, thank you for the yarn, I shall never be able to repay you!* "Zemya, it's me—it's Marya, and you're not dead after all, and neither am I! No silver on your chest or mine. Come and kiss me!"

"I think you have me mistaken." The little man laughed. "That's

my name, no fear, but I've never seen your own self in all my days,
nor your friend there."

No, no. No magic, no ugly curses. "But Zemya, we've known each
other all our lives."

"I doubt it! But I can introduce you to a good vodka, and leave
you to get acquainted. I take no offense—I have a face people take
a liking to. But don't let my wife hear you asking for kisses!"

"Your wife?"

"My sweet, tall Naganya, how do I love her! Like a gun loves
bullets, that's how. Half-blind without her glasses and what a one
for swearing, but she's mine and I'm hers. Only she remembers
how long we've been married." He poured a generous glass for
both of his guests.

"Fifteen years, Zem, and you have every one written on your
belly." A voice like the air in a flute floated through the room.
Marya and Ushanka turned towards it as towards the sun. A slender, pale-haired woman with deep, elegant lines in her face laid
her gloves on the bar. Her eyes were painted to match the glass of
wine she poured herself. She was clearly the dressmaker whose
shop sparkled outside the windows. Her cool white dress swept
around her, tailored perfectly, and a fan of rather dingy, but still
lovely, swan feathers gathered at her hip. "See you get home to her
in good time tonight. Nasha has never learned patience, no matter
how I try to teach it."

"Lebed!" Marya gasped, and as if she were still a girl, as if she
had never starved until her stomach shriveled up, tears came, running messily to her chin. "Lebedeva, I've missed you so! But I'm
here now, you see; it's all right."

The dressmaker put an ivory cigarette holder to her mouth.
"That's rather familiar, Officer. Have we met?"

Marya had lost all her composure, all her care whether Ushanka
knew her secrets or not. "Of course we've met! Madame Lebedeva,

you taught me about cosmetics, and magic, and we ate cucumber soup that day in the cafe!"

"I think the heat must be on you, my dear. I can't abide cucumbers. Or anything green, really." The pale-haired woman sipped her oily red wine. "I do wish you'd get something good in here one of these days, instead of this endless Georgian swill."

Zemlehyed shrugged amiably, as if to say, *We drink what we drink.*

"Perhaps you should go and see the butcher, Officer. He knows everyone in town. I'm sure he can help you find . . ." The lady paused meaningfully—or perhaps not. Marya could not tell. "Whoever you're looking for. I can only assure you it isn't me." Madame Lebedeva tapped her fingernails against her glass, neatly excising Marya and Ushanka from her concern. "Nasha has rabbits' hearts in a pie for dinner, Zem." She changed the subject brightly. "She said I could join, if I brought mushrooms."

The butcher shop possessed little else but a slab of cutting stone and a glassless case with a single ruby-colored steak on display, marbled with fat, quite a specimen. The rest of the place slowly fell apart around them, so slowly it managed to give the illusion of standing firmly upright. The floorboards did not fit together right; a lonely fan missing one propeller spun wobbly from the ceiling lamp.

Ushanka rang the bell obnoxiously—but Marya found everything she did obnoxious. No one appeared.

"Come on out or I'll requisition that rib eye!" hollered the sergeant. Nothing moved in the amber afternoon shadows of the back room.

"No one's here, Ushanka." Marya ran her hand along the case. Her fingers turned black with old dust. She still shook from seeing her old friends. And they *were* her old friends—she was not mistaken, could not be. Her heart hid down deep in her belly. *Who will the butcher be?*

"We don't have an assignment in this town, Major-General. If you want a bit of beef, have at it, and let's be off." The staff sergeant slapped a fly on the counter and held her cupped hand over it, listening to it buzz uselessly.

A young woman appeared behind the counter, flushed, her pale gold hair frizzing out around a sweet, round face. Her pink lips made a little heart of apology and surprise.

"I'm sorry to have kept you waiting, Officers! Sometimes a nap lands on you and you just can't get out from underneath."

"Laziness is the enemy of industry." Ushanka sniffed.

Marya stepped subtly but emphatically in front of her junior officer. "What is your name?" she asked.

The girl blushed for no apparent reason at all. "Yelena," she said with a nervous laugh.

Marya made her face as smooth as she could. Her mind tripped over itself. Oh, the Yelenas with their terrible amber eyes! Did she know this one, among all of them? She could not remember. *But she's free, she's speaking—something's happened, and everything's all right. This woman means everything's all right, doesn't she?*

"Where are you from, Yelena?"

"Oh, here. Well, not here, exactly. I don't have a very good memory! But I lived for a long time in the women's collective on the northern border of town." Marya knew without asking that the collective would have a horse-bone door and an iron balcony.

Ushanka narrowed her eyes at the girl. "You did not enjoy communal living?"

"Oh, no, you don't understand. We ran a textile mill together, and it provided for all our needs. We ate each other's bread, drank each other's water. We lived like sisters, like a family with no head, no authority, only love." Ushanka blinked slowly. Her face colored darkly. Marya stared at her while Yelena went on. "And do you know, by the most extraordinary coincidence, we were all named Yelena? This world has such strange stories to tell! My sisters still weave up beyond that hill, and I bring them candies and stewed tomatoes on Revolution Day. Some of them are old, old babushkas, with watery eyes and blue scarves. They don't even remember how old they are, or where they were born. I wash their hair, when I don't have to watch the counter here. I would still live there, if not for falling in love. I got married—it happens." The girl shrugged.

Marya frowned. But really, how could she be one of the Yelenas she knew? And whom did she marry? "How long did you live in the collective?"

"All my life." Yelena shrugged again, her rosy cheeks dimpling.

"Surely you were not born in a women's collective. Conventional wisdom holds that a male is necessary for that sort of thing," Ushanka needled.

Yelena's pretty freckled brow furrowed. She tugged at her curly hair. "I don't . . . It's so hard to remember! I just . . . always lived there. Always. Until I met my husband. I mean, I'm sure you're right, Officer—I don't mean to contradict you. I must have been born somewhere else. But I was little. I don't remember. Who remembers being born?"

"Not a soul on this earth," replied Ushanka coldly.

Yelena looked as though she might cry, her big brown eyes full of confusion.

"I don't want to offend! Please, take some meat and enjoy the sunshine. If you want something other than the rib eye, you'll have to see my husband, though. Times are tight."

"Tight as a coat; tight as a glove; tight as a shoe," whispered the staff sergeant, her face closed up, unreadable. Marya Morevna cleared her throat. They were getting nowhere.

"I think my comrade is suffering in the close air of your shop,"
she said. What could be the officer's trouble? "Tell us where to find
your husband and we'll leave you."

"I'm sure he's with Auntie about now." She smiled. "That's his
sister. We all call her Auntie. She runs the canteen down the road.
The most amazing soups, I swear! Like gold on a spoon. You really
must try her ukha. I promise, you've never tasted the like."

Marya thanked her. *This is Buyan,* she thought. *I know it is. I
can smell it. The yarn stopped here. What has happened? I am human;
my memory got old and needs a cane. But them? They should know me.
Why do they not know me?*

"Tell me," said Marya Morevna, her hand on the door, the
rusted bell caught half-ring. "What is your husband's name?"

"Koschei Bessmertny," she said with the pride of a nesting hen.
"He'll be so pleased to meet you, I'm sure."

30

The Country of Death

They strode down a long, thin road which must be Skorohod-naya Road, which could not be other than Skorohodnaya Road—yet Marya was sure that if they could ask it, if they could whip it and curse it into sitting up and opening a dusty, stony mouth, it would profess no memory of ever having been called such a thing. The eternal twilight of summer nights in the north country splashed gold and rose onto the street.

"Sergeant, what is wrong with you?" Marya asked. She wished the wretched woman would vanish. Everyone else had—why was she stuck with the one soul who refused to do her the courtesy? Ushanka kicked the dirt.

"I thought you were meant to be some brilliant soldier. I thought you would have figured it out. I'm bored with walking between shitty buildings while you nosh at this town like an imbecile cow! I was told you were brilliant. I demand that you be brilliant!"

Marya rubbed her temples, a place she had given over to Ushanka, the place that hurt whenever she talked. "I have no idea what you're talking about."

Ushanka stopped in the middle of the road. The sun blazed on her brass buttons, her brass medals. She took off her cap and hooked one long finger into the side of her mouth. The staff sergeant yanked hard, and Marya winced at the vicious ripping sound of her skin splitting. But Ushanka was laughing, laughing while she tore her face open, all her teeth suddenly white and bare. No blood flew or dripped or seeped. Instead, threads popped open, stitches burst, a seam in her face split, and the linens of her cheeks hung down in tatters.

"Not a soul on this earth remembers being born." Ushanka grinned. "But I remember coming to Leningrad for you. It took me so long to get over the mountains, but I did it. To watch you. To question you. I remember losing you when you went into the damned egg, and finding you half-dead on the barricades—not so lucky as me, no, but with your blood all coming out like stuffing. I remember you in the sniper corps, and how they never guessed, not once, that you were anything but a poor starving Leningrader like all the other poor, starving Leningraders. I got myself assigned to your detail, and I've done so well, so well for a suit of clothes stitched by a damned Yelena! I've done as I was told. I watched you, and I brought you back here. It took me longer than I thought to make you miserable enough to use that yarn. That butcher's bitch—or one of her sisters, makes no difference—made me. Made me for you."

Marya had known, but she had not known. She had known Ushanka was wrong, was broken—but what human was whole? "Why didn't you tell me, that day in the parlor? We could have been friends. We could have been a comfort."

Ushanka shrugged. "They didn't tell me to comfort you." She started walking again, towards the canteen. "Do you know what he did when you left? He stopped the Yelena mill. He pulled them all out and made them sit in a room in the Chernosvyat, all in rows like students, and he dragged Likho out from wherever she liked to slink before she died, and made her teach them. Like a skinny old black-wool-and-chalk schoolmistress. And do you know what he wanted taught? How to turn a Yelena into a Marya. He made them read that awful black book you had, and make friends with leshiyi and vintovniki and vilas, and shoot firebirds. Everything you ever did, he made them repeat, hoping one would show promise, be his star pupil. But they couldn't stop their weaving as easy as winking, and all the while they just kept moving their hands like they were still working at the looms. Eventually, he gave up. That, quite frankly, is practically the worst thing I've ever heard of a husband doing, but it only goes to show what the flesh will do when it's grieving. Better to have organdy and linen and silk, if you ask me. Silk doesn't love; linen doesn't mourn."

Ushanka banged open the door of the canteen and dropped herself insolently into a chair by a little table with one leg shorter than the others. She let her face hang open, as though it didn't trouble her a bit. Marya wanted to strangle her until she told her everything she'd ever known. No one came to ask them what they wanted to drink, to eat, anything. They were alone with the sunlight pouring in like the light after an air raid.

Marya hissed at her comrade, "Why are you so angry? It's me that's come home to find all my dead friends don't know who I am, and nothing as I wanted it."

"Who cares how you wanted it? I'm a golem, Marya Morevna. A golem with no masters left. What am I to do now? My mission is over, and all I've got to show for it is a dolt of a mother in a butcher shop who can't even remember that she is my mother."

Marya snatched Ushanka's hand and dug in her nails, though it couldn't hurt her, not really, unless organdy could suffer. "Where are we?" she hissed. "It's not Buyan, but it is." And then she knew. She understood. The revelation moved in her like death. But it was too big; she could not hold it. She let go of the sergeant's linen hand.

"This is Viy's country, isn't it?" she whispered, afraid to say it and make it so. "And the war is over. We lost. In the end, between Germany and the wizard with the mustache in Moscow, the one I told them about all those years ago—the two of them ate us alive. The dead overwhelmed us. While we were counting our ration cards, Buyan and Leningrad and Moscow and everything was shriveling and blowing away." And her heart recited from the black book as she had once recited from Pushkin as a girl: *Viy made his country as like the living world as he could, even to building film houses where silvery images of the war showed, so that the dead might be grateful, and not wish to return to life.*

Marya put her hand on her heart. It hurt as though it were being cut out. Ushanka nodded, and for once her face grew sad and soft, like an old, oft-washed dress.

"It's over, Marya. Koschei's country has passed from the face of the earth. It doesn't show silver on the streets anymore because the streets are gone. It's all silver. It's all dead. When the mud came up in the spring and mired the German tanks and broke them, do you think anyone thought, *That must be the vodyanoy, rising up to protect their country, to fight alongside us?* No, they thought it was weather. And so it was. The future belongs to the dead, and the makers of the dead. Men like Viy, who are blind to the deeds of their own hands, who reach out for souls. Our kind belong to him, now. We wander, lost, and you cannot even see the silver on our chests anymore, because all the human world is the Country of Death, and in thrall, and finally, after all this time, we are just like everyone else. We are all dead. All equal. Broken and aimless and believing we are alive. This is Russia and it is 1952. What else would you call hell?"

But they're all here, Marya thought, her head heavy and hot. *Everyone I love is here. Except Ivan, and who is to say he is not here: a sheriff, a policeman, a cigarette maker, something, forgetful as the rest of them? And is there a nurse in a clinic called Kseniya, with a precocious daughter? Oh, I could find them. I could find them and make them know me.*

Someone moved in the kitchen, banging pots together.

"Who do you think Koschei's auntie is?" Ushanka continued. "This is Baba Yaga's kitchen. Look under the porch and you'll see the slats of this place gnarling and twisting—a little like chicken legs, yes? All her soups, all her cauldrons bubbling away, and oh, you *must* try the ukha!" Ushanka wallowed in Marya's torment with glee. She leapt in it, turned somersaults. "What a place, where the Tsaritsa of Night runs a canteen and steals bites of carrot from her own soup."

Marya thought she might throw up. She felt hot and sick all together. Her body wanted to do something in the face of it all, to throw something back at it. She looked uncertainly toward the kitchen.

"Then he is here, too. Visiting his sister. Discussing the week's cuts of meat, the potato harvest, what sort of soup she might make tomorrow."

Ushanka's smile faded like a stain. She looked sorry for Marya.

"Koschei died. Well, he always dies. And he always comes back. Deathless means deathless. He dies and plays out the same story again and again. How many people have told you that? The Country of Death looks so much like the Country of Life. So now he lives in Viy's possession, and he has a little wife he spirited off from her family, and thinks he is a man. A man, like he always wanted to be. It's a good joke, if you have the right humor for it.

He won't remember you. He's not strong enough. Viy was always the better of them. Inexorable, that's the word. Life is like that. Death sweeps it away. That's what death is for. That's why they keep telling this story. It's the only story. He will look at you and think you are a woman of rank getting on in years, and wouldn't you like to try the kvass?" Ushanka put her hand back inside Marya's grip, making it into an intimate touch, full of pity. "Marya," she sighed. "No one is now what they were before the war. There's just no getting any of it back."

The kitchen door creaked, and an old woman emerged. She wore a bloody leather apron, streaks of beef and fish blood crisscrossing themselves, making patterns on her bosom. Her white hair was pulled back into a savagely tight chignon. She looked directly at Marya Morevna, her eyes twinkling as if anticipating some particular amusement.

"How can I help you, Officers?" the woman said. Her dry lips cracked as she grinned at them.

Ushanka tucked her cheek in. "I want nothing," she said curtly. "I have done as I was asked. I did not like it, but I did it. I want only to rest." For a moment she did not move, staring at the floor with an expression of stubbornness that Marya knew so well, as a mother knows her child's angry stomp. Then Ushanka rose, walked away from them, out the door of the canteen and onto the twilit road. As she walked, her head straight and high, a long golden thread unspooled from her foot, faster and faster, zipping up through her calf, her thigh, leaving little cairns of thread behind her. By the time she reached the center of what had once been Skorohodnaya Road, and perhaps still was, her hair and scalp were unraveling, and the wind blew through the strands, carrying them off towards the mountains.

The old woman turned back to Marya Morevna. "But certainly," the crone continued, unperturbed, "certainly I can help *you*, madam."

Marya Morevna looked up, and she felt so old, so awfully old and worn, and so young all at once, raw as a wound. *Let it be over,* she pleaded within herself. *Let it never have happened—any of it. Let me be young again, and the story just starting.* She glanced at the walls, at the faded old Party posters, each showing a man or a woman or a child with a narrow, hungry face and a finger laid over their mouths, abjuring some distant soul to be silent, be still. No slogans shouted from them; no moral directive told Marya how to behave, who to be in this place. And so she was herself—a bitter thing, and sour as onions in brine.

"When have you ever helped anyone?" she snapped. She could not sit there and let Baba Yaga pretend she was some ridiculous shopwoman.

"Oh, I help," said the Tsaritsa of Night, her voice curling like ram's wool. "Sometimes. It depends on the story. But I do help. When a girl has proven herself. When she's kept my horses well or swept my floors or lifted my cauldron with just her own two arms. Or when her perversity has made me proud. How did she turn out, the woman you might have been?"

"You know me?" But the thought arrived inside her like a train: Marya Morevna, all in black, here and now, was a point at which all the women she had been met—the Yaichkan and the Leningrader and the chyerti maiden; the girl who saw the birds, and the girl who never did—the woman she was and the woman she might have been and the woman she would always be, forever intersecting and colliding, a thousand birds falling from a thousand oaks, over and over.

The old woman shrugged expansively, as if to demur. *Who is to say what I know?*

And Marya Morevna recalled the raskovnik, and the black gold, and the mortar with its pestle grinding beneath her. To remember it hurt her; pinpricks stabbed at her chest, her fingers.

The posters hushed her from the wall, and in her memory an orange flower bristled with white needles opened.

Baba Yaga leaned down so that their faces stood close as secrets.

"Listen, long-past-soup. There is a room in the dark. Where a ceiling fell through, and a floor, until all that was left was a hole leading down into the earth, into a basement. Into the shadows, peacock tapestries fell dusty and burning. A table lies broken down there, and a great chair of bone. You should go there. At night, when no one can see you. I could never guess what you might find in the frozen mud and shattered walls. I am not a betting woman these days. But you know, in the end, you can only be yourself in a basement, in the black, underneath everything, where no one can find you."

The blister below Marya's eye, that old scar, pulsed—twice, three times. "Is it because Viy rules you? Is that why you will not say my name? Are you afraid of him, like a wizard with a mustache? Why the posters say *quiet, quiet, don't breathe a word*? Because if all the world dwells in the Country of the Dead, I should not remember either, and yet I do—though it hurts like starving to do it."

"I don't know what you mean. I would never engage in underground, antirevolutionary activities," purred the crone. "I am only suggesting a thing for you to see, the way an old lady with a sprung back and a greasy little cafe might do when tourists blow through her town. I say nothing; I know nothing; I certainly don't remember a thing." She put her withered hand, spotted as a leopard's flank, onto Marya's sternum, between her breasts. Marya felt something heavy and hot growing between them, like a bullet. "I would never attend meetings in dank, moldering cellars. I would never importune the character of your colleague, who tells the tale as powerful ears want to hear it. I would never mince about and pantomime a life full of dressmaking and marriages and a successful butcher shop so as not to be caught committing the crime of remembering that anything existed before this new and righteous regime. It's so much easier when we say, *There was never an old world. Everything will now be new forever.* I am hurt that you look at me and assume such criminal tendencies in a nice babushka with only your best interests at heart." The thing like a bullet between their skins burned at the heart of Marya Morevna, drawing heat from her, giving nothing back. "And on my life I would never suggest to you that stories cannot be forgotten in the bone even when a brother or a wizard or a rifle says you must, you must forget, it never happened; there is only this world, as it is now, and there has never been another, can never be any other."

"Babushka," Marya said, and she meant it, here, at the end of everything. "I am so tired. I am so finished with it all. How can I live in this? I want to be held by everyone I have loved and told that it is all forgiven, all done, all made well."

"*Tscha!* Death is not like that. The redistribution of worlds has made everything equal—magic and cantinas and Yelenas and basements and bread and silver, silver light. Equally dead, equally bound. You will live as you live anywhere. With difficulty, and grief. Yes, you are dead. And I and my family and everyone, always, forever. All dead, like stones. But what does it matter? You still have to go to work in the morning. You still have to live." The crone lifted her hand from Marya's breast. In it was no bullet, not hot nor heavy, but a red scarf, bunched and knotted together. She tucked it into the flap of Marya's uniform, next to her skin. She pulled her pinched, wrinkled, sullen face back on carefully, her practiced, amiable gaze.

Marya Morevna let her breath go. She made her face blank and unreadable. She looked up at her babushka as though she were a stranger—interesting, perhaps: such a face—but no relation of hers. After all, Marya was so good at games. She stood and walked out of the canteen, down a long, thin road toward the wreckage of some shattered black palace turned to rubble by endless shelling. The dust beneath her feet spangled in the evening light. She did not waver in her path, toward a place underground, down, down into the merciful dark, in a basement where a man with black curls flecked with starry silver would say her name like a confession; and in the place where their hands would touch, Marya Morevna could already see diamonds and black enamel swelling huge and gravid, yolk seeping from their skin like light.

Acknowledgments

There is no way to begin an accounting of those who contributed to this book except to say that my husband, Dmitri, and his family have included me in their lives for five years, engaging in the dangerous activity of telling a writer their stories and histories, and for that I am grateful beyond any mortal measure. It has been one of the most extraordinary things in my life, listening to their tales and jokes and being welcomed into their world. This book sprang from that very fertile ground, and from Dmitri especially, who in addition to acting as a human English-Russian dictionary and font of priceless details, first read me the story of Marya Morevna and Koschei the Deathless, leading to that immortal question: "Wait, what? Why is he chained up in her basement?"

Thank you also to the women of the Siege of Leningrad Museum in St. Petersburg, who humble everyone with the strength of their memory, and who were kind enough to speak with a young American; and posthumously to Anna Ahkmatova, the patron of Leningrad, whose work pierces and commands my soul; and Harrison Salisbury, whose seminal work *The 900 Days* was vital to my research and is responsible for many of the physical details of wartime Leningrad. And thank you to Anna Vasilevskaya, whose music accompanied me during long nights of writing.

Thank you to all those who have provided succor, advice, and encouragement to an admittedly grumpy writer without a paid cafe card, especially Tiffin Staib, Michael Broughton, Ferrett Steinmetz, Gini Judd, Amal El-Mohtar, Lee Harrington, and Claire Cooney, who kindly read an early draft.

Thank you to my agent, Howard Morhaim, and my editor, Liz Gorinsky, as well as my assistant, Deb Castellano, and the tireless Evelyn Kriete.

Thank you as ever to S. J. Tucker, my sister-tsarevna, who makes my world so bright, teaches me so much about authenticity and magic, and makes my books into such astonishing sorceries, and to her partner, Kevin Wiley, logistical god and dear friend.

And finally, to Rose Fox, *il miglior fabbro*.